"SAINTS, BUT YOU TEMPT ME," DUNCAN MURMURED.

He gathered her into his arms and gently lowered her into the silky warm waters of the bath. "Ne'er in my life have I desired a woman more." Without taking his eyes off her, he kneeled beside the tub and softly brushed his lips back and forth over hers.

Lulled into contentment by the sheer magic of his kisses, Linnet felt herself melting. But a tiny voice deep inside scolded her for being a wanton fool. A brazen piece willing to barter her pride for a man's touch, for the feel of his lips on hers. In truth, she'd sunk lower than a bawd for the thrill of a few moments in the arms of a man who'd never love her—even though he was her husband.

"Duncan, wait," she pleaded the moment he broke their kiss to feather lighter ones down the curve of her neck. "Please, I cannot do this after all."

"Shhh," he urged, "*of course* you can. Hush, dinna speak." He placed two fingers over her lips, silencing her. "Just *feel*."

DEVIL IN A KILT

Sue-Ellen Welfonder

WARNER BOOKS

A Time Warner Company

WARNER BOOKS EDITION

Copyright © 2001 by Sue-Ellen Welfonder

Cover art by John Ennis
Lettering by Carol Russo

Warner Books, Inc.
1271 Avenue of the Americas
New York, NY 10020

Visit our Web site at
www.twbookmark.com.

For information on Time Warner Trade Publishing's online publishing program, visit www.ipublish.com.

W A Time Warner Company

Printed in the United States of America

First Printing: August 2001

10 9 8 7 6 5 4 3 2 1

This book is dedicated with love and appreciation
to my husband, Manfred, my real-life hero.

Handsome and noble as any fictitious knight
in shining armor, he slays my dragons daily
and makes all my dreams come true.

acknowledgment

this book was inspired by my visit to Eilean Donan Castle in the Scottish Highlands and I want to offer sincere appreciation to Patricia Suchy, founder of Novel Explorations, for taking me there, and also for showing me the Clava Cairns.

Extraspecial thanks and deep appreciation to Kathryn Falk, Lady Barrow, of *Romantic Times Magazine* and Lady Barrow Tours, for introducing me to her friend, Miss Mary MacRae, whose family are the hereditary chatelaines of Eilean Donan Castle. Miss Mary's father was Captain Duncan MacRae, Younger of Eilean Donan. Considering how the book's hero came to me so vividly the day I visited her castle, and Miss Mary's claim that her father had a marvelous sense of humor and would have enjoyed having the book's hero named after him, well, I can't help but wonder. . . .

Deepest appreciation to my fantastic agent, Pattie

Steele-Perkins, for her belief in me, her support, and for having enough faith in Duncan to send him up against the big boys. And heartfelt appreciation to my first editor, Maggie Crawford, for this chance, her expertise, and for that very special night at Vidalia's. Our time together was brief, but my appreciation will last forever.

1

Dundonnell Keep, Western Highlands
Scotland 1325

"It is said he's merciless, the devil's own spawn." Elspeth Beaton, unspoken seneschal of the MacDonnell keep, folded her arms over her substantial girth and glowered at her laird, Magnus MacDonnell. "You canna send the lass to a man known to have murdered his first wife in cold blood!"

Magnus took another swig of ale, seemingly unaware that most of the frothy brew dribbled into his unkempt beard. He slammed his pewter mug onto the high table and glared back at his self-appointed chamberlain.

"I dinna care if Duncan MacKenzie is the devil hisself or if the bastard's killed *ten* wives. He's offered for Linnet, and 'tis an offer I canna refuse."

"You canna give your daughter to a man said to possess neither heart nor soul." Elspeth's voice rose with each word. "I willna allow it."

Magnus guffawed. "*You* willna allow it? You overstep yerself, woman! Watch yer mouth, or I'll send you along with her."

High above the great hall, safely ensconced in the laird's lug, a tiny spy chamber hidden within Dundonnell's thick walls, Linnet MacDonnell peered down at her father and her beloved servant as they argued over her fate.

A fate already decided and sealed.

Not until this moment had she believed her sire would truly send her away, especially not to a *MacKenzie*. Though none of her six older sisters had married particularly well, at least her da hadn't plighted a single one of them to the enemy! Straining her ears, she waited to hear more.

"'Tis rumored the MacKenzie is a man of strong passions," Elspeth pronounced. "Linnet knows little of a man's baser needs. Her sisters learned much from their mother, but Linnet is different. She's e'er run with her brothers, learning their—"

"Aye, she's different!" Magnus raged. "Naught has plagued me more since the day my poor Innes died birthing her."

"The lass has many skills," Elspeth countered. "Mayhap she lacks the grace and high looks of her sisters and her late mother, may the saints bless her soul, but she would still make a man a good wife. Surely you can purvey her a more agreeable marriage? One that won't so sorely imperil her happiness?"

"Her happiness matters naught to me. The alliance with MacKenzie is sealed!" Magnus thundered. "Even if I wished her better, what man needs a wife who can best him at throwing blades? And dinna wax on about her other fool talents."

Magnus took a long swill of ale, then wiped his mouth on his sleeve. "A man wants a consort interested in tending his aching tarse, not a patch of scraggly herbs!"

A shocked sputter escaped Elspeth's lips and she drew herself to her full but unimpressive height. "If you do this, you needn't tax yourself by banishing me from the dubious comforts of this hall. 'Tis gladly I shall go. Linnet will not be sent to the lair of the Black Stag alone. She'll need someone to look out for her."

Linnet's heart skipped a beat, and gooseflesh rose on her arms upon hearing her soon-to-be husband referred to as the Black Stag. No such creature existed. While animals of certain prowess often adorned coats of arms and banners, and some clan chieftains called themselves after a lion or other such noble beast, this title sounded ominous.

An omen of ill portent.

But one she had little time to consider. Rubbing the chillbumps from her arms, Linnet pushed aside her rising unease and concentrated on the discourse below.

"'Tis glad I'll be to see your back," her father was ranting. "Your nagging willna be missed."

"Will you not reconsider, milord?" Elspeth changed her tactic. "If you send Linnet away, who will tend the garden or do the healing? And dinna forget how oft her gift has aided the clan."

"A pox on the garden and plague take her gift!" Magnus bellowed. "My sons are strong and healthy. We dinna need the lass and her herbs. Let her aid the

MacKenzie. 'Tis a fair exchange since he only wants her for her sight. Think you he offered for her because she's so *bonnie*? Or because the bards have sung to him of her womanly allures?"

The MacDonnell laird's laughter filled the hall. Loud and mean-spirited, it bounced off the walls of the laird's lug, taunting Linnet with the cruelty behind his words. She cringed. Everyone within the keep would hear his slurs.

"Nay, he doesna seek a comely wife," Magnus roared, sounding as if he were about to burst into another gale of laughter. "The mighty MacKenzie of Kintail isn't interested in her looks or if she can please him or nay when he beds her. He wants to know if his son is his own or his half brother's bastard, and he's willing to pay dearly to find out."

Elspeth gasped. "You know the lass canna command her gift at will. What will happen to her if she fails to see the answer?"

"Think you I care?" Linnet's father jumped to his feet and slammed his meaty fists on the table. "'Tis glad I am to be rid of her! All I care about are the two Mac-Donnell kinsmen and the cattle he's giving in exchange for her. He's held our clansmen for nigh onto six months. Their only transgression was a single raid!"

Magnus MacDonnell's chest heaved in indignation. "'Tis a dullwit you are if you do not realize their sword arms and strong backs are more use to me than the lass. And MacKenzie cattle are the best in the Highlands." He paused to jeer at Elspeth. "Why do you think we're e'er a-lifting them?"

"You'll live to rue this day."

"Rue the day? Bah!" Magnus leaned across the table, thrusting his bearded face forward. "I'm hoping the boy *is* his half brother's brat. Think how pleased he'll be if he gets a son off Linnet. Mayhaps grateful enough to reward his dear father-in-law with a bit o' land."

"The saints will punish you, Magnus."

Magnus MacDonnell laughed. "I dinna care if a whole host of saints come after me. This marriage will make me a rich man. I'll hire an army to send the sniveling saints back where they came from!"

"Perhaps the arrangement 'twill be good for Linnet," Elspeth said, her voice surprisingly calm. "I doubt the MacKenzie partakes of enough ale each time he sits at his table to send himself sprawling facefirst into the rushes. Not if he's the fine warrior the minstrels claim."

Elspeth fixed the laird with a cold stare. "Have you ne'er listened when the bards sing of his great valor serving our good King Robert Bruce at Bannockburn? 'Tis rumored the Bruce hisself calls the man his champion."

"Out! Get you gone from my hall!" Magnus Mac-Donnell's face turned as red as his beard. "Linnet leaves for Kintail as soon as Ranald has the horses saddled. If you want to see the morn, gather your belongings and ride with her!"

Peering through the spy hole, Linnet watched her beloved Elspeth give Magnus one last glare before she stalked from the hall. The instant her old nurse disappeared from view, Linnet leaned her back against the wall and drew a deep breath.

Everything she'd just heard ran wild through her mind. Her da's slurs, Elspeth's attempts to defend her, and then her unexpected praise for Duncan MacKenzie. Heroic acts in battle or nay, he remained the enemy.

But what disturbed Linnet the most was her own odd reaction when Elspeth had called the MacKenzie a man of strong passions. Even now, heat rose to her cheeks at the thought. She was embarrassed to admit it, even to herself, but she yearned to learn about passion.

Linnet suspected the tingles that had shot through her at the notion of wedding a man of heated blood had something to do with such things. Most likely so did the way her heart had begun to thump fiercely upon hearing Elspeth's words.

Linnet's cheeks grew warmer . . . as did the rest of her body, but she fought to ignore the disquieting sensations. She didn't want a MacKenzie to bestir her in such a manner. Imagining how her da would laugh if he knew she harbored dreams of a man desiring her chased away the last vestiges of her troublesome thoughts.

Resignation tinged by anger settled over her. If only she had been born as fair as her sisters. Lifting her hand, she ran her fingertips over the curve of her cheek. Though cold to the touch, her skin was smooth, unblemished. But while her sisters had been graced with milky white complexions, a smattering of freckles marred hers.

And unlike their hair, always smooth and in place, she'd been burdened with a wild mane she couldn't keep plaited. She did like its color, though. Of a bolder tone than her sisters' blondish red, hers was a deep shade of copper, almost bronze. Her favorite brother, Jamie, claimed her hair could bewitch a blind man.

A tiny smile tugged at her lips. Aye, she liked her hair. And she loved Jamie. She loved each of her eight brothers, and now she could hear them moving through the hall below. Even as her father's drunken snores drifted up to her, so did the sounds of her brothers making ready for a swift departure.

Her departure from Dundonnell Castle. The dark and dank hall of a lesser and near-landless clan chief, her ale-loving da, but the only home she had ever known.

And now she must leave for an uncertain future, her place at Dundonnell wrested from her by her father's greed. Tears stung Linnet's eyes, but she blinked them away, not wanting her da to see them should he stir himself and deign to look at her as she exited his hall.

Squaring her shoulders, Linnet snatched up her leather herb pouch, her only valued possession, and slipped from the laird's lug. She hurried down the tower stairs as quickly as she dared, then dashed through the great hall without so much as a glance at her slumbering da.

For the space of a heartbeat, she'd almost hesitated, almost given in to a ridiculous notion she should awaken him and bid him farewell. But the urge vanished as quickly as it'd come.

Why should she bother? He'd only grouse at her for disrupting his sleep. And was he not pleased to be rid of her? Worse, he'd sold her to the laird of the *MacKenzies*, the MacDonnells' sworn enemies since long before her birth.

And the man, king's favorite and strong-passioned or nay, only wanted her for the use of her gift and because he'd been assured she wasn't bonnie. Neither prospect was flattering nor promised an endurable marriage.

Linnet took one last deep gulp of Dundonnell's

smoke-hazed air as she stood before the massive oaken door leading to the bailey. Mayhap in her new home she wouldn't be suffered to fill her lungs with stale, ale-soured air. "Oh, bury St. Columba's holy knuckles!" she muttered, borrowing Jamie's preferred epithet as she dashed a wayward tear from her cheek.

Before more could fall, Linnet yanked open the iron-shod door and stepped outside. Though long past the hour of prime, a chill, blue-gray mist still hung over Dundonnell's small courtyard . . . just as a pall hung over her heart.

Her brothers, all eight of them, stood with the waiting horses, each brother looking as miserable as she felt. Elspeth, though, appeared oddly placid and already sat astride her pony. Other clansmen and their families, along with her da's few servants, crowded together near the opened castle gates. Like her brothers, they all wore sullen expressions and remained silent, but the telltale glisten in their eyes spoke a thousand words.

Linnet kept her chin high as she strode toward them, but beneath the folds of her woolen cloak, her knees shook. At her approach, Cook stepped forward, a clump of dark cloth clutched tight in his work-reddened hands. "'Tis from us all," he said, his voice gruff as he thrust the mass of old-smelling wool into Linnet's hands. "It's been locked away in a chest in your da's chamber all these years, but he'll ne'er know we took it."

With trembling fingers, Linnet unfolded the *arisaid* and let Cook adjust its soft length over her shoulders. As he carefully belted the plaid around her waist, he said, "My wife made it for the Lady Innes, your mother. She wore it well, and it is our wish you will, too. 'Tis a bonnie piece, if a wee bit worn."

Emotion formed a hot, choking lump in Linnet's throat as she smoothed her hands over the *arisaid*'s pliant folds. A few moth holes and frayed edges didn't detract from the plaid's worth. To Linnet, it was beautiful . . . a treasure she'd cherish always.

Her eyes brimming with tears, she threw herself into Cook's strong arms and hugged him tight. "Thank you," she cried against the scratchy wool of his own plaid. "Thank you *all*! Saints, but I shall miss you."

"Then dinna say good-bye, lass," he said, setting her from him. "We shall see you again, never worry."

As one, her kinsmen and friends surged forward, each one giving her a fierce hug. No one spoke and Linnet was grateful, for had they, she would've lost what meager control she had over herself. Then one voice, the smithy's, cried out just as her eldest brother Ranald lifted her into a waiting saddle. "Ho, lass, I've something for you, too," Ian called, pushing his way through the throng.

When he reached them, the smithy pulled his own finely honed dirk from its sheath and handed it to Linnet. "Better protection than that teensy wench's blade you wear," he said, nodding in satisfaction as Linnet withdrew her own blade and exchanged it for his.

Ian's eyes, too, shone with unusual brightness. "May you ne'er have cause to use it," he said, stepping away from her pony.

"May the MacKenzie say his prayers if she does," Ranald vowed, then tossed Linnet her reins. "We're off," he shouted to the rest of them, then swung up into his own saddle.

Before Linnet could catch her breath or even thank the smithy, Ranald gave her mount a sharp slap on its rump and the shaggy beast bolted through the opened gates, putting Dundonnell Castle forever behind her.

Linnet choked back a sob, not letting it escape, and stared straight ahead. She refused . . . *she couldn't* . . . look back.

Under other circumstances, she'd be glad to go. Grateful even. But she had the feeling that she was merely exchanging one hell for another. And, heaven help her, she'd didn't know which she preferred.

Many hours and countless leagues later, Ranald MacDonnell signaled the small party behind him to halt. Linnet's pony snorted in protest, shifting restlessly as she reined him in. She shared his nervousness, for they'd reached their destination.

After a seemingly endless trek through MacKenzie territory, they'd reached the halfway point where Ranald claimed her husband-to-be would meet them.

Inexplicably beset by a tide of self-consciousness, Linnet patted the linen veil covering her hair and adjusted the fall of her mother's worn but precious *arisaid* around her shoulders. If only she hadn't coiled her long plaits around her ears, hiding them from view beneath her concealing headgear. Her betrothed thought her plain, but her tresses were bonnie.

Her brothers were e'er claiming her hair color rivaled the reds and golds of the most brilliant flame.

Would that she'd worn her hair loose. 'Twas embarrassment enough to meet her new husband, enemy or nay, garbed in little more than rags. At least her mother's bonnie plaid lent her a semblance of grace. Even so, she could have kept a wee bit more dignity by flaunting, not concealing her finest feature.

But regret served no purpose now, for the forest floor already shook from the pounding hooves of fast-approaching horses.

"*Cuidich' N' Righ!*" The MacKenzie battle cry rent the air. "*Save the king!*"

Linnet's pony tossed its head, then skittered sideways in panic. As she struggled to calm him, a double line of warrior-knights thundered into view. They came straight toward her party, forming two columns at the last possible moment, then galloping past Linnet and her small escort, enclosing them in an unbroken circle of mailed and heavily-armed MacKenzies.

"Dinna you fret, lass," Ranald called to her over his shoulder. "We willna let aught befall you." Turning in his saddle, he shouted something at her other brothers but the loud cries of the MacKenzies swallowed Ranald's words.

"*Cuidich' N' Righ!*"

Their bold shouts echoed the MacKenzie motto. The proud words were emblazoned beneath a stag's antlers on banners held by mounted standard-bearers. Unlike the warriors who'd charged forward, the young men held their mounts in check a short distance away. Four abreast, their standards high, they made an impressive sight.

But naught near as imposing as the dark knight who so self-assuredly broke their ranks.

Clad in a shirt of black mail, broad sword at his side and two daggers thrust beneath the fine leather belt slung low around his hips, he rode a huge warhorse as black as his armor.

Linnet swallowed hard. This intimidating giant of a man could only be Duncan MacKenzie, the MacKenzie of Kintail, her betrothed.

She didn't need to see the green-and-blue plaid fastened over his hauberk to know his identity.

Nor did it matter that the helm he wore cast his face in shadow, almost hiding it from view. His arrogance came at her in waves as his assessing gaze scorched its way from the top of her head to the scuffed brogans on her feet.

Aye, she *knew* 'twas he.

She also knew the fierce warrior-laird was displeased with what he saw.

More than displeased . . . he looked outraged. Anger emanated from beneath his armor, his gaze traveling over her critically. She didn't need her gift to know his eye color. A man such as he could have naught but eyes as dark as his soul.

Her finely tuned senses told all. He'd taken a *good* look at her . . . and found her lacking.

Sweet Virgin, if only she'd heeded Elspeth's advice and let the old woman dress and scent her hair. 'Twould have been much easier to raise her chin against his bold appraisal did a veil not hide her tresses.

When he rode forward, making straight for her, Linnet fought the urge to flee. Not that she stood a chance of breaking through the tight circle of stone-faced MacKenzie guardsmen. Nor could she get past her brothers . . . at the dark knight's approach, they'd urged their horses closer to hers. Their expressions grim, their hands hovering near the hilts of their swords, they warily allowed her betrothed's advance.

Nay, escape was not an option.

But pride was. Hoping he couldn't detect her wildly fluttering heart, Linnet sat straighter in her saddle and forced herself to match the glare he aimed at her from beneath his helm.

'Twould serve him well to know she found the situation displeasing. And 'twas undoubtedly wise to show she wouldn't cower before him

Duncan raised a brow at his bride's unexpected display of backbone. Rage had fair consumed him when he'd seen her threadbare cloak and worn shoes. Even the fine-looking *arisaid* she wore bore holes! All the Highlands knew her sire was a drunken worm of a man, but ne'er had he dreamed the lout would shame his daughter by sending her to meet her new liege laird and husband dressed shabbier than the poorest villein.

Leaning forward in his saddle, Duncan peered at her, glad for the shadows cast by the rim of his helm, thankful she couldn't see his face clearly. She'd no doubt think he'd found fault with *her* rather than guess it was her sire's blatant disregard that stirred his ire.

Aye, her raised chin and defiant glare pleased him. The lass wasn't meek. Most gentleborn females would hang their heads in self-pity and embarrassment 'twere they caught dressed in rags. Yet she'd met his perusal with a show of courage and spirit.

Slowly, Duncan's frown softened and, to his amazement, the corners of his mouth rose in the beginnings of a rare smile. He caught it, though, clamping his lips together before the smile could spread. He'd not taken the lass to wed so he could find favor with her.

He only wanted her to put an end to his doubts about Robbie, to care for the lad, and keep him from his sight should his suspicions prove true. Her character scarce mattered beyond her suitability as a new mother for Robbie. But it pleased him to see steel in her blood.

She'd need it to be his wife.

Ignoring the glares of her escort, Duncan urged his steed forward. He reined in mere inches from her scrawny pony.

Linnet squared her shoulders at his approach, refusing to show the awe she felt for his magnificent warhorse. Ne'er had she seen such an animal. The beast fair towered over her shaggy Highland pony.

She hoped her awe of the man was well hidden, too.

"Can you ride farther?" The dark knight's deep voice came from beneath his steel helm.

"Should you not be a-kissing her hand and asking if she isna weary from riding afore you ask if she can go on?" Jamie, Linnet's favorite brother, challenged the MacKenzie. Her other brothers echoed Jamie's sentiments, but Linnet's own bravura faltered when instead of answering Jamie, her betrothed swept them all with a dark glare of his own.

Did he not think enough of her to give her a proper greeting? Was she so low in his esteem he'd forgotten the rules of chivalry?

Still, she kept her shoulders back and her chin up, angry at his lack of courtesy.

" 'Tis Linnet of Dundonnell I be." She lifted her chin a notch higher. "And who be *you*, milord?"

"Now is not the time for pleasantries. I would that we make haste from here if you are not too weary."

She was *bone weary*, but she would rather perish afore she'd admit weakness.

Linnet glanced at her pony. His coat was slick with sweat, and heavy breathing bespoke the toll the long day's exertion had cost the animal. "I am not weary, Sir *Duncan*, but my mount canna continue. Can we not make camp here and journey onward on the morrow?"

"Marmaduke!" The MacKenzie shouted rather than answered her. "Hie yourself over here!"

All the proud resolve she'd mustered fled when the object of his bellowing rode forward. The knight with the harmless-sounding name was the ugliest and most formidable man she'd ever seen. Marmaduke wore the MacKenzie plaid over his hauberk, and, like the other guardsmen, his only headpiece was a mail coif. But in *his* case, Linnet wished he'd donned a concealing helm like her betrothed.

His disfigured face presented a visage so terrifying, her toes curled within her brogans. An ugly scar made a wide slash across his face, beginning at his left temple and ending at the right corner of his mouth, pulling his lips into a permanent downward sneer. Worse, where his left eye should have been, 'twas a frightful mound of puckered pink flesh!

Linnet knew she should feel naught but pity for the brawny warrior, but the fierce expression in his good eye, which was disconcertingly focused on her, only filled her with terror.

Fear sent her blood rushing so loudly through her ears that she did not hear what Sir Duncan told the man, but she knew it concerned her, for the one-eyed Marmaduke kept his feral gaze trained on her, nodding once, before he turned his horse and galloped off into the woods.

Her relief at his abrupt departure escaped in one quick breath. If the saints were with her, he wouldn't return.

Unfortunately, her relief was short-lived for Duncan MacKenzie shot out one arm, scooped her off her pony, and plunked her down in front of him on his great charger. With his free hand, he snatched her mount's reins. She could barely breathe, so firmly did his arm hold her in place.

A great roar of protest rose up from her brothers, Ranald's voice a shade louder than the rest, "Handle our sister so roughly again, MacKenzie, and you'll be dead before you can draw your blade!"

In a heartbeat, her betrothed wheeled his mount toward her eldest brother. "Cool your temper, MacDonnell, lest I forget this was meant to be a friendly assignation."

"I will not tolerate anyone manhandling my sister," Ranald warned. "Especially you."

"Be you Ranald?" The MacKenzie asked, boldly ignoring Ranald's ire. At her brother's curt nod, he continued, "The kinsmen you seek are in the woods beyond my standard-bearers. They've been assured any further raids onto my land will be punished with a worse fate than being held hostage. The cattle your sire awaits are in your men's care. I have kept my word. We shall leave you here."

Ranald MacDonnell bristled visibly. "We mean to see our sister safely to Eilean Creag Castle."

"Think you I canna protect her on the journey to my own keep?"

"What you propose is an insult to my sister," Jamie protested. "We meant to stay a few nights to discuss the wedding preparations. Our father expects tidings upon our return."

Duncan adjusted his hold, pulling Linnet backward against his chest. "Inform your sire all has been arranged, the banns read. We shall wed the morn after we reach Eilean Creag. 'Tis no need for Magnus MacDonnell to bother himself with the journey."

"Surely you jest!" Jamie's face colored. "Linnet canna marry without her kinsmen present. 'Twillna—"

" 'Twould be wise to remember I do not jest." Duncan turned back to Linnet's elder brother, tossing him her pony's reins. "See to your sister's mount and be gone from my land."

Ranald caught the reins with one hand, his other going to the hilt of his sword. "I dinna ken who be more the bastard, you or my father. Dismount and unsheathe your blade. I canna—"

"Humor an old woman and cease bickering, all of you!" Her gray hair badly disheveled from the journey, and her plump cheeks red with exertion, Elspeth Beaton spurred her pony through the circle of men. With a shrewd gaze, she turned first to the MacKenzie guardsmen, then to the MacDonnell brothers. "Unhand your blade, Ranald. 'Tis no secret your sister would enjoy her wedding more without the likes o' her father present. 'Twould be foolish to shed blood over what we all know to be better for the lass."

She waited until Ranald let go of his sword, then stared straight at Duncan. "Will you not allow the lass to have her brothers present at her wedding?"

"And who are you?"

"Elspeth Beaton. I've cared for Linnet since her mother died birthing her, and I dinna mean to stop now." Her voice held the confidence and authority of a well-loved and devoted servant. "Your broad shoulders speak o' hard training, milord, but I am not a-feared of you. I willna allow anyone to mistreat my lady, not even you."

Turning to gaze up at him, Linnet saw a corner of her betrothed's lips rise at Elspeth's words. But the faint smile vanished in a heartbeat, quickly replaced by . . . nothing.

Suddenly she knew what had bothered her the most since he'd hauled her onto his horse.

The rumors were true.

Duncan MacKenzie possessed neither heart nor soul. Naught but emptiness filled the huge man who held her.

"'Tis I who decide who sleeps under my roof. Linnet of Dundonnell's kinsmen may rest here this night and depart MacKenzie land at daybreak. You, milady, shall continue with us to Eilean Creag."

Duncan signaled to a young man, who promptly rode forward leading a riderless gray mare. Turning his attention back to Elspeth, he said, "The mare was meant for your mistress, but she shall ride with me." He gave the squire a curt nod. "Lachlan, help the lady mount. We've tarried long enough."

The squire, young but well muscled, sprang from his own horse and plucked Elspeth off her pony as if she weighed no more than a feather. In one fluid motion, he hoisted her onto the saddle of the larger gray. As soon as she'd settled, he made her a low bow, then swung back onto his own steed.

Elspeth blushed. No one else would notice—for her cheeks were already mightily flushed from the long ride and her anger.

But Linnet *knew*.

Her beloved Elspeth had been charmed by the squire's gallantry.

Then Duncan MacKenzie gave the order to ride. In a daring move, her brothers spurred their horses forward to block the way. "Hold, MacKenzie! I'll have a word with you first," Ranald yelled, and Linnet's betrothed reined in immediately, having no choice unless he cared to plow through the wall of horseflesh made by her brothers.

"Speak your piece and be quick about it," the MacKenzie said curtly. "Do not think I will hesitate to ride straight through you if you try my patience over-long."

"A warning, naught else," Ranald called. "Know this. Our father is not the man he once was, and he may not care for Linnet as he should, but my brothers and I do. These Highlands won't be big enough to hide you should you harm a single hair on our sister's head."

"Your sister will be well treated at Eilean Creag," came Duncan MacKenzie's terse reply.

Ranald gave him a sharp nod, then, one by one, her brothers freed the path, and the MacKenzie warriors kneed their horses. The lot of them surged forward as one. Linnet barely managed to bid her brothers good-bye. Their own shouts of farewell were lost in the thunder of hooves, the clank of heavily armed men, and the creak of saddle leather.

Her betrothed held her well and 'twas glad she was for his strong grip. Ne'er had she sat upon a beast so large, and the distance to the hard ground speeding past beneath them was daunting.

But while Duncan MacKenzie's firm hold kept her secure, and his mighty presence kept her physical body warm, he exuded an unholy chill that went straight to her core. 'Twas a deep cold, more biting than the darkest winter wind.

A shudder shook her and, immediately, his arm tightened, drawing her nearer. To her surprise, the gesture, whether meant to be protective or done out of sheer instinct, made her feel secure. It warmed her, too, making her belly feel all soft and fluttery.

Warm.

Despite the cold of the man.

Linnet sighed and let herself rest against him . . . only for a moment, then she'd straighten. He *was* a MacKenzie after all. But ne'er before had she been held in a man's arms. None could blame her if she relaxed for just a wee bit and tried to understand the unusual sensations stirring deep within her.

Several hours later she awoke, stretched out upon a bed of soft grass, her leather pouch of herbs beneath her head. Someone had wrapped her in a warm wool plaid.

She found herself in the midst of a camp full of MacKenzies.

All in varying stages of undress.

Elspeth slept nearby, next to a crackling fire, and Linnet did not fail to notice the old woman's snores sounded quite content.

Too content.

Apparently her beloved servant had accepted their predicament. Pushing herself up on her elbows, Linnet peered at the sleeping woman. Elspeth might be swayed by the courtly flirtations of a MacKenzie squire, but she wouldn't be.

She didn't care how many MacKenzie men played the gallant. Nor did it matter that being held by her husband-to-be's strong arms had nigh turned her belly to mush. The pleasurable feeling had surely been caused by her relief upon knowing he wouldn't let her be dashed to the ground.

Ne'er would a MacKenzie arouse stirrings of passion in her. Nay, 'twas unthinkable.

And, unlike Elspeth, she found naught appealing about being surrounded by the enemy.

Especially near-naked ones!

"Lachlan, help me off with my hauberk." Her betrothed's voice, deep and masculine, came from the other side of the fire.

"As you wish, milord." The young man scrambled at the MacKenzie's command, fair falling over his feet to do his master's bidding.

Linnet stared as her future husband pulled his helm from his head, revealing a tousled mane of lustrous dark hair.

Praise be the saints he stood with his back to her, for she'd begun to tremble.

As she watched, he let the steel headgear fall to the ground with a heavy thump, then removed his gauntlets. With both hands, he ran his fingers roughly through black hair that fell in thick, sweat-sheened waves almost to his shoulders.

Linnet swallowed hard, uncomfortably aware that her stomach was beginning to grow mushy again. Could the man be a spellcaster? Had he bewitched her? With hair as dark as sin, and glossy as a raven's wing, she supposed the rumors about the devil spawning him could be true.

'Twas common knowledge beauty and evil often walked hand in hand.

When his squire pulled the black mail hauberk over Duncan MacKenzie's head, her breath left her in an audible rush, and she feared her heart would stop beating. The sight of Sir Duncan's broad back captivated her as thoroughly as if a sorcerer had indeed cast an enchantment over her.

Flickering light from the campfire played upon finely honed muscles that rippled with each move he made as he bent to aid his squire in removing the rest of his garb. Not even Ranald's fearsome build matched Duncan MacKenzie's.

Her heart sprang back to life, leaping to her throat as he rolled a pair of thin woolen braies down his muscular legs. Faith, even his buttocks appeared fierce and proud! Linnet wet her lips and gulped, hoping to ease the sudden dryness in her mouth.

She'd seen every one of her eight brothers and a

goodly number of her cousins unclothed. But nary a one had looked as intimidating as the giant who stood across the fire from her.

Nor as fine.

As she gaped, unable to tear her gaze away, he stretched his arms above his head. Powerful shoulder muscles rolled and bunched beneath skin burnished deep gold by the firelight. Faith and mercy, naught in her score o' years had prepared her for such a sight! He could pass for a pagan god, so magnificent was his form.

The thought of being *bedded* by such a man filled her with more trepidation than if she'd been ordered to tame one of the sea monsters known to dwell in Highland lochs!

But even *that* fear dwindled in the face of the terror that seized her when he turned around. She didn't even spare more than a quick glance at the impressive array of virility displayed proudly at his dark groin.

Nay, 'twas her first good glimpse of his face what chilled her to the very marrow of her bones and brought back a long-suppressed memory.

With horrible clarity, she realized why she'd gotten gooseflesh upon hearing her betrothed referred to as the Black Stag.

St. Columba and his host of holy brothers preserve her condemned soul: She'd been sold to the man of her most frightening girlhood vision.

The man without a heart.

2

$a$ll through the night, fragments from Linnet's most unsettling girlhood vision plagued her, robbing her of sleep and alarming her more than if she'd been visited by a thousand nightmares.

Long-suppressed images of a mortally wounded stag, black with its own blood, its heart torn from its body, rose in her mind, and she relived the shocking scene she'd endured on the day of her last unmarried sister's wedding.

She'd fled the drunken merrymakers at the *ceilidh* celebrating Caterine's nuptials, escaping to Dundonnell's bailey where the vision overtook her at the courtyard well. Ne'er had she suspected she was seeing her own betrothed!

As vividly as then, Linnet saw herself nearing the stag, hoping to ease its pain. But before she could help, the animal had transformed itself into a man. A fierce-looking but handsome warrior, and like the stag, he was covered with blood, his heart missing. The man had stared at her with pain-filled eyes, beseeching her to help him. He'd reached out to her, but terror had consumed her, and she'd run away.

As she must run now, for the frightful creature was nigh upon her. She could almost feel his bloodied hands on her flesh. With a scream, Linnet came fully awake. The image that greeted her was almost more upsetting than her long-ago vision.

Duncan MacKenzie straddled her, his iron-hard thighs pressed tight against her hips. His broad shoulders loomed above her, and light from the moon glinted off his dark hair. And he was unclothed . . . fully naked!

Linnet's pulse quickened, and an unexpected thrill of excitement shot through her at the feel of his warm, well-muscled body so intimately close to hers.

"Saints, Maria, and Joseph, lass," he swore then, his breath coming hard and fast, his rough words breaking the spell, reminding her who he was. "I thought you'd ne'er cease fighting me," he panted. " 'Tis trying to calm you I was, not harm you."

Calm her? Linnet swallowed hard. How could she be calm with *that* part of him mere inches from her belly?

Slowly, her wits cleared, and the remaining dread from reliving the vision eased out of her, but these strange new sensations increased. A pleasurable ache began deep inside her, its center low in her abdomen near where the MacKenzie's male parts almost touched her. Then *that* part of her started pulsing, and she knew.

'Twas desire she felt.

Her first true stirrings of passion . . . and ignited by a MacKenzie!

Indignation ripped through her, followed by an alarming thought: Did he feel the same things he'd awakened in her? Her gaze flew to his face, and she saw he did. He still scowled, but the look in his eyes revealed his lust.

As did the rigid shaft of his manhood, no longer relaxed, but boldly riding hard against the darkness of his groin.

Linnet squirmed to break free of him. "Release me! I dinna need this sort of calming."

"Ho, Duncan! Is aught amiss?" came a deep voice from the far side of the camp.

"Nay, all is well," the MacKenzie called back. "The lass had a bad dream. 'Tis over now."

The heat she'd glimpsed in his eyes a moment before had vanished, but his frown remained. "Sssshh," he warned her, placing his fingers over her lips. "I willna have you waking my men with your cries. They need their rest."

Releasing her at last, he pushed to his feet. Though he gave her a look of greatly taxed patience, a muscle jerked in his jaw and revealed the effort his stone-faced expression cost him.

"Can you return to sleep?" he wanted to know, seemingly unaware or uncaring that his manhood yet gave proof of what had just transpired between them.

"Aye." Linnet nodded and hoped the saints would forgive her the lie. Relief filled her when he nodded back, then left her to return to his own sleeping place on the other side of the low-burning fire.

Again and again as she awaited the dawn, she'd cast furtive glances at her betrothed as he slept . . . half-expecting him to shapeshift into a mortally wounded stag, black with its own blood. Or that he'd roll to face her, and she'd see a gaping hole in his chest where his heart should be.

Or worse, that she'd drift to sleep, then awaken to find him crouched over her again . . . naked.

But he'd not stirred, sleeping on, while she'd spent the remainder of the night beseeching the saints to grant her the fortitude she'd need to wed the man whose disturbing image had haunted her girlhood nightmares.

And now, as they rode through the rain toward the MacKenzie stronghold, Linnet huddled deeper into her cloak, seeking whatever warmth the threadbare garment would give her.

But it wasn't truly physical comfort she sought. Since her da had e'er spent what meager funds he had on stocking Dundonnell's stores of ale and throwing raucous *ceilidhs* for his friends, she'd never worn aught but handed-down gowns of thin, scratchy wool, and she'd learned long ago to ignore the blisters caused by ill-fitting passed-along shoes.

Nay, bodily discomfort did not bother her overmuch. And, despite the lashing wind off the loch and the pelting rain with its bone-chilling damp, her betrothed held her securely before him, shielding her well from the elements.

Turning her head to the side, Linnet stared out across the storm-tossed water, but the landscape of sea, loch, and islands was little more than a silver-gray blur as the MacKenzie's great steed carried them at a thundering pace along the shingle-lined edge of the loch.

From the distant shore, a seabird trilled to its mate. The lonely sound drove home her own forlorn state of mind. Whilst the solitary bird sought to call through the mists to its partner, *hers* could not be nearer yet ne'er had she felt more alone.

Mayhaps, under other circumstances, time would have erased her grudges against the MacKenzies. If she looked deep into her soul, she knew most of the sharp reprisals they'd suffered upon her clan had usually been dealt after the MacDonnells had gone raiding, not afore.

And ne'er without cause.

Her soon-to-be husband was stern, and sparse with words, but he did not seem the ruthless man she'd expected.

Aye, in time, she could have put aside her ill will toward the MacKenzies. And she knew he could teach her about passion.

But she didn't know if she could live with his face, dinna ken if she could e'er look upon him and not see his chest ripped open, his heart missing.

Nor did she know if she could ignore the peculiar physical impact he had on her either.

Uncomfortable with the strange and conflicting feelings he stirred within her, especially those he'd aroused in the night, she squirmed, and immediately, he tightened his grip on her. The feel of his mail-covered chest so close against her back and his well-muscled thighs pressing so intimately against hers made her belly go all soft and mushy again. As they rode on, Linnet grew acutely aware of every place their bodies touched.

With a weary hand, she brushed aside the rivulets of rain coursing down her forehead. Secretly, she welcomed the cooling wetness, for her cheeks had become very hot. Squinting, she tried to peer through the drifting sheets of fog, and at the same moment, the mists parted, revealing a massive keep on an island in the middle of the loch and still some leagues away.

The imposing castle could only be Eilean Creag, her new home.

Forbidding walls of gray stone rose straight up from the dark waters of Loch Duich and she caught a brief glimpse of a stone causeway leading to the heavily fortified stronghold before the mists engulfed the bridge once more, making the castle appear as if it were floating above the loch.

Aptly named for the island of rock it stood upon, Eilean Creag presented itself as a gray and solemn mass of stone isolated from the rest of the world.

A dead place, void of life and love.

Even at a distance, Linnet's gift let her sense the cold hanging over the austere castle Duncan MacKenzie called home. Its chill enveloped her like a shroud.

An empty chill that had naught to do with the foul weather, an impression so intense it lifted the fine hairs on the back of her neck. Indeed, she feared none but the most barren of souls could survive in such a place.

Abruptly and without warning, Duncan reined in his horse as a single rider bore down on them from the direction of the castle. Linnet resisted the urge to cross herself as the rider neared and she recognized him.

St. Margaret stay her by . . . 'twas the one called Marmaduke.

Despite the unease she felt toward the MacKenzie, she pressed herself back against his chest. Although she knew her fear of the disfigured knight was unfounded, his fearsome visage filled her with trepidation.

A sidelong glance at Elspeth did naught to ease her mind. 'Twas obvious she could not expect help from *that* quarter. Seemingly impervious to her soaked garments, the old woman beamed at the young squire, Lachlan, and several other MacKenzie guardsmen, listening eagerly to their tales of Sir Duncan's heroic adventures with the good King Robert Bruce.

Linnet caught boasts of how the Black Stag had rallied the contingent of Highlanders prior to the king's great victory at Bannockburn. According to his men, her betrothed had persuaded the chiefs to abandon their feuds in the face of their common enemy, then helped the Bruce to train the men who would form the king's own battle division.

'Twas highly doubtful the well-loved king had required her betrothed's assistance in dealing with the Highlanders, but that wasn't near as far-fetched as his mens' claims he'd used naught but a battle-ax to best twenty English knights who'd seized Scotland's most sacred relics from the Abbot of Inchaffray! And, of course, the Black Stag had fought his way back to the Bruce's side, returning the king's precious reliquary box, unharmed.

Linnet's brows drew together in a frown. Her beloved childhood nurse appeared totally unaware of her distress. Elspeth had let the bonnie faces and glib tongues of the MacKenzie men bewitch her.

"Were you successful?" Her betrothed's deep voice

sounded behind her, tearing her attention away from Elspeth. The one-eyed knight had drawn up before them. "I
expected you sooner."

"The chest was locked, and Fergus took his bloody
time fetching the key." Marmaduke fixed Linnet with a
sharp look from his good eye, then patted a leather
satchel fastened to the back of his saddle. "I regret the
delay, milord. I meant to make haste because of the rain,
but I've brought all you desired."

"'Tis good of you and well you intercepted us before we reached the gates." Duncan's hands suddenly
grasped Linnet's waist. "Will you help the lady dismount?"

"'Twould be an honor." The battle-scarred knight
swung down from his horse and strode forward.

Then, before Linnet could utter a word of protest,
Duncan lifted her in midair, passing her into Marmaduke's upraised hands. The fearsome warrior knight
did not toss her over his shoulder and abduct her as she'd
half feared, but deposited her most gently on her feet. He
even made her a low bow.

"Sir Marmaduke Strongbow, milady," he said in a
voice too chivalrous to match his frightening appearance. "I am pleased to be of service to you."

Linnet gasped upon hearing his voice clearly for the
first time.

Sir Marmaduke was a Sassunach!

Surprise made it impossible for her to do more than
nod in answer. An Englishman! Ne'er had she seen one,
and she couldn't imagine why the MacKenzie would
have a Sassunach in his guard.

Shivering with cold, she watched Sir Marmaduke

lift Elspeth from the gray mare. He held the stout woman as if she weighed no more than a sack of goose feathers and carried her to where Linnet stood, setting her down with great gentleness. After bowing to Elspeth, too, he returned to his steed and retrieved the large leather satchel.

The MacKenzie also dismounted and joined him. While Sir Marmaduke held the pouch open, her betrothed glanced inside and nodded in apparent approval. Linnet watched him pull a length of fine dark blue wool and a pair of half boots out of the satchel. He laid the wool over his arm and made straight for her.

"This cloak belonged to my sister," he said. "Remove the sodden one you wear, and I shall fasten this one about your shoulders. 'Tis better made than yours and should keep you warm and dry for the remainder of the journey."

Beyond where they stood, she saw the Sassunach help Elspeth out of her own drenched mantle and assist her in donning a dry one almost as fine as the one her betrothed held ready for her.

Shame and guilt flooded Linnet. The one-eyed knight had departed so hurriedly yestereve to fetch raiments for her and Elspeth.

And on the MacKenzie's orders.

Despite the chill rain and the soggy *arisaid* she'd insisted on draping over the new cloak, heat spread up her neck. She hadn't imagined her husband-to-be capable of thoughtfulness. She'd only noted the emptiness he carried inside and had cringed in terror upon recognizing his face.

She'd been unjust to the scar-faced Sassunach, too.

Regardless of the reason he found himself in the Highlands, far from his native land, he'd proved himself a
gallant and she'd thank him for his good deed.

As for the MacKenzie, she'd thank him, too, but reserve further judgment until she understood his motive.
Mayhap he simply didn't want his people to see her own
lowly garments when she entered his hall?

"These are newly crafted," he said, handing her the
footgear. "If they do not fit, I'll order another pair made
for you."

Linnet glanced at her scuffed brogans, embarrassed
to see her big toe poking through the worn and cracked
leather. "Thank you," she said stiffly, exchanging the
butter-soft boots for her old ones.

"'Tis not necessary to thank me." His voice sounded
flat, void of emotion. He nodded toward Elspeth. "If
you're both prepared to continue, we will ride on. We are
nigh upon Eilean Creag."

Although the fine cloak shielded her well from the
rain and wind as they rode along the shore, it did naught
to protect her from her growing sense of unease.

While the forbidding stone castle loomed larger with
every mile they covered, Duncan MacKenzie seemed to
grow more distant the closer they came to his home. The
barrier of ice Linnet sensed he'd built around himself intensified, becoming colder, more impenetrable, now that
they had almost reached his formidable domain.

Despite the heavy woolen mantle, Linnet shivered
as if it were the dead of winter and not midsummer.

She prayed silently as the heavily burdened horses
clattered under the raised portcullis of a fortified gate-

house and continued across a long stone causeway to the island fortress.

The atmosphere was bleak, dismal, and pressed in on her from all sides. Again, she suppressed the urge to flee. Yet, even if she could spring from the MacKenzie's mighty horse, where would she go? On either side of the low bridge, the dark waters of Loch Duich churned angrily, while strong gusts of chill wind sent low, rain-leaden clouds scuttling across the loch's wind-whipped surface.

Undoubtedly Eilean Creag would appear more majestic than gloomy on a fairer day, but to Linnet, the somber gray of its massive walls and the evening's murkiness seemed a most appropriate home for the solemn-faced man she must wed.

At the end of the causeway, they paused before the final gatehouse, a massive twin-towered structure, while yet another portcullis rattled upward. Linnet's spirits sank lower as they rode beneath the steel-tipped spikes and into the yawning darkness of a tunnel-like passage.

Her breath caught in her throat, near choking her, at her first glimpse of the keep itself. It stood across a cobbled bailey, grim and unwelcoming.

A stone fortress on an island of stone, ruled by a man whose heart had turned to stone—if indeed he still had one.

Linnet had her doubts for a tangible air of unhappiness, powerful enough to crush anyone's heart and soul, pervaded Eilean Creag. The oppressive atmosphere bore heavily on her shoulders, the sheer strength of it making her almost physically ill.

Not a soul stirred within the courtyard or near the

outbuildings clustered around the outer walls as they rode across the cobbled bailey, halting at the keep's broad stone steps. Duncan MacKenzie quickly dismounted, plucked her from his horse, and set her down beneath an arched entrance bearing the MacKenzie coat of arms.

As if in a hurry to be rid of her, he let go of her immediately and mounted the steps. At the top, he opened a large, iron-studded door, then turned to face her.

"Lachlan will take you to Robbie," he said. "I would speak with you in my solar after you've seen him."

Linnet opened her mouth to speak, but he'd already stepped into the gloom beyond the door. She followed him, entering a dimly lit vaulted hall of enormous proportions. Without further acknowledgment of her presence, he strode briskly past rows of trestle tables and benches, elbowed his way through a knot of servants busily decorating the raised dais at the far end of the hall, and disappeared up a shadowy stairwell.

Speechless at being fair abandoned in a yet-strange hall, Linnet stared after him, grateful the sputtering rush torches did not provide enough light for those present to see how her cheeks flamed at his callous dismissal.

She bristled. Whether the arrangement pleased either of them or nay, she was entitled to be treated with civility. Apparently her husband-to-be considered a warm cloak and newly cobbled shoes adequate adherence to the codes of decency.

"'Tis not personal, my lady. He hasna been himself for a long time," his squire, Lachlan, said, stepping up beside her. "If you'll follow me, I'll show you where you may refresh yourself. After you've had a light repast, I'll take you to Robbie."

Elspeth joined them, placing her hands gently on Linnet's shoulders. "Dinna look so lost, child; you've carried yourself so well thus far. Unless my perception is failing me, the man's behavior just now has naught to do with you. Simply be yourself, and all will be well."

"I hope you're right," Linnet replied, more to herself than to Elspeth. "For the love of St. Margaret and all that's holy, I hope you're right."

"If you'll allow me, I shall take you to meet Robbie now." Lachlan the squire appeared just as Linnet finished a small portion of fish stew and pushed aside the empty bowl. " 'Twas my master's wish you see the lad as soon as possible."

Linnet stood, patted her still-damp head veil and readjusted the dampish folds of her mother's *arisaid*, then let the squire grip her elbow and guide her through the great hall. He skillfully dodged hordes of scurrying servants as they rushed about, their arms laden, no doubt tending to preparations for the next day's wedding festivities. Some sent shy glances her way, others stared more openly.

Hopefully they'd think she still wore her rain-dampened garments because she was too tired to change clothes after the long journey. She didn't want their pity should they guess she'd brought little with her besides what she had on.

At least, her new cloak was fine and well hid her ragged gown. And, blessedly, unlike her veil and precious *arisaid*, the splendidly woven mantle had stayed fairly dry . . . just as her betrothed had assured her it would.

Aye, let Duncan MacKenzie's servants gape at her. Until she was more ready to face them, the cloak and her veil shielded her well.

The assessing perusals of dining clansmen followed her as well, their curious stares taking in her every move as Lachlan led her past their tables toward a spiral stone staircase barely visible beyond a darkened archway in a far corner of the hall.

Something lurked in the shadowy stair tower . . . a palpable air of sadness so well defined it seemed to have taken on a life of its own. It wasn't the same kind of emptiness that filled and surrounded her husband-to-be, but a feeling of great dejection laced with a very faint trace of hope.

Linnet's instincts told her the oppressive atmosphere had to do with the boy, and suddenly she knew, without yet seeing the child, that he was indeed Duncan MacKenzie's true son.

Ne'er had she been so sure of herself.

The higher they climbed, the more certain she became.

When they reached the third landing and Lachlan made no attempt to halt their ascent, she yanked on his surcoat.

"Aye, milady?"

"Why is the lad hidden away in such a dismal corner of the castle?"

"'Tis not for me to say."

Linnet folded her arms, driven to assertiveness by a sudden overwhelming desire to ease the great pain already reaching her from somewhere higher up in the tower. It came at her like a dark cloud and thickened with each step she took.

"I know Sir Duncan doubts Robbie is his son. Be that the reason he's kept so far from the hall and in such a dark place?"

The flickering glow of a wall torch revealed the squire's discomfort. "Indeed it causes my lord pain to look upon the lad, but I canna say why he's quartered here. 'Twas my master's orders, and I would ne'er venture to question his motives."

At the fourth landing, Lachlan led her down a dim passage, stopping before a heavy oaken door. "He may be asleep."

"Then I willna disturb him," Linnet said in a hushed voice, stepping past him into the shadow-filled chamber the moment he opened the door.

The cloud of sadness she'd sensed on the stairs fair knocked her back into the passageway, so heavily did unhappiness permeate the room. The very walls seemed saturated with distress, and it cost all of Linnet's strength to keep from crumbling to the floor under the sheer weight of the boy's anguish.

Although a fire burned in the stone hearth, it took a moment for her eyes to adjust to the darkness. Purposely, she went to the small chamber's one window and threw open the shutters. When she turned around, she knew her instincts had been correct.

On a canopied bed against the far wall, a small boy slept, one arm flung around an ancient-looking mongrel. The dog glanced warily at her, but the child slept on, unaware she'd entered the room.

Covered by a thick plaid woven in MacKenzie colors, and with only the back of his dark head visible, Robbie MacKenzie didn't stir as she stared across the room at him . . . stared at him and the image of a stag's head hovering in the air above him.

A loud buzzing sounded in her ears and the vision intensified in clarity until it seemed to glow from within. Then the whirring noise stopped, and the image vanished as if it had never been there.

"Are you ill, milady?" Lachlan hurried to her side. "'Tis pale you are. Shall I fetch you a draught of mulled wine? Or escort you to your lady servant?"

Shivers still raced up and down her spine, but she shook her head. "Nay, I am fine now."

"Would you like to rest here afore I take you to Sir Duncan? Robbie will likely awaken at any moment. He doesna sleep well."

Linnet glanced at the child. "Then we dinna want to disturb his rest, do we?"

The squire made no move toward the door, and a light pink tinge colored his cheeks. "My liege had hoped you'd spend some time . . . ah . . . getting to know Robbie."

"'Tisn't possible to do that when the lad's sleeping, now, is it?" Linnet announced, exiting the room. "You can escort me to your liege instead."

"But Sir Duncan—"

"—asked to speak with me afore I retire, did he not?" she persisted, deliberately evading the real reason she'd been ushered to Robbie's chamber. "Will you take me there or nay?"

"Of course, milady," he said, hurrying to join her in the passage.

As she followed him down the stairs, Linnet sent silent prayers to all the saints. She hoped they'd grant her the wisdom to choose her words wisely when she faced the mighty MacKenzie of Kintail. She knew what he wanted from her, and she knew the answer, too.

But she meant to keep her knowledge a secret.

She had a plan, and if the merciful saints were with her, it just might work.

Duncan heard her outside his private chamber long before she chose to make her presence known. She'd waited until his squire's footsteps faded before she rapped on the door. But when he'd called out permission to enter, she'd hesitated.

While he waited, he glanced about the solar, his best-loved room. The only place where he could truly re-move himself from the world.

Escape from the misery that was his life.

Except for the rich silk tapestries on the walls, the solar was austere. A small wooden table, one uncomfort-able chair, and a large strongbox made up the furnish-ings. No cushions adorned the window seats and even the sweeping views of the loch did scarce little to ease the bleakness of the chamber. Only the fire in the hearth provided a semblance of comfort and warmth.

Not that he cared. 'Twas old Fergus, his seneschal, who insisted on keeping the firelog burning. Duncan liked the room sparsely furnished and cold . . . it matched his barren soul.

He'd purposely chosen to meet with his bride-to-be

here, where the severity of the setting would emphasize the image of himself he wished to convey to her.

No longer wearing his sword, but still clad in his hauberk of black mail, he knew he made a daunting presence that would rattle her to her maidenly core despite her repeated displays of courage on their journey.

'Twas better for her if she thought him as cold and immovable as the thick walls of his castle.

He moved to the hearth and stood with his back to the door, waiting. After a moment, he called out again. This time she entered.

When he heard her close the door, he turned around. "Do you know why I chose to take you as my wife?"

For what seemed an eternity, the crackling of the fire made the only sound. Finally, she nodded. "Aye, 'tis because of my gift."

He nodded in return, satisfied.

"You should know I canna make use o' the sight at will. The visions—"

"Your soothsaying abilities are well-known in the Highlands," Duncan cut her off. He'd seen an indefinable expression flicker across her face and didn't want to hear whatever she'd meant to tell him. "I have no doubt you shall provide me with the truth of that which plagues me."

He paused before posing the question he must ask. His dread of her answer sent more terror racing through his veins than he'd e'er felt when facing a full battalion of mounted English knights and their ever-present Welsh archers.

Still, he had to know. "You've seen the child?"

"Aye."

Splendor of God, the wench said no more!

Simply '*aye*.'

Dinna she know he burned for an answer?

"And what did you see?" The words fair burst from his lips.

Rather than answer him, she smoothed her palms on the folds of her cloak and stared at the floor. With her obvious discomfiture, realization dawned. Duncan breathed a sigh of relief. He'd intimidated her more than was his intent, his warrior garb and the bleak solar made her feel small and insignificant.

That had to be the reason for her silence.

Moving to the small table, he filled two jewel-encrusted chalices with a blood-red liquid and handed her one. "'Tis herbed wine. Let us drink to a union that shall be beneficial to us both."

She raised her glass and took a small sip, but the small gesture of welcome Duncan had hoped would put her at ease seemed to have the opposite effect for her hands shook, and she spilled a bit of the wine onto the rushes at her feet.

"I would like to ask a question if I may," she said, her voice steady despite her slight trembling.

Duncan took a long sip of his wine before answering. "What would you know?"

"Our clans have ne'er been friends. Why did you not just kidnap me? Why marriage?"

"Knowing the truth of Robbie's parentage is not the sole reason I chose you." Duncan dragged a hand through his hair and drew a deep breath. Merely speaking about the lad caused him great pain. "Whether he is mine or naught, he needs the care of a loving adult. You shall provide that care."

"And you, sir? A child needs both mother *and* father. A boy-child, especially, should have his father's love. 'Tis not right to withhold it."

At her boldness, Duncan's fingers tightened around his chalice. "You are not here to question my motives."

"I would only know why you need me? A nursemaid could do the same. Or you could foster him to a trusted ally."

"Do not speak of that which you know naught."

She raised her chin at him. "Of loving children, I know much, milord."

Love for a child was something he, too, knew about, but his feelings were no concern of hers. Fighting the anger she stirred within him, Duncan set down his wine and folded his arms.

"So tell me what you saw. Is the lad mine?"

Looking suddenly nervous, she wet her lips before she spoke. "I canna say. Mayhap I need time to know him before my gift will show me."

Not wanting her to see his searing disappointment upon hearing her words, Duncan returned to the fireplace and kept his back to her until he was certain his face bore no emotion.

Finally, he turned around. "How much time?"

"I canna say," she repeated.

Fury, ominous and chilling like a dark wind, consumed him but he said naught. He needed her, for her abilities were genuine. His spies had sworn it. If he must, he'd wait to learn the truth.

But it was nowhere writ he must be pleased at the prospect.

By Saint Peter of Rome, he'd wanted the answer this night.

"When you know, you are to inform me immediately," he said, his tone clipped. "Your duties are to look after Robbie and warn me of any treachery you may foresee. Naught else shall be expected of you."

"Naught else?"

Duncan shot a glance at her. He'd thought she'd be relieved, but she gaped at him as if he'd grown horns and a tail. Then she lowered her head and began poking at the floor rushes with the toe of her new boot.

"I see," she said in a small voice. "You dinna want me as a true consort."

Thunder of heaven! Surely she wasn't upset because he didn't mean to seek her bed?

"Pray do not be offended, lady. It has naught to do with you." He crossed the room and took her chin in his hand, lifting her head so she had to look at him. "I swore upon the death of my first wife ne'er to wed again. By keeping you chaste, I shall not completely break that vow."

Her lower lip began to tremble, but she met his gaze. "As you wish."

" 'Twill not be an unpleasant arrangement," Duncan assured her. "You shall have your own chamber, the leisure to do as you please, and my protection. Mayhap you'll come to enjoy living at Eilean Creag. It canna be as bad as what you've left behind."

"Aye, 'tis grateful I am to be out of my father's hall."

"Good, 'tis settled then." Letting go of her chin,

Duncan stepped away from her and went to the door, opening it. "Can you find your way to the hall? Lachlan should be waiting there to escort you to your quarters. Rest well this night, for tomorrow shall be a long day."

Although he held the door wide, she didn't move. She stood staring at him with the queerest look on her face he'd e'er seen. When a single tear rolled down her cheek, Duncan silently cursed himself and stepped forward, intending to comfort her as best he could, to explain he didn't mean to reject her *personally*.

He didn't want *any* wife.

A score of dancing sirens, all naked and one more desirable than the next, wouldn't persuade him otherwise.

But before he could tell her aught, she dashed past him and fled down the passageway. Duncan waited until the sound of her running footsteps grew faint before he shut the door and slammed his fist against its cold oaken panels.

Again, he swore.

She'd run as if the hounds of hell and the devil himself chased after her.

Duncan pressed his lips together in a grim line.

Mayhap he *was* the devil.

At the moment, he certainly felt like it.

3

"**S**he refuses to come down, sir." Lachlan joined Duncan near the chapel steps, a decidedly uncomfortable look on his youthful face.

Duncan dragged a hand through his hair, then glanced up at the gray morning sky. 'Twas not a good day for a wedding. A chill wind blew from the north, and if the ominous-looking clouds in the distance were any indication, the light drizzle they'd endured since dawn would soon be a full-fledged downpour.

Nay, 'twas not a good day to start a marriage.

And now, in addition to her inability to ease his mind about Robbie with the swiftness he'd hoped, his bride-to-be would humiliate him in front of his men as well.

Dressed in their best plaids and armor, his kinsmen and knights stood in a semicircle before the castle steps, waiting to escort their new mistress to his side. Others formed a long line that stretched from the keep to where he stood in front of the small stone oratory.

They'd all been waiting since dawn.

Duncan glanced over his shoulder at the priest. The holy man stood serene, his hands clasped before him, his whole countenance fair oozing patience. Just beyond him, inside the chapel, dozens of burning candles did naught to dispel the gloom of the dreary morn.

And the clusters of Highland flowers, meant to symbolize fertility and joy, merely emphasized the travesty of what was about to take place.

Only the proximity of the priest prevented Duncan from uttering a string of blasphemous oaths.

"Is she dressed?" he finally asked his squire.

"Aye, milord."

Duncan turned to Sir Marmaduke. The disfigured Sassunach knight lounged against the arched entrance to the chapel, looking for all the world as if he were highly amused by the morning's unusual turn of events.

"Cease gloating like a dim-witted woman," Duncan snapped at him. "'Tis naught funny about the wench playing stubborn."

Marmaduke smiled as best he could. "Do not vent your anger on me. Mayhap you should ask yourself what you did to her to make her choose to stay in her chamber this morn?"

"What I did to her?" Duncan scowled. "I've done naught. 'Tis grateful she should be. I've rescued her from a drunken sire and gifted her with chests of finer gowns than she's likely ever seen, much less possess."

"Then what transpired in your solar yestereve to

make her come running down to the hall as if a horde of banshees pursued her?"

Duncan forgot the priest and swore.

Marmaduke walked over to Duncan and slapped him on the back. "There is your answer, my friend. Whatever you said was not to her liking. I always told you to use more finesse with the ladies."

"I said naught to upset her," Duncan repeated, glancing up at the tower window he knew to be her chamber. "I simply told her very little would be expected of her."

"And how did you word that?" Marmaduke pressed further.

Duncan blew out a breath. "For the love of St. Mungo, you persistent swine, I only said naught else would be asked of her except the use of her sight and tending to Robbie."

Marmaduke whistled, then slowly shook his head. "'Tis worse than I feared. How could a man who's spent so much time in the company of Robert Bruce manage to make a blundering fool of himself with a woman?"

Something that sounded suspiciously like suppressed laughter came from Lachlan, then rippled through the ranks of his men, earning them each a furious glare.

By the heavens, they were laughing at him!

"If you think you are such a charmer, English, then why don't *you* hie yourself up to her chamber and fetch her down here?"

"'Twould be my pleasure." Marmaduke made him a low bow, then headed toward the castle. After ten paces, he stopped and looked back. "Mayhap someday I shall give you lessons in how to treat a lady."

To Duncan's surprise, Marmaduke emerged from the keep a short time later, followed by his bride and her servant. Immediately, his pages blasted their trumpets and his knights fell into place behind the trio as they crossed the cobbled bailey, the lot of them cheering as if they were about to witness a real wedding and not a farce.

The nearer they came, the more Duncan began to regret his decision to make the MacDonnell lass his wife. Aye, he should have kidnapped her, forced her to quell his doubts about Robbie, then sent her back to Dundonnell. Instead, he'd soon be burdened by a second wife he did not want.

'Twas only a small comfort she looked equally unhappy about the situation.

Everyone else present seemed determined to make fools of themselves.

His men cavorted about like a group of silly women. Shouting jests and cheering, they behaved as if they were all simpleminded. Even his bride's old servant beamed, blushing at his men's antics as if she were a young girl of ten-and-four and not a mature woman long past her prime.

"She's a fetching sight, aye, milord?" Lachlan commented, as Marmaduke escorted the two ladies nearer.

Duncan kept silent. He did not want to admit, even to himself, that Linnet MacDonnell did indeed make a lovely bride.

She wore a heavy silk tunic of deep blue, fastened at her waist by an intricate girdle of gold. A full-length cloak of the same blue protected her from the rain and a jewel-encrusted circlet held a long golden head-veil in place. She'd kept her hair unbound, letting it spill from beneath her veil to flow in a shining curtain of bronze waves to her waist.

Duncan uttered a silent oath, angry at himself that, even for a split second, he'd wondered what it would feel like to run his hands through such tresses.

By the saints, 'twas like spun gold!

Ne'er had he suspected she would have such glorious hair. Why, 'twould tempt St. Columba himself!

Thunder of heaven, he'd have an explanation for this. He'd been assured the lass was plain, as unappealing as a sow's hindquarters.

He didn't want a comely wife.

Never again.

Not after Cassandra and the suffering she'd wrought with her evil ways.

Nay, 'twas not a fetching wench he'd wanted, but it appeared he'd gotten one despite his wishes to the contrary.

Ignoring the way her hair flowed over obviously full breasts which he'd not truly appreciated earlier because of the ill-fitting garments she'd worn on the journey, Duncan set his face in what he hoped to be a fierce grimace as Marmaduke guided her up the chapel steps.

He would simply force himself to see her as she'd appeared the day before: plain and garbed in rags.

Aye, he would concentrate on that image and not look at her hair. In fact, he'd insist she wear her red-gold tresses braided and wrapped around her head *and* hidden beneath a veil at all times.

As for her breasts . . . he'd simply pretend they weren't there.

He only hoped his men did not insist on a bedding ceremony. They knew full well why he was marrying the lass. The subject had been much discussed of late. If they'd conveniently forgotten his reasons and expected him to perform the role of besotted and eager groom, he'd personally challenge each of them to a round of swordplay in the lists and cheerfully carve them to ribbons!

"'Tis time, milord." Marmaduke propelled his bride toward him. "Do you not want to escort your lady up the chapel steps?"

Duncan glowered, not bothering to hide his displeasure. The only place he wanted to escort Linnet MacDonnell was back to her father's miserable keep. Instead, he offered her his arm and took small satisfaction in the fear he read in her large brown eyes.

If she feared him, she wouldn't regret his absence from her bed.

Unfortunately, he'd noticed more than the expression in her eyes. He'd also noted they were flecked with gold and would likely be most appealing were they lit by a smile rather than dulled by resignation.

Then his men pressed forward, giving him no alternative but to guide his unwanted wife-to-be up the few stones steps to where the priest waited before the opened chapel door.

As if the holy father knew Duncan would flee if given the slightest chance, he immediately began the ceremony that would bind the MacDonnell wench to Duncan for the rest of his days, God willing.

Sheer curiosity, nothing more, made Duncan steal a glance at his bride during the opening prayer. Sooty lashes rested on her cheeks . . . cheeks that, if possible, had grown even more pale since the priest had begun his sacred monologue.

Her lips moved in silent prayer, and, saints preserve him, he couldn't help notice how full they were. Luscious and supple-looking, she had lips he would've claimed in a swift and possessive kiss in earlier years.

Before he'd cast aside such foolhardy notions.

Unshed tears clung to her thick lashes, and at the sight of one of them breaking away to roll down her cheek, the cold knot in his stomach tightened and some accursed muscle in his jaw began to twitch with a vengeance.

By Lucifer's knees, surely the prospect of wedding him wasn't *that* unbearable?

He was the one getting the lesser end of the bargain, after all, not her. She had much to gain.

One look, though, at the way she clasped her hands tightly before her, assured him she did indeed dread becoming his wife.

Duncan fought the urge to swear. He was not an ogre, and he had tried to offer her comfort last night. He couldn't be faulted because she'd sped from the solar before he'd had the chance.

Many were the women who would gladly throw themselves at his feet. At least in the old days before Cassandra's perfidy had ruined his life. And in the years he'd fought alongside the Bruce, there'd not been a single night during their forays across the land he'd had to sleep alone . . . unless he chose to do so.

His prowess in bed had been almost as legendary as that of his king's.

'Twas grateful the MacDonnell wench should be to become his bride.

Not that he intended to consummate their marriage.

As the priest droned on, Duncan's gaze fell upon Linnet's breasts. They rose and fell with her breathing, and only a blind man would not notice the alluring curves they made beneath the heavy silk of her gown.

A loud clearing of someone's throat, and the sharp jab of an elbow in his side snapped his attention back to the ceremony. By St. Ninian's breath, 'twas almost over! He'd scarce been aware of speaking his vows, barely recalled the blessing and exchanging of rings.

Yet there the priest stood, holding a rolled parchment and waiting expectantly for Duncan to take the proffered quill and sign his soul away.

As if an unseen force guided his hand, Duncan scrawled his name on the document and handed the quill to his bride. She did the same, then before Duncan realized what was happening, they'd been ushered into the chapel for mass and holy communion.

'Twas over.

A few words, a signature, mumbled blessings he'd scarce registered, and he was once more married. Bound, at least in name, to a new wife who looked at him with huge brown eyes as if he was about to carry her into the very depths of hell.

And, he admitted bitterly, mayhap he was.

But for some reason he could not fathom, he felt an undeniable urge to prove he was not the demon she apparently thought him to be. For a very brief moment, Duncan desired to see her gold-flecked eyes shining with joy rather than staring at him in dread.

'Twas a good thing he'd chosen a chamber for her that was as far as possible from his own. Everyone in his household knew he wanted naught of her. Pride alone would keep him from crossing the great hall to reach the stairs leading to her quarters.

If his men thought he'd changed his convictions and would chase after her like a rutting stag, they would be sorely disappointed. Let *them* make fools of themselves, he decided, as they crowded around her the minute they stepped from the chapel. They were the ones who claimed 'twas time he sought the love of a virtuous woman, not he.

Aye, let them make blithering idiots of themselves if it so pleased them.

Only Sir Marmaduke had the good grace to remain by his side. Unfortunately, Duncan suspected the man stayed near only to prevent him from riding off somewhere, rather than out of any sense of loyalty. Considering the way the Englishman preened himself in her presence, acting more chivalrous than the most adept French courtier, Duncan had no doubt but that Marmaduke had appointed himself Lady Linnet's champion.

Not that she needed one.

Even though she'd appeared subdued and unhappy during the wedding ceremony, his new wife had a mind of her own. She'd proven the strength of her nerve yestereve in his solar.

Turning, he fixed his friend with an unflinching glare. "What did you say to get her down here?"

Sir Marmaduke folded his arms and had the bad taste to look mightily pleased with himself.

"Well?"

"Naught but what I thought the lady wanted to hear."

Duncan resisted the urge to throttle the Englishman. "Pray enlighten me what that might have been."

"Simply that you meant not all you said to her in your solar yestereve, that you spoke out of consideration for her maidenly state, not wanting to unduly frighten her."

The sudden pealing of the kirk's bells and the equally loud cheering of his clansmen drowned out Duncan's black oath. He frowned as he watched his men practically tripping over their own clumsy feet as they vied for his bride's attention.

St. Columba preserve him, had they forgotten the treachery and intrigues that had poisoned Eilean Creag the last time a Lady MacKenzie had resided within his castle?

Deliberately hanging back, Duncan watched the boisterous crowd of merrymakers surge toward the hall, his new wife ensconced in their midst. Let them act the fools and drink themselves senseless at the wedding feast. He, for one, had no desire to celebrate.

He'd offered for the MacDonnell wench because she was the seventh daughter of a seventh daughter and therefore gifted with the sight. All he wanted was the use of it.

Naught else, as he'd made clear to her.

He didn't care how many tall tales Marmaduke had told her. She need only supply him with the answer he needed, warn him of impending danger to his clan, see to Robbie, and he would leave her in peace.

'Twould be simple enough to avoid her in a castle the size of Eilean Creag.

So why did he have such a nagging feeling in his gut? Scowling, lest anyone dare think he was anything other than displeased, Duncan glared across the bailey, watching the rowdy celebrants file into his keep.

"Are you ready to join the festivities?" Sir Marmaduke clamped a hand on Duncan's shoulder, urging him down the chapel steps. "'Tis no such thing as a wedding feast without the bridegroom."

"Aye," Duncan darkly agreed. "I daresay I canna make myself scarce, can I?"

As they crossed the bailey, the cause of his foul temper became more clear with every step he took. He feared Linnet MacDonnell would prove more than he'd bargained for.

Much more.

And that was a notion he did not care for at all.

"Out of our way, make way for the lady," Lachlan shouted, forcing a path through the knot of merrymakers blocking the entrance to the castle. Once inside, he tried to propel Linnet forward, but she stopped him by digging her heels into the rushes spread upon the floor.

"Is aught amiss, milady?"

"That is what I would know." Linnet raised her voice to be heard above the din in the great hall. "I dinna see Robbie in the crowd nor in the chapel."

"Nay, you wouldn't have," the squire said, raising his voice as well.

"Why not? Surely he should have been—"

Lachlan suddenly grabbed her arms and lifted her out of the way as two wrestling Highlanders lurched past them. "Here is not the best place to stand, milady. Please allow me to escort you away from the door, then I'll explain about Robbie."

Without further explanation, the squire ushered her toward the raised dais at the far end of the hall. While crowded upon her arrival the night before, the great vaulted chamber was now fair bursting with revelers. Ne'er had she seen aught to compare with such an elaborate celebration.

Someone had even strewn the floor rushes with fragrant meadowsweet, rose petals, and thyme. 'Twas a grand spectacle that made her father's feasts at Dundonnell seem paltry.

A score of trumpeters, high above in the musicians' gallery, competed with the gay shouts and laughter that filled the vast room and a trio of minstrels paraded among the celebrants, loudly singing bawdy songs.

Trenchers of bread and numerous silver jugs of ale and wine already stood upon the trestle tables while an endless stream of servants carried in platters of every imaginable delicacy from the kitchens.

But Linnet wouldn't let the finery or tempting array of festive dishes sway her purpose. When they reached the high table, and Lachlan pulled back an elaborately carved high-backed chair, she remained standing.

"Where is Robbie?"

"In his bed, milady," the squire told her. "'Tis sick he is."

"What ails him?" she asked. "Do you know?"

"Aye, it's his stomach. Cook allowed him to eat too many custard pasties."

"Then I shall go to him," Linnet stated, stepping back from the table.

Her intention appeared to make Lachlan nervous, for he shot a quick glance across the hall toward the entrance they'd just left. "Sir Duncan willna be pleased if you're not at your place when he enters the hall."

"And I could not partake of a single morsel of food if I dinna look in on the lad. Do you know if your liege laird has sent anyone to see to him?"

"Cook sent one o' the laundresses up to his chamber earlier, but Sir Duncan willna ken the lad's abed." Once again, Lachlan glanced at the far door. "He angers easily, so we try not to bother him overmuch about Robbie."

"Bother him?" Linnet eyed the squire sternly, the self-pity that had overcome her in the chapel now replaced by anger. "I'd say 'tis the wee lad who's bothered if his belly is hurting him."

Lachlan nodded but said nothing.

"I would ask a favor if I may?"

"You have only to state your request." He bowed low. "'Tis pleased I am to serve you."

"Do you remember where my chamber is?"

"Of course, milady."

"Then please fetch my leather satchel. When you return, I should like to be escorted to the kitchens." At the look of bewilderment on the squire's face, she explained, "It contains my medicinal herbs. I want to brew a *tisane* of watermint for Robbie. The concoction will ease his stomach pains."

Lachlan nodded, but a look of discomfort crossed his features. He made no move to leave.

"Is my request too difficult?"

"Nay." A pink tinge stained his cheeks. "'Tis only that my lord will expect your presence at the high table."

"Then make haste on your errand, and I shall have no need to tarry." Linnet arched a brow at the squire, amazed at her own nerve. "The sooner Robbie can drink the *tisane*, the sooner he and I can take our places at your master's table."

Lachlan's jaw dropped, and his eyes grew round, but he bowed again and hurried away.

A short time later, after he'd returned with her herbal pouch and escorted her to the kitchens, Linnet made her way to Robbie's dismal tower chamber with a steaming beaker of watermint. Lachlan followed silently behind her, lighting the way with a rush torch.

Preferring to be alone with the boy, Linnet entered the room and closed the door, leaving the squire to wait in the corridor. Robbie slumbered peacefully, so she took a moment to glance around the chamber. She found it sorely lacking in warmth and almost as bleak as her new husband's solar. Mayhap more so because no tapestries graced the walls.

Only the embroidered bedcurtains gave the stark room a semblance of color. A child-sized ladderback chair stood near the hearth, and a small table of dark oak had been placed next to the bed. A clump of wilted wildflowers lay upon the tabletop, and the ancient-looking mongrel slept curled at the foot of the child's bed.

As before, the dog opened one eye, looked at her, and went back to sleep. Satisfied the enormous beast posed no threat, she crossed the room and gazed down at the sleeping child.

Her new stepson.

A child apparently as shunned by his father as she had been by hers . . . albeit for very different reasons.

Her heart ached at the small boy's plight. Unable to help herself, she reached out and stroked his hair.

Immediately, he rolled onto his back and opened his eyes, staring up at her with dark blue eyes so like his father's her breath caught in her throat. Except her husband's eyes held such a perpetually dark expression she'd initially mistaken their color for black.

Linnet let out her breath on a gentle sigh and gave the lad a tender smile. She couldn't yet speak, could only stare in wonderment at the sheer perfection of the boy's face. In truth, Robbie MacKenzie looked so much like her husband she broke out in gooseflesh.

How could the man doubt the lad was his own flesh and blood? 'Twas impossible not to see the resemblance.

Robbie was a miniature version of his handsome father. But where the father's beauty was marred by grimness and distrust, the son had the face of an angel.

Trusting, good, and pure.

An incredible feeling of compassion welled up in Linnet, filling her with warmth and a fierce desire to protect the child from harm.

And from unhappiness.

Especially from unhappiness.

All of a sudden she was very glad she'd come to Eilean Creag. No matter what Duncan MacKenzie thought of her . . . whether he found her too homely to bed or not, his child needed her and she would do her best to assure Robbie received the love and happiness he deserved.

As she gazed down at him, very close to tears, so overwhelmed by emotion was she, the boy pushed himself up on his elbows. "Are you my new mother?" he asked. "Cook said you were coming."

"Aye, Robbie, I suppose I am. Your father and I were wed this morn." Linnet took a seat on the edge of the bed. "Would you like me to be your new mother?"

He regarded her solemnly for a moment before answering. "Aye, I would. You have the bonniest hair I've e'er seen."

Linnet's heart swelled, and heat stung the backs of her eyes. None save her brothers had e'er paid her compliments and even those were few and far between. She didn't know what to say to Robbie, and even if she did, she doubted she could speak past the thick lump that had lodged in her throat.

Robbie glanced at the table and frowned. "I gathered flowers for you, but got sick before I could give them to you. I'm sorry they're not pretty anymore." He picked up the wilted bouquet and placed it on her lap.

"Oh, nay, Robbie lad, 'tis lovely flowers they are. The most beautiful I've ever seen." Linnet's voice trembled as she held up the bouquet and admired it. She knew her tears were spilling unchecked down her cheeks. It was the first bouquet she'd ever received.

"You're crying," he said, concern clouding his eyes. "Did I do something wrong?"

Reaching out, Linnet gently smoothed the back of her hand down his cheek. "Nay, child, you've done naught to displease me. 'Tis happy I am. You're a most gallant lad, and I thank you for the flowers."

"You willna go away, will you?" he asked, his brow still creased with worry.

Linnet's heart twisted. "Nay, I shall not e'er leave

you. 'Tis here to stay I am," she promised. Without taking her gaze off him, she reached for the mug of watermint she'd placed on the small table beside the bed. "I've brought something to soothe the ache in your belly."

Later, as Linnet followed Lachlan down the stairs, Robbie's little hand held tightly in her own, the squire's most recent warning about her new husband's temper went round and round in her mind. '*Sir Duncan willna like you bringing Robbie to his table*,' he'd cautioned her in a low voice so the boy wouldn't hear. '*He's mighty fearsome when angered*,' he'd added just before they'd begun their descent back to the hall.

'*Is there aught what doesna rile him?*' Linnet had asked, hoping her voice didn't reveal her fear of vexing her formidable husband. But her own anxiety was of little importance compared to the need of the child who'd slipped his hand into hers so trustingly. For his sake, she had no choice but to be bold.

"I hope you've thought this through, milady," the squire said, stopping so abruptly at the bottom of the stairs Linnet fair collided with his back.

"I have, Lachlan, dinna worry," she said with more conviction than she felt.

Her fingers clenched around the bundle of limp flowers she held in her free hand. Aye, she'd thought her actions through and knew what she was doing.

Unfortunately, she also knew she was about to unleash the wrath of the devil.

4

"Have you seen her hair?" Duncan leaned back in his canopied seat at the high table and aimed a pointed glare at Sir Marmaduke.

To his irritation, the Sassunach either ignored, or didn't hear, his question. Instead, his most stalwart knight appeared completely engrossed in watching Eilean Creag's craggy old seneschal, Fergus, order about his troupe of servitors as they filed through the crowded hall.

Each one shouldered a great platter of some kind of elaborately dressed game bird or a sizable haunch of roasted meat, all prepared with special care for the wedding feast.

Perturbed, Duncan reached across the conspicuously empty seat to his left and gave his friend a sharp jab in the ribs. Raising his voice above the ruckus, he tried again, "I said, have you seen her hair?"

"Hare?" Marmaduke fixed him with the most innocent look possible considering his disfigurement. "'Tis certain Fergus will have ordered a goodly number. If we're lucky, mayhap he's prepared them with his special onion-and-saffron gravy."

"'Tis *her* hair I speak of, you conniving fox," Duncan fair roared, not caring if all at the high table and beyond heard him. "I'll have an explanation, Strongbow. *Now* before her ladyship sees fit to join us."

"Explanation?" The eyebrow above Marmaduke's good eye rose a notch.

"Dinna repeat my words like a blithering fool or I'll have you replace the jester Fergus hired to entertain us this afternoon."

Marmaduke lowered his brow immediately. "What troubles you, my friend?"

"'Tis plain she be, as unappealing as a sow's behind,'" Duncan quoted, his wrath at being misled sorely testing his temper. "Would you deny those words?"

"Nay," Marmaduke stated with great calm, offering his chalice to a young squire who promptly refilled it with spiced wine. "And 'twas true enough of her appearance the day I called at Dundonnell. She'd been in the bailey, teaching a small lad how to brandish his wooden sword when I arrived. Rain had turned the ground to a sea of mud. Both she and the lad were covered with it, but she did not seem to mind. I had the impression the boy's squeals of laughter mattered more to her than a bit of mud on her gown."

Duncan swallowed the angry words he wanted to fling at his friend. The even-tempered Englishman was the only man alive who managed to make him feel guilty, even when he was in the right.

Like now.

'Twas *he* who'd been culled, made the fool.

He whose world had tilted at the sight of her unbound hair this morn.

A wife with such glorious tresses spelled trouble, despite Marmaduke's chivalrous attempts to paint her as a half saint, fawning over children and ignorant of the effect her hair would have on any mortal man beneath the age of eighty and mayhap a few beyond.

But rather than embarrass himself further by commenting on Marmaduke's pretty speech, undoubtedly designed to emphasize his new bride's goodness of character, he clamped his lips together in a grimace. He'd content himself with giving the Sassunach knight another cold, hard glare.

"If I recall, you questioned me about how she'd appeared that day, and I told you true," Marmaduke continued, obviously taking great delight in Duncan's displeasure. "Had you inquired if I thought she'd wash up well, my answer would've been much different."

That did it. Duncan curled his fingers tightly around the armrests of his chair. If anyone else had dared taunt him so, he'd have grasped the sharp blade resting on the table before him and cut out the offender's tongue.

Better yet, he'd use a *dull* blade.

"Whose side are you on, English?" he finally asked, his hands still gripping the chair as if he sought to snap the sturdy oaken armrests in twain.

"Why, yours, milord," Marmaduke gallantly replied,

lifting his chalice in a silent toast. "As ever, your well-being is my most steadfast desire."

Duncan snatched his own drinking vessel, an intricate silver chalice fashioned like a sea dragon and encrusted with precious gemstones, and took a long draught of hippocras, a heady mixture of red wine and spices Cook had concocted especially for the wedding feast.

After a goodly amount flowed past his lips, he slammed down the goblet. The specially prepared treat tasted as sour as his mood, its delicate combination of flavors lost on him.

Fouled by his own malcontent.

"Is aught amiss?" Marmaduke asked, his good brow arching upward.

"Nay," Duncan snapped, unwilling to voice that *all* was amiss, yet unable to put his finger on exactly what bothered him the most.

Everything bothered him.

"You look . . . pained," Marmaduke observed. "Here, have some more hippocras."

Duncan held out his chalice while Marmaduke, ever the gallant, refilled it with a liberal dose of the spiced wine. But Duncan cared naught for drinking and even less for celebrating.

Truth be told, he desired only to escape the confines of the festively decorated hall and retire to a quiet corner of the castle.

Alone.

Without his new bride.

Without his cares.

And without his pack of dunderheaded clansmen and their silly chatter.

A quick glance around the high table told him no one else shared his displeasure. Everyone present, from his most trusted friends and kinsmen to the lowliest of his servitors, all grinned like witless villeins.

Buffoons every last one of them.

Senseless fools jesting amongst themselves about the bride's lengthening absence. The bolder ones, those already deep in their cups, loudly proclaimed she'd no doubt heard tales of the MacKenzie's legendary prowess in bed and had bolted herself in her chamber, cowering in fear, yet secretly waiting to be ravished.

As if he desired the wench! He wanted naught to do with her.

Tresses of silken flame or nay.

And not that he cared, but where *was* she anyway?

By the blessed martyrs, 'twas time she took her place beside him. But, nay, she dallied again, leaving him to look the fool even as she had this morn whilst he'd stood waiting upon the chapel steps.

His displeasure mounting, Duncan scanned the smoke-hazed hall. Straining his eyes, he sought to catch a glimpse of her coppery hair, hoping to see her hurrying toward the high table, looking suitably contrite for her tardiness.

But she was nowhere to be seen.

And where was his first squire?

Off making moon eyes at the new lady of the castle, no doubt. Duncan frowned. If it weren't for his pride, he'd be tempted to go fetch them hisself.

He wouldn't demean himself by doing so, though. A laird had a certain dignity to uphold.

Nay, he'd deal with his bride in good time, and in private. As for Lachlan, the youth was too softhearted for his own good. If he'd allowed himself to be cajoled into helping his wife escape to Dundonnell, he'd have the lad scour the cesspit till it shined like a bairn's arse!

And mayhap he'd have his new wife help him!

For the first time all day, Duncan smiled.

If he *really* wanted to improve his mood, he'd order Marmaduke to assist them. 'Twould serve the lout right for playing him the fool.

Aye, he'd have words with them all—later. For now, he had little choice but to suffer through the day's festivities so he could retire to the sanctuary of his chamber.

And woe be to any hapless dolt who might try to stop him.

"You wear an expression darker than the black mail you favor. 'Tis no wonder the lady has chosen to linger far from your side." Marmaduke gave him a hefty thwack on his shoulder. "Come, let us drink to a happy future for you and your bride."

"*A happy future?*" Duncan narrowed his eyes at his friend. The severe head blows Marmaduke had once received must've addled his senses. "You ken better than most why I took her to wed, so cease your dunderheaded banter. I care naught about a shared future with her, content or otherwise."

Duncan paused to draw a breath, and the moment he opened his mouth to further rebuke his friend for such ridiculous sentiments, all present let out a collective gasp.

Then the hall went still.

Except for one foolhardy simpleton who cried out, "Great Caesar's Ghost!"

'Twas her.

It had to be her.

Even though the smoke from the fires made it difficult to see much farther than just beyond the high table, he knew.

And judging from the gaping of his clansmen he *could* see, she'd done something most displeasing.

Or bold.

But what?

Had she rolled among the pigs, soiling the fine gown he'd provided for her? Or had she hacked off her glorious tresses, thinking to spite and embarrass him by coming to the wedding feast bald as an old hairless man?

If so, she'd be surprised, for he'd be pleased . . . she would have saved him the trouble of shaving her head himself. The saints knew he was sorely tempted to do so.

"'Tis him! She's brought the lad with her."

Clear, sharp, and going straight to his heart like a well-aimed arrow, the quickly whispered words cut through the fog of his frustrations.

Duncan froze.

It mattered naught who'd uttered the words. He'd ne'er know and didn't care.

'Twas the *meaning* behind them what stopped him cold.

He didn't realize he'd loosened his grip on his chalice until it hit the top of the table with a dull thud, its contents staining the tablecloth the deep red of spilled blood.

Dropping his wine seemed to break the spell of un-natural silence, too, for the moment he looked up from the ruined tablecloth, the entire hall erupted into pande-monium.

A cacophony of voices.

Sheer chaos.

And through it all Duncan heard but one word: Robbie.

The lass had done what not a single of his clansmen would have dared.

She'd brought the lad before him, into his hall, and chosen a time when he could do naught about it. Not with the priest sitting to his right and his men watching his every move.

'Twas no secret what they thought of his behavior toward the child, scarce little they cared his heart had been wrenched from his chest and trod upon, ground into the dirt.

Duncan's blood ran hot and cold as he searched the shadows, trying hard to catch a glimpse of his bride and the lad he'd once thought his son.

Dread filled him as he anticipated the moment his gaze would fall upon them. Yet deep inside, anticipation made his heart pump ever faster whilst anger at his own weakness pulled his brows together in a fierce grimace.

His new wife best be thankful for her sex. Were she a man, he'd flay her within an inch of her life for such flagrant disregard of his orders. Not a soul under his roof would've attempted such an affront.

He felt Marmaduke grip his arm and heard him speaking to him, but he couldn't make sense of the words. His head pounded, and the blood rushing through his veins turned all sound into an unintelligible buzz.

All except the one word that caused him so much pain and cut straight through his defenses as if they were naught but butter.

Robbie, Robbie, Robbie . . . the name echoed around the cavernous hall, bouncing off the stone walls, reverberating in his ears until he feared his head would burst asunder.

If only he could see better, but the haze from the hearth fires and wall torches filled the vaulted chamber, blurring his vision, making it hard for him to spot them.

Not that he wanted to.

Still, may God have mercy on him, his traitorous gaze searched the darkness. It'd been nigh onto two years since he'd closely looked upon the boy, truly *seen* him.

Breaking away from Marmaduke's iron grasp, Duncan pushed back from the table and stood. He leaned forward, planting his hands firmly on the table to keep from sinking back into his chair . . . a humbling possibility considering the way his knees threatened to buckle on him.

With the last reserves of his willpower, he forced his legs to cease trembling while he scanned the crowded hall.

Then, of a sudden, the murky air seemed to clear, and he located his wife almost immediately. Her unbound hair, shining brighter than the most brilliant flame, gave her away. His first squire stood next to her, and he, too, resembled a flame, but 'twas his face what glowed, not his hair.

Aye, Lachlan knew well his master would be mightily displeased.

And his contrition was well justified. But Lachlan's punishment would be dealt later. At the moment, he cared naught about his squire and less about his new lady wife.

His entire attention focused on the small boy she held by the hand.

Taller and sturdier than the chubby bairn Duncan used to bounce on his knee, Robbie'd grown into a handsome lad. Someone had draped a child-sized plaid in the green-and-blue MacKenzie colors over his left shoulder, tucking it in place under a finely tooled and obviously new leather belt.

A belt *he* should have fashioned.

Duncan blinked back the stinging sensation in his eyes as he stared at the beautifully crafted belt. The last thing he'd made for Robbie was a toy sword he'd carved from wood for the lad's fourth birthday.

He could still recall the look of wonder on Robbie's face when he'd given it to him.

It seemed like a hundred years had passed since then.

Without warning, a red-hot throbbing started in the back of Duncan's neck then spread lower to grip his chest in a stranglehold that fair squeezed the breath out of his lungs.

The longer he stared at the boy, the more painful the tightness became, but he couldn't tear his gaze away.

At six, Robbie looked every bit a miniature version of a fine MacKenzie warrior. 'Twas no denying the clansblood ran thick and proud through his veins. Even from across the hall, it was plain to see the lad bore a sharp likeness to Duncan.

Nay, he looked *exactly* like Duncan.

And how proud he'd once been of the undeniable resemblance.

The pain in Duncan's gut intensified, hurting as fiercely as if someone had thrust a knife into his belly and now twisted the blade, cruelly upping the torture, taking advantage of a besieged man already on his knees.

A deep groan welled in his throat, and he disguised it as a cough. All would have been so simple if Kenneth MacKenzie, his hated half brother and his first wife's lover, couldn't pass for his twin.

Indeed, fate had shown no mercy in stealing all he'd ever loved. Should he and his foe stand with the child between them before the wisest of men, there wouldn't be one among them who could say whether the seed that begot Robbie had sprung from his or Kenneth's loins.

And the doubt was killing him.

Had killed him, for surely his life hadn't been worth living since the day he'd learned of Cassandra's treachery.

But mayhap an end to his suffering was close at hand. High were his hopes Linnet MacDonnell—nay, *MacKenzie*—would soon put an end to his days, and nights, of despair.

As he stared at the boy, a great weariness bore down on him. A heavy, crushing weight, pushing aside all else, leaving only a desperate need to lower himself into his chair.

By the Rood, he couldn't bear to stand and watch their approach.

'Twas too much.

With great effort, he sank back down, letting out his pent-up breath in a deep sigh the moment he rested his back against the cushions of his canopied master seat.

Ever chivalrous, Marmaduke poured him a liberal dose of wine he gladly accepted, gratefully curling his fingers around the heavy silver chalice.

Clutching the drinking vessel provided a good way to hide the trembling of his hands whilst he waited. He only hoped, once his wife wove her way through the hall and took her place at his side, she'd finally grant him the answer only she could give.

And by the power of the Holy Rood, he prayed he'd like what she'd have to tell him.

Her new husband was drunk!

Or so angry sheer fury twisted his features and glazed his deep blue eyes, turning them into dark pools that stared right through her rather than at her.

Linnet scooted as far away from Duncan MacKenzie as she dared considering circumstances deemed she occupy the seat of honor, a smaller duplicate of his own canopied chair, and also share a trencher with him.

Trying hard to hide her nervousness, she peered at him from beneath lowered lashes, watching as he held tight to his chalice with one hand and gripped the edge of the table with the other. The whiteness of his knuckles and the rigid set of his jaw made her believe it was ire and not an overindulgence in spirits what ailed him.

She swallowed hard but kept her back straight.

Ne'er had she thought he'd be so vexed, so distant and cold.

He'd barely acknowledged her as she'd taken her place beside him. His greeting to Robbie had been even more sparse. A few words, a curt nod, and then he'd ignored them both. He conducted himself as if he were many leagues away and not so close she could smell the distinct masculine scent of him with each breath she took.

Linnet stole another glimpse at his uncompromising profile. He stared straight ahead, purposely avoiding her eyes . . . and those of the child she'd drawn onto her lap.

He didn't even bother to hide his displeasure, giving his ill will free rein to thrum through him. 'Twas visible for all and sundry to see.

Anger of her own simmered deep within her at his dismissive behavior. She slid a sidelong glance at him, seeing the grim expression on his handsome face and feeling his wrath over her daring to bring his son before him.

"Lady?" an expectant voice interrupted her thoughts, and she turned, extending her hands to a young squire who held ewer, basin, and towels. "May I?" he asked, respectfully inclining his head before pouring scented water over her hands.

Grateful for the distraction, Linnet thanked the squire, then assisted Robbie in washing his hands as well. For *his* sake, she tried to ignore the tension emanating from her husband, but doing so was hard.

Despite herself, Linnet's heart wrenched at the sight of the mighty Laird MacKenzie.

His son's presence wouldn't affect him thus did he not truly love the child.

This man needed to be taught an important lesson. If only she could open his eyes and heart, make him realize and admit he cared for the lad whether or nay his blood ran true in Robbie's veins.

Only then would she tell him the truth.

A small tug on her sleeve caught her attention. "Should I leave, lady?" Robbie's eyes were rounded, full of an unwanted child's vulnerability. "I'm not supposed to come near the high table."

"What nonsense," Linnet disagreed. "Someday you will be laird. All chiefs, present or future, must sit at the high table."

Linnet shot a quick glance at her husband. "Is it not so?"

His jaw twitched, and he took his time answering, but finally he grudgingly admitted, "Aye, 'tis the accustomed way."

Sitting up straighter, Linnet smoothed Robbie's hair and said, "Be assured, son, 'tis your place here as well as mine."

"*Son* you say," Duncan leaned close and whispered into her ear. "And is he, I ask you?"

Turning to face him, her breath caught in her throat, so intense was his stare. "I canna yet see, milord," she lied, once more begging the good saints to guide her. "Mayhap if I saw more of you both together I could tell."

She wouldn't have deemed it possible, but the expression on his face grew darker. "Mayhap if you would hone your gift such wouldn't be necessary?"

"And if you, milord, would but look into your heart,

a gift such as mine would not be needed," she whispered back, not caring if she raised his ire further. "But then, 'tis said you do not possess one."

From the other side of her, Linnet heard the Sassunach offering Robbie sugared wafers. Anxious to avoid further confrontation, she turned her back on her liege husband lest he grow so riled he raise his voice, hurting the child with his cruel words.

Yet even facing away from him, she felt enveloped by his dark presence.

Linnet shivered. Mayhap 'twas more good fortune than insult that he didn't want her for a *true* wife. She'd rather stay a virgin all her days than be bedded by a man so cold-hearted as Duncan MacKenzie.

Gazing at the boy on her lap, she prayed for wisdom. She'd oft heard none were given a burden heavier than they could carry, yet she mightily doubted her ability to shoulder this new one she'd taken upon herself.

Her instincts told her both father and son needed her, both husband and stepson suffered great pain.

But could she aid them without unduly hurting either?

Would she hurt *herself* in attempting to do so?

'Twas this truly the reason she'd been sent here . . . or was she merely interfering where she had no right to meddle?

Robbie shifted his position on her lap and the cuddly, warm weight of him softened her heart and strengthened her resolve. Glancing at him, she saw he sat rigidly, innocently mimicking his father, glancing neither left or right, his hands fisted tightly in his lap.

He stared fixedly at the mug of goat's milk a servant

had placed before him, his face, so like his father's, now pale and tense. He obviously struggled as diligently to ignore his sire as he in turn struggled to ignore his son.

It was unnatural for a lad to be so nervous, yet how could he be aught but shy and frightened of a father who'd shunned him?

And it was equally unnatural for a father to shun his son.

Gently, Linnet rubbed Robbie's shoulder, hoping to soothe him, extraordinarily pleased when he didn't pull away, but leaned into her hand as if he welcomed her touch.

His acceptance of her filled her with a contentment she'd never known, swelling her heart with love for the child she could now call her own.

If her husband would respond as willingly to her overtures, mayhap she'd have half a chance at bringing the two of them together. The occasional covert glances he slid his son's way gave her hope.

But one look at his unyielding profile left no doubt as to the enormity of her task. Still, even if he cast her aside as a woman, denying her a child of her flesh, she'd be forever thankful for his giving her his son to love.

With a tender hand, she smoothed Robbie's hair from his forehead. On her honor, she pledged to bring warmth and love into his life. As long as she could remember, she'd tried to believe all things happen for a reason.

A good reason.

'Twas oft difficult to see at first, but she'd found if one practiced patience, time usually revealed the answer. Duncan MacKenzie's son needed her, and if the saints had seen fit to send her to help him, she'd humbly accept the challenge.

A tiny voice deep within told her she needed him, too. She didn't doubt it either.

With a single finger, she touched the exquisite belt circling the lad's small hips. "'Tis a bonnie belt you wear, Robbie," she said, hoping to ease him out of his shyness. "I dinna think I've e'er seen one so fine."

She was rewarded by a bashful smile that faded all too quickly. "Fergus made it for me," he told her.

"And who is Fergus?"

"He's Papa's sene'chal," Robbie piped in answer. "He gave me my plaid, too."

"Did he now?" Linnet said, not missing the way her husband chose the moment to loudly clear his throat as if to drown out the boy's words. "And a handsome plaid it is. Do you know what the colors mean?"

Robbie nodded solemnly, then began to recite, "'Tis green for the forest and fields, and blue for the sky and sea, drawn through with white for . . . for—" he stumbled over the words, looking up at her with troubled deep blue eyes so like his father's Linnet's heart constricted.

Biting his lower lip, the lad struggled to recall the lines of the verse.

Her husband drew a deep, audible breath, then supplied, "White for purity, red for blood and bold warriors . . ."

". . . and all mean freedom, fairness, honor, and courage," Robbie finished, his small chest appearing to swell with pride upon each word. Afterward, he bestowed a look of pure hero worship on his father.

But though he'd helped the boy remember the words, Linnet had sensed rather than felt Duncan MacKenzie stiffen beside her at each line of the verse his son had so valiantly recited.

"And after that fine recital, I'm thinking 'tis time for you to go abovestairs to your bed," Marmaduke said, pushing back from the table. With a pointed look at Duncan, he lifted Robbie into his arms. "A future laird needs his sleep if he is to grow broad enough shoulders for his future position, does he not?"

Duncan nodded stiffly but said nothing. Only when the Sassunach and Robbie were a good ten paces away, did he call out to them. "'Twas good to hear you recite the meaning of our colors, lad."

Though a clear afterthought, the words heartened Linnet. 'Twas a start. Robbie's gaze clung to his father as Marmaduke carried him away. The sight made Linnet's heart contract.

Before he carried Robbie abovestairs, Marmaduke turned. "Ho, Duncan, do not let Fergus fetch the marriage stone until I return."

"Plague take the fool stone and I'll have Fergus's hide if he brings it," her husband groused even as the hall erupted in good-natured clamor, all present calling for the stone.

Scowling, Duncan shot to his feet. "Cease shrieking like simpletons," he roared above the din. "There will be no marriage stone ceremony."

"*Marriage stone ceremony?*" Linnet asked when he sat back down.

Rather than answer her, he pressed his lips into a tight line, his whole demeanor stiffening.

"What ails you, Duncan? There's ne'er been a MacKenzie wedding feast without one!" A rowdy voice suddenly bellowed from the depths of the hall. "And 'tis o'erlong we've waited to see you drink with yer bride!"

"Aye! A drink wi' the bride!" A chorus of MacKenzie men chanted in boisterous rhythm, raising their voices to rival the accompanying trumpet blasts. "Long life and many bairns to the lady Linnet!"

Duncan stared at the table, clearly growing more uncomfortable with each raucous shout. As Linnet peered at him, Marmaduke slipped back into the seat beside her. Through the commotion, Linnet thought she heard Marmaduke whisper she had naught to fear, all would be well, but when she looked his way, he was calmly sipping his wine and didn't appear to have said aught.

"Long life and many bairns to Lady Linnet!" the clansmen continued to chant, thumping their drinking cups on the tables and stamping their feet as a crusty-looking elder clansman strode through their midst, a great silver goblet raised high above his head.

Four brawny warriors followed him. Together, they carried a large blue-tinted stone. Elongated in shape and carved with ancient Celtic runes, its surface was smooth except at the bottom. The stone's base appeared ragged as if it'd been wrested from its original location.

But what most caught Linnet's attention was the hole in its center. Her husband's ill-tempered grousing wasn't needed for her to know this was the 'marriage stone.'

And now she knew its ceremonial purpose, too.

The stone was a swearing stone. A *talisman*. The ancients believed if couples clasped hands through the opening in its middle, their marriage would be blessed.

A joyous union filled with love, harmony, and many healthy bairns.

Linnet's back stiffened at the implication. Now she knew why her husband had bristled at the mention of the stone. He did not care to perform the ancient ceremony with her, did not want to risk the chance the old gods' magic might exert an influence over their union.

A union he didn't even care to properly consummate!

A fresh new burst of stamping feet and shouts dispelled Linnet's thoughts. The seneschal and the four men bearing the stone had arrived at the high table. Stopping before Duncan and Linnet, the old seneschal turned in a slow circle, holding up the ceremonial chalice for all to see. The men with the marriage stone held back, waiting until the couple partook of a shared drink before carrying the stone forward.

A jubilant cheer sounded when Fergus plunked down the huge drinking vessel, filling it to the brim from the jug of hippocras.

"Hold, Fergus," Marmaduke spoke up, staying the seneschal's arm, "the hippocras may be too potent for the lady. What say you we dilute it with water before she partakes of it?"

Fergus's bushy brows snapped together in a fierce scowl, and he yanked his arm from Marmaduke's grip. "Mayhap 'tis too strong for a Sassunach lass, but not for one born of our own Highlands," he scolded, pouring the blood-red brew into the wedding cup. "I mixed it mesself for the occasion," he added, as if daring Marmaduke to contradict him.

All but the English knight roared with approval as her new husband dutifully lifted the unwieldy chalice to his lips and drank from it.

"Leave some for your bride!" someone boomed from the back of the hall. " 'Twill prime her for the bedding!"

Bedding? Linnet's gasp was swallowed by the ear-splitting laughter and jeering that filled the hall. Heat flooded her as the image of her naked husband straddling her flashed across her mind. Again, she saw him looming above her, his arousal boldly proclaiming he'd felt the same stirrings she had.

Yet he'd told her forthrightly he did not want her as a true consort . . . as a woman.

With a bluntness that cut to her core, he'd taken the bruised feminine pride she hadn't known she possessed and dashed it to the ground.

And now his men would call for him to mount her, make her a woman before their lusting eyes in a bedding ceremony?

A new kind of chill stole over her. One of fear, a maiden's natural apprehension at being mounted the first time.

And one of shame should he be forced upon her by his men.

For she couldn't bear it if he cringed in revulsion at being made to perform the act of love with her.

"Ye've dallied long enough, Duncan!" Someone suddenly yelled. "Pass yer bride the wine, let her drink, and then, by thunder, make her a MacKenzie!"

"Aye, make her a MacKenzie!" others joined in.

Ribald laughter rose to the vaulted ceiling, and the floor shook from a furious chorus of foot stomping. And, try as he might to ignore the bad memories, the gay ruckus reminded Duncan of another wedding feast long past and best forgotten.

A time when he'd been young and thought himself in love.

Nay, besotted.

And the worthless marriage stone ceremony had failed to spare him grief!

Saints, he'd been so thoroughly beguiled by his first wife's beauty and grace, he'd ne'er have believed her perfidious nature had Saint Peter himself warned him.

Pushing all thoughts of Cassandra from his mind, he dutifully offered his new wife the heavy wedding chalice. "Drink so we can have done with this foolishness," he said, his tone more harsh than he'd intended.

"I care not much for spirits, sir," she said, taking the great chalice with both hands but making no move to drink.

A dark oath almost passed Duncan's lips before he remembered she was the daughter of a drunkard. "You must not partake of much, only a sip," he told her, surprised at the protectiveness he felt toward her upon recalling her lout of a father. "I shall drink the rest."

He watched closely as she raised the chalice and drank. He doubted she'd taken more than a wee sip, but the potent wine left her lips looking soft and red.

Sweet.

Not enticing as another woman's lips had looked on another wedding day, but sweet . . . innocent.

And more tempting than those of any practiced siren he'd e'er had the misfortune to come across.

Faith, but she tempted him beyond all reason.

Even though, by all rights, he should be angry, and *was*, over her parading the lad under his very nose. Tearing his gaze from her, Duncan gave in to the urge and swore.

Mayhap he should have sought a wife at court, an accomplished and cultivated beauty whose polished charms would have reminded him so thoroughly of his first wife, he wouldn't have had difficulty ignoring her.

Instead, he'd burdened himself with a toothsome Highland lass whose lush comeliness and blatant innocence intrigued him.

"I canna drink more, sir," she said, setting down the chalice, the honeyed softness of her voice fair unmanning him.

Fighting to quell the desire she so unwittingly unleashed in him, Duncan snatched the chalice off the table and downed its contents in one hefty swig. A loud roar of approval went up from his men when he plunked down the empty chalice.

Despite the look of alarm on her face, he refilled the large drinking vessel and emptied it again before Fergus could launch into the marriage stone ceremony. As if the disobedient lout had read Duncan's mind, his seneschal grasped the curved horn he wore around his neck, brought it to his lips, and gave a sharp blast.

At once, the feasters fell silent. Those who sat, leaned forward, and those who stood, inched closer. "The tale, Fergus," someone yelled from the back of the hall, "tell us the tale!"

Lachlan handed Fergus a *cittern*, and as he strummed a few chords to test it, Duncan overheard the Sassunach whispering to Linnet.

"Fergus acts as the clan *filidh*, or *fili*," Marmaduke told her. "He never studied the bardic arts, so can't claim the true title, but he is a born storyteller and deserves respect. At every MacKenzie wedding, he tells the legend of the marriage stone."

Duncan glared at his friend. "Aye, and dinna forget that is all it is . . . a legend. Naught but words."

"Then you canna be harmed by it, can you, milord?" his lady said, displaying another glimpse of the fire he'd admired on the journey from Dundonnell.

"I do not fear the stone or its silly legend," Duncan snapped.

"'Tis glad I am to hear it," Marmaduke countered, a mischievous gleam in his good eye, "for then you have no reason to deny us the pleasure of watching you and your fair lady wife perform the ceremony."

Another blare from Fergus's horn silenced those still speaking and spared Duncan from responding to Marmaduke's cheek. "'Twas long ago," Fergus began his tale, his gnarled fingers deftly strumming the *cittern*. "Old gods still ruled and their ways were yet respected. A proud Celtic king lived not far from where we sit this night. He was a powerful man, and none dared defy him. He feared no man or creature, and some say neither did he fear the gods."

Fergus paused to sip from a brimming cup of ale. "This king had four daughters, and being as wise as they were beautiful, they, too, feared him. All save the youngest daughter . . . his favorite."

As Fergus recited the legend, Duncan leaned back and folded his arms. Folded his arms and closed his ears. He knew the foolish prattle by heart, and the most annoying part of the story was almost upon him.

". . . so certain was the fair maid of her father's love, she saw no reason to be secretive about having lost her heart to a young man she knew would not meet her father's approval. Though a braw and bonnie lad, strong of muscle and pure of heart, he was without means or prospects. The proud king became outraged upon learning his favorite daughter desired a man so unworthy."

The words flowed over Duncan, seeping into his ears despite his best efforts to ignore them. Saints, he wished the old fool would finish so they could have done with the rest of the ceremony.

The part he dreaded . . . the hand-holding and kissing part.

"Aware her father would never allow the marriage," Fergus went on, "but unable to deny her heart, the lass and her true love ran away to the marriage stone. A swearing stone, ancient even then. Its magic was strong and true." Fergus paused and took another sip of ale. "But the father was warned, and he caught up with them just as they thrust their hands through the opening in the stone's middle."

Pausing again, Fergus looked around the hall, his sharp eyes wise and knowing. Duncan closed his own eyes before the wretched graybeard's piercing gaze could reach him.

". . . The king's fury gave him more strength than a mortal man should have and he ran at them, tore the stone from its base and cast it into the sea . . . the young man with it." The seneschal's voice rose as he neared the legend's climax. "Shocked, for he hadn't meant to kill the lad, the king fell to his knees and begged his daughter's forgiveness. But her loss was too great. Without even glancing at her father, she walked off the cliff, joining in death the love she was denied in life.

". . . So angered were the old gods by the king's disrespect for the stone's sanctity, they repaid him in kind, destroying his stronghold so thoroughly, none can say where his court truly stood."

Duncan opened his eyes as the seneschal finished the tale. "But all was not lost," Fergus's voice rang out. "Many years later, the marriage stone washed ashore on our fair isle and has been at Eilean Creag ever since. Its power is stronger now, and all newly married MacKenzies who grasp hands through the stone's opening and share a kiss afterward, are blessed by a powerful bond no man can destroy, for the old gods themselves shall favor and watch o'er them."

The hushed silence seemed to deepen, broken only by a sniffle or two from the few womenfolk present. Then deafening applause erupted, soon joined by the inevitable chant: "Bring on the stone! Bring on the stone!"

Fergus's chosen buffoons paraded the stone thrice around the high table, finally halting behind Duncan's great chair. Other clansmen, grinning like dimwits, yanked Duncan and Linnet from their seats and pushed them before the stone.

"Take her hand!" a voice rose above the babble. Others quickly joined in. "Aye, take her hand!"

Duncan blew out a furious breath and thrust his hand through the hole in the stone. 'Twas his duty, he supposed, and nary a soul present would cease to bedevil him until he'd done his part. But then his wife placed her hand in his and Duncan no longer heard his men's fool prattle.

Her hand was surprisingly warm and strong, yet her touch unsettled him. Saints, but her warmth stole into him. It sprang from where their clasped hands touched, making its way brazenly up his arm to flow through him like warmed mead.

Before she could bewitch him further, Duncan shouted the words he must, "See, all here present, we are joined! Honor to the old gods, may they bless our union!"

To end this part of the ceremony, he laced his fingers with hers and gave her hand a light squeeze. She gasped, a tiny breathy sound, but he heard it. Even above the hoots and foot stomping of his men. Following his lead, she tightened her fingers over his and Duncan's heart slammed against his ribs.

"The kiss! The kiss!" his men roared.

Spurred on by his wish to have done with this spectacle and an overwhelming desire to do just what the men urged him to do, Duncan released her hand but grasped her arm and drew her close. "We must kiss," he told her, taking hold of both of her arms. "Afterward we shall have our peace."

Something indefinable sparked in her eyes, but she lifted her chin to await his kiss. With a low groan that couldn't possibly have come from him, Duncan caught her hard against him and pressed his mouth against hers in the most possessive kiss he'd given a woman in years.

When, in her innocence, she parted her lips and the

tip of her tongue fleetingly touched his, a burst of raw desire flared in Duncan, and his loins tightened with pure, heated need.

The sort of need he did not want to be burdened with.

At once, he broke the kiss and set her from him. "'Tis done," he vowed. Lifting his arms above his head, he turned in a circle and raised his voice so all could hear him. "Let no man claim we have not asked the old ones' blessing."

"May they e'er watch over you!" his clansmen answered the ritual chant. Still hooting and full of themselves, those who'd crowded round made their way back to their places, those still seated reached for jugs of ale or wine and refilled their drinking cups. At last, the clamor died down as the celebrations turned to the more serious amusements of supping and imbibing spirits.

Back in his own seat, Duncan purposely turned his attention to the delicacies and great platters of succulent meat spread upon the table. He didn't trust himself even to glance at his bride, for beneath his braies, his body was still uncomfortably aroused. Saints, even the soft sound of her breathing and her sweet, feminine scent were enough to keep him stirred.

Nay, 'twas wiser to concentrate on the feast before him. Fergus had outdone himself, bringing forth a wealth of finer victuals than Duncan had seen in longer than he cared to remember. The old seneschal had set a table good enough for the Bruce himself.

Duncan reached for the hippocras. Mayhaps if he partook of enough of the potent brew and ate his fill, a sound sleep would help him forget he'd bound himself to another wife this day.

A wife whose purpose was *not* to quicken his loins.

"Make haste and eat, will you? You've not touched a morsel," he admonished her, nodding to the choice pieces of roasted stag he'd carefully selected for her. "The sooner we've had done with our meal, the sooner we can be gone from this table."

"I am not hungry, milord."

"Then I shall eat for you," Duncan said irritably, lifting a succulent piece of meat off their shared trencher and popping it into his mouth.

Anything to take his mind off the conflicting emotions whirling through him, driving him near mad.

Anything to steer his thoughts away from his manhood, still fully charged and pressing hard against the confines of his hose.

He'd wanted naught more than a docile and plain bride who would but answer the question that burned ceaselessly in his mind. He'd gotten a maid who fired his loins without trying and who'd defy every rule he'd laid down in his household.

A maid whose sight was likely little more than Highland gossip . . . a minstrel's exaggeration.

And he'd fallen for it.

A maid whose purity his clansmen roared, at this very moment, for him to take.

And, by St. Columba's holy bones, he burned to do so.

But he'd learned a burning in the loins is fast quenched and forgotten whilst a searing of one's soul lasts an eternity.

Once more, Duncan refilled the enormous wedding chalice and downed its contents in one long gulp.

If his men insisted on a bedding, they could have one.

But without him.

He intended to sleep through it.

5

'twas nigh onto midnight as Linnet paced the length of her chamber, naked save the linen sheet she'd snatched off the bed and wrapped around herself like a shroud.

In the distance, even through the heavy oak door, she could hear the retreating footsteps of her new clansmen as they noisily made their way back to the hall after unceremoniously depositing both Linnet and her husband atop her bed.

Her cheeks flamed with indignation at the way the tumultuous merrymakers had cheerily divested them of their raiments.

To her dismay, even Elspeth had participated, clucking like a mother hen, calmly reminding Linnet that such was the way of things, as she'd deftly peeled off each and every layer of Linnet's clothing—not even leaving her the modesty of her undertunic.

Ignoring Linnet's protests, her trusted old nurse had stripped her bare, leaving her fully unclothed, as unprotected as she'd been on the day her mother had birthed her.

Totally exposed.

Elspeth had even snatched Linnet's precious *arisaid* as she'd exited the chamber. Someone had also locked the large chest containing Linnet's new gowns.

Not that it mattered to aught but the walls and few scant pieces of furniture, for her husband appeared to have fallen into a deep slumber the moment his dark head hit the pillows.

Still, being locked in a room, without a stitch of clothing, with an equally unclothed man, was a bit disconcerting.

She was cold, too.

Freezing.

"Do you intend to stalk back and forth all night?" her husband's deep voice boomed from the bed, startling her so much she nearly dropped the sheet she held clutched to her breast. "'Tis more noise you're making than my fool clansmen below."

"I'm moving about to keep warm, sir," Linnet snapped, angry at the way her heart responded to the sight of him sitting upright in the bed, his bare chest broad and powerful-looking. Too late, she wished she'd drawn the bedcurtains, thus hiding his masculine splendor from her view!

Faith, but he was magnificent.

MacKenzie or nay.

Cold-hearted or not.

"'Tis a pity none among your men thought to stoke

the fire," she ventured, pulling the sheet tighter about her breasts. "'Twould appear they were too intent on undressing us to think about such a minor thing as our comfort."

She regretted the sharp words the moment they passed her lips, for her husband threw back the coverlet and sprang to his feet. "Then *I* shall do it."

Handsome and breath-stealing as a pagan fertility god come to life, Duncan strode across the room, as comfortable with his nakedness as she was uncomfortable with hers.

Light from a brace of tallow candles burnished his skin, casting dancing shadows up and down his well-muscled back as he knelt before the hearth.

Like a lovestruck damsel from a French romance, she gawked helplessly at his noble form, her heart beating faster the longer she stared.

Then, as if the angels above wished to save her the embarrassment of having him catch her ogling him like a brazen bawd, a chill gust of sea wind swept through a window, extinguishing the candles and plunging the chamber in darkness.

The sharp tang of brine and the darker scents of a damp night laid heavy in the air as Linnet stood perfectly still, waiting for her eyes to adjust to the gloom.

She fair jumped out of her skin when strong, warm fingers curled about her elbow and something even warmer, nay, *hot*, brushed lightly against her hip.

Her breath caught in her throat at the brief contact. 'Twas *that* part of him, she was sure.

What else could fair scorch her through the linen sheet she'd wrapped around herself several times over?

What else would send tingles all the way to her toes?

What else indeed but that mysteriously masculine part of him he meant to keep from her.

"Come," he said close to her ear, his breath warming her cheek. "I'll guide you to bed," he added, his voice steady and firm . . . *normal*.

As if he hadn't realized what part of him had just touched her so intimately.

Or, mayhap closer to the truth, he simply didn't care.

Linnet yanked her arm from his grasp. "I canna yet sleep."

"And neither can I if you dinna cease poltering about," Duncan grumbled, snatching back her arm and pulling her forward.

Linnet dug her heels into the rushes. "Then I shall sit in the chair by the fire."

"By the Rood, wench, 'tis cold, I am weary, and my head aches. Dinna rile me further." Fair dragging her to the bed, he flung back the covers. "Climb in. I willna touch you if that's what's bothering you."

She bristled at his harshly spoken words, but scrambled onto the bed, quickly scooting to the far side and drawing the coverlet to her chin.

To her surprise, rather than getting into bed himself, he hastened to the wall where he took down one of the hanging tapestries. As she looked on, he spread the heavy cloth on the floor and began rolling it up.

"What . . . what are you doing?" Linnet asked from the bed, although his intentions became humiliatingly clear as he carried the unwieldy column closer and plunked it down in the middle of the bed.

"Naught but assuring myself an undisturbed night's

rest," he said, then settled himself onto the bed . . . on the other side of the tapestry barrier. "After this night, I shall sleep in my own chamber, and you will not be disturbed."

Feeling chastised and as insignificant as if he'd just informed her he found her less appealing than a gray mouse, Linnet lay stiff and quiet, fearing the slightest movement or sound would only serve to further inflame his ill humor.

Merciful saints, did he think she'd fall upon him in the night?

Would that she had the courage to flee.

Exit the chamber and seek refuge elsewhere.

She would, too, were it not for the boy.

For his sake, she remained motionless, not daring to even take a deep breath lest she disturb her husband.

If she meant to help Robbie, she must achieve some semblance of a relationship with his father.

Even if that meant suffering through such indignities as knowing he'd likely prefer taking a ewe to bed than her.

Aye, her own feelings mattered scarce little.

Besides, she was used to being unloved.

But for the good of the lad, she must be strong. Duncan MacKenzie could bully her to the gates of hell and beyond, she wouldn't reveal what she knew about Robbie unless he softened toward the boy.

Until then, she'd maintain a firm stance, anger him if need be. His opinion of her wasn't of consequence.

'Twas the lad who needed him, not her.

Linnet swallowed the long sigh that almost escaped

her lips. Could she e'er bring her husband to accept Robbie?

To admit his love for the child?

Afore he learned the truth? Her husband should love Robbie for himself . . . regardless of whether he'd sired the lad or nay.

Such was her goal, but could she achieve it?

She did not know, but she meant to try. Even if the effort cost her last breath.

Outside, wind caught the shutter of one of the windows, slamming it against the tower with a mighty bang that echoed and reechoed in the shadowy chamber.

Linnet sat up with a start, coming instantly awake and realizing she must've fallen asleep despite her doubts of being able to do so. Pearly gray moonlight shone through the one unshuttered window, bathing the room in a silvery glow.

She shot a glance at the man beside her, half-afraid the loud noise might've startled him awake, too, but he slept soundly, his breathing deep and regular.

Indeed, he appeared completely at ease, without a care, as he lay sprawled in resplendent nakedness across his side of the bed.

Despite herself, her gaze sought and rested upon his sex, relaxed now, yet no less imposing in its dark virility. As she stared, an exquisite warmth began to curl languidly through her belly.

An aching, pulsing heat that intensified the longer she looked upon him.

Heat stole into her cheeks as well, and, embarrassed, she tore her gaze away. Very slowly, the pulsing warmth in her most feminine core ebbed, and the room's damp chill claimed her once more.

Only now she felt empty as well as cold.

Bereft and hollow, as if for a brief moment, she'd had something unique and wonderful in her grasp, only to have it cruelly ripped away from her.

A very faint fluttering still rippled through her and, instinctively, she pressed her thighs together to ease the ache she didn't understand.

She wanted naught to do with such stirrings.

Not from a man who did not want her.

A man she aught despise for his name alone, lest all his other shortcomings.

To her great relief, anger gradually replaced the disturbing sensations gazing at his nakedness had aroused in her.

Praise God he hadn't awakened and caught her eyeing him.

Would he have been able to tell her belly had gone liquid and warm at the sight of his virility, his blatant maleness?

Could he have guessed how she'd yearned to reach out and touch him?

She shuddered.

The possibility he might be able to read her thoughts was unthinkable.

Shaming.

She would've died of mortification.

Another loud bang reverberated around the room as the wind once more flung the loose shutter against the tower wall. This time her husband gave a slight groan and rolled onto his side.

Not wishing to risk his waking, Linnet crept from the bed as carefully as she could and refastened the loose shutter. To her alarm, the rusty latch made a loud grating noise that brought another mumbled groan from the direction of the bed.

Linnet froze in place, her hands on the cold metal latch, determined not to move until she was certain he slept soundly again. Fortune was with her. The sound of his gentle snores soon blended with the hollow whistle of the wind, the patter of rain, and the low drone of nesting bees.

Nesting bees?

The tiny hairs on the back of her neck prickled, standing suddenly on end as unease crept up her spine.

She'd not noticed so much as a spider in the chamber. Nor had she seen signs of bugs or vermin in the floor rushes. Truth to tell, they appeared newly strewn. Someone had even scented them with fresh meadowsweet.

Had the bees swarmed into the room to escape the rain? Warily, lest she make a noise, she drew her husband's blue-and-green plaid off a chairback and draped it loosely around her shoulders against the chill as she cautiously scanned the chamber for the bees.

Her gaze darted about, but she saw naught.

Even though the whirring noise grew so loud her temples began to throb.

The room was empty.

Nothing moved save the shadows dancing along the walls.

With dawning comprehension, Linnet stared at the oddly elongated shadows, watching as they took shape, forming themselves into a copse of pine trees.

The buzzing reached a piercing level, hurting her ears. Then a cloud of mist rose up from the floor, its shifting tendrils blocking out all but the circle of pines . . . and the bed.

Fear constricted her throat, and her heart slammed against her chest as beads of moisture sprang onto her forehead. 'Twas only a vision, only a vision, she repeated to herself, trying desperately to cling to the knowledge it'd pass in a moment.

They always did.

But this one was different.

Different, yet frighteningly familiar.

Biting her lower lip till she tasted blood, Linnet struggled to stifle the scream building inside her. She mustn't cry out, mustn't awaken her husband.

Her lot with him was precarious enough without him seeing her in the throes of one of her fits, as her da called them.

Biting harder on her lip, she squeezed her eyes shut, hoping the vision would dissipate by the time she opened them again. But the pressure in her head and the humming in her ears only increased.

She had to look.

The nightmare wouldn't end until she did.

Dread consumed her, pressing the breath from her lungs, but she opened her eyes and sent her gaze where it had to go.

Straight through the mist to the prone shape stretched upon her bed.

The image there beseeched her with eyes so filled with pain and sorrow their powerful impact near bent her double.

'Twas the black stag.

The beast whose heart had been ripped from its body.

Blood ran down her chin as her teeth sank deeper into her lip, filling her mouth with a brassy, metallic taste.

She tried to look away, but couldn't. Frozen in place, bound by a force stronger than she, Linnet watched the terrifying spectacle unfold.

Then the wretched creature on the bed shifted, changing shape as she'd known it would. Before her eyes, the stag became the man.

One whose identity she now knew.

Her husband.

The man without a heart.

And like the beast, Duncan MacKenzie beseeched her with his eyes.

Troubled eyes holding her spellbound, forbidding her to look elsewhere.

As before, he reached for her with blood-soaked hands. But this time his mouth worked soundlessly, forming silent words whilst his tormented gaze held her captive.

"Please . . . I need . . ." he pleaded, his voice raw, broken.

His anguish wrapped itself around her, suffocating her in a stranglehold from which she couldn't break free. She could only stand immovable as stone and pray the vision end soon lest she perish from fright.

"*Please* . . ." he said again, but the word faded, ending on a ragged gasp.

The mists dissipated, too. No longer dense, the thin,

curling wisps receded into the floor whence they'd come. And the tall shadows against the walls were once again just that, shadows.

Gone, the dark copse of trees she'd seen but moments before.

She still heard the whirring noise but it, too, lessened as the normal night sounds returned: the light patter of rain against the closed shutters and the sigh of the wind chasing away the unholy drone that accompanied such visitations.

Only *he* lingered on, his ravaged state growing in terrifying clarity with each breath she took, his anguish a living thing.

'Twas so real she could smell the blood gushing from the wound in his chest, almost feel the damp warmth of the deep red stains on the bedclothes, hear his lifeblood dripping onto the floor, where it formed a pool, staining the rushes.

Aye, 'twas real.

Too real.

Linnet's fingers dug into the plaid, holding it tight as if its nubby wool could shield her from the nightmare before her.

In desperation, she turned away, staring instead at the tightly shuttered windows. She must keep her wits, dared not do aught to awaken her husband.

Or shatter the frightening image.

Ill tidings came to those who tampered with visions such as hers.

A soft rustling sound made her glance fearfully back to the bed. To her horror, she saw he'd moved, raised himself up on his elbows.

Pinning her with his stare, he struggled to speak, but his mouth only formed silent words.

And he tried to lean forward.

Why? To reach her?

A shudder passed through her at the thought. Pure terror welled inside her, demanding release. Trembling, she clamped a hand over her mouth.

Then he spoke.

Garbled words she couldn't understand.

With tremendous effort, he took a deep breath, holding it within as if to gather strength before he released the air on a rush.

The words that burst forth from his lips curdled Linnet's blood.

"Give back my heart!"

Linnet jumped back and released the cry she could hold back no longer.

'Twas an earsplitting shriek that echoed through the castle and was surely heard all the way to the farthest shores of the loch.

A bloodcurdling scream rent the night's quiet, instantly banishing the sweet oblivion of Duncan MacKenzie's deep slumber. With a curse, he sprang from the bed, his hands reaching for his sword.

Sweet Mother of God, they were under attack!

"Man the walls!" he roared. "We're under siege!"

Frantically, he searched for his arms. Naught was where it should be. Thunder of heaven, where was his blade? In his haste, his bare foot collided with a misplaced chest, shooting a red-hot arrow of pain up his leg.

"By Lucifer's knees, who rearranged my chamber?"

he cursed, limping toward his sword. It was propped against a wall near the door, with his dagger and belt on the floor nearby.

As if they'd been carelessly flung there.

Puzzlement drew his brows together. Ne'er would he have cast aside his arms so clumsily. 'Twas his way to lay his weapons atop his carefully folded plaid each night.

Within easy reach.

His confusion grew.

Where *was* his plaid?

Something foul was afoot and if the castle women would cease shrieking and his head didn't ache as if it'd been cleaved in twain, mayhap he'd get to the bottom of the matter.

But first he had to see to the safety of his clan.

Unclothed, if need be.

Fastening his belt around his bare hips, Duncan thrust his dagger beneath the wide leather band, then made ready to dash from the room, anxious to join the fray.

But the door wouldn't open.

'Twas locked from the outside!

Unease seized him at the same moment a shrill cry sounded behind him—he hadn't heard the castle wenches screaming, the cries came from within the chamber! Brandishing his sword, he whirled around only to . . . freeze.

A banshee stood before the hearth!

Her flame-colored hair wild about her shoulders, blood dribbling down her chin, her vacant eyes staring at him from a face pale as a week-old corpse, the *bean shith*'s wail turned his very bones to water.

And, saints preserve him, she wore his plaid!

"Dinna come closer!" the banshee cried.

As if *she* feared *him*, she threw up her arms in a defensive gesture, letting loose of the plaid as she did so. It fell to the floor, pooling around her ankles.

Realization hit him with the force of a wind straight from hell, stealing his breath. His heart skipped a beat, and his jaw dropped.

Eilean Creag wasn't under attack, nor had a *bean shith* penetrated its thick walls.

The banshee was his wife!

And she stood before him in *her* chamber, not his.

"By the lance of God, what goes on here?" Duncan thundered, his heart hammering in his chest. "Saints alive, woman, you've blood dribbling down your chin!"

Visibly shaken, his bride lifted a hand to her lips. Her trembling fingers came away smeared with red. "I did not intend to disturb your sleep, my lord," she said, examining her bloodied fingertips rather than look at him. "I am not oft visited by such alarming manifestations."

"The blood . . ." Duncan let his question hang in the chill air between them. For the love of St. Mungo, he still felt as if he was teetering on the threshold to hell's antechamber.

"I bit my lip, 'tis all, sir. You've no need fetch the leech."

Duncan's alarm eased upon the realization she'd been in the throes of a vision. But blessed knowledge didn't slow the blood racing through his veins. He blew out a ragged breath. Every muscle in his body screamed with tension.

Including ones he hadn't known he possessed.

Needing to do something . . . anything . . . he set his weapons aside and strode to the bed. He ripped a strip of cloth from the bedcurtains, closing his fingers around the makeshift bandage with the same fierceness a certain question squeezed his innards.

"Did you see what I must know?" he asked, still facing the bed. "Is the boy mine?"

Silence answered him.

Duncan curled his hands to fists. Was he ne'er to be granted surcease from his doubts? Not even now after binding himself to a lass whose abilities were sung throughout the Highlands?

A lass who, though gifted with the sight, seemed to have lost her tongue. Duncan's ire grew. A speech-deprived seeress served him naught.

"I canna tell you if Robbie is yours," came her reply at last. "The vision had naught to do with what you want to know."

Want to know? Duncan glanced heavenward and swallowed an oath that would've curled the devil's own tail.

Did she not realize he *needed* to know?

His impatience got the better of him, and Duncan spun around, the strip of cloth dangling from the fingers of his outstretched hand. "For your chin," he said, but the sharp-toned words died on his tongue as a very different type of need assailed him.

Throat of Christ, was he growing as blind as a

cloudy-eyed graybeard? How had he missed noticing the maid stood before him wearing naught but a blush?

A blush that deepened as she snatched the cloth from his fingers and pressed it against her lower lip. "Thank you," she said, but Duncan scarce noticed. Blood surged to his loins, intense desire, hard and swift, causing his too-long-neglected arousal to lengthen and swell.

He let his gaze roam over her, drinking in the sight of her freely displayed bounty, inch by intoxicating inch. Doing so was torture in its most exquisite form, but so pleasurable, he couldn't deny himself.

The soft glow of the dying embers in the hearth illuminated her unclothed body in all its naked glory, taunting him with the fullness of her breasts and the gentle curve of her hip, whilst a lush tangle of curls beckoned to him from betwixt her thighs.

Curls the same color and every bit as alluring as the luxuriant red-gold tresses cascading to well below her waist.

A man less skilled in the arts of love would've spilled his seed just looking upon her!

His shaft now fully engorged and aching, Duncan nearly joined the ranks of such depraved and ignoble souls when he glanced at her face and caught her peering intently at his swollen sex. His maleness bucked under her innocent perusal, filling and lengthening even more beneath her gaze.

Saints, but she fired his blood!

"I thought you had no desire to bed me, milord?"

The confusion in her voice banished the haze of Duncan's desire, deflating his passion and stealing the rampant lust she'd stirred in him. Ne'er had it been his intent to confuse or hurt her, yet he'd behaved like a stag in rut and done just what he'd vowed he wouldn't.

"You have seen I desire you," he replied, unable to keep the thickness from his voice. "But naught has changed. It would not be wise and was never my intent to take my ease with you."

"I see," she said in the same tone of voice she'd used in his solar when they'd first discussed what was to be expected of her.

Duncan scowled at the memory of that ill-fated meeting.

He did not want to desire her. Ne'er had he expected her to stoke flames he'd thought were long extinguished, flames powerful enough to do more damage than merely supply his neglected tarse with its ease.

The most lackluster-brained dolt would see the danger of slaking one's lust upon his lady's bountiful offerings. A man who dared would lose more than his seed on her . . . he'd lose his soul.

And Duncan didn't have one to give.

A pestilence on his men for convincing him to fetch her. He'd wanted an ill-favored bride, not one whose charms would tempt a monk!

With an oath, he raked both hands through his hair. Using one hand to shield his arousal as best he could, he snatched his plaid off the floor with the other, then tossed it at her.

"Cover yourself," he ordered, his tone harsher than he'd intended. Turning his back to her, he added, "It is not wise for me to look upon you."

He waited until the soft rustling of wool ceased before he spoke again. "Be you covered?"

"Aye," came her shaky reply.

He wheeled back to face her, but focused his gaze on the wall, just to the left of her head. "Return to your bed, I shall not disturb you. The chair will serve me well for the remainder of the night."

For once she didn't contradict him, but fairly flew across the room, his plaid clutched tightly to her breast. The stricken look on her face twisted the knife in his gut, making him despise himself for the heartless bastard he'd become.

But if he'd had to gaze upon her another moment, he'd have lost control and tossed her upon the rushes, not even bothering to carry her the few steps to the bed.

Splendor of Heaven, she'd looked like a mythical water nymph risen from the depths of the loch, all wild and lush and tempting.

Too tempting.

Duncan waited until all grew still beneath the bed-covers, then lowered himself into the high-backed chair beside the hearth, stretching his legs out before him.

The long-dead fire left not a pretense of warmth but he was too drained to start another.

Nor did he relish passing the long hours till morn sitting naked, cold, and uncomfortable, in his wife's bedchamber.

He scarce recalled his men half-carrying, half-dragging him up the stairs, then stripping him of his clothes and tossing him upon her bed, but he'd think on the matter of their boldness later—when his head hurt less.

Scowling, he looked about for something with which to cover himself.

Anything capable of providing even a semblance of warmth.

But the room was scant furnished and held none of the elaborate trappings his first wife had kept about her chamber.

Naught but his new wife's worn leather herb satchel caught his eye. It rested on the floor, close to his chair. Duncan regarded the pouch with bitter irony.

How fitting for him to contemplate using the soft leather satchel to warm himself when his bride slept, chaste and alone, not four paces away.

She might as well be four leagues away for all the comfort she spent him!

With a muttered oath, he snatched up the pouch and settled it across his loins. The butter-soft leather would keep his tender parts warm if naught else.

Not that he need concern himself with keeping *himself* warm.

Truth be told, he could share his bed with *ten* wenches, pile sheepskins high atop the lot of them, and *still* freeze.

Inside.

Aye, the room's chill mattered little.

'Twas a paltry discomfort compared to the cold he carried within.

6

Some bold whoreson sought to put out his eyes with red-hot needles! Duncan shot to his feet, ready to fend off the foolhardy knave who'd dare attempt such a foul deed, only to slump back into the chair he'd spent half the night in. The quick motion nigh caused his head to burst asunder.

Leaning back, he let out an agonized groan. The pain was great, but at least he'd not been set upon by a needle-wielding assailant.

Nay, 'twas merely the bright morning light slanting through the cracks in the shutters what made his eyes smart as though they'd been set afire.

By his blessed mother's grave, what had befallen him? He hadn't partaken of *that* much spiced wine yestereve.

Or had he?

By the saints, he'd never felt more wretched.

And why had he awakened in a chair and not his bed?

With a ragged moan, he lowered the arm he'd flung across his aching eyes. Squinting against the sun's infernal glare, he peered about the chamber, looking for his first squire, Lachlan.

The lad usually slept on a pallet before the fire, but he was nowhere to be seen.

Nor was his pallet.

And the hearth Duncan eyed was not his own!

By the Rood, he'd awakened in a strange bedchamber.

Nay, not quite, for, with dawning comprehension, he recognized his surroundings.

His gaze flew to the bed and the lustrous flame-colored tresses spilling over the edge of the coverlets. Duncan pressed his lips together. There could be no doubt as to whose quarters he'd awakened in.

Thanks be to the powers above, his new wife yet slumbered.

He wasn't in any mood to bid her a good morn.

Not naked as he was, clad only in the belt fastened about his hips.

A further glance about the chamber showed his plaid lying in a heap beside the bed, whilst his sword and dagger rested atop a table next the door.

A door that stood ajar.

Slowly, realization filtered through the throbbing pain clouding his senses. Little by little, the events of the day before—*his wedding day*—came back to him.

He'd wanted naught but to have done with the feasting, mayhap address his bride about Robbie again, then escape to the solitude of his solar.

But it wasn't meant to be.

Instead of the docility he would've preferred, his new wife had flaunted her position by bringing the child to his table even though someone in his household had surely warned her he'd given strict orders the boy was to be kept from his sight.

Aye, she had to have been told.

Yet she'd defied him.

And so had his men.

The faithless bastards had blatantly disregarded his wishes. They'd culled him into performing the marriage stone ceremony, then later, boldly carted both him and his bride to bed in the hopes of cajoling him into performing an act they knew fair well he'd expressly stated would not take place.

Not yestereve and not in the future. Not with this woman.

Duncan squeezed his eyes shut and pressed his fingers against his throbbing temples. He should never have brought the wench here, ne'er done such a fool thing as wed her.

She hadn't been under his roof but a scant few hours and already she'd wrought havoc and caused him grief.

A muscle twitched in his jaw, its jerking making him uncomfortably aware of the tension coursing through him. The woman had gone too far, overstepped her bounds, on her first day as lady of Eilean Creag.

Of her first *night*, he remembered precious little beyond being lugged up the stairs and stripped.

And that which he *did* recall, he wished to forget, for the fleeting images flashing through his mind were unsettling.

Disturbing in a manner he didn't care to examine.

Even now, with his head feeling as if it'd been split in two, his traitorous loins quickened at the memory of her standing before him in all her naked glory, her red-gold hair swirling about her like a sea siren straight out of a lovestruck bard's silly tale of unquenched love and desire.

Recollections of barred doors and screams in the night came back to him, too, chasing away the unwanted lust his too-fetching bride aroused within him.

He didn't want to desire her.

Didn't want to need her.

'Twas far easier—safer—to slake his need for a woman's velvety warmth and softness with a village bawd.

For a few pieces of coin, they'd barter their wares, let him partake of their well-worn charms. But even such whores couldn't keep the revulsion, the fear, from their eyes as he mounted them.

Their expressions e'er bespoke the words they'd never dare voice to his face. They, too, believed he'd pushed Cassandra to her death.

Thought him a murderer.

Duncan swore. In death as in life, his beautiful first wife had the power to make him miserable. In truth, she'd killed him with her treachery.

Not that he'd cared aught about her infidelity.

At least not after the first few years of their marriage. The saints knew, he'd stopped loving her long before he'd discovered her indiscretions. 'Twas only when she'd taunted him about Robbie's true parentage that she'd stolen his heart, his very soul.

That, and her part in the death of his sister, Arabella.

Duncan dragged a hand over his face, then pinched the bridge of his nose. Might God forgive him if his suspicions were unfounded, but not few were those under his roof who, like him, wondered if the witch-woman had also had a hand in the mysterious death of his lady mother as well.

Proven or nay, the deeds were done, irreversible. His beloved sister, cold in the ground, his sweet mother resting not far from her daughter's side.

As for Robbie being Kenneth's son, deep inside Duncan knew the truth of the spiteful words Cassandra had flung at him on the last day of her life. What pained him was the tiny shimmer of hope he'd never been able to extinguish.

A desperate wish to discover she'd lied . . . a notion only a fool would cling to.

Duncan's hands clenched to fists, and he drew a ragged breath. Cassandra had taken his life as surely as she'd lost her own by tripping on the hem of her gown and plunging from the battlements as he'd looked on, unable to stop her fall.

In her grave, she'd found peace, freedom from whatever madness had made her so wicked, but he could not run from his demons.

His torture was a living death.

Ne'er would another woman cause him such pain again.

Not in a thousand lives.

Even if protecting himself caused his new bride anguish. It couldn't be helped. He wanted only peace. She would have to seek other ways to fill her heart and days.

Her *nights* mattered less; they were no concern of his.

Duncan glanced across the room at her. She slept soundly, blessedly unaware of the turmoil her very presence had wrought upon him. A tiny twinge of guilt made a slight chink in the wall around his heart, but that only made him all the more determined to keep away from her.

Using great care lest he jar his aching head, or make a noise and awaken his bride, Duncan pushed himself to his feet. 'Twas time he sought answers, but not yet from his wife.

'Twould take a stronger man than he to face her down and question her whilst she still had the vulnerable look of a sleeping angel about her.

He'd press her about Robbie later.

When he had his wits full about him . . . and his manhood safely ensconced within his braies.

Although not in his best form, he wasn't befuddled enough not to ken his bride wasn't the only one who owed him explanations.

She hadn't barred the bedchamber door from the outside yestereve.

Nor could she have opened it from the inside come the morn.

He didn't need a sage to know a certain one-eyed, ugly-faced Sassunach was the culprit. 'Twould be just like Strongbow to have concocted such a scheme. Duncan bit back an oath. What a fine and ignoble bit of trickery it'd been . . . locking him naked in a chamber with an equally bare-bottomed wife!

The English lout had undoubtedly thought they'd give in to their baser instincts and spend the night in wedded bliss, locked in a fevered embrace.

Against his better judgment, Duncan shot another glance at his new lady. Faith and hypocrisy, it didn't help his mood any to know how close he'd come to doing just that.

How much he'd *wanted* to.

On his life, only his iron resolve had kept him from making Linnet truly his.

He shook his head, heedless of the pain the slight motion caused him. Sir Marmaduke's uncanny knack for knowing his innermost thoughts was positively frightening at times.

Annoying in the extreme.

He must have words with him.

Stern words.

Eager to challenge the Sassunach he loved like a brother, truth be told, Duncan cautiously retrieved, then donned his plaid. As quietly as he could, he snatched up his weapons and hastened from the chamber.

It wasn't till he'd bounded halfway down the stairs that he realized he'd used his bride's given name.

Linnet awoke to a bright morn, much relieved to find herself alone in her bed. The saints must've smiled upon her, for she doubted she'd been able to face her husband so soon after the queersome happenings of the night.

Later, aye.

After she'd had time to compose herself.

But not yet.

'Twas a relief, too, to see the door stood open a crack and some goodly soul had unlocked the strongbox containing her new clothes so she'd be able to dress. Even her *arisaid* had been returned, its soft woolen length carefully folded and draped over a chair.

With great haste spurred by the chill morning air, Linnet made use of a ewer of scented water to bathe, hurriedly pulled on the first gown she withdrew from the chest, and slipped from the chamber.

Yet even properly dressed, she shivered as she hurried down the spiral stairs. Although no longer murky and dim, the curving stairwell was clammy and damp, heavily permeated with wet sea smells from the night's storm.

Indeed, she feared it would take more than a new day's sun to banish the blackness lying so heavily over Eilean Creag.

And neither woolen blankets nor a blazing hearth fire would e'er ease its cold.

Not so long as its master carried darkness in his heart.

Lifting her chin, Linnet hastened down the remaining stone steps. If only for Robbie's sake alone, she meant to bring light and warmth to this grim island fortress.

'Twas a feat she meant to accomplish, no matter the cost.

But her determination faltered when she neared the

hall and she saw what looked very much like her under-tunic being brandished about like a trophy of war.

Even the servants, painstakingly collecting refuse from the floor or sweeping ashes from the hearths, were all atwitter, boasting along with her husband's clansmen about the blood-smeared state of her undergown!

Lingering in the shadows of the hall's arched entry, she peered hard at the displayed garment. It was indeed hers. The very one Elspeth had fair wrested off her the night before.

Linnet pressed her hand against her breast while her heart hammered with embarrassment. But confusion warred with logic: the garment *couldn't* have been bloodied.

It wasn't her woman's time and Duncan MacKenzie had been asleep long before Elspeth had left the chamber with Linnet's clothes.

Someone had to have purposely stained the tunic after it had been taken from her room.

Would Elspeth do such a thing?

And if so . . . why?

Or had she merely imagined Elspeth had near forced her to remove the undergarment, then departed with it? Sometimes, with the onset of her spells, her mind went fuzzy. Afterward, too. There were times she'd lost hours because of the toll her visions exacted from her.

And she *had* been visited by a most powerful one yestereve, that she couldn't deny.

She blew out a shaky breath. Truth was, she could well have confused the events of her wedding night.

But even if Elspeth hadn't taken the tunic, it couldn't

be stained with her maidensblood. To her best recall, her husband had slept most of the night. First on the other side of his improvised tapestry barrier, then in a chair by the hearth.

'Twas true her vision had disrupted his slumber, and he'd confronted her but hadn't laid a hand on her.

Or had he?

A hazy recollection of him naked and aroused played through her mind. Vaguely, she remembered watching his manhood swell, the whole of it growing thicker and longer beneath her gaze, but the titillating image was too elusive to grasp.

As if the devil himself meant to taunt her, she couldn't remember aught else.

Not for sure.

Could her husband have ravished her during her vision? Or after? When her mind had still been too fogged for her to take proper heed of what might have happened between them? The image on the bed *had* reached for her, demanded she 'return his heart.' Had Duncan MacKenzie taken in the flesh that which his vision-likeness couldn't claim?

Was it possible to be bedded by a man and not have any recollection of the act?

A shudder passed from the crown of her head to the tips of her toes. She didn't know the answer but knew who would. Determined, she took several deep breaths to calm her still-racing pulse, then pushed away from the wall. Drawing back her shoulders, she entered the hall with as much grace as she could muster.

Thomas, a strapping lad who couldn't speak, spot-

ted her first. The youth blushed to the roots of his unkempt hair and nodded to her as she passed.

Everyone else fell quiet, suddenly appearing overly
intent on whatever task they could find to occupy themselves. Some gave her respectful nods as poor Thomas
had, a few of the younger serving maids smiled timidly.

But no one moved except the tale-spinning
seneschal, Fergus. *He* roughly plucked the tunic from
the hands of a scarlet-faced clansman and brought it to
Linnet.

"You'll be wanting this," he said, handing it to her
with much solemnity, as if the undergown were a precious reliquary and not a sullied piece of linen. " 'Tis the
way of the clan for the lady to save the proof of her
virtue. We thank you and Duncan for sending it to the
hall for us to see."

Linnet took the proffered tunic, quickly scrunching
it into a ball to hide the smears of blood. "But I
dinna—"

" 'Twas not our wish to embarrass you," he broke
in, his commanding voice loud in the unnatural silence
of the hall. " 'Tis pleased we are to know you came to
Duncan a pure and virtuous bride."

Of a sudden, a raucous chorus of cheers broke the
stillness, and Linnet flushed crimson. The MacKenzies
were acknowledging her as their own . . . as their laird's
lady.

Thanking her for her virtue.

Only, until a few moments ago, she hadn't known
she'd relinquished it!

She still didn't know for certain.

But she *did* know she hadn't sent her undergarment to the hall for all and sundry to examine.

Blood-smeared or no.

Aye, that much she knew.

"Where be Elspeth?" she asked, amazed her voice sounded so calm.

"Where be *who*?" Fergus placed a cupped hand behind his left ear and leaned forward.

"My servant," Linnet said louder. "The grizzle-headed old hen I thought I trusted," she added under her breath.

"*Grizzle-headed*, eh?" Fergus folded his arms and narrowed his eyes at her. "'Tis a fine woman, she be, your Elspeth. I havna seen aught grizzled about her." He paused, fixing her with a hard look as if daring her to challenge him. "You'll find her in the kitchen. Just go through the screens passage and follow your nose."

"I thank you, sir." Linnet didn't bother to tell him she'd already visited Eilean Creag's vast kitchen. "A good morrow to you," she added, again marveling her tone hadn't betrayed the emotions swirling inside her.

A fine woman, he'd called Elspeth. The three words echoed in her head as she made her way from the hall, her soiled gown tucked tightly beneath her arm. Could the crusty old seneschal be smitten with Elspeth? 'Twas too ludicrous to consider.

Or was it?

Eilean Creag seemed a place where naught was too odd to happen.

But she pushed the notion aside as she rounded a corner and neared the kitchen. She had other matters to discuss with Elspeth. It concerned her not if her childhood nurse had been making moon eyes at her husband's legend-chanting steward.

If her suspicions proved true, Elspeth *deserved* to tie herself to a bandy-legged MacKenzie ancient whose fierce glares would curdle vinegar!

Linnet spotted Elspeth the moment she entered the kitchen. The stout old woman stood before one of the three enormous hearths, using a long-handled ladle to spoon something from a cauldron into a smaller earthenware pot held by a young lad.

Careful to hide the soiled tunic behind her, and especially not to make any noise, Linnet crept up behind her.

"Since when must you stir pottage like a kitchen maid, or think you I wouldn't look for you here?"

Elspeth jumped and spun around. The ladle flew from her fingers, landing on the stone floor with a clatter. "Faith, but you startled me," she gasped, bringing a hand to her breast much as Linnet had done herself outside the hall. "I thought you'd still be abed."

"And why should you think that?" Linnet wanted to know, no longer trying to keep her voice level. "Perchance because you believe the MacKenzies' fabled marriage stone has already begun to work its magic?"

For the first time Linnet could recall, Elspeth avoided her eyes. "Why . . . 'tis the morn after your wedding night. . . ."

"And you're hoping it *was* a wedding night, aren't you?"

Elspeth smoothed the apron she'd tied around her thick waist before she met Linnet's gaze. "I willna lie to you, child. Aye, 'tis true I'm hoping you found favor with one another."

Linnet leaned forward till her nose almost touched Elspeth's and lowered her voice, "And how was that supposed to happen betwixt meself and a man who finds me less appealing than a kirk mouse?

"Or were you supposing he'd downed a sufficient amount o' hippocras at the wedding feast to make himself fuzzy-headed enough to bed me?" she went on, anger knotting her belly. "Mayhap allow him to overlook the homeliness of my freckle-nosed face?"

Elspeth shook her head. "You're talking nonsense, child. 'Tis a bonnie bride you were. More beautiful than any I've e'er seen."

"Then why wasn't it left to my husband to carry me to his bed if he so desired? 'Twas no mistaking he didna want a bedding ceremony, that he—" Linnet paused, lifting a hand when Elspeth opened her mouth to protest. "Whilst I can understand his men getting out o' hand since 'twas deep in their cups they all were, I canna condone your participation in a scheme what could only end with my humiliation."

Elspeth glanced left and right before she spoke in a barely audible whisper. " 'Twas the Sassunach's idea, not mine. Though I did listen to him, for I truly believed he meant well."

"So the two of you conspired to leave us unclothed and locked in my bedchamber in the hopes we'd find favor with another?"

A pink tinge stained Elspeth's round cheeks. She nodded. "Aye, that was the way of it."

Anger and humiliation raced through Linnet so

quickly she feared steam would escape from her ears and blood from her nose. "And did you never consider how humiliated I'd be to have him reject me when I stood afore him wearing naught but my skin?"

She paused to catch her breath. "Did you not think he'd be furious o'er being forced to spend the night with me?"

"We acted on good faith, with your best interests at heart."

"And be *this* what you call good faith?" Linnet whipped the undergown from behind her back. "Do you care to explain?"

Tiny beads of perspiration appeared on Elspeth's forehead, but she didn't flinch, obviously as determined to defend herself as Duncan MacKenzie was to avoid consummating his marriage.

"We thought 'proof' would make it easier for you," Elspeth finally replied. "You're both too stubborn to see beyond your own noses. 'Tis a perfect union, yours; but neither of you is capable of seeing into the other's heart. We only meant to help."

Linnet dangled the gown in front of Elspeth as if it was as distasteful as a barrel of half-gnawed and fly-covered fish carcasses.

"Help me?" Linnet smothered a bitter laugh. "Have you forgotten 'twas you who warned Da not to barter me to the 'spawn o' the devil' . . . a possible *murderer*?"

Elspeth wiped her hands on her apron, then rested both on Linnet's shoulders. "Aye, to help. And I dinna believe the MacKenzie took his first wife's life."

"And how do you profess to know?" Linnet demanded, still riled but her chest no longer heaving in agitation. "You don't have the sight."

"Nay, I do not. I dinna need it. At my age 'tis possible to tell a man's character by simply looking at his eyes. Duncan MacKenzie isn't a murderer of women."

Linnet compressed her lips. She, too, doubted the dark tales spun about her husband. If he *had* murdered his first wife, she would've sensed it. Such vile acts clung to a person, forever blighting them, darkening the circle of luminous light she sometimes saw around a person's physical body.

While an air of blackness *did* surround her husband, 'twas not the mark of murder.

A different kind of darkness surrounded him . . . one borne of much sorrow and grief.

But that didn't excuse his treatment of Robbie, nor his callous rejection of her as his true consort.

Still, he wasn't a murderer.

Of that she was certain.

"So we agree he dinna kill her," she said at last. "But no matter how painful, the bitterness in his soul 'tis no writ to turn his back on the child, Robbie, nor to treat me poorly."

Elspeth's eyebrows rose. "Are you saying he handled you roughly?"

Linnet shook her head. "He . . . he dinna . . . touch me at all," she stammered, ashamed, angry, and relieved, at the same time. "I mean, I dinna ken if he . . . if he . . ." She let her words trail off, unable to voice the conflicting emotions tearing her apart. "I canna remember all what transpired."

"My poor bairn," Elspeth cooed, drawing Linnet

into her arms. "I should have explained to you about what happens between a man and his lady wife. Some gentleborn women are too delicate to withstand their husband's needs. 'Tis sorry I am if he hurt you."

Linnet extracted herself from the motherly embrace. Elspeth meant well, but she didn't understand. "I dinna ken if he hurt me or nay. As best I remember, he slept most of the night and dinna come to me at all. 'Tis impossible to recall aught of what did or didn't happen."

She paused, deliberately leaving out mention of the disturbing visitation. She *especially* left out what little she could remember of what had happened after the vision: the brassy taste of blood in her mouth and watching the swollen fullness of her husband's sex buck and lengthen beneath her curious gaze.

Even now, just the thought of such a wonder sent a pulsing hunger curling through the lowest part of her belly. The most womanly part of her grew heavy and warm even as Linnet's vexation bubbled and boiled inside her.

Her ire over her husband not wanting her overpowered and dispersed the fragile beginnings of her long-awaited introduction to passion.

"All I remember is waking up in bed, unclothed, and with blood on my hands," she snapped, temper and hurt lending an irritable edge to her voice.

Elspeth's brows lifted. "Blood on your hands?"

"Aye, and on the bedsheets as well. I bi—"

"Bless the saints, child, 'tis a mystery no longer," the old woman cut her off, a glimmer of relief crossing her face. "Or do you suffer your woman's time?"

"Nay, 'twas a full sennight past when I last bled."

Elspeth smiled. "Then 'tis as I hoped . . . Laird MacKenzie duly consummated your marriage."

"But I canna—"

"It matters naught if you've pushed the memory from your mind. The first time is ne'er pleasant," Elspeth assured her. "Many years have passed since my Angus died, but 'tis well I recall the early days of our marriage. The pain will lessen, dinna worry. Then you'll see what a wondrous thing the love between a man and woman can be."

Linnet's cheeks flamed. She'd wondered about the dried blood on her hands and the bedcoverings, but had assumed it'd been from biting her lip. Still, could a wee cut on the inside of her lip cause so much blood? She doubted it, but how else could the reddish smears have gotten on the bedsheets . . . unless they'd mated?

The possibility seemed more than remote, but she couldn't deny the blood.

She was gifted with the sight, but she wasn't a spellcaster, capable of conjuring physical manifestations. 'Twas beyond her talents to create blood where there was none.

Whether she liked the implications or not, 'twas likely the Black Stag had indeed come upon her while she was still dazed from the vision.

The saints knew she'd seen the might of his arousal.

"There's no reason to blush," Elspeth crooned. "Shame doesn't suit a new bride. In a few days, 'twill be happiness, not embarrassment, coloring your cheeks."

Grasping any excuse to change the subject, Linnet picked up Elspeth's ladle off the floor and handed it to her. "You haven't told me what brought you to the kitchen? Eilean Creag has a goodly number of servants. 'Tisn't necessary for you to tend the cookfires. Who sent you here?"

"No one, 'twas my own meddling," Elspeth said, the concern in her eyes replaced by a bright twinkle. "Fergus, the seneschal, was ordering the preparation of alms baskets for the abbey, and I offered to help. He's a most able man, dinna misunderstand, but after a wedding feast, there is much to do. I'm glad to make myself useful."

Linnet heard only half of what Elspeth said. Certain comments caught her attention, joining those uttered by Fergus.

A most able man.

A fine woman.

The significance behind the simply spoken words burned brighter than a beacon, leaping out at her and dimming all else either of them had said.

The notion struck her as wildly absurd, but even without the giveaway words, the piercing stare Fergus had fixed her with and the girlish gleam in Elspeth's eyes told their own tale.

". . . I asked if you want to ride along to the abbey?" Elspeth broke into Linnet's musing. "Fergus tells me 'tis a pleasant journey. One of the monks is said to be an unrivaled herbalist. Fergus claims the monk, Brother Baldric, visited the Holy Land and brought back many unusual plants. Mayhap he'll show you his garden?"

Linnet stifled a smile. Elspeth always knew how to entice her. "'Tis true I'd enjoy seeing the abbey gardens, and a ride would suit me well. Perhaps Robbie would like to accompany us." She paused to glance at the assortment of foodstuffs set upon the table, ready to go. "Why aren't the alms distributed here? Even Da's almoner handed out Dundonnell's meager offerings from the castle gate."

Rather than respond to Linnet's question, Elspeth made a great show of wiping her wooden ladle clean. After a few swipes with a cloth, she held it up, perusing it as if searching for an overlooked speck of dirt.

Recognizing the familiar ploy, Linnet prodded for an answer, "Why do the poor not come to Eilean Creag to collect the almsgivings? 'Tis the usual way."

"Fergus said 'tis no need to employ an almoner."

Without failing to notice Elspeth had once more started a sentence with 'Fergus said . . .' Linnet bored deeper. "And why not? Did the all-knowing *Fergus* say?"

"Aye," Elspeth conceded, her expression inscrutable.

"And what be the reason?" Linnet asked testily.

"The poor willna come here. Not since the death of your husband's first wife has any villager dared cross the bridge. 'Tis said they fear the laird."

Linnet squared her shoulders, surprised by her indignation over needy villagers accepting her husband's charity but shunning *him* with their refusal to collect almsgoods from his door.

Her own feelings aside, it was becoming clear to see why the man was so embittered.

"All the more reason for me to go to the abbey." Linnet skimmed her fingertips along the top of the kitchen table. "I shall inform the burghers there shall always be alms aplenty, but henceforth they must collect such offerings here . . . as is custom."

Elspeth looked aghast. "Your lord husband may not care for your intrusion into the matter."

"I doubt Duncan MacKenzie knows what he should or shouldn't care about."

But mayhap she'd be able to show him. An ember of hope sparking within her, the demons of the night banished for the moment, she left the kitchen to retrieve her herb satchel and fetch Robbie. A sense of calm and purpose settled over her as she went. If her husband could learn to care again, perhaps he'd find the heart his vision-likeness seemed so desperate to have returned.

For a brief moment, the wee spark of hope inside her flared brightly as a small voice, one that had naught to do with her gift, told her his heart wasn't missing . . . it just was buried too deep for him to recover it alone.

Bracing himself against the bright daylight beyond the shadowy confines of his castle walls, Duncan stepped outside and headed straight for the lists.

"Cease pandering about like a woman!" a deep voice commanded from the training ground. "If you desire to earn your spurs, have at me like a man!"

Duncan hurried his gait upon hearing Marmaduke barking commands at the young squires he was instructing in how to handle a sword.

Not that he wouldn't have known where to locate his brother-in-law.

He'd have found him even if the brisk sea wind did not carry his booming English voice across the bailey. The scar-faced Sassunach spent nigh onto his every waking moment training in the lists. Some of Duncan's men jested they'd glimpsed him there in the wee hours, sparring against moonbeams. Duncan didn't doubt it either.

Martial skills such as Sir Marmaduke Strongbow possessed were only wrought from years of long hours spent at practice. Few men could claim his prowess as a warrior, and fewer still could best him.

Duncan's late father, of a certainty, when in his prime. Duncan himself . . . when the saints chose to grant him such favor. But never did he know beforehand the outcome of a good round of swordplay with his best champion. Only one had ever taken the Sassunach down . . . the debased whoreson who'd carved out Marmaduke's eye and left his handsome face a twisted mask.

The selfsame miscreant who'd wrought untold misery in Duncan's own life, his half brother Kenneth MacKenzie.

Just the thought of him made Duncan scowl.

Aye, no one understood better than Duncan what drove Marmaduke to hone his skills.

Duncan, too, was driven by bitterness.

But not for revenge. He cared naught about retribution. He only wanted to be left alone.

The ring of steel against steel and a barrage of heartily uttered oaths brought his mind back to the present. Entering the lists, he suppressed the admiration that always rose in him upon seeing his brother-in-law at training and strode forward, determined to settle the issue at hand: the Sassunach's undoubted role in locking him in his wife's bedchamber yestereve, unclothed and befuddled from too much hippocras.

"Strongbow!" he bellowed, pulling up a safe distance behind the sword-wielding Englishman. "Order a pause, for I'd have a word with you, you scheming heap of trouble."

"Merciful saints," Marmaduke exclaimed, wheeling around. "You know better than to come up on a man's back when he's at training. I could have sliced your squire in twain."

"'Tis *you* who'll be rent in two if you dinna explain yourself . . . *now!*"

Marmaduke cast his blade aside, then dragged his arm across his dripping brow. With a nod, and a fearsome glance from his good eye, he sent the circle of young men scattering.

Turning back to Duncan, he said, "What demon has crawled under your skin this fair morn, my good friend?"

"If good friends e'er go against one's wishes and conspire to thrust one into the arms of a maid one has no intention of bedding, then I dinna need enemies, do I?"

Marmaduke made to speak, but Duncan stayed him by raising his hand. "What goal did you seek to accomplish? Have you forgotten I've sworn not to touch my lady wife?"

"Nay, I have not forgotten, little that I care for the notion," Marmaduke said, then paused to wipe more sweat from his forehead. "But 'tis not your vow that concerns me, 'tis your *happiness*."

"And you thought to secure my marital bliss by locking me in Lady Linnet's bedchamber?"

Marmaduke's ravaged lips twisted in an attempt to smile. "The ploy bore success."

Duncan's brows shot upwards. "What the saints do you mean, *success*?"

"You bedded her, did you not?" Marmaduke stepped forward and slapped Duncan on the shoulder. "Ah . . . 'twas a fine sight to see your men so pleased when her blood-smeared gown was passed around the hall this morn. You should have heard them cheer."

"But I dinna touch her, I swear it. 'Tisn't possible. I—"

A loud commotion behind them cut off his protest as a lone man on a heavily winded horse entered the lists from the bailey. He rode forward, reining in before Duncan and Marmaduke.

Duncan recognized him as one of the men who watched and protected the MacKenzie boundaries.

"Sir, I bring grim tidings," the man said the moment he swung down from his saddle. "We found one o' the outlying cottages torched. Naught remains, the bastards even butchered the milk cow."

"Which family? Were they all killed?" Duncan's level tone belied the anger roiling through his veins.

"'Twas the Murchinsons. Some managed to escape into the wood when they saw the raiders approaching, but most of them, God rest their souls, were slaughtered."

Rage, hot and fierce, ripped through Duncan, and a sickening feeling churned deep in his gut. A ghastly possibility cast an ugly shadow on the day, but he didn't want to accept it. For years, his wife's ragtag band of brothers had harried his borders, but ne'er had they pillaged and murdered.

The MacDonnells were simple cattle thieves, and not well skilled at that. Still, he had to know.

"Did any of the survivors recognize who did this? Were they MacDonnells?"

"Nay, sir, they weren't MacDonnells. 'Twas far worse."

"Worse?"

" 'Twas *him*," the man said, clearly uncomfortable. "Your half brother Kenneth and his men."

7

Several leagues away from the confining walls of Eilean Creag, Linnet followed a well-trampled footpath through a copse of ancient yew trees. She sought the burial cairns Brother Baldric had said marked the spot she'd find the herb, ragwort. The well-traveled monk had assured her the healing plant grew in profusion next to a sacred well near the cairns.

Robbie and his dog, Mauger, trailed behind her, the boy carrying a linen sack the monks had given her to collect the wild-growing ragwort. They'd generously filled her own leather pouch with a large assortment of cultivated herbs from their herbarium.

"'Tisn't much farther," she told Robbie when she spied a rounded pile of stones beyond the edge of the grove. "I can see the cairns." Upon her words, Mauger trotted ahead to sniff at the low heaps of lichen-covered stones.

"There won't be any spirits about, will there?" Robbie hung back as if reluctant to exchange the cool shade of the copse for the grassy clearing with its collection of burial mounds.

"None what will harm you," Linnet assured him, reaching for his hand and drawing him into the late-afternoon sunshine. "All what rest here, sleep peacefully. 'Tis a good place, guarded by those who've gone before us and blessed with a holy well. You've naught to fear."

Robbie did not look convinced, but he let her lead him forward. Still, he peered with rounded eyes at each cairn they passed. "Be you sure?"

"Were I not I wouldna brought you here." Linnet stopped to tousle the boy's dark hair. "More danger abounds on the road where the others wait for us than here with our ancestors."

But not much later, as she bent to gather more of the yellow-flowering ragwort from the banks of a tumbling burn, she was no longer so certain. She tensed, her skin prickling despite the day's warmth and the sweet fragrance of the wildflowers that grew with abandon amongst the tall grass.

Something . . . *someone* . . . watched them from the shelter of the trees, and whoever it was came from the land o' the living, not the shadow world of the dead.

And they weren't friendly.

Although the sacred ground upon which they stood was hushed and deceptively peaceful in the afternoon haze, Linnet's pulse quickened, and she deeply regretted coming to the cairns unguarded save Robbie's elderly dog.

The old mongrel shared her unease, for he'd abandoned his exploration of the cairns to hasten back to their sides. Low growls rumbling deep in his chest, the coarse fur between his shoulders raised, Mauger kept close to them as he scanned the edge of the woods with wary eyes.

A trickle of moisture rolled between Linnet's breasts. Plague take her for disregarding Fergus's offer to accompany them. She'd selfishly wanted to have Robbie to herself, to savor being alone with him in a special place.

Now, she'd brought them both into danger.

Straightening, she dropped an apronful of ragwort into the sack Robbie held open for her. Without letting him notice, she hoped, she scanned the edges of the clearing but saw nothing except the glossy, reddish brown trunks of the great yews and their overarching mass of leafy branches.

Yet she *knew* someone hid there.

Someone who meant them ill.

"Give me your hand, Robbie lad," Linnet said as calmly as she could. "'Tis time for us to go."

"But the sack isna full."

"We've enough for the salve I want to make." She took him firmly by the hand. "'Tis good to take only what we need, you see, and now is not the best time to collect herbs anyway. Early morn is far better."

She kept up a stream of chatter as they crossed the clearing. Perhaps by doing so Robbie wouldn't sense her nervousness . . . or his dog's. She also hoped he hadn't noticed she'd slipped her new dirk from the pouch attached to the band of her apron. Its finely honed blade was far superior to her old herb dagger and would serve her well should she need to make use of it.

At the thought of such a possibility, Linnet tightened her grip on Robbie's hand and silently thanked Dundonnell's smithy for his gift . . . and his foresight.

Then she spotted Duncan. He stood in the green shadows where the footpath reentered the wood. Her relief upon seeing him was so great her knees fair gave out on her. The rapid pounding of her heart took on another meaning, too, for never had her husband appeared more handsome.

Minus his black mail and permanent scowl, and with the MacKenzie plaid slung proudly over his bare shoulder, the sight of him stole her breath away. Faith, he was even smiling at her.

"Praise the saints!" She dashed forward, pulling Robbie behind her. Mauger barked fiercely, but Linnet was blind and deaf to all save the magnificent-looking man before her.

All the conflicting feelings he stirred in her vanished in the face of the sheer terror that had consumed her mere moments before. Naught mattered except the comforting reassurance of his presence. "Sir," she called, nigh breathless, "'tis glad I am to see you!"

Robbie tugged fiercely on her hand and the force of his strength surprised her. Spinning around to face him, she almost lost her balance. "'Tis your father, lad, do you not see him? There, by the path?"

The boy shook his head, edging backwards and trying to pull her with him. "He isna my papa. 'Tis *him* . . . the bad one. 'Tis Uncle Kenneth."

Linnet's heart plummeted, and the terror returned,

more ominous than before. Turning slowly around, she saw that the smiling man who could pass for Duncan MacKenzie's twin had left the cover of the trees and came stealthily toward them.

Still smiling, and still heartstoppingly handsome, much more so than her battle-worn and grim-faced husband could ever hope to be, but evil to the core.

His true nature was frighteningly apparent because, now that he'd stepped into the sunlight, Linnet clearly saw a sickly greenish black glow shimmer all around his body before it flared and disappeared.

A shudder skittered down her spine. She'd seen that shade only once before and had hoped never to see it again.

Unlike the darkness of despair she'd glimpsed once or twice about her husband, the dark marring Kenneth MacKenzie's beauty was the mark of an evil man.

A murderer.

"The lad doesna want to believe it, but he is mine," Kenneth MacKenzie said, pausing to fold his arms in a gesture that perfectly mirrored the favored stance of his half brother. "And you can only be the lady Linnet? I was told my brother had married a . . . healer, but no one informed me of your beauty, milady."

He made her a gallant bow. "Kenneth MacKenzie, at your service," he said with a silky tone and a knowing smile that didn't quite touch his dark blue eyes. " 'Tis good fortune indeed to make your fair acquaintance since Duncan did not extend me the courtesy of an invitation to your wedding."

"I am sure he had his reasons for not doing so," Linnet stated as calmly as she could. Beside her, Mauger growled his displeasure. His hackles rose again and he bared his teeth menacingly, but made no attempt to attack, only to protect and defend.

Linnet tightened her grip on the dagger she kept hidden in the folds of her gown. "You will excuse us. My husband's guardsmen await our return."

"Not if they're sleeping as soundly as the one I passed on the footpath. 'Twas the tongueless Thomas, I believe. He may have been coming for you, but it seems the overgrown lad walked into a tree."

The corners of his mouth twitched as if he meant to laugh, and he raised a hand to rub his chin. "At least I canna think of another reason for the nasty lump I saw on his forehead."

Fear tightened Linnet's chest, but she forced herself to remain calm. Her sixth sense told her their lives depended on her keeping her wits. "Then we must bid you good day and be on our way so I can assist Thomas back to the cart."

"Ah, but 'tis such a fine afternoon," Kenneth lamented, coming closer. "Surely you willna deny me a visit with my own son?"

Ignoring him, Linnet yanked Robbie closer and made to rush past the man, but he whistled sharply and a band of unsmiling, filthy men stepped from the trees around the clearing, successfully blocking any path of escape she'd hoped to take.

Kenneth smiled and shrugged his shoulders. "My men dinna mean any harm, milady, but you'll understand they ken how much I've been missing my wee lad here."

"You're not my papa!" Robbie shouted, balling his

fists and struggling to break free of Linnet's grasp. "I'm not yours!"

"Of course, you are," Kenneth fair crooned, the wild light in his eyes warning Linnet he wasn't right in his head. "Just look at you, full of fire and ready to fight. Were you Duncan's get, you'd be cowering behind Lady Linnet's skirts, hiding the way my brother hides behind the walls of his keep."

White-hot anger shot through Linnet with the speed of a lightning bolt, chasing away her fear. "And I say 'tis the mark of a coward who'd slander a man afore his wife and young son. Or would you spew such lies in the face of my lord husband?"

Kenneth steepled his fingers and brought them to his chin. "Ah . . . I see you've fallen under his spell. My late father suffered the same affliction, I'm afraid. Ne'er could he see my brother's shortcomings whilst my own were e'er falling from his tongue."

"My sympathies. Now step aside and let us pass," Linnet demanded, whipping out her dagger. "If you do not, you'll give me no choice but to plant my blade between your eyes."

Kenneth threw back his head and laughed. "What-ho! 'Tis not only the lady's tongue what be sharp. So you would threaten me with your dirk?"

"Nay, Sir Kenneth, 'tis not threatening you I am," Linnet said, dragging Robbie behind her. "'Tis *warning* you what I'll do if you do not cease accosting us."

A look of fierce anger flashed across his handsome face, but it vanished almost instantly as he swept low in another courtly bow. When he straightened, he wore a wolfish grin.

"You've no need to wax noble with me, *Lady* Linnet, for I canna claim the title of *sir*. My father, rest his soul, did not see the need to bestow knighthood upon me. Nor will any other noble capable of performing the deed. I bear the stigma of being baseborn, you see." He paused and flung his arms up in the air as if for emphasis. "It matters naught, though, for an adubbement as knight isn't necessary for a man to be chivalrous."

"And it'll matter less after I take aim at you," Linnet shot back. " 'Twill be hard to appear gallant with the hilt o' my dagger protruding from the top of your nose."

Kenneth laughed again, a full-bodied, rich kind of masculine laughter that would have made her laugh, too, did his mirth reach his eyes . . . and if her gift hadn't let her look deep into the depths of his twisted soul.

" 'Protruding from the top o' my nose,' you say?" he roared, bending backward in his levity. "I vow that snarling beast at your side poses a greater threat. Fair lady, if you can land your blade anywhere within an arm's length of where I stand, you, the lad, and his hell-dog, may leave this place unhindered."

His fingers caressed the hilt of his own dagger, tucked jauntily beneath a wide leather belt. "Or mayhap I shall relieve you both of the wretched hound now? The cur's barking sorely annoys me."

"And if I can slice off a lock of your hair, will you give me your word that we—all three of us—may leave here unharmed?" Linnet challenged him, hiding her fear that he'd harm Robbie's pet behind bold words, instinctively aware she must concede to his image of himself as a gallant if they hoped to gain a safe retreat.

"A lock of my hair?" His black brows shot heavenward. "Lady, if you can do that, you shall have my solemn word."

"Then pray choose the lock of your choice and hold it high."

An expression very much like admiration curved his lips in a smile that would've been irresistibly seductive to any other woman. Without taking his gaze off her, he raised his hand and lifted a portion of thick black hair from the top of his head.

"Take aim, but be warned," he said, his voice smooth as sun-warmed silk, "if you lose, I shall demand a kiss."

"I never lose," Linnet countered. "My brothers taught me well."

Concentrating, she focused her gaze on the man who looked so like her husband she almost had second thoughts about throwing a knife at him. But he wasn't Duncan. He was a man whose envy and warped logic made him capable of unspeakable acts of treachery.

The colors of the darkness she'd glimpsed clinging to him when he'd first stepped from the trees revealed his true nature beyond a doubt.

The thought of Robbie falling into his hands was beyond unbearable. The lad's grief should harm befall his beloved dog, a cruelty she must attempt to spare him. Her heart, too, would ache should Kenneth make good his threat against Mauger. She had no choice but to defend them all as best she could.

Grateful to Ranald for training her in the art of knife throwing, and to the saints for giving her the patience to learn, Linnet sent a quick prayer skyward, asking the divine powers to guide her hand.

Then she took a deep breath, narrowed her eyes, and let her dagger fly.

It seemed the blade had no sooner left her fingers, then a collective gasp erupted from Kenneth MacKenzie's men and *he* stood gaping at her, one hand clamped atop his head. Then he bent and scooped up her knife . . . and his lock of hair . . . from the ground at his feet.

He stood for a moment, staring down at the two items in his hands, then turned his gaze on her. This time there could be no mistake about the admiration in his eyes. A look of sheer amazement replaced his flamboyant smile.

"You kept your word." He came toward her, the dark lock of hair and her knife offered to her on the palms of his outstretched hands. "I shall do no less. You may go."

Hoping he couldn't see how she trembled inside, Linnet took her blade and tucked it beneath the band of her apron. She made to leave, but he stepped before her, blocking their way. "Please take this as a token of my admiration," he said, holding out the lock of hair. "I should be vastly injured if you decline."

Linnet accepted his offering with a curt nod. She'd dispose of it as soon as they were a safe distance from him.

Holding her head high, she led Robbie away, trying hard not to show the fear knotting her stomach now that the unpleasant encounter was almost over. Mauger trotted along beside them, casting wary glances over his shoulder as they went. At the edge of the clearing, just before they reached the path back to the road, Kenneth MacKenzie called out once more.

"Do not think you've seen the last of me, lady. I like

a woman with fire in her blood," he shouted. "Aye, lass, we shall meet again. Be certain of it."

Many hours later, in the gray and quiet time between midnight and daybreak, Linnet stood before the narrow arched windows of her chamber and stared out at the night-darkened landscape. Far below, Loch Duich lapped gently at the sturdy castle walls, the lake's surface tranquil and smooth at this late hour.

In the wan light of a slim crescent moon, the loch resembled a polished silver mirror set down and forgotten in the midst of the wilder landscape of rugged mountains rising around its shoreline.

Pressing her forehead against the damp coolness of the window's stone tracery, Linnet closed her eyes and breathed in the sharp smell of sea tang that seemed to permeate every inch of her formidable new home.

How like her husband were his lands of Kintail. Cool and unruffled on the surface, yet beneath, she sensed a man of brute strength, capable of deep emotion. A man whose anger was no less dangerous to the unwary than scaling the peaks of Kintail's mountains would be to a Lowlander unaccustomed to treacherous terrain.

Winning his heart, his love, would be a triumph as rewarding as reaching the summit of a high mountain after a difficult climb. A triumph she wanted, and one she'd fight to achieve.

Linnet smoothed the tips of her fingers along the cold stone at the window's edge. Its chilled dampness was undeniable, a tangible thing, yet come a fine summer's day filled with warmth and light, the stone would grow warm and glow beneath the transforming rays of the sun.

Hope burgeoned bright in Linnet's heart. As the sun was always there, even on days turned gray and forbidding, so, too, thrummed the fire of her husband's passion beneath the self-erected barriers he thought were so inviolable.

Resting her cheek against the molding of the arch-topped window, Linnet let the brine-laden night air cool her cheeks. 'Twas necessary, for anytime her thoughts turned to Duncan MacKenzie, fierce yearnings shot through her, boldly sweeping aside any maidenly reserve she may have possessed and flooding her with a need that demanded to be quenched.

A need the strong-passioned Black Stag seemed determined to ignore.

A burning urgency she suspected raged as strong as the raw sexual hunger that swelled her husband's sex each time she'd had the intoxicating pleasure of glimpsing it!

Linnet blew out an agitated breath and pressed her thighs together in a fruitless attempt to suppress the intensely arousing tingles dancing over her woman's flesh. Like a thousand fired needles, the sensations ignited a blaze of pleasure across her tender parts whilst, from within, came an equally exquisite heaviness, a deep pulsing ache.

Then, with slow but persistent success, irritation conquered the wild stirrings that bedeviled her. Irritation born of annoyance at her husband for not wanting her. Anger at herself for desiring him.

Gradually, another type of ache made itself known,

too. Refusing to be further ignored, Linnet's exhaustion bore down on her, but she welcomed its diversion. Reaching her arms high above her head, she stretched her entire aching body, seeking relief for the stiffness in her limbs and the red-hot knot of tension between her shoulders.

She'd spent the day and most of the evening tending to poor Thomas's head wound and trying to offer solace to the Murchinson survivors. They'd arrived at the keep tired and shaken some hours past. The tales they'd told had unsettled Linnet more than she cared to admit.

Weary, she pressed a hand to the small of her aching back. 'Twas no wonder exhaustion robbed her of the energy to do more than stand and gaze out her window, engaging in fantasies. Elspeth and Fergus had fair dragged her to her bed, insisting she rest, contending she'd done more than she possibly could until the morn, but sleep eluded her.

And not because of her bone-aching fatigue. 'Twas worry what stole her rest and had sent her thoughts galloping full tilt toward her husband. Alarm had eaten away at her ever since she'd returned from the abbey and discovered that Duncan, Sir Marmaduke, and Eilean Creag's best men had ridden in pursuit of Kenneth MacKenzie and his assemblage of undesirables.

She'd tried to use her sight, to focus on her husband and glean a sign of what had happened, but she'd been able to cull nothing. Her efforts continually met an impenetrable wall of reddish haze. A representation, she knew, of fury and outrage. Unfortunately, she could discern naught else.

And, having seen the crazed look in Kenneth

MacKenzie's eyes, and after having learned of the vile acts he and his followers had committed at the Murchinsons' small holding, sheer terror had accompanied her every breath and still did.

She wouldn't rest until she knew her husband and his men were safe within the castle walls.

When at last she heard him bolting up the tower stairs, the pent-up tension she'd borne all day left her in a rush so powerful she sagged against the window. Not for a moment did she doubt the thundering footsteps were his, for a red cloud of rage preceded him, warning her, letting her feel his anger, long before he approached her chamber door.

Nor did she concern herself that his wrath could be directed at her. She'd done naught to rouse his ire. All beneath his roof would vouchsafe she'd spent hours working hard to assuage the damage caused by Kenneth and his raiding party.

But her confidence was challenged the moment Duncan burst into her room, slamming the door against the wall so violently she feared the heavy oaken timbers would splinter.

A daunting sight, he seemed to fill the open doorway. His powerful limbs were streaked with dirt, the plaid draped over one massive shoulder, bloodstained and torn, his dark mane of hair, wild and tangled about his unsmiling face.

"Thunder of heaven!" he roared, expelling his relief upon knowing her safe in the guise of a curse. "I thought I married a *sensible* lass?"

"And I, sirrah, thought I'd married a man who'd make me his wife," she had the cheek to counter.

Bloodlust still thick in his veins, Duncan crossed the room with four swift strides, closing the distance between them before she could even think about letting loose another insult. Grasping her by the shoulders, he stared down at her, daring her by sheer power of will to vex him again.

"You *are* my wife and dinna e'er doubt it," he seethed, already regretting he'd so impulsively grabbed hold of her. Her unbound hair flowed thick and smooth over her shoulders, and he'd thrust his fool hands right into the silken mass of it!

His traitorous loins tightened in response whilst his equally faithless imagination fair hummed with a hundred different things he'd like to do with her lustrous tresses. Erotic, arousing, *lascivious* acts, the very thought of which aroused him to near bursting. Her uncanny ability to bring him to his knees from sheer lusting for her also fanned the fury that'd sent him storming up to her chamber.

"Christ's blood, woman," he roared. "Do you know the danger you placed yourself in this day?"

"You are pulling my hair, Sir Duncan," she said simply, the impertinent tilt of her chin giving lie to the calm tone of her voice. "Pray, release me."

He did and immediately wished he hadn't when she smoothed the flame-colored tresses off her shoulders, allowing the cascading mass to tumble down her back.

Thus freed of the shielding curtain of her hair, naught save the thinness of her night rail stood between him and the sweet mounds of her full breasts. Their tips pressing against the near-translucent fabric of her gown.

The sight of them near robbed him of the last shreds of his waning self-control.

A brace of tallow candles burning on the room's single table cast a flickering pattern of light and shadows over her lush form, the candleglow scant but sufficient for him to see the darker shadows of her intimate places. And what he saw made his mouth go dry with pure need.

No doubt brazenly following the direction of his gaze, she needled him again, "Did you come to chastise my foolishness this day, my husband, or are you here to try and peer through the cloth of my gown to peruse what lies beneath it?"

Duncan's gaze flew from the shadowy apex of her sweet thighs to glare furiously into the depths of her amber-flecked eyes. "That tale-spinning graybeard, Fergus, and my entire household are singing your praises, milady," he said, barely containing his ire. "I would know if it was your sharp-edged blade or your tongue that bested my half brother?"

"Both," she said, her chin still tilted at an angle . . . an angle perfect for kissing. "And both served me well."

Thunder of heaven, did she not comprehend how gravely she'd imperiled herself? Riled beyond reason, and not just with her, Duncan captured her hands and raised them above her head. Pure lust, base and raw, stormed through him. He burned to kiss her senseless, and to keep at it until he, too, was consumed by mindless and blissful release.

Saints, he ought do more than plunder her lips after having lived through this day. Naught else would better banish the loathsome images of the butchery at the Murchinsons' cottage, unspeakable horrors what might have happened to her and Robbie had they not escaped Kenneth's clutches.

Duncan blinked hard to rid himself of the images. Blessedly, they receded. But his desire raged on. Indeed, it would aid forgetfulness and help him ignore his screaming muscles if he could but sink himself into the silken heat of her woman's sheath—an act his men seemed convinced he'd already indulged in. Not that he recalled the pleasure.

And, by the Rood, now was not the time to refresh his memory.

Not with his lady wife all prickly and her tongue full of pepper.

Saints preserve him, he wanted her quivering in lust beneath him, her tongue sweet, eager, and doing delicious things to him.

He swallowed a groan as something raw and deeply elemental in its intensity broke and twisted within him. Bringing his face to within inches of hers, he stared fiercely into her eyes, trying, by force of sheer will, to vanquish whatever it was that made her seek to vex him at every turn.

But instead of sweeping aside her obvious distaste for him, he only seemed to upset her all the more. She matched his glare, her eyes snapping in fury, her stubbornness apparent with every agitated breath she took. After a long moment, she broke the stare and lifted her chin in a clear gesture of defiance. Turning her face away, she stared pointedly out the window.

"Mother of God, lass, cease bristling and listen to me." He grasped her face with both hands and forced her to look at him. Leaning so close he could taste the sweetness of her breath, he said, "Never—I repeat *never*—leave these walls without my knowledge again."

This time she nodded, and the motion caused the soft weight of her well-rounded breasts to rub against the sensitive skin on the inner side of his forearms. Desire, immediate and all-consuming, shot through him.

As if acutely aware and affected by the unexpected contact as he'd been, she squirmed against his hold on her. In one valiant attempt to break free, she twisted her head to the side, and her mouth, her tender lips caught half-opened, slid across the palm of his hand.

The sensation rocked him, the honey-soft sweetness of her lips on his skin shooting straight to his engorged shaft and unleashing a powerful need not only in his groin but also in the secret place he kept locked, barred, and buried.

He suspected she'd felt something, too, for a quizzical look flashed over her face. Then she began to tremble, but not from defiance, he could tell. He also recognized the softening of her features as she gazed at him. When she parted her lips, he knew his instincts hadn't deceived him.

He couldn't recall the last time a woman had looked at him thusly, but he did remember the look.

His lady wife wanted to be kissed.

And he burned to oblige her. But, might the raging fires of hell take his accursed soul, he didn't *want* to want her! If he gave in to the temptation she offered, he'd be lost, for he wouldn't settle for a mere kiss.

He'd carry her to the bed, disgrace himself by the urgency of his need, and promptly lose the heart he didn't have to give.

His passions ran too rampant, went far beyond her innocent desire for a kiss. Duncan dug his fingers into her fiery hair and choked back an oath. He couldn't fall upon her like a rutting beast, wouldn't take her whilst lust raced uncontrolled through his blood.

If he e'er took his ease with her . . . and he had no intention of doing so . . . he must be gentle with her, show her mating is more than his unremembered claiming of her maidenhood. Nor is it the wild abandon he'd unleash upon her should he give in to his baser instincts and mount her this moment.

Nay, she deserved a slow and thorough pleasuring.

But he wasn't sure he was capable of initiating her in the finer pleasures of lovemaking even if he wanted to. Too distant was the memory of the last time he'd seduced a woman with tenderness. In truth, mayhap he never had. And he didn't intend to learn with his wife. Doing so would only cause them both grief.

Drawing a ragged breath, Duncan stepped back. He placed his hands firmly on her shoulders to keep her an arm's length away from him.

A safe distance and far enough for her not to feel the hard swelling beneath his braies.

Steeling himself against the female scent of her and the intoxicating silkiness of her hair as it swirled freely over the backs of his hands, Duncan willed all emotion from his face save the darkest frown he could muster.

"I will have your word you'll not venture forth alone again."

The tip of her tongue appeared, to wet her still-parted lips, and the sight of it made his loins tighten to a painful degree. "But I wasna alone, milord," she stated, disagreeing with him yet again.

"Lucifer's knees!" Duncan exploded, fighting the urge to shake her so she'd comprehend the danger she'd put herself and the boy in. "You were accompanied by an old man, a crone, a mute lad, and a nigh ancient dog! Do you not ken what could've happened?

"Answer me!" he commanded when she remained silent. "Do you ken?"

"I do now, aye, and so do all beneath your roof, for even the dead would hear such bellowing," she pronounced, her expression as dark as he knew his own to be. "But for the sake of peace, you have my word, sir. It will not happen again."

Duncan released her. "Faith, 'tis killed you could have been. And dinna tell me about your show of bravery . . . I've already heard. The whole castle speaks of naught else. But listen well to my words: my half brother was playing with you. *Playing* with you, do you hear?"

"Aye, that, too, I realize, milord."

"Had he wanted, he could have carted you off before you'd even had a chance to *think* of pulling your dagger on him." He scowled at her, hoping to drive in the gravity of his warning. "Do you understand me?"

"I do, sir."

"Then come to me when you wish to ride out again, no matter where or for what reason. I shall see you are accompanied by my best guardsmen." Wheeling around, Duncan stalked to the door lest he abandon his control totally and ravish her upon the bare rushes as he was sorely wont to do.

But before he left the chamber, he had one more

issue to settle with her. 'Twas only a small thing, but of a sudden it mattered a great deal.

"Linnet?" he called, his voice husky despite his best effort to keep it neutral.

"Yes, milord?"

"My name is Duncan. Not 'milord' or 'sir,' but *Duncan*. Please use it."

Then he left her alone before the foulness of his mood caused him to say more, to reveal feelings he hadn't known he still possessed and certainly didn't care to set free. The anguish he carried within was painful enough. Letting loose its poison upon his innocent bride, pepper-tongued or nay, would be a grievous act beyond pardon.

A burden he had no right to place upon her shoulders, regardless of her status as his wife. Besides, he was nowise certain she would e'er be willing to care for a man said to be so unblessed as he, much less endeavor to help him past the ache in his soul.

Much later, Duncan stood upon the battlements and scowled down at Loch Duich's silent waters. After leaving his wife's chamber, he'd paced the wall walk for hours, glaring holes into the dark night, seeking answers but finding none.

Save one.

He'd remembered something his king had once told him. A great secret he could use oft and well if he so desired, the Bruce had promised.

Women go weak in the knees at the sight of a battle-stained warrior.

Such was the most plausible reason his wife had appeared to want a kiss after her sweet lips had slid so temptingly over his palm.

At that moment, she'd indeed looked upon him with favor, albeit for a very fleeting instant. She'd gazed at him with the same moon-eyed adoration he'd seen upon the faces of young, and not so young, noblewomen at the tournaments he'd competed in years ago in France.

And he'd been too bewitched by the unexpected softening of her features to realize her look of veneration was not for him as a *man*, but for his warlike appearance and bloodied plaid.

He'd deceived himself, seeing naught but what he'd wanted to see.

But fool that he was, he'd harbored hope.

Hope that the unexpectedly enchanting lass he'd wed—sometimes defiant, sometimes proud, and definitely more desirable than he'd imagined a woman could e'er be—could come to care for him, could teach *him* to care again.

Heaven help him, he'd wanted to believe that she possessed enough bravery to not only face down his half brother but to stand against the demons that ravaged his soul and feasted on the remnants of his heart.

Hope she'd assure him Robbie was his true son, convince him his doubts had been for naught.

And, even if he admitted it only to himself, hope she'd somehow make him whole again.

But for now, he wanted nothing more than to retire to his bedchamber, alone, and lose himself in the deceptive oblivion of sleep.

Every fiber of his being longed to return to her chamber, seek her bed, and lose himself deep inside her heated softness. A near-overpowering urge to have her force him to admit his feelings consumed him, but Duncan crushed the unwanted sentiments as easily as if they were of no more substance than eggshells.

Pushing away from the stone merlon he'd been leaning against, he crossed the wall walk and let himself back inside the tower.

Then, as soundlessly as he could, he headed in the opposite direction from her quarters, making for his own chamber and the empty bed awaiting him there.

a naked man slept in his bed!

Duncan squeezed his eyes shut and ground his fists against his eyelids, certain the unclothed ox reposing upon his bed was a figment of his imagination, brought on by his extreme weariness. Or the shock of the icy water he'd just sluiced over his head.

But when he looked again, the lout was still there.

Appearing more comfortable than a man had a right to be, Sir Marmaduke lolled on his back atop the covers, limbs akimbo, his misformed mouth slack and emitting loud snores.

"Damnation!" Duncan thundered. "Awaken and explain yourself, lest I haul your arse onto the floor!"

Just as he reached the bed Marmaduke pushed himself up on his elbows and yawned. Duncan leaned forward, his anger barely contained. "Be you too drunken to know where you've laid yourself to rest, or do you seek to deliberately rile me?"

Marmaduke yawned once more and peered groggily at Duncan with his good eye. "Rile *you*? 'Tis not I bursting into another man's bedchamber and stealing his sleep."

"Have a care, Englishman, for I tire of the riddles you speak of late," Duncan countered tersely. "'Tis *my* chamber and *my* bed in which you find yourself."

"Indeed?" Marmaduke drawled, no longer drowsy-looking, but alert, his one intact brow arching upward. "Mayhap 'tis you who's partaken of too much wine?"

"Dinna speak to me of spirits, you bold whoreson, for I have not yet forgotten how you persisted in replenishing my hippocras at the wedding feast." Duncan planted his hands on his hips. "I've had not a drop of ale or wine this eve though I now regret it. A befuddled state would have eased the offending sight of your nakedness sprawled across my bed."

"Think you I find your appearance any more pleasing? Here I seek naught but a well-deserved night's rest and awaken to find a wild-eyed, raving hulk, clothed in a bloodied plaid and torn braies, charging my bedside." Marmaduke drew himself into a sitting position and slung the bedcovers over his lower body. "Nay, 'twas not a pleasant sight, my friend."

Duncan raked his fingers through his damp hair. "Has the world gone mad? I came to my chamber desiring scarce more than to wash the grime from my body, then sleep in my own bed. Yet I find it occupied by you." He paused to glare at the Sassunach. "And you dare to spout nonsense rather than hie yourself out of here."

"I beseech you to cease bellowing. When you have, I shall gladly remind you of that which today's turmoil has apparently caused you to forget."

Duncan folded his arms. "Pray speak."

"The explanation is simple." Marmaduke spoke as if placating the village idiot. "During the feast, you generously granted me use of your chamber now that you are gainfully and blissfully rewed. Do you not remember?"

"Nay, I do not!" Duncan stormed. "Further, 'tis not wed I feel . . . gainfully, blissfully, or otherwise."

"Then perhaps you should seek your lady wife's bed and attempt to address that . . . er . . . failing?"

"By the Rood!" Duncan grabbed Marmaduke's arm and yanked him to his feet. "The only failing I have is suffering the madness that's overtaken this household since the MacDonnell wench set foot in it!"

"Tsk, tsk," Marmaduke chided, shaking his head. "You should have taken better heed of the way Robert Bruce charms the womenfolk. You'll never win your lady's favor if you think of her thusly, milord."

"Plague take her favor, I do not want it," Duncan raged, his temper close to boiling. "I want my bed and now! Take yourself to your own good chamber afore I toss you over my shoulder and carry you there myself."

"You know I've not slept there since Arabella's death. From that day forth, the chamber only houses my arms and, on occasion, serves as a training room for your so— . . . er . . . the lad, Robbie's, instruction in handling a sword. Otherwise, I strive to avoid setting foot there." He paused, a look of feigned perplexity on his scarred face. "Have you forgotten that as well?"

"I've forgotten naught except why I call you my

most trusted friend," Duncan exploded, his throat becoming painfully hoarse from hollering. "Be you wise, I sorely suggest you join the men sleeping on the floor rushes below, as we both ken you're usually wont to do, because you are not staying here." His patience at an end, Duncan propelled Marmaduke toward the door. "Better still, steel your backbone against the ghosts what haunt you and reclaim your old quarters. 'Tis a fine chamber and shouldn't be empty."

"I cannot do that."

"Why not?"

"I offered the chamber to Fergus."

"What?" Duncan let go of Marmaduke's arm in his surprise. "You and Fergus are ever at each other's throats."

Marmaduke shrugged. "For all his bluster, the old goat is getting on in years. He shouldn't sleep on a bench in the hall each night." Rubbing his arm where Duncan had gripped it, and avoiding Duncan's eyes as if suddenly self-conscious, Marmaduke went on, "I thought mayhap giving him the chamber would smooth the waters between us."

"'Tis noble of you, then, but I still canna let you have this chamber, for it is mine. Nor will I share it with you." Duncan crossed his arms. "And even if I wanted to, I do not see how you can desire to sleep here, with *her* gazing down at you."

Marmaduke's one-eyed gaze latched onto the image of a beautiful raven-haired woman smiling serenely at them from above the hearth. Beautiful beyond words, blessed with an ethereal loveliness even the angels would envy, Duncan's first wife Cassandra's elegant grace was captured forever on the smooth panels of painted wood.

'Twas an exquisite piece of art, its rendering wrought by a famed Irish illuminator who had come years before to paint saints upon the chapel walls. But rather than holy figures, he'd immortalized a she-devil.

Bile rose in Duncan's throat at the memory of the way she'd thrown herself upon the artist. None within miles of Eilean Creag had doubted the methods she'd used to persuade the man to paint her likeness.

"Your brain is addled," Duncan said, convinced he spoke the truth. "The sight of her will rob your sleep."

"Nay, my friend, you err," Marmaduke's tone was colder than the deep waters of Loch Duich, black and silent beyond the chamber's arch-topped windows. "'Tis because of her, I welcomed your generosity in granting me these quarters."

"How so?" Duncan asked, fearing he'd just lost the battle whether he recalled giving away his bedchamber or not.

"Similar to your own reasons for keeping the likeness, her presence shall keep me steadfast in my quest for vengeance." Marmaduke ran the tip of his middle finger down the puckered scar marring his once-handsome face. "But unlike you, I have not sworn to forsake all women because of the wickedness of one."

Marmaduke drew back his mighty shoulders, then walked over to the hearth and stared up at the painted beauty. "With your new marriage, 'tis forgetfulness you must master. You must put the pains of the past behind you and look forward. But I have yet to avenge Arabella's death. If the face of her murderer is the last thing

I see at night and the first I see upon awakening, I shall never slacken in my attempts to see justice done . . . to send Kenneth to join his lewd ladyship in the pits of hell."

Duncan stared at Marmaduke's broad back, saw the well-developed muscles bunch with tension. When his friend's shoulders sagged, Duncan knew he'd lost the battle.

And his bed.

" 'Tis a master of words you are, Strongbow. How can I deny you the chamber after such a silver-tongued speech?"

"I but spoke my heart," Marmaduke said, turning around. " 'Twould be wise if you would do the same."

"I dinna have one, or hasn't the news reached your English ears?" Duncan couldn't stop the bitter retort. " 'Tis the devil himself they call me."

"And you've a very fine angel sleeping in a cold bed on the other side of this castle. I vow she'd gladly banish your demons if you'd but let her," Marmaduke said. "Or would you be called a fool as well as the devil?"

His aim perfect as always, Marmaduke's sagely spoken words slipped through the chinks in Duncan's armor to skewer the heart he wasn't supposed to have.

"Tongue-waggers' prattle matters naught to me," Duncan groused, knowing his friend knew better.

"Then cultivate her favor simply for yourself. I vow were such a treasure mine, she would not sleep alone."

At the Sassunach's admonishment, a parade of his lady's enticements marched through Duncan's mind. Her lips, warm and pliant beneath his when he'd kissed her during the marriage stone ceremony. Candleglow casting a gleam upon the smooth gloss of her hair, and not just the glorious tresses springing from her fair head! Nay, the luxuriant wealth of fiery curls at the tops of her thighs caught the light well, too.

Too well.

Enough to make him burn to drop to his knees before her and press a thousand kisses against their lush softness *and* the fragrant sweetmeat hidden beneath!

Hellfire and damnation! Duncan roared the silent curse, letting it swell and expand in his mind until every last vestige of beckoning bronze nether curls was vanquished.

'Listen to his heart' Marmaduke had advised. Ha! Only one malediction plagued him at present and it had naught to do with his heart. Hoping Marmaduke's all-seeing eye for once didn't see *everything*, Duncan adjusted a fold of his great plaid to hang a bit more conveniently.

His lustful cravings thus disguised, another image flashed across Duncan's mind, and this one was even more alarming because it had the power to stir more than his physical arousal.

'Twas the fleeting look of adoration and desire he'd glimpsed in her gold-flecked eyes earlier on, when her expression had gone all soft and she'd looked as if she ached for him to kiss her.

By Saint Peter's holy tomb, if he heeded Marmaduke's sentimental advice, he wouldn't care if an entire garrison of men-at-arms took possession of his bedchamber. They could have it, and all his holdings, if only he could inspire his lady wife to gaze upon him thusly—and genuinely mean it.

But, alas, 'twas well he knew it had merely been a woman's weakness for a battle-weary warrior that had made her momentarily forget her dislike of him and naught more.

He also knew his own masculine pride had made him believe, for a brief moment, that she would shower him with such attention, would welcome his devotion and love in turn.

Thankfully, he'd caught himself in time, remembered loving a woman was a dangerous endeavor fraught with more peril than a lusty dip betwixt their thighs was worth.

Nay, he'd let Sir Marmaduke woo the women if he was wont to do so. *He* wouldn't be persuaded—or seduced—into forgetting himself again.

Scowling once more, Duncan snatched one of the bedcovers and tossed it over his arm. "Dinna attempt to advise me on matters of the heart, English. 'Tis a wise man who doesna wear his feelings on his sleeve. I'm a-thinking you've buried your nose in too many French romances and spent too many nights listening to lovesick bards croon their insipid ballads to all who'll toss them a coin."

Duncan jerked his head toward his squire who, amazingly, slept soundly on his pallet before the fire. "Save your romanticism for young lads like Lachlan, but spare me such nonsense. 'Tis a grown man I am, and I know from experience what comes on the heels of losing one's heart."

"You know naught, my friend," Marmaduke said, sadly shaking his head. "A man *gives* his heart, and gladly. Never does he lose it, for in the giving, he gains a wealth of love in return. But, you are right, 'tis a grown man you are, and one too weary, and accustomed to his comfort, to stalk into the night with naught but a thin length of wool to warm your bones. If you will not seek the Lady Linnet's bed, take your own. I can join Lachlan on the floor."

Duncan hesitated, tempted to accept Marmaduke's capitulation, but the memory of his friend's shoulders sagging as he'd gazed at the painted image above the hearth soured Duncan's small victory.

He shot a glance at the perfection of his dead wife's face, and his gut twisted with revulsion. Mayhap the likeness had served its purpose as far as he was concerned and would now better serve Marmaduke. He didn't need to stare at the infernal painting to be reminded of Cassandra's perfidy.

Indeed, had Marmaduke not expressed a desire to keep the whoring beauty's accursed likeness, he'd wrest it from the wall this moment and cast it out the window, letting it sink into the cold, dark waters of the loch.

Naught would please him more than to know Cassandra's likeness rested in the muck at the bottom of Loch Duich. Preferably facedown so her loveliness would be forever ground into the mud.

'Twould be a fitting revenge for the way she'd stomped his heart and soul into the dirt.

Duncan didn't acknowledge Marmaduke's offer until he reached the door. Turning, he gave his friend a tired smile. "Nay, you keep the bed and the chamber—though I still deny granting them to you."

An expression very much like guilt washed over Marmaduke's face, but it was hard to tell given the sad extent of his disformity. He opened his mouth to speak, but Duncan stayed him by raising his hand.

"Dinna say it. The saints alone know what you and the others conspire to achieve with your intrusions into my affairs, but I do not believe your motives are corrupt." He paused to open the door. "I think your intentions are well-meant and good, albeit misguided."

"Hold a moment, wait," Marmaduke protested, coming forward. "For the love—"

For the love. The three words propelled Duncan through the door and made him shut it tight behind him. He didn't want to hear whatever Marmaduke had wanted to say. And he especially didn't want to discuss love.

Not love of the saints or angels, not love of any kind, and definitely not love of a man for his wife.

Nor of a man for his son.

A muscle in his jaw twitched at *that* thought, and he increased his pace down the shadowy passageway. He wanted naught to do with love of any kind and felt a pressing need to put a great distance between himself and his too-wise Sassunach friend.

The one-eyed Englishman had the uncanny knack of making him feel as if he could see into his very soul at times. Faith, he should have married Marmaduke to discover Robbie's true parentage! His new wife's failure to satisfy him in that regard deepened the scowl he already wore.

At the end of the corridor, just before the stairwell that led down to the hall, Duncan stopped to lean against the cold and damp stone wall. His jaw twitched and jerked almost uncontrollably, and frustration made him grind his teeth together so brutally, he wouldn't have been surprised if he chipped one of them.

He shivered, too, for before he'd found Marmaduke in his bed, he'd doused himself with chilled water in an attempt to wash the blood and grime from his aching body.

And he smelled, for the unsettling discovery had put a premature halt to his much-needed ablutions.

Above all, he was absolutely miserable. Even more than he'd been when he'd left the battlements and headed for his chamber, desiring naught but to rest his weary bones.

Uttering a dark oath, he pushed himself away from the wall. With heavy steps, and a heavier heart, he began the winding descent to the hall. He'd spend the remainder of the night sleeping on a bench or make do with the rushes as did most of his men. But halfway down the stairs, he halted.

The perverse irony of his situation would have made him laugh in younger years . . . back when he'd still possessed a hearty sense of humor.

He had sought the hand of Linnet MacDonnell. *He* had brought her to Kintail in the hopes she'd rid him of his doubts and prove herself a useful, if not cherished, wife.

Instead, she'd turned his world upside down, and utter chaos had ruled his household from the moment she first passed through the castle gates. He was laird, yet *he* alone crept through the night-darkened keep, chilled to the bone and reeking to the heavens, without a bed to claim his own.

She slept in one of the castle's finest chambers, the

one that had belonged to his parents, and their parents before them. *She* was likely lost in a dream world of valiant knights, gracious ladies, and cherubic babes, while *he* skulked about like an outcast in his own home.

The injustice of it made his hands clench, while his lips formed a thin, tight line.

From below, the faint sounds of his men's snores carried up the circular stairwell, along with the scurrying sounds of his hounds foraging for scraps of food amongst the rushes. Fainter still, the crackling of the fires in the hall's three great hearths and the ever-present sound of Loch Duich's waves, gentled by the late hour, lapping against the castle walls.

An ordinary night for all who called Eilean Creag home.

All save its liege laird and master.

Duncan flexed his fingers a few times, then balled them into tight fists once more. He needed the slight pain of his nails digging into his palms, welcomed it, lest he pound his hands to pulp against the wall.

Everyone but himself had peace this night. Marmaduke rested well in Duncan's . . . *former* . . . chamber, his men slumbered as always below, and old Fergus no doubt enjoyed the luxury of finally having a bed to call his own in Marmaduke's relinquished quarters.

He didn't know where his wife's protective lady servant slept, but she, too, had assuredly found more calm than he.

Feeling much the fool, and angrier still, Duncan took two steps downward, then stopped. He'd be a bigger dolt if he spent the night in the hall. Come the morn, his men would make jests, speculate amongst themselves his reasons for abandoning the warmth of his bride's bed.

Duncan winced at the ramifications. Giving his men fodder for gossip would only increase his misery. Without taking time to consider the consequences, Duncan turned and headed back up the stairs.

'Twas true, his lady wife's chamber was on the opposite side of the keep, attainable only by crossing the hall and climbing yet another set of spiral stairs, but he was laird of this island stronghold and as such he knew its every stone . . . and secret.

Such as the narrow passage cut within the castle walls.

An escape route connecting a few of the castle's rooms before winding downward to a hidden cave on the island's rocky shore.

A slight tugging pulled at the corners of his mouth in what could've been the beginnings of a smile—if he were wont to smile, which he wasn't. But it pleased him greatly to have decided to take matters into his own hands.

He was, after all, laird.

It was beneath his dignity to scramble about in the middle of the night, seeking a place to lay his head.

Nay, he'd exercise his rights as the present MacKenzie of Kintail and reclaim the chamber his father and all the clan chiefs before him had used as their own.

Including the bed.

"My faith, but you startled me!" Sitting bolt upright in her bed, his bride clutched the covers to her breasts and stared at him, round-eyed and aghast as if he'd risen up from the floor like a wraith or other such unwelcome creature of the night. "I must not have heard your return."

Nay, you wouldn't have for I did not arrive through the chamber door!

The unspoken quip and the exhilaration of sneaking into her chamber through the secret wall passage, something he hadn't done in years, brought a wolfish smile to Duncan's lips.

'Twas the first genuine smile he'd allowed himself in the devil knew how many years, and the feel of it was unexpectedly good.

His wife tilted her head to the side as if she meant to take full measure of such an odd phenomenon as the great MacKenzie of Kintail grinning. "Then why did you?" she asked finally. "Return, I mean."

"Of a certainty, not to joust words with you, my lady."

"Am I needed below?" She peered sharply at him. "Has something befallen Robbie? Or one of the Murchison survivors?"

Aye, you are needed, lass. By me.

The heart he didn't possess and Marmaduke would have him listen to, spoke.

Duncan ignored it.

"The boy is well and the Murchison party sleeps soundly, or so I've been informed," he answered as laird, and continued to work the shoulder clasp that held his plaid in place. He also continued to enjoy the view.

The thin woolen coverlet his wife grasped so tightly did more to pleasingly frame the fullness of her breasts, emphasize their lushness, than to hide them, as was surely her intent.

"What are you doing?" Apprehension stained her cheeks with a flattering wash of color.

"Be it not obvious?" The devilish smile almost returned, but this time he resisted.

"You appear to be readying yourself for bed, milord."

"*Duncan.*"

"You appear to be readying yourself for bed, Duncan, sir," she corrected, her voice soft yet piercing the wall around his heart as expertly as if her words were carried on the sharpest and most swift of arrows.

"And so I am," he confirmed, more serious now, the rare moment of unanticipated frivolity past, replaced by a sharpening of his senses caused by the fetching way moonlight gilded the silken skein of her unbound hair. "I dinna usually sleep fully clothed."

"But I thought . . . you said—"

"I know what I said," Duncan finished for her. "But I've been compelled to change my mind about where I lay my head. You needn't look so alarmed. 'Tis sleep alone I want."

"Oh." Her cheeks promptly turned a brighter shade of red. "'Tis not alarmed I am, sir, only confused. I thought you preferred your own quar—"

"My chamber, milady, has been sequestrated by a certain one-eyed demon of rascality."

Surprise, nervousness, or mayhap because the saints inspired her to help rob him of his sanity, she pushed a strand of hair behind her ear, and in doing so, let slip the edge of the coverlet. In the instant it took her to realize what she'd done and yank the coverlet back in place, Duncan caught a most tantalizing view of one deliciously peaked nipple.

His loins fired immediately, his shaft filling at the sight. Dusky rose in hue and tightly rouched, the exposed nipple, even glimpsed so briefly, sent desire crashing through Duncan. Driven by pure male hunger, he strode forward, ready to abandon his ridiculous monkish vows and take possession *both* of his wife's nipples and everything else she had to offer.

And this time he intended to remember every minute detail of the pleasuring of her!

But the quick flare of panic that flashed across her face at his approach stayed him. Staff of Columba, fire in his tarse or nay, he would not force his rusted attentions on a wife who dreaded his touch.

Slaking his lust betwixt the spread legs of a bawd willing to service him even whilst her eyes revealed what she truly thought of him was a necessary part of Duncan's life. There wasn't a man on this earth who didn't need his shaft milked on occasion. But, even a well-fired groin couldn't bring him to thus use a gentleborn woman and most certainly not his wife.

Duncan's mood darkened. What madness had let him imagine the sweet puckering of her nipples had been caused by arousal over his presence? Nay, the room's chill air had been responsible and not his brawn. Simply the cold, and that sobering knowledge quickly tempered his own flare of desire.

But how he wished he had been the cause.

Breath of the Apostles, but he wanted to rouse her far beyond the mere peaking of her breasts. He wanted her to writhe and moan beneath him. To welcome his embrace . . . and more.

But would she ever be able to look past the cold man she thought him to be and see the heated longing he carried deep within?

Would she e'er sense his need?

And if she did, would she be willing to assuage it?

Did he even want her to try? Hadn't it been just such wild longings that had given Cassandra such power over him? Duncan stared at her, transfixed by the look of her. His respect for the danger he knew desiring her would bring seemed to dwindle with each breath he drew. Saints, but he'd started down a treacherous path!

Half-angelic with her wide-eyed innocence, she had purity written all over her upturned face, yet with her fiery gold hair swirling about her naked shoulders, her bewitching charms so provocatively displayed, she was half temptress as well.

Something broke loose inside him, rending another tear in his carefully woven shield. Another damnable gap in the wall. But caution be damned, he *wanted* her to see the man beneath his stern looks and gruff words, *needed* her to rescue him from himself and his private hell.

He just wasn't able to admit it, couldn't bring himself to let her close. Yet every time he glimpsed her, he wanted nothing more than to do just that. He was a man split in twain, cast by his own fool machinations into a world of turmoil and disorder. And he was at a pretty loss as to how to make things aright.

Before he could catch himself, Duncan swore. The furious words of an oft-muttered oath tumbled from his lips as if they had a mind of their own. A black and hearty epithet that would have sent his most fearsome foes scrambling for cover.

His wife scrambled, too, scooting backwards upon the bed, forgetting to hold on to the covers in her haste to put distance between them.

Her breasts, now fully exposed, were so inviting in their ripeness a tonsured monk would abandon his psalm chanting to taste of them! Duncan's self-control flagged and his shaft lengthened and swelled to an unbearable degree. His curses became a groan and, overcome by need, he worked free the clasp holding his plaid in place and let it fall.

As quickly, he dispensed of his travel-stained hose and kicked them aside.

His bride gasped, and the look of innocence and confusion in her beautiful eyes changed swiftly to wariness. And this time the expression of dismay wasn't fleeting. Or was it a look of repugnance? Not sure, Duncan studied her face, acutely aware of the unflattering gaze she'd fixed upon his jutting manhood.

He swallowed the string of oaths he burned to let loose. 'Twas impossible to discern what she thought of him, but he knew it wasn't good.

The delight and wonder he'd oft seen upon the faces of women when they'd gazed upon his nakedness and realized the size of him was once again painfully absent from his wife's reaction. Duncan's pride crumbled. Truth be told, he'd not seen a woman's face alight with passion since he'd last shared a few lusty wenches with his king.

And that had been a goodly number of years ago . . . before Cassandra.

At the thought of his first wife, his manhood began

to wither. Cursing again, he spun around before Linnet could see. Yet, from her sharp intake of breath, he suspected she already had.

Fuming, his face hot with humiliation, Duncan stalked to the hearth and glared at the dying embers. His hands clenched at his sides and his entire body tightened like a bowstring . . . all except *that* part of him.

His manhood, the most intimate part of himself which he'd just hoped to proudly display to his new bride, to *woo* her, to *seduce* her with his manliness and prowess, had let him down. Disgraced, embarrassed, and shamed him by shrinking before her very eyes.

Saints and martyrs, but he'd made a mess of things! The sight of his unclothed body inspired his wife to look upon him first with distaste, he was sure of it, and then, as he'd diminished in size, with shock.

Such a performance had likely done irreparable damage to his chances of ever winning her affection. And all because of *her*. If he could, he'd damn the ghost of Cassandra to eternal hell, but he highly suspected the devious she-devil already resided there.

Ne'er would Linnet believe it'd been the thought of his first wife that had so rapidly stilled his desire. Duncan knew enough of women to know she'd put the blame on herself, think he found her unappealing.

Or she'd think him incapable.

He didn't know which notion upset him more.

"Sir?" came her voice, its hesitancy twisting Duncan's innards. "Have I offended you?"

"Nay, wife," he said, his own voice rough in his throat. "You've done naught to displease me. 'Tis only weary I am."

"But yo—"

"I am consumed by a raging need for sleep," he snapped, ill humor making him clench his hands to fists. Mother of God preserve him did the woman dare to pursue his embarrassment.

"Sir, I have heard of su—"

"Naught is amiss," Duncan ground out, spinning around to still her lips with a fierce glare.

Lucifer's knees! She still sat with her breasts exposed! Were he any other man, he'd march across the room and bury his face between their fullness, drink in her sweetness in great greedy gulps, then settle his mouth over first one nipple, then the other, drawing deeply until he was utterly filled with the taste of her.

He ached to taste her elsewhere, too, and would, now, this instant, were he not so consumed with rage and pain, even the love of a good woman wasn't strong enough to banish the demons eating away at his soul.

She peered curiously at him but made no move to cover her breasts. Duncan fought not to move either. Doing so might make her yank up the coverlet. Considering the disharmony of their alliance thus far, the heavens only knew when he'd be blessed with such a glorious sight again.

"You said you meant to sleep," she said then, blessedly abandoning her pursuit of discussing the state of his manhood. She cocked her head to the side as she spoke, and the rounded globes of her breasts swayed a bit with the movement.

Swift and powerful, Duncan's lust returned. He swallowed hard, his gaze fastened on the tight little nipples thrusting so prettily toward him, fair begging for attention. Christ's blood, but she'd cast some kind of dark witchery over him, dulled his very wits.

". . . Did you mean *here*, in this bed?" she asked, apparently unaware of what she did to him. "With *me*?"

Duncan knew the meaning of her innocent words, but despite himself, the last two she'd uttered went straight to his loins. Aye, he wanted to sleep with her . . . but not how she meant. He wanted to spread her sweet thighs, look his fill upon her, drive her wild with his hands and mouth, pleasure her until she was dripping with need, then plunge himself into her again and again and again until his release shattered every last one of his fool reasons for keeping himself from her.

But the ghost of Cassandra and her perfidy still lurked near enough to halt the swell of his tarse.

"Are you going to fetch down the tapestry again?"

It took Duncan a moment to comprehend her words. When he did, ire drove him to snap at her. "Have you not seen I pose no threat to you this night?"

His sharp words widened her eyes and sent her scooting even farther away from him. To Duncan's perverse delight, her flight across the broad expanse of the bed freed even more delectable treats for his hungry gaze to feast upon. For one very brief instant, he tried to resist, but how could he not allow his gaze to devour a bounty so deliciously displayed?

Although she'd doused the brace of candles for the night, a wide band of moonlight fell through an unshuttered window, casting a pattern of light and shadows across her.

The saints must have meant to vex him apurpose, for she'd tangled the bedcoverings to such a wild degree, she'd unwittingly exposed the triangle of lush red-gold curls between her thighs. Bathed in moonglow, the core of her womanhood, cleft and all, was clearly visible, every sweetly pouting fold sharply illuminated by the moon's silvery light.

And with her bent knees slightly parted, she unwittingly allowed him a more-than-ample eyeful!

'Twas as if, unbeknownst to her, the sweet mound of hair and tender, gently swollen flesh begged for a man's touch.

His touch.

He had but to take her. Saints, he already had, once!

But then the bush of fiery curls turned sooty black before his eyes and Duncan's blood ran cold. Sweet Jesu, help him, he even imagined he saw Cassandra's long, slender fingers toying idly with her own sex as she'd oft done to torment him, taunting him until he'd craved her more fiercely than a stag in rut.

Unable to move, Duncan stared at his new wife's sweetness but saw the black spread of a wicked she-wolf's wiles. From the very bowels of hell, he conjured the images that had once driven him to such heights of erotic bliss: his first wife's hand plucking lightly at her raven-colored nether curls or trailing a slow-moving finger down the pouty length of her cleft, driving him mad with lust as she'd performed her uninhibited acts of sheer wantonness.

Then Linnet moved, and the ghastly memories shattered. Whirling around, lest she see the horror he knew had to be etched into his face, Duncan stalked across the room to the bank of tall arched windows. Mother of God, seldom had he been so shaken. Careful to hide his turmoil, he took long, deep breaths of the chill night air until he was certain he could get words past his lips.

"Pray, straighten the bedcoverings, for I want naught but to rest now. 'Tis only the bed I want you to share," he said, feeling more ancient and worn than Fergus. "I'll ask naught else of you."

And if I freely give what my heart tells me you seek? Linnet's heart spoke the words she chose not to say aloud. She would've shouted them, but she'd seen his eyes glaze with some inner turmoil, and her gift had picked up the surge in the dark torment she knew he carried on his broad shoulders. So she chose silence this once and simply did as he bid her.

She'd concede this night's battle, but ne'er would she admit total defeat. Not even to demons the likes of which she couldn't begin to fathom.

Yet she knew they existed, for the darkness that filled his soul spilled over into the bedchamber, blocking out the soft light of the moon and weighing down the atmosphere with its malignancy.

An intangible, elusive presence, but real. A cruel and relentless foe, and partly of his own making. That much she knew. But whatever agonies possessed him, they were too powerful for her to conquer.

Not that he'd let her try. She'd seen his manroot shrivel while he'd looked upon her. Shame and regret pressed down upon her until she could scarce breathe, so heavy was the weight of her humiliation.

No wonder he'd taken advantage of her dazed state during one of her visions to consummate their marriage. Such was the only way to have done with the act as swiftly as possible.

She still found it difficult to believe he'd touched her at all, for she remembered none of the pain her sisters had sometimes spoken about in hushed whispers. Nor had she experienced the joy, the great passion, of which the bards e'er sang. She'd experienced naught of such wonders, and it was difficult to believe she ever would.

For hadn't her liege husband stared long at her naked breasts, and with such fierceness she'd thought his gaze would singe her bared skin, yet it was clear he'd found her unworthy.

Untutored as she was in intimate matters, she knew enough to understand what had happened to his manroot.

And the reason for it.

Yet with him making no secret about finding her lacking, why did she still get all aflutter and soft inside each time he turned his dark countenance her way? Why did she ache with a need for something she couldn't discern?

Something that seemed so close, yet out of her grasp.

Unless she reached out and took it.

She turned her face away as he eased himself onto the bed and stretched out beside her. She didn't want him to see her hurt and confusion. His reaction to her body, his rejection of her as a woman, had been embarrassment enough.

For a very long time, Linnet lay still in the darkness. The moon had long since sailed on, taking with it the soft glow its silver-blue light had cast over the bedchamber. Not trusting herself to move lest the simple rise and fall of her chest shatter the fragile peace that accompanied her husband's sleep, she allowed herself to take only tiny, shallow breaths.

Until, finally, Duncan's own slow and steady breathing assured her he'd fallen into a deep slumber. Only then did she relax, carefully rolling onto her side to face him.

He rested a good arm's length away, but the heat from his body reached her, warming her. His masculine scent teased her senses, unleashing the powerful urges she was only beginning to understand. Having him so close disturbed her greatly, but not in an unpleasant manner, merely a perplexing one.

She wished to explore the feelings he aroused in her, relish the new discoveries he could undoubtedly teach her. But their union wasn't congenial enough for her to risk him knowing the power he held over her.

Nor did she need him to tell her what was happening to her, to her heart.

She knew.

Or at least she had a strong suspicion.

And if her emotions were so clear to her, how could she expect to keep them from him?

Her brothers had oft teased her, claiming she could ne'er hide her feelings. Would Duncan guess the truth? Had he already done so? Could he have sensed how she'd trembled in anticipation when she'd awakened to find him standing so unexpectedly before her?

Could he have known her pulse had quickened? Guessed the thought he'd come to spend the night in her arms had sent delicious shivers rippling down her spine?

Would he ever abandon his demons, ever seek to

make their marriage work? Did he suspect how fervently she wished they could do just that?

Did he know she was coming to care for him?

Her heart winced at the thought. He was a man who wanted naught to do with gentler emotions. A man who had no place for love in his heart. And Linnet was convinced he possessed one. He'd merely locked it away.

Staring at him to assure herself he truly slept, she lightly traced the hard line of his jaw with her fingertips, then smoothed her hand over his tangled mane of black hair. She touched him with careful tenderness, for she knew instinctively that was what he needed most.

And if e'er she'd doubted it, she knew now. As daunting a figure he made, stretched upon her bed in all his magnificence, his sleep-relaxed face bore a look of vulnerability that called to her in a way she couldn't resist.

Gone now, the fearsome and proud warrior with his booming voice and critically narrowed eyes. Stilled, too, his frequent bouts of anger. Sleep had banished the grimness, leaving in its place a man whose face appeared so unguarded, so pure in its dark beauty, she couldn't resist leaning across the bed and raining gentle kisses on his untroubled brow.

Only a few because she didn't want to steal the rest she knew he needed nor could she have stood it if he'd awakened and resumed the uncompromising expression he favored in waking hours.

With a soft sigh, Linnet shifted onto her back and closed her eyes. But not to sleep. Too many cares drifted through her mind for her to rest this night.

Cares she could not control nor do aught about.

Now, though, after seeing the mighty MacKenzie of

Kintail, the Black Stag, with his guard down, she understood only too well why she found herself fearing him less and caring more.

Casting a furtive glance at him, at his handsome face, fair boyish in sleep, her hold on her own emotions slipped farther out of control. The vulnerability gracing his features was a discomfiting image paired with the raw, brute strength of his powerful body, the sheer might and vigor she knew coursed through his well-muscled limbs.

Closing her eyes again, she took a deep, ragged breath. She supposed being drawn to him was inevitable.

Her fate, deemed by the saints long before she'd taken her first breath.

For ne'er had she been able to resist taming wild creatures. She'd always felt a burning need to aid injured beasts, to nurse them back to health, then set them free.

But Duncan MacKenzie was one beast she doubted could e'er be fully tamed.

Certainly not by her, though she did mean to try.

And if by some divine miracle she *could* heal her husband's heart, letting him go would surely break her own.

9

On a mist-hung morning a sennight later, Linnet
let herself into the tiny herbarium old Fergus had grudgingly relinquished to her care. She closed the gate securely behind her, the screech of its rusty hinges overly
loud and intrusive against the rhythmic whoosh of the
tide washing over the shingled beach just beyond the
garden's thick stone walls.

Pushing back her head veil, she turned her face skyward. The cooling moisture of the early-morning fog felt
good upon her skin, its gentle softness welcome. Healing, too, the rich scent of freshly turned earth and the
more pungent sea smells carried on the light breeze.

Eager to get on with her work, she scanned the neat
rows of vegetables and herbs she'd carefully weeded
over the past seven days. She'd accomplished much and
was pleased with her progress.

If only she could be pleased with her marriage, too.

But, alas, whilst she could work fair magic with plants, turning a long-neglected plot of rock-strewn earth and overgrown herbage into a wondrous physic garden of which even the gifted monk, Brother Baldric, would be proud, her special talent for nurturing living things seemed to have no effect whatsoever upon her husband.

She took a deep, cleansing breath but barely had time to expel it before she heard a rustling movement in a dark corner of the garden.

"Who goes there?" she called, turning toward the sound.

"'Tis only me." Her husband stepped out from the shadows, and Linnet's heart leapt at the sight of him. His tall warrior's body, resplendent in his gleaming black hauberk, seemed almost overpoweringly masculine in the morning peace of the small garden. "I came to bid you farewell," he said.

"Farewell?" Linnet took a step forward. "You said naught about going away when we awoke this morn. What is amiss?"

He strode toward her, his plaid slung boldly over his left shoulder and not one but two long-bladed knives thrust beneath his low-slung belt. A telling precaution that matched the grim set of his jaw. His deep blue eyes had darkened to a shade very close to the steel mesh of his mail shirt and appeared equally cold.

Very much aware of the coiled power and strength he held so masterfully in check, and the anger simmering below the surface of his tightly controlled demeanor, Linnet waited until he reached her before she voiced her suspicion. "Is it Kenneth?"

As if unconsciously, Duncan's hand strayed to the

hilt of the broadsword hanging from his sword belt. "Aye, it would seem so. I've received word from my friend and ally, John MacLeod, that Kenneth has been harrying the kinsmen who dwell on the outmost fringes of MacKenzie land. The MacLeod is a good man and would not spread false rumors. He would not have sent warning if the danger was not earnest. I shall leave with a patrol anon."

Linnet swallowed her ill ease at his confirmation of what she'd feared and simply nodded. He needn't carry her worry with him when he rode through the castle gates. Keeping her tone as unruffled-sounding as she could manage, she said, "May God go with you, milord."

A flare of something indefinable sparked in his eyes, and he touched her face, letting the backs of his fingers glide down the curve of her cheek. "'Twould please me more if He remained here to watch over you."

A tingling shiver of pleasure rippled through her at his unexpected gentleness, but the gravity of his journey didn't allow her the luxury of considering the implications of the simple but tender gesture. Instead, she lifted the hem of her kirtle to display the sharp knife Dundonnell's smithy had given her. As she usually preferred, she wore it tucked jauntily into the top of her boot.

She lifted her chin and met his gaze full on. "I am not afeared of your half brother," she declared, letting her skirt drop back into place. "Nor will I hesitate to use my blade if need be."

He grasped her upper arms and squeezed, his fingers like bands of iron, firm and strong, yet incredibly comforting, his warmth easily reaching through her sleeves and chasing away the chill that had begun to curl around her at the mention of Kenneth.

"May the saints hinder you'll ever come that close to the bastard again," he vowed.

"'Tis a fine shot I am with a crossbow as well," she said, inwardly alarmed by the tension thrumming through him. It sprang from his hands and entered her blood, a living, crackling sensation as wild and furious as the heavens gripped in the talons of a fierce summer storm.

Deliberately keeping her voice light in the hope she could dispel, at least, his concern for her, she boasted, "Not one of my brothers can best me."

"Truth tell?" Her bravura was rewarded by a flash of amusement in his eyes and the upward turn of the corner of his lips. Not quite a smile and so fleeting she may have imagined it, but for the brief instant the almost-smile had touched his handsome face, the power of it had flared so bright it fair blinded her.

And certainly set her needy heart to thumping.

"I swear it on my mother's grave," she said, emboldened by his not-quite-a-smile smile and hoping to assure him of the truth of her claims.

No sooner did the words leave her lips, did his expression grow stony again. Letting go of her, he said, "I dinna care if you can shoot the tail off the devil, you shall remain within these walls. I'll not have you wandering about and inviting trouble. I've ordered a guard to stand watch at your door, and I deem it best I escort you there now."

"Surely I am safe in the garden?"

Rather than answer her, Duncan remained silent, his

lips thinning into a tight look of displeasure . . . or disapproval.

The same closed-face look she'd observed each time he'd caught her heading for the little herbarium. The last whirling eddies of pleasure his presence always seemed to set loose in her fizzled out, his dark mood vanquishing them as swiftly as two fingers can snuff out a smoldering candlewick.

"I like it here, sirrah," she said, straightening her back and the set of her shoulders. "Tending the garden gives me purpose." She gestured toward the neat rows of newly planted herbs. "I came to prepare an elixir for Sir Marmaduke. The ragwort poultices I've been giving him have worked so well, 'tis my hope an elixir will benefit him even more." On impulse, she laid a hand on his arm. "Have you not noticed the change?"

A grudging smile slowly spread across his face, transforming it and stealing Linnet's breath away. "Aye, I have, and if I hadn't, the vain blackguard would have made certain I did notice."

"Then you are pleased?"

He smoothed a stray lock of hair off her face, and let his fingers skim along the line of her neck. A tender, gentle touch, light as a breeze but mighty enough to curl Linnet's toes and send a wash of pleasurable sensations spilling through her. "'Tis fine work you've done," he said, his fingers toying with the hair at the nape of her neck. "The swelling around Marmaduke's missing eye has all but receded, and I'm mightily impressed with your talent. Still, if you must work with herbs, I'd rather you collect them from the brothers at the abbey than grow them here."

"But why?" Linnet glanced around the little garden. It was just beginning to look well tended . . . *loved* . . . again. " 'Tis true the garden needs much care, but I do not mind. The work is a pleasure to me, a joy. Your mother—"

"Who spoke of my mother?" Duncan cut her off, his fingers stilling their pleasure-spending caress.

"No one, except, that is . . ." Linnet stammered, confused. "Fergus said she'd cared for the garden and I thought, since it's gone so long untended, you'd appreciate—"

"It went untended on my orders."

"I'm afraid I do not understand."

"Nay, you do not and cannot." Stepping away from her, Duncan strode to the gate, where he remained standing with his back to her, his hand resting on the rusty latch.

Linnet stiffened at the cold dismissal she read in his stance, but something about the way he lingered, hesitating as if waiting for her to come forward, made her go to him.

"I would like to understand, Duncan," she said softly, unaccustomed to using his given name. But somehow it felt right on her tongue.

He rewarded her by resting his arm about her shoulders and drawing her near. Yet his touch felt awkward, stiff and wooden, as if holding her close made him uncomfortable. "You have naught to do but have a care when here. And I shall have your word you ken each and every plant . . . every seed . . . what grows here."

She pulled back to look at him, surprised by the reproach in his voice. "Why, sir, I've been familiar with herbs since afore I could walk. I assure you there is not a single plant here what can be used for aught but good."

"And so I wish it shall remain."

"Do you worry I would cause someone ill?" A chill washed over her at the thought he could think so poorly of her. "Ne'er would I—"

"It is not you I distrust," he said, cupping her chin in his large hand. "'Tis only that unhappy memories linger here and spoil this place for me." He paused as if weighing his words before he continued. "My mother and sister both died of tainted food. 'Twas believed the poison came from this garden."

"Merciful saints!" Linnet's hands flew to her cheeks. "'Twas surely an accident?"

Her husband waited a moment before he answered. "I canna say. Naught could be proven, for the person we suspected perished before any questions could be raised."

"I did not know." She paused to wet her lips. "If it pleases you, I shall abandon my work here."

He hesitated, then smoothed his knuckles lightly over her cheek. "Nay. 'Tis perhaps time the garden once more enjoys the attention of a gentle lady."

Linnet nodded, too moved by his unexpected tenderness to speak.

Without warning, he stepped closer and took her face between the palms of his hands. He lowered his head and touched his lips to hers in an achingly sweet kiss, its tenderness stealing Linnet's breath away. Then, even as she melted against him, parting her lips to gladly accept a deeper, more urgent joining of their lips, he released her and was gone.

Linnet remained where she stood, her fingers pressed lightly to her still-tingling lips, until the sound of his receding footsteps was swallowed by the morning fog.

Shaken and awed by the force of passionate need his kiss had unleashed deep inside her, Linnet bent to pluck several fat snails from a newly cleared bed of mint and thyme. Mayhap her nightly efforts to breach the barriers he held against her were having effect?

She couldn't deny the tenderness of his parting kiss nor the concern that had laced his words just now.

Did he suspect how she'd lain awake night after night, waiting for him to settle into a deep sleep? Had he unwittingly sensed her tracing the noble lines of his face with the backs of her fingers? Had he merely feigned sleep whilst she'd tenderly explored his hard-planed warrior's body with her questing hands?

For only then, in the quietude of the dark, did she dare hope to gentle him with the tenderness of her touch.

To win his heart when he was unwary and perhaps too weary from the day's toils to resist her affections.

Only then did she allow herself to dream.

Straightening, she wiped her hands on her apron. Faith, but she'd grown bold. Each night she'd become more daring, first stroking his hair, then moving on to the breadth of his shoulders, and finally caressing the rock-solid muscles of his arms.

Once, she'd even smoothed her fingertips down the hard planes of his chest and abdomen, stopping just short of the thick black hair that sheltered his manhood.

There, her fingers had hovered while tingles had raced up her arm, surging through her, alighting her senses, before pooling in the depths of her belly. The sensations had warmed her, urged her to explore that most masculine and mysterious part of him.

But she'd desisted, pulling back her hand as if she'd been scorched.

Too frightened of his possible reaction and too unsure of herself to risk discovery.

She winced at the very idea of his awakening to find her running her hands over him, exploring his body as if she were the lowest sort of village bawd. She couldn't imagine his reaction, but knew he'd not appreciate her boldness. He'd made no secret of his desire to keep himself from her.

A great shudder passed through her at the tremendous chance she'd taken in daring to touch him thusly.

Yet he'd come to the garden to bid her farewell, shown her the kind of gentleness she wouldn't have dreamed possible, voiced his desire to know her safe.

Had given her cause to hope.

Suddenly, a thick sheaf of hair slipped forward and fell across her eyes. With well-practiced ease, she tucked it in place and sighed.

If only she had more to commend her than her supposedly bonnie tresses!

Not that she considered her hair as lovely as some claimed.

Ne'er would it stay properly coifed, being far too weighty for the plaits Elspeth so painstakingly arranged each morn. The hour of terce was not yet upon them, and already Elspeth's handiwork had come undone. Aye, her tresses were e'er difficult to tame. And its color was far too immodest a red, a shade better suited to a woman of lesser morals. Or as her da oft accused, a sorceress.

Had fate been kind, she would've been blessed with her sisters' quiet beauty. Instead, she'd been born with a plain face and errant locks, lips much too full, and skin, whilst fair enough, marred by freckles inherited from her sire.

A drunken lout of a man who'd no doubt revel in the stinging humiliation she'd found by coming to care for a man who didn't want her as a husband should. She craved more than tender kisses, she burned to experience true passion, a total abandonment to the fires her husband ignited inside her. Aye, her da would convulse with laughter if he could see her now, yearning for Duncan MacKenzie's favor.

For despite his concern for her well-being, her husband's only true interest in her was the answer to the question he posed her every morn . . . and every night.

But she'd remained silent, keeping her secret even as he fell into sullen silence over her apparent failure to see the truth he sought.

Yet with each rising sun, she awoke with new hope.

Hope for herself, and hope for Robbie.

But with the coming of the night, she went to bed knowing her attempts to please had been hopelessly ineffective regardless of what she did. Her efforts to make him want her and to acknowledge, unconditionally, his love for his son, remained sadly futile.

With a mumbled curse, full-bodied enough to have made her brothers proud, Linnet kicked a stone out of her way, then strode straight for the haven of the little stone workshop built against the garden's seaward wall.

Here, and with the lad, Robbie, she found solace.

This morn, as on others, the burden of the great task she'd taken upon herself felt lighter the moment she stepped into the low-ceilinged workshop, with its bundles of dried herbs hanging from the rafters.

The many shelves crowded with bottles, jars, and earthenware pots, along with several worktables holding an assortment of pestles, mortars, and wooden bowls, the variety of which Linnet had never seen, gave her great comfort.

In a corner cupboard, she'd even found a precious set of metal scales, a collection of small wooden boxes ideal for storing her medicinal preparations once dried, and even several rolls of fairly clean linen for bandaging wounds if e'er she must.

Linnet took a deep breath, filling her lungs with the pungent air. Her heart warmed immediately. In the quiet of the dim workshop with its comforting scents of herbs and peat smoke, she'd found a sense of peace she'd not expected to find at Eilean Creag.

Even the earthy smell of the well-trodden dirt floor and the tang of briny sea air drifting in through the one tiny window calmed her and gave the workshop an indefinable air of sanctuary.

Taking an earthen jug from a high shelf, she poured a measure of ragwort elixir into a small flagon. She'd concocted the special unguent especially for Sir Marmaduke, taking great care with the selection of its ingredients. On impulse, she added a few drops of other herb essences to the ragwort in the hopes of bringing even more relief to the puckered and angry welts upon Marmaduke's face.

Satisfied, she carefully sealed the flagon so not a drop of the precious elixir would be lost.

Tucking the flagon into a small purse tied to her apron, she turned and nearly stumbled over a large hound stretched upon the floor behind her. She smiled upon recognizing Mauger, the ancient mongrel wont to follow her stepson wherever he went.

But she'd heard neither of them enter. Nor did she see Robbie anywhere in the workshop. Puzzled, Linnet bent down to scratch the hound's large head, scanning the shadows as she did so. "Robbie? Are you here, laddie? You've no need to hide from me."

Although he didn't answer her, a slight rustling noise in the far corner revealed his hiding place. Robbie sat on the floor, beneath a table, his small form barely visible in the deep shadows.

More puzzled still, Linnet closed the short distance between them and knelt on the earth floor. Despite the dimness, 'twas plain to see the boy was much distressed. He'd drawn his knees to his chest, wrapping his arms tightly about them. To her dismay, he kept his face averted.

But what troubled her most was the way his shoulders shook. Robbie was crying, and his silent tears rent her heart in two. Edging forward, she reached under the table and tried to touch the lad's arm, but he ignored her and continued to cower against the wall.

"Robbie, lad, what's happened? Will you not come out and tell me what's troubling you?"

A muffled sniffle came in reply, but he did twist around to glance at her. Pity seized her at the sight of him, his eyes red-rimmed and swollen, his cheeks pale and wet with tears.

Thinking only to comfort him, Linnet snatched him to her, cradling his trembling body against hers. As gently as possible, she smoothed her hands over his dark hair, then used the edge of her apron to dab the moisture from his cheeks. "What ill has befallen you, laddie? Tell me, for I promise it canna be so bad as it seems."

He sniffled again and didn't attempt to speak, but the way he tightened his arms around her encouraged Linnet to keep probing. "Why aren't you with Sir Marmaduke?" she asked gently, stroking the back of her hand down his damp cheek. "'Tisn't this the hour he instructs you in handling a sword?"

"Uncle Marm'duke rode out with the patrol," Robbie blurted, swiping at his eyes as he spoke.

Uncle Marmaduke? Linnet tucked that interesting bit of information into the back of her mind for later clarification and concentrated on discovering what ailed the boy. "If you dinna have a lesson this morn, what are you doing about so early?"

Again, silence answered her. But the anguished look in his dark blue eyes, eyes so very like her husband's, was all the clue she needed to know something had hurt him sorely.

Of a sudden, Mauger nudged her from behind, almost knocking her off-balance as he came forward to rest his great dome-shaped head upon Robbie's lap. The old dog whined pitifully, staring up at Linnet with mournful brown eyes as if begging her to ease his young master's pain.

"'Twould please Mauger if you'd tell me what's

amiss," she tried, resting one hand upon the dog's shoulder. "There's no one here but he and I, and you know how much we both love you."

Fresh tears sprang to Robbie's eyes, but he nodded and began to speak. "I went to the kitchen 'cause Fergus said Cook was baking spiced cakes and . . . and . . ."

"And?"

"A few of Cook's helpers were lighting the fires and I heard them talking. They said you would give Papa a new son and then . . ." Robbie drew a great, shuddering breath, then seemed to crumple in her lap. His next words came out in a rush, ". . . and then he'd ne'er want me at all."

Linnet's heart twisted, his fears lancing her very soul. Taking his face between her hands, she forced him to look at her. "Hear me well, child, for what I say is true: Your father loves you more than his own life. Do not ever doubt it, nor that you *are* his son. Have you forgotten what I told you the day we met his half brother in the woods?"

Robbie shook his head but looked far from reassured.

"Good. All ken you are your father's son. I saw it, too, when first I laid eyes upon you, and I've told you 'tis only the truth I see in such a way."

She paused, getting to her feet and drawing Robbie up with her. She also searched for the right words and when she found them, she placed her hands firmly on his shoulders.

"'Tis hard, I know, but mayhap the saints wish to strengthen you so you'll be better able to face the responsibilities of being next laird. Those above ne'er give us heavier burdens than we can bear." Stepping back from him, she crossed her arms. "If e'er I am blessed with a babe, 'twould be a brother or sister for you to love . . . a child who would naught but love you. And respect your place as future laird."

"But why can't we tell Papa?"

For the first time, Linnet doubted the wisdom of keeping such a secret. But her sixth sense told her 'twas the only way, and never had her instincts led her falsely.

"Because," she began, hoping he'd understand, "your father must find the truth himself. 'Tis a powerful ache he carries within, and only he can heal it. If we tell him, we'll be taking away the lesson the saints have ordained he must learn. Does that make sense to you?"

Robbie hesitated, digging at the hard-packed dirt floor with the toe of his shoe. "Do you think it will take him long to learn that lesson?"

"Nay, I do not, for your papa is a well-learned and wise man," Linnet assured him, praying to the heavens above not to prove her wrong.

At Robbie's age, a mere sennight 'twould seem like forever.

"You think Papa is wise?"

"Oh, aye, I do," she agreed, pleased when the lad stood a bit straighter upon hearing her words. Even Mauger's ears perked up as if the old hound understood her. "'Tis well-known he's the mightiest of Highland warriors, too. The most revered in all the land. I'd heard of his daring feats in battle, of his valor, long afore he brought me here."

A pink stain tinged Robbie's cheeks and he took his lower lip between his teeth. Then, looking sheepish, he said, "But you're a MacDonnell. How would you know?"

Her heart swelled at the way the lad instinctively puffed out his chest, pride in his MacKenzie heritage replacing his earlier distress.

"'Tis likely there are none who do not know of him," she said, gently tugging his tunic into place over his hose. "A grievance, even a long-standing one as betwixt our clans, doesna mean they hear naught of each other. Many are the traveling minstrels who sing your father's praises, as they sang of his father before him."

"Have you heard them sing of my papa?" Robbie asked, his voice full of awe.

"More oft than I welcomed," she told him, a wry grin curving her lips. "The courage and spirit of the MacKenzie men is legend, and no matter what plaid a man flings o'er his shoulder, 'tis not a Highlander worthy of the name who willna respect another man's valor, enemy clan or nay."

"Do you think the bards will e'er sing about me?"

"I know they will." She tousled his silky dark hair, then slipped her hand under his chin, lifting his face so she could glory in the hope she saw there. "'Tis a tall legacy you must follow, Robbie, but I dinna doubt you'll make a fine laird one day."

He seemed to grow taller before her eyes, but Linnet could see something still troubled him. "I am sorry I cried," he blurted. "Men dinna cry."

"And who told you that?" Linnet peered intently at him. "'Tis only a very brave man who is not afeared to show he cares."

At that, Robbie rushed forward and threw his arms

around her legs. "I am so happy you're here," he said, gazing up at her, the ardor in his words melting her heart.

"'Tis glad I am too," she admitted, speaking the truth she couldn't deny. Despite everything. "Would you like to help me sow a bed of cabbage seeds?" she asked, changing the subject. "A future laird must ken the workings of his castle just as he must learn to wield his sword and lance. So, will you assist me?"

Robbie nodded. "But . . . will you . . ."

"Will I what?" Linnet queried, gathering her supplies from the worktable.

He shot her a shy look. "Will you teach me to throw a dagger the way you threw yours at Uncle Kenneth?"

Linnet laughed and plunked a small sack of cabbage seed into Robbie's hands. "Aye, lad, I shall teach you that and more."

Then she opened the workshop door, holding it wide so the boy and his dog could step out into the morning sunlight. She followed close on their footsteps, the flagon of Sir Marmaduke's elixir tucked away in her purse, totally forgotten.

It wasn't until after vespers and a light repast of pickled herring, bread, and wine, that Linnet remembered the special herbal remedy she'd concocted for the Sassunach.

He'd never be soothing to look upon, but her remedies seemed to be working well, and with a lessening of the swelling and a diminishing of the redness, traces of the handsome man he'd once been were becoming visible.

His gratitude had been immediate, and he'd been

presenting her with flowers, or ewers of the finest wine nigh onto every day since she'd first offered to help him.

But none of the gifts he'd showered upon her had pleased her more than when she'd come upon him two days past, bent over the outside well, carefully examining his reflection in the circle of water. Not wanting to embarrass him, she'd slipped quietly back inside the keep, but not before the pleased expression on his ravaged face had sent a warm glow spreading through her.

From behind her, the unexpected sound of clanking metal made her spin around, and she gasped in surprise at the sight of Fergus. The bandy-legged old seneschal stood before her garbed in a rusty mail shirt much too large for his scrawny bones. The much-used gear appeared more ancient than he himself.

He carried a sword in one hand, a mace in the other. Linnet doubted he had the strength to use either, but the fierce set of jaw warned that *he* felt he could.

"Fergus," she cried, "whate'er are you about so armed?"

He puffed out his chest as best he could under the ill-fitting hauberk. "'Tis on my way to make my round of the walls, I be, lady. With our laird and the Sass—, I mean Sir Marmaduke, on patrol, 'tis my duty to see to your safety and that of all within."

Linnet couldn't bite back a smile. "Aren't the sentries keeping watch?"

"Aye, and well they should be." He fixed her with a hawklike stare. "They ken what will happen if I find them away from their posts."

"But . . . I've never seen you armed thusly." Linnet

tried to keep her voice earnest. "Do you truly expect trouble?"

The old man glanced furtively about, his sharp gaze probing the vastness of the great hall as if he thought the apparition of Edward Longshanks and his mounted knights would sally forth out of the shadows and fall upon them any moment.

"Nay, milady, dinna fear. 'Tis only"—his voice dropped to a whisper—"if the bastard Kenneth discovered your husband and Sir Marmaduke be both gone, 'tis evil and daring enough he be to launch an attack."

"And you want to be prepared to stand upon the battlements and defend the castle."

"Aye." He answered solemnly. "'Tis still a good sword arm I have."

"I'm sure you do," Linnet conceded, her smile genuine, for she admired his devotion and valor. Were Dundonnell faced with a siege, her sire would have taken to his bed with a generous supply of ale.

He nodded respectfully. "By your leave, lady, I shall be on my way," he said, turning to mount the stairs to the battlements.

"Wait, please, sir," Linnet stayed him, remembering the flagon she still carried in her purse. "I've made an elixir for Sir Marmaduke and would like to leave it where he'll find it when he returns. I've heard he has a chamber of his own. Can you tell me where it is?"

"I can, and 'tis a new chamber he has." A gleam appeared in the seneschal's eye, making him look years younger. "He's taken your liege husband's old quarters . . . now that our good laird sleeps elsewhere."

Linnet thanked him, grateful the dimness of the hall

shielded the blush warming her cheeks. She waited until Fergus disappeared around the first curve in the stairwell, then hastened to Duncan's solar.

'Twas well she remembered the austere room where they'd had their unpleasant altercation the night of her arrival. Her husband's former bedchamber had to be beyond the closed door she'd noted in a corner of the solar.

Not that she must deposit the flagon *there*. She needn't intrude into the sanctity of her husband's former sleeping chamber. The adjoining solar would serve as well.

A short while later, upon entering the small room, she immediately noted the changed atmosphere. That her husband no longer used the solar was glaringly apparent. The air of grim severity she'd sensed upon her first visit was gone.

Now, the chamber seemed warm and welcoming. A finely carved chessboard sat atop the small table, and cushions adorned the window seats and single chair. Even the colors of the wall tapestries appeared brighter, despite the grayness of the damp night darkening the tall windows.

And this time the oaken door in the far corner stood ajar.

Staring at it, an irresistible urge to view Duncan's former bedchamber seized her, curiosity propelling her forward. She withdrew the flagon from her purse as she went, telling herself she could place it upon the bed, grasping any excuse to sanction an intrusion into her husband's privacy, and Sir Marmaduke's.

At the door, she paused to draw a deep breath. Although convinced of the innocence of her errand, and the urgency of her need to see where Duncan had spent a goodly number of hours, her knees shook and her heart knocked against her ribs.

Then, before she could change her mind, she eased the door completely open and stepped into the dark chamber.

The room's chill brought gooseflesh to her skin, and she rubbed her arms vigorously to warm herself. But she attributed the cold to the stiff wind rattling the window shutters and the rain pelting the tower walls.

'Twas unnaturally dark because of the storm raging outside yet here, too, the Sassunach's benevolent presence had already left its mark.

Still, something bothered her.

Gradually, her eyes adjusted to the murkiness and her gaze was drawn to the massive bed across from where she stood. 'Twas the most magnificent bed she'd ever seen. It boasted a great embroidered canopy and heavy curtains of a sumptuous material she supposed was fustian.

Vaguely, she became aware of other furniture, equally fine and noble, but the bed called to her, not releasing her until she crossed the room and tested the thick softness of its several feather mattresses with her hand.

'Twas like touching a cloud.

At the thought, an image of her husband, naked and laboring atop a dark-haired woman whose face she could not see superimposed itself upon the richly embroidered coverlet. Crying out, Linnet snatched her hand from the bed. Her fingers burned and tingled, smarting as if she'd thrust her hand into a bucket of hot coals.

Anxious to leave the bedchamber, and the unholy memories it housed, she wheeled around, only to cry out once more.

Directly before her, mounted above the hearth, was the painted likeness of a beautiful woman.

The one from her brief vision.

With sickening dread, and even though she hadn't seen the woman's face, Linnet knew the painting was of *her*.

Cassandra.

Her husband's first wife.

Linnet's breath stocked, and her chest grew painfully tight, aching as if a heavy weight pressed against her, squeezing the life from her.

With a dull thud, the little flagon slipped from her fingers and a keening wail filled the chamber, making her fear Lady Cassandra's shade had manifested behind her . . . until she realized 'twas her own cry she'd heard.

Never had she seen a more exquisite creature. Not even the shadowy chamber could detract from the woman's radiance. She was sheer perfection, her tresses expertly coifed and gleaming like black silk, her face, hauntingly beautiful.

Whilst a moment before Linnet's heart had fair stood still, it now lurched out of control, thumping wildly against her chest. And the breaths she'd had diffi-culty taking now came in deep, shaky gulps.

The lady Cassandra had been everything she was not and never could be.

If a mere painted image could exude such grace and elegance, she could only imagine the splendor of the liv-ing woman. As Linnet stared at her predecessor, a sick feeling roiled and churned in her stomach until she was sure she'd lose her supper.

Unable to resist making comparisons, she glanced from the woman's elegant gown to the plain brown kirtle and apron she herself wore. She'd worked too long in the herbarium to change before hurrying to the hall to dine.

Feeling more a peasant's wife than a laird's, she smoothed her work-stained apron, then wished she hadn't, for she couldn't help but notice how stubby her fingers appeared compared to Lady Cassandra's slim and delicate-looking ones.

How could she have thought to seduce her husband by smoothing such clumsy hands over his magnificent body?

How could she have thought the tenderness he'd shown her in the garden this morn had meant aught?

How could she have believed he might be beginning to care?

Her heart wrenched at her naïveté. Ne'er could she replace the beautiful woman who had claimed his heart first.

With excruciating clarity, Linnet suddenly understood why he'd shunned her as a true consort. The consummation of their marriage, an event she still couldn't recall, must've cost him dearly.

A convulsive sob escaped her, and she fell to her knees before the hearth, gripping her middle as she fought to swallow her anguish rather than cry before her foe. Wood and paint or nay.

Finally, as naught but quiet whimpers escaped her lips, Linnet looked again at the woman's likeness. Tears blurred her vision, but not so much she didn't notice the change.

Whether caused by her imagination, the poor lighting, or her gift playing a cruel trick on her, the painted image was no longer smiling so sedately.

Lady Cassandra, her husband's stunningly beautiful first wife, appeared to be gloating at her.

10 ◆

Her cloak wrapped tightly about her, Linnet stood atop the battlements and tried hard to remain impervious to the chill bite in the damp and briny air. Far below, a group of poor burghers crossed the castle bridge on their way back to the village.

For three days she'd kept herself busy observing their comings and goings, used the distraction to chase the sneering visage of Duncan's first wife from her mind.

At first only a few came, barely a trickle, as if still wary of the dread laird of Eilean Creag. But, gradually, their numbers increased until at times a steady stream of them paraded back and forth across the narrow stone bridge.

All come to collect alms at the castle gates . . . as was custom.

And her liege husband was still absent and could not see this small victory she'd won for him.

A strong gust of sea wind tore back her veil suddenly and she shook out her tresses, not caring how wet or wind-tossed she appeared.

The saints knew, her looks mattered scarce little. She could plait her hair with spun gold ribbons and dress in a gown fashioned of moonbeams, and Duncan would still find her unappealing.

And how could she blame him?

What man would desire *her* when he'd possessed a woman so beautiful a queen would be covetous of her?

Nay, her appearance was of no consequence. But she wished Duncan had seen the return of the needy to his castle door. Mayhap their show of trust would erase some of the darkness from his soul?

Truth to tell, though, she wasn't sure it would make a difference. Perchance the wounds beneath the grim mask he oft wore were already too deep.

Too raw.

Too solid, the wall he'd built to protect himself.

Yet he'd allowed her fleeting glimpses of the man within.

"Will you not come inside, milady? 'Tis a fierce storm approaching," Lachlan entreated, coming up beside her. "My master will flay me alive if you fare ill, and he learns I could not dissuade you from bringing harm upon yourself."

"'Tis good of you to be concerned, but my cloak keeps me fair dry and my hair matters naught." Linnet gave her husband's first squire a wan smile. "As yet, 'tis only a light rain and does not bother me."

Lachlan glanced at the roiling black clouds racing ever closer across the loch. "I beseech you, lady, for my lord would indeed be mightily displeased, and I would not seek to foul his temper so soon upon his return."

And when is his temper not foul? Linnet swallowed the bitter retort dancing on the edge of her tongue, grateful the shrill cries of a passing flock of seabirds prevented her from taking out her frustration on the well-meaning squire.

Instead, she laid her hand gently on his sleeve and shook her head. "Nay, Lachlan, I fear you place too much importance upon my worth to your liege. We are alone and 'tis old enough you are to ken why he married me. He will not care if the ague takes me, nor will he punish you if I dinna do as you bid."

The squire shook his head. "I beg your pardon in disagreeing, but you are mistaken. Sir Duncan cares deeply for you."

Turning away, Linnet clutched the cold stone of the parapet wall. "Please do not speak that which is not true. 'Tis cruel and, I would have thought, beneath you."

"My words are not lies. I swear it upon all the holy relics in the land," Lachlan implored her, his tone sincere enough to make Linnet's heart skitter out of beat. "'Tis naught but the truth and all know it."

All save your laird. Her own truth echoed in her head, mocking her with the futility of Duncan mayhap caring for her yet not knowing it himself. Pressing her palms more firmly against the cold, wet merlon, she wanted to cry out at the hopelessness of her situation.

Even if she did believe Lachlan, and she wasn't sure

she should, she still didn't know how to breach the walls her husband held against her.

How to win his heart.

A heart she feared rested in Lady Cassandra's grave.

"Lady, please," Lachlan urged again, "do not think I tell falsehoods, for I would rather be struck dead than lie to you."

Unable to resist the squire's chivalrous tone, Linnet turned back to face him. "Are all MacKenzie men, save my husband, gifted with silver tongues?"

Lachlan's handsome young face flushed pink, and he made her a slight bow. "So it is claimed, but I am not a MacKenzie. I am a MacRae. My father sent me here to be fostered when I was but seven."

"More than enough time to learn their ways," Linnet teased, amazed the squire's glib charm had raised her mood. Soon, she'd be as addlepated as Elspeth, hearing naught but pretty words, no longer capable of seeing the truth.

Linnet lifted her chin a notch. She'd not make a fool of herself as Elspeth did, fawning after old Fergus, making moon eyes at him. But, then, the crusty seneschal seemed to welcome Elspeth's attention.

She could not say the same of her husband.

He'd simply shown her the same concern he'd have over anyone within his domain.

"Tell me, Lachlan," she asked, before she could lose her nerve, "Why do you think Sir Duncan cares for me?"

"Allow me to escort you inside, lady, and I shall explain," he said, offering his arm.

Linking her arm through his, Linnet couldn't help but smile. "I see you are clever as well as chivalrous."

"My master teaches me well," he said, guiding her toward the tower door, which stood ajar.

He did not speak again until he'd escorted her to her chamber. After opening the door with an exaggerated flourish, he made her a sweeping bow, then, before she could guess his intent, he seized her hand and brought it to his lips.

"The answer to your question is obvious to those who know my master well," he said upon releasing her hand. "You have only to observe how his face tightens, as if becoming a mask, whene'er he comes upon Robbie."

Her brows drew together in a frown. "I do not understand."

"Do you not? Truly?" One of the squire's brows shot upward in a perfect imitation of her husband's frequent gesture.

"Nay, unless—" a sudden thought, nay . . . hope . . . popped into her mind, but she didn't dare voice it lest she be wrong.

"Aye, milady," Lachlan fair laughed, a wide grin spreading across his face, proving he'd read her thoughts. "Duncan loves Robbie dearly, but is too blinded by anger and pain to realize it. Yet we all do. When he looks upon you, 'tis the same expression he wears when he looks at his son."

Linnet opened her mouth to speak, but she couldn't get the words past the hot lump swelling in her throat. Tears sprang to her eyes, blurring her vision, but she managed to give Lachlan a tremulous smile.

Smiling back, he laid a hand on her shoulder. "Now do you understand?"

"I . . . want . . . to," she stammered.

"You must," he told her, stepping back, his tone and expression serious once more. "For only by understanding him can you heal him. 'Tis the one thing he's never had and needs the most."

Linnet nodded, wishing she could reassure the young man, but how could she make promises she doubted she'd be able to fulfill? Understanding what troubled her husband wasn't difficult.

Knowing what to do about it, was.

And far more difficult was believing he cared for her.

Lachlan had to be mistaken.

Long after the squire had rekindled the fire in her hearth and left her on her own, Linnet stood gazing into the flames. She watched them grow and lick around the firelog, their crackling, and the distant rumble of thunder, not near so loud as the thudding of her heart.

If only she could warm Duncan's soul as easily as the flames warmed her outstretched hands.

If only she could ignite his passions.

If only Lachlan's words were true.

But she'd been too long alone, too long unloved to dare hope.

'Twas late when Duncan and his men returned from patrol, and later still when he finally made his way up the circular stairs to his wife's bedchamber.

He would've gone immediately after downing a welcome draught of ale in the hall, but Marmaduke had barreled back down the stairs from whence he'd retired shortly afore, predicting doom and despair if Duncan sought his wife's presence without first consulting with him.

Tired and irritable, Duncan had waited for the Sassunach to speak. His patience was thin, for he was eager to join his lady wife in bed.

And not merely to sleep, but to partake of the tender ministrations she wasn't aware he knew of.

But instead of speaking, his friend handed him a flagon, telling him where he'd discovered it.

No other explanation had been necessary. With a growing sense of dread deep in his gut, Duncan understood: Linnet had ventured into his former bedchamber.

She'd seen the panel-painting.

Waves of hot anger and cold chills had washed over him in turns. Anger at himself because he hadn't destroyed Cassandra's likeness years ago, and chills at his brother-in-law's grim prediction of how looking upon it would affect Linnet.

As if from a great distance, Marmaduke's deep voice had droned on, advising him how best to approach his lady.

But Duncan had scarce listened. Only he knew of the sweet comfort she rained upon him each night, thinking he slept. His lady was good and pure, yet possessed of an inner fire and strength Duncan greatly admired. And she was . . . sensible.

Although his friend had meant well, Marmaduke had not the experience to know the heart of a robust and strong-willed Highland lass like Linnet. He'd been wed to Arabella, Duncan's sister. A high-spirited woman, beauteous and gay, as skittish and excitable as Linnet was earthy and unruffled.

And before Arabella had blossomed and captured Marmaduke's attentions, he'd dallied with the jaded ladies of the tourney circuit. Or the worldly women at the Bruce's court.

Aye, his friend knew women, but not Linnet. *She* wouldn't be distressed upon seeing his first wife's great beauty. Appearance mattered little to his lady wife. Such things were of no significance to her.

She'd be more upset to find her precious herbarium destroyed than to gaze upon the loveliness of a woman she knew to be dead.

But his confidence evaporated the moment he entered their bedchamber and saw her sitting before the fire.

She looked as though she'd been out in the rain the entire time he'd been away. Her hair fell loose about her shoulders and was badly snarled from the storm winds, while her gown was wrinkled and damp, the leather of her shoes dark with waterstains. Only the worn *arisaid* she clutched about her appeared to be dry.

"By the Rood, woman, must I watch over you every minute?" Duncan asked sharply, forgetting the bland words he'd meant to utter before slipping into bed to await her sweet explorations of his body. "What have you done to yourself?"

"I . . . I have been—"

"I ken where you've been." He strode toward her, holding the little flagon in his outstretched hand.

Her eyes widened, but she said not a word, only gaped at him from troubled eyes.

"Have you naught to say?" Duncan prodded, leaning

so close he could smell the sea brine in her wildly tangled hair.

But for once she didn't spout pepper at him. She only shook her head and stared at the fire. Why didn't she speak up for herself, show him the vinegar she'd exhibited nigh onto every day since he'd first brought her to Eilean Creag?

Why didn't she revile him for pining for his dead wife?

Marmaduke had warned him that Linnet would believe he *was* pining and, as always, the one-eyed bastard had been right.

And he doubted Linnet would ever believe how far from the truth her assumptions lay.

Duncan swore, an oath blacker and more ominous than the storm-darkened night lurking beyond the thick tower walls. As if the heavens understood his frustration, a loud crack of thunder sounded, its resounding boom drowning out his curse. His wife jumped as if struck, but as quickly reassumed her rigid posture.

No doubt she'd jumped because of him, not the thunder.

Whether she'd heard his curses or no.

'Twas well aware he was of his untamed appearance. But *he'd* had reason to be out on such a night. He'd sought to ferret out Kenneth and his followers, banish them from his lands once and for all time. Hoped to send his half brother to the most vile abyss in hell for his many crimes.

But more, for his lady's sake.

To protect her from harm at Kenneth's hands.

Yet she shrank away from him as if *he* were the one to be feared.

Stepping close enough to tower over her chair, Duncan planted his hands on his hips and gazed down at her. "If you will not speak of what I know weighs on your mind, then tell me why you look as if you've been swimming in the loch."

"I did not leave the castle, sirrah," she snapped, showing a spark of her usual backbone. "I was on the battlements, watch—"

"That, too, I know, milady, for 'tis none under my roof what dinna tell me what wondrous feat you've accomplished." He paused to drag a hand through his own damp and disheveled hair. "I suppose their hunger has grown greater than their dread of a murderer."

Something flared briefly in his lady wife's eyes, and he couldn't tell if it'd been anger, frustration, or pity. He hoped it wasn't the latter, but whatever it'd been, she now sat ramrod straight in her chair, regarding him from eyes that no longer looked so haunted.

"And did you?" she blurted, piercing him with a gaze as all-seeing as his annoying arse of a brother-in-law's.

"Did I what?" Duncan shot back, fully aware of her meaning.

He grew rapidly uncomfortable under her sharp perusal. 'Twas *she* who now steered their discourse . . . and in a direction he did not care to venture.

"Did—I—*what*?" he repeated in a tone that would've warned a more prudent soul.

"Did you murder your first wife?"

Duncan's face flushed with heat at her blunt question, and his stomach tightened into a cold, hard knot. "What do you think?" The four words dropped between them like tiny chips of ice.

Faith, how he wished she'd abandon the cheek he'd yearned for only moments ago and return to her prior stubborn silence. The lass riled him more than any man should be made to endure.

"*You* are the seventh daughter. Can you not see the answer to your question?" he challenged, his temper barely in check.

She looked away then, and for a long moment, the rumble of thunder and soft popping of the fire made the only sound. Keeping her gaze averted, she finally said, "I already know the answer. Still, I should like to hear it from you."

"If you can see the answer to a matter of such gravity, why can you not divine if Robbie is my true son or nay?"

"That answer, too, will come in time, milord. And it was not my gift that told me you did not kill the lady Cassandra," she said, returning her gaze to his. "It was my heart."

"Then you canna know for sure, for hearts lie," Duncan contradicted.

"Nay, they do not," she said simply, folding her hands in her lap and peering up at him with that strange look in her eyes again.

Unable to stand her close scrutiny, Duncan turned away from her and crossed the chamber to the bed, shrugging off his drenched cloak as he went. His back to her, he drew his tunic over his head, then began removing his soggy shoes when she stayed him with one sentence.

Stiffening, Duncan asked her to repeat the softly whispered words he hoped he'd misunderstood.

"I said, actions dinna lie either."

"What actions?" *Not that he wanted to know.*

"The action of a bereaved man keeping his dead wife's likeness in his bedchamber," she said, her tone as bland as if she were commenting on the rain hammering against the shutters.

Duncan crossed the room in a heartbeat. He grasped the arms of her chair so tightly it wouldn't have surprised him if the heavy oak had snapped in twain beneath his fingers.

Leaning forward until he could taste her breath upon his lips, he said, "You cannot know why I kept the panel-painting, and I will not speak of it. I *will* tell you whatever tale you've conjured up as a reason 'tis untrue."

She gasped, pressing herself into the back of the chair, but keeping her jaw defiantly lifted, her injured gaze level with his furious one.

"God's blood, wench!" Duncan cursed, straightening. "Must you e'er vex me?"

"I understand, milord. Truly. I've never seen a more beautiful woman."

"You understand naught, do you hear me?" He grabbed her arms, pulling her to her feet. "Naught, I say!"

"You are hurting me, sirrah," she cried, and he released her immediately.

Rubbing her upper arms where he'd gripped her, she persisted, "But I do. It is not difficult to comprehend. At least why you haven't touched me since our wedding night. What I do not understand is how you can even bear to look upon me after being married to her?"

"Will you drive me to the brink of madness?" Duncan groaned, then closed his eyes, forcing himself to draw a long, calming breath.

When he felt able to speak again, he opened his eyes, determined to guide their evening to a swift and peaceful close. "'Tis tired and wet we both are, Linnet," he said, his voice surprisingly calm. "I am going to bed. I bid you to do the same." He paused for emphasis. "And remove those damp garments afore you join me. It suits no purpose for either of us to become ill."

Returning to the bed without sparing her another glance, Duncan rid himself of his shoes at last, then stripped off his braies until naught but the chill air of the room was next to his bare skin.

Hearing no telltale rustling of clothes, and heedless of his nakedness, he turned to face her. "If you are not out of those sopping rags and into bed by the time I've doused the candles, I swear I shall divest you of them myself."

She eyed him warily as he went about pinching the candlewicks, but made no move to rid herself of her rain-dampened garments. "My clothes are merely damp, not sopping, and I've no intent to remove them. I beseech you to leave me be," she said, her voice so low he barely heard her. "Please."

Duncan took two steps forward, then halted at the look on her face.

Gone, the brief flaring of temper, a condition he

much preferred . . . except now. In its place, she wore an expression he first thought to be shyness.

Yet such modesty made scarce sense for she'd slept fully unclothed beside him for many nights now.

And during those nights, she'd done deliciously wicked things to his senses, her innocent explorations arousing him more than the wiles of the most skilled harlot he'd e'er paid to lift her skirts.

Duncan stared hard at her, suddenly recognizing it was shame clouding her gold-flecked eyes, turning their normally enchanting color a dull brown.

Shame making her seem to shrink into herself as he strode forward again. And that knowledge sent a pointed shard of regret lancing through him, for he knew what had put the abashment on her face and self-doubt into her soul.

The all-knowing Sassunach had told him.

"And why can you not undress?" he queried, as if he must torture himself by hearing the words from her own lips. "What has changed since I left that you will no longer disrobe before me? 'Tis oft enough I've seen your naked flesh." He glanced briefly at his own nakedness, thankfully at rest. "As you have seen mine."

"Everything has changed." She turned her face away from him.

Biting back another furious oath, Duncan closed the distance between them and took her chin in his hand, forcing her to look at him. "Naught has changed save the foolishness you've allowed to overrule your good sense."

"Nay, 'tis my good sense that has opened my eyes to

the truth. The only foolishness I am guilty of is . . . is . . . having thought you could care for me."

He hadn't expected to feel such a painful stab of regret, but he did. By the Rood, he *did* care for her. He *desired* her, too. But the stirrings of his body were naught but lust. What man could lie still each night whilst a maid ran her gentle hands o'er his flesh and *not* quicken with animal need?

Aye, he cared, but not in the manner she wished.

Not in a romantic sense.

Such folly was best left for young squires like Lachlan, yet to earn their spurs.

Yet to have their hearts ripped out and trod into the dirt.

"I do care, lass," he said, hoping to soothe her. " 'Tis the highest regard I have for you. Think you I've not seen all you've done here? Now cease fretting o'er a dead woman who means naught to me, remove your gown, and come to bed."

Instead of having the effect he'd desired, his words only seemed to make her more miserable. And when, in frustration, he reached to help her undress, she pulled away from him, crossing her arms over her chest as if to ward off a demon straight from the bowels of hell.

"Dinna touch me," she warned. "I will not stand ungarbed before you again. You can do naught but compare me to the lady Cassandra yet . . . yet . . . there can be no comparison. I am not beautiful."

"Splendor of Christ!" Duncan fair exploded. "Did you not hear me say I care for you? Must I tell you I desire you, too? Is that what you wish to hear?" In one quick motion, he pulled her hard against his chest. " 'Tis true, do you hear? *I—desire—you!*"

"I do not see how you can."

"Damnation, but you try my patience," he said, wrapping his arms tightly around her. "Saints alive, lass, think you truly I've slept these past nights? What kind of a man do you hold me for that I could lie there, unfeeling, whilst you let your fingers roam all o'er my body?"

Her jaw dropped. "You knew?"

"Aye, I knew," he breathed, resting his chin atop her head and reveling in the warm, womanly feel of her. He smoothed his hands up and down her back, letting them roam lower each time until he cupped her lower buttocks and molded her so tightly against him she couldn't deny the evidence of his arousal. " 'Tis half-mad you've been driving me."

"And 'tis mad you shall make me, if you dinna release me at once." Her hands were flattened between them and she pressed hard against his chest. "Have you forgotten your own arrangement? Was it not you who said you did not wish a true consort?"

" 'Tis well I remember the words, but I believe I shall exercise my rights as laird and change my mind." He slipped one hand beneath the damp curtain of her hair and began caressing the nape of her neck.

"Mayhap you can run your hands o'er me now, whilst you ken I'm awake? Then I will not have to hide my arousal from you," he suggested, the idea borne to him on the pounding waves of intense need surging through his groin. " 'Twould be a much more interesting experience if I didn't have to feign sleep."

Her eyes widened, either from shock at his suggestion or from the deliberate intimacy of his slow-moving fingers upon the soft skin of her neck. She appeared more perturbed than pleasured, but Duncan couldn't pull his hand away. The heavy silkiness of her hair flowing so sweetly over his hand made retreat an impossibility.

As did the softness of her belly pressed so temptingly close to his fully charged shaft.

"So what say you, wife?" He let go of her and stepped back, opening his arms wide. "Would you care to explore me now?"

"Oh, nay, I could not," she breathed, the words scarcely audible over the loud patter of rain against the shutters.

"You can and you shall." Duncan curved his mouth into the seductive smile he'd used so successfully in the past, but she still gaped at him, clearly alarmed.

"Shall I prove it to you? Perhaps with a kiss?" he persisted, lowering his arms.

Her eyes sparked protest, but when Duncan stepped forward and grasped her shoulders, she merely stiffened but did not seek to jerk away as she had before. Encouraged, Duncan pulled her close and caressed first her shoulders and back, then her hips and sweetly rounded bottom until he felt her resistance lessen.

"Aye, I think I shall kiss you," he said, as her body reacted to his caresses. She grew soft and warm in his arms, almost seeming to melt into him despite the smoldering embers of anger still visible deep in her eyes. "One kiss, my lady, to prove the power of your passion."

Lowering his mouth to hers, he settled his lips over hers in a soft and gentle kiss that nearly cost him his last reserves of self-control. With all the restraint he could summon, he let his tongue ease her lips apart, and gradually deepened the kiss until a breathy little sigh escaped her.

Satisfied, Duncan eased the kiss to an end. He framed her face between his hands and rested his forehead lightly against hers. "That wasn't so painful now, was it?" he asked, still reeling from the sheer sweetness of her lips. "'Tis my desire to kiss you all the night through, sweeting. *All of you*."

"Nay . . . please, sir," she protested, her breath soft and warm against his skin, the way her body melted into his giving bold lie to her spoken words of denial. "Dinna do this."

"Do you fear me?" Duncan hated to ask, but he had to know. Fire in his loins or nay, he would leave her be if she feared his touch.

"Nay, sir, I do not," she said, and the heart Duncan wasn't supposed to have, soared. "I have told you why I am not desirous of your attentions." She met his gaze full on, her voice surprisingly firm. "I will not compete in a battle I have no fair chance of winning."

Duncan bit back the dark invective that rose in his throat. "There never was a battle, lass, and if there had been, you would have won."

As tenderly as he could, Duncan set her away from him. Her pulse fluttered wildly at the base of her throat, and the sight of it made him vow to take her gently, to use restraint. With an iron will, he pushed aside his own misgivings, his reluctance to breach his self-imposed pledge of monkishness, and concentrated on winning his lady wife's trust.

That she no longer tried to bolt away from him, emboldened him much, but she'd surely go scrambling for cover if he unleashed the full fury of the passion she stirred in him. Never had he kissed a woman with such tenderness, never had it been more difficult to hold himself back.

But if he meant to thoroughly pleasure her, and he did, he must proceed slowly and make use of every scrap of knowledge he possessed about seduction. Duncan resisted a bitter laugh at the thought. Whatever such skills he'd e'er made use of, was long ago and all but forgotten.

Concentrating, he delved deep into his past, to the distant time before Cassandra. Slowly, bits and pieces came back to him, but they were fleeting and too elusive to grasp, drifting away before he could make any use of the memories he'd deliberately suppressed.

Then he remembered something his king had once shared with him. The Bruce had sworn that *speaking of love* primes a lass faster than all else. A slow smile curved Duncan's lips. Aye, he'd follow his liege lord's advice and woo his lady wife with words.

Feeling more pleased with himself than he had since entering the chamber, nay since *years*, Duncan took one of his wife's hands and smoothed it languidly down his chest. Encouraged when she didn't attempt to withdraw from his grasp, he began to guide her hand in slow circles, letting her feel the texture of his skin, the contours of his muscles.

A sudden, loud crack of thunder shook the window shutters and a burst of lightning lit the chamber, its eerie whitish silver glow lasting just long enough for Duncan to see Linnet had closed her eyes and parted her lips.

As if awaiting, *desiring*, another kiss.

His loins tightened at her increasing responsiveness. Very gently, lest he break the spell he felt stirring between them, Duncan brought her hand to rest against his pounding heart. "Can you feel how you make my blood race? Do you like the feel of me beneath your hand?" he asked, his voice husky. "Is touching me pleasing to you?"

She hesitated, then nodded.

'Twas not a vigorous nod, but it'd been one just the same.

"Would you like to touch all of me?"

She almost nodded, but stopped mid-nod and turned her face away. Duncan could almost feel the furious heat of her blush.

"You've no reason to be shy with me, Linnet," he said, smoothing the backs of his fingers down her cheek. "I will never ask you to do aught you do not wish to do." Taking her chin between his fingers, he turned her face back to his. "But you have learned you can enjoy touching me whilst I'm awake, have you not?"

Duncan narrowed his eyes at her, trying to hold her captive with the power of his gaze. "And you are enjoying this, are you not?"

"Aye," she admitted after another long moment's hesitation.

A tremendous feeling of triumph coursed through Duncan. "Would you deny me the same?"

Taking her lower lip between her teeth, she slowly shook her head.

"Good. Then shall we finally have done with your damp garments?"

She still looked uncertain, nay, *embarrassed*, but she removed her *arisaid*, then raised her arms to accept his aid with the rest. At her acquiescence, the pull at Duncan's groin became unbearable. Fighting hard to keep a hold on his mounting passion, he made haste to rid her of her gown.

When at last he'd drawn her thin undertunic from her body, his need raged sharper than ever before. The sight of her, standing naked before him, freed to his gaze, and not attempting to shield herself, nearly undid him. He knew it was hard for her to remain still, arms at her sides, whilst his gaze raked over her.

Yet she did, and her very willingness to comply with his wishes despite her unfounded shame awakened a deep and primitive need he'd thought long dead.

The need to truly please a woman.

And to be as one with her.

Her unassuming manner, so innocent and pure, so very *uncontrived*, stirred to life something buried deep within him. The devil might take him for being a fool, but he even suspected she desired him.

Truly wanted him.

Something akin to happiness pumped through him at the possibility. An empowering and uplifting sensation that sent a portion of his pain tumbling away, freeing him, and shining a beacon of light into the darkest region of his soul.

A wondrously giddy, pleasure-laden feeling as powerful and deep-reaching in its emotional intensity as the sharp pull at his groin was fiercely carnal.

An unfamiliar emotion he'd not thought to experience, had never hoped to achieve. Not with Linnet, not with any woman. So soundly had his first wife crushed the dreams of his youthful heart.

Never truly enjoying passion, she'd taken her pleasure in the knowledge her beauty and uninhibited sexual appetites was a potent enough mix to make him, or any man who caught her eye, crave her lascivious charms.

Yet just *gazing* at his new lady, so unaffected and innocent, aroused him more than Cassandra's practiced wantonness ever had.

His comely Linnet with her rounded curves and fire-bright hair stirred him so, even the thought of *her* could no longer chase away his desire.

Drinking in his wife's lush enticements, so different from Cassandra's sleek form, Duncan swallowed hard, his mouth gone dry with need.

How had he ever thought his first wife's slender body so desirable? Not once had she enflamed his blood the way Linnet did. Ne'er had he yearned to love Cassandra as sweetly, as thoroughly, as he meant to pleasure Linnet. As if testing the strong attraction he felt for her, Duncan fastened his gaze onto the luxuriant nest of red-gold curls at the juncture of her shapely thighs.

Saints, but he ached to touch her there, to build her passion with his fingers, then feast upon her sweet woman's flesh with his lips and tongue until she moaned her bliss, fully consumed by the thundering release he meant to give her. Only then would he slake his own lust.

Sharp bolts of white-hot longing shot through him at the mere thought of all the ways he wanted to pleasure her. The urgency of his need gripped him so strongly he felt it clear to the tips of his bare toes. If he didn't take his ease soon, he would burst asunder.

"Sir," his lady's voice cut through the haze of his passion. "Do you still mean to kiss me again?"

His brows rose in surprise, but, truth to tell, her directness pleased him and fired his blood even more. "Aye, I do," he said, his voice heavy with passion, his shaft so full, so eager, he could scarce speak. "I shall kiss you all the night through, and not just upon your lips."

She drew a sharp intake of air at his last words, and Duncan caught a fleeting glimpse of her tongue. 'Twas enough. Nay, too much. With a ragged groan, he pulled her into a savage embrace, slanting his mouth over hers in a hard, deep, and possessive kiss.

A kiss meant to hurl away the last vestiges of her doubts and awaken the ardor he suspected would burn as brightly as his own. Reining in his own desire as best he could, Duncan focused only on hers. He meant to assault her senses until she surrendered completely, and began assaulting his in return. He wanted full, total abandonment from her.

Proving the fire she possessed, her mouth suddenly opened wider beneath his and she boldly met the thrustings of his tongue, tangling hers with his in an erotic dance that sent the remaining shards of his restraint spiraling out of control.

Driven by urges more powerful than he'd ever known, he swept her into his arms and carried her to the bed. Without breaking their kiss, he used his shoulder to shove aside the bedcurtains and eased her down, careful not to crush her beneath his weight. For a long moment, he remained poised atop her, fair drowning in the honeyed nectar of her mouth, seared by the heat of her body, consumed by his burning need to possess her.

Their kiss became fevered, their very breath mingling as one until it seemed he'd lose his soul in the taste, feel, and scent of her.

And, might the saints help him, he wanted to!

Like a desperate man, too long starved of sustenance, he ravished her lips, slaking his thirst, his hunger, as one possessed.

She cried out in protest when finally he pulled away. "Dinna cease," she whispered, her soft plea going straight under his skin, gouging another hole in his defenses.

"I shall kiss you many times over this night, lady," Duncan said, smoothing his hands over and around the well-rounded globes of her breasts, reveling in the glory of them. "But first I shall give you the same pleasure you've given me. And this time 'tis my hands that shall do the roaming, *I* who shall explore. *You* shall lie back and allow me."

She seemed to melt, to soften, upon his spoken intent. Staring at him from eyes no longer a dull brown, now a rich, molten amber, she offered herself to him. Her thighs were still tightly pressed together, and she said not a word, but Duncan knew.

He had but to take and she would give.

His arousal at the sight she made, so temptingly displayed beneath him, and her willingness to accept his need, made him forget all else.

He pushed up to sit straddling her thighs, then stared down at her, devouring her with his gaze. Never had a woman been better suited for a man's ardor.

Never had a woman fired his passion more.

And never had he felt more helpless, more victim to the pulsing heat at his fevered loins.

Half-crazed with wanting her, and the need to go slow, Duncan brought his fingers to his lips and licked the middle finger of each hand, thoroughly wetting the ends of each. As she watched him, her sweet lips parting in growing desire, Duncan touched his moistened fingers to the hardened tips of her breasts.

A sharp cry burst from her lips at the contact. Pleased beyond measure, Duncan used the dampened tips of his middle fingers to lubricate her nipples with slow, little circles. Idly, he toyed with them, plucking gently, or simply grazing the tip of one finger back and forth over each taut peak until his wife's hips lifted off the bed, her woman's mound instinctively seeking the same aching pleasure he showered upon her aroused breasts.

Her hips began moving in a gentle rocking motion, and consciously or unconsciously, her thighs parted. When they opened wide enough for him to see all of her, the very last dredges of his ridiculous vows of abstinence flew, scattered to the four winds and swept away as thoroughly as if he'd tossed them into the full force of a raging summer gale. With a deep groan that started in his very bones, Duncan realized he was lost. Naught would keep him from having her.

Not now, not with her sweetness spread open so invitingly beneath him.

She was his wife.

He'd already taken her virginity.

Why should he deny himself pleasure? Or her?

Didn't she seem to crave his attentions? To abstain was nonsense and would serve no one.

The saints knew, he'd favor her well.

And teach her to favor him.

Theirs would be a lusty and enjoyable union. Mayhap he'd keep her abed for a sennight, pleasure her until she was limp with exhaustion and begged him to cease.

He'd give her his all . . . all except his love.

That, he could give no one, for he did not believe in such fool emotions. But he would give her pleasure.

Nights and nights of pleasure.

She tensed beneath him then, the rocking motion of her hips slowing, her legs stretched taut. The warm, musky essence of her arousal drifted up from her as she instinctively sought her release, the deep womanly scent nigh driving Duncan wild. Then she moved again and the silken flesh of her thighs brushed against his swollen sex. The contact, fleeting as it'd been, nearly caused him to spill his seed.

"I'm sorry, lass, I canna withhold myself much—" his words broke into a ragged groan as his lady rested two fingers against his lips.

" 'Tis as well, sir, for neither can I."

Locking her gaze with his, she arched upward, boldly rubbing herself against him, her body leaving no doubt of what she, too, needed. She opened her thighs to him, not quite fully, but in an invitation no man could deny.

Still, Duncan paused before he urged them wider. He searched her eyes, looking for fear and found none.

Only desire.

"It may hurt, once is not enough for a maid to accept

a man without pain," he cautioned, his voice deep with raw emotion and desire.

"It does not matter. I will not shatter," Linnet encouraged, her gaze steady on his. Then she closed her hand around the length of him, guiding him to her sweetness, arching her hips up to welcome him.

Duncan's control fled in an irretrievable rush at her touch, her show of complete and utter acceptance. Unable to deny himself any longer, he plunged deep inside her. Greedily, he took all she offered . . . including her virginity.

His heated shout of passion froze on his lips, blending with her sharper cry of pain even as he tore through the barrier he'd thought no longer existed.

But it had, and they'd both been duped.

The consummation of their marriage had ne'er taken place.

Until now.

11

Hellfire and damnation!

Duncan remained poised above his lady wife, frozen in place, afraid to even breathe lest he hurt her more.

Helplessly, he watched several fat tears leak from beneath her tightly closed lashes and roll down her cheeks, leaving silvery tracks in their wake.

"Sweeting," he breathed, his voice ragged. He stared down at her pulse, its rapid beat clearly visible at the base of her throat and saw how her lower lip trembled ever so slightly, the signs of her pain twisting his heart. "Linnet, I—"

Her eyes opened then, and she regarded him with a gaze the color of molten bronze. "Dinna say you're sorry. Please."

As tenderly as he could, he brushed the tears from her cheeks with the side of his thumb. " 'Tis only sorry I am that I've hurt you. For the rest, and the gift you've given me, 'tis grateful and awed I am."

Lifting her hand, she curled it around his neck, tangling her fingers in his hair. "The pain is not so great."

By the Rood, he'd meant to *seduce* her, not cause her pain no matter how sharp or small. He'd wanted simply to win her over with the prowess he'd once been so proud of.

And what had he done?

Stormed into her virginal sheath with all the finesse of a rutting stag!

In one out-of-control moment, he'd proven himself no better than the wild beast she seemed to hold him for at times.

"Lady, I do not believe you," he murmured against her temple. "But I promise you, ne'er shall you suffer the pain again. You wouldn't have this time, at least not so acutely, had I been more gentle."

But, saints have mercy on him, how could he have known?

He'd truly thought he'd taken her in a hippocras-induced haze on their wedding night.

Cautiously, Duncan began easing his still-swollen shaft from the tight heat of her body. His lady tensed at the movement, stiffening beneath him and the fleeting wince she hadn't been able to hide lanced his conscience with the sting of a newly sharpened sword.

Instantly, he froze, the tip of his manhood still within her, the warm silkiness of her woman's flesh intoxicating him, urging him to plunge back into the heated softness of her core.

Instead he swallowed an oath, remaining where he was, rigid and unmoving.

He opened his mouth to tell her he wouldn't mount her again lest absolutely certain she was ready for him, but she reached up to stroke his jaw, her fingertips sliding lightly over his lips, silencing him. "You could not have known, my husband. I, too, thought I was a maid no more."

A maid . . . a *virgin*.

His manhood throbbed, jerking at the very thought.

His *heart* melted.

Ne'er had he been the first with any woman. Not with Cassandra and certainly not with the paid bawds he'd used to assuage his need in recent years.

Truth to tell, he'd doubted virgins existed, had not expected his new bride to be one.

Hadn't even cared.

Yet now, as they lay joined together still, guilt at his clumsiness roiled through him, twisting his gut even as an incredible feeling of joy coursed through his veins.

A feeling so powerful, he wanted to race to the battlements and cry out in triumph.

Shout his gladness for all to hear.

For as surely as her virtue pleased him, the willingness she'd displayed in the moments before he'd plunged into her meant more.

Much more.

Her welcoming acceptance filled him with such happiness he felt as if some great hand had ripped aside a dark veil, allowing light to stream into the dark void he carried within.

His entire weight resting on his elbows, Duncan

feasted his eyes on her. She lay as if cut from marble, her beautiful eyes staring up at him, her full lips slightly parted, her cheeks still pale and damp from her tears.

The wan light seeping through the shutters cast a lustrous glow to her smooth skin, and the dying fire reflecting in the tangled mass of hair spread across the pillows, turning her tresses the color of dancing flames.

A dusting of freckles stood out against the creaminess of her skin, and he ached to kiss each and every one of them. He'd start with the ones sprinkled like stardust across the bridge of her nose and end with the ones adorning the swell of her wonderfully full breasts.

Duncan drew a deep, steadying breath, totally awed. Ne'er had he seen a more beautiful sight.

Ne'er had he desired a woman more.

And ne'er would he have believed he'd come so close to loving again.

"On my life, lady, I wouldn't have used you so roughly had I known," he breathed, lowering his lips to the warm skin of her neck. "But I . . . I thank you."

"'Tis *I* who am grateful," his wife said, her voice so soft and low Duncan doubted he'd heard her correctly.

Taking his full weight onto his arms, he pushed himself up, easing his manhood completely out of her. "What did you say?"

Rather than answer him, Linnet used the tip of her tongue to wet her lips. She gave him a shaky smile, then sighed and pressed her hand against his cheek. "'Twas naught I shall repeat, but I will ask why you pulled away." Her words were barely audible above the din of the storm outside. "'Tis a wondrous feeling, this, and I would that it does not cease." She smiled again, brighter this time. "I told you I would not shatter."

Deep inside Duncan, something swelled and *did* shatter. Another great portion of the wall around his heart. "You would that we go on?"

Her gaze steady on his, she nodded, then moved against him. The feel of her damp, intimate curls brushing against his shaft nearly drove him past the bounds of restraint.

"I must warn you, it will not stop hurting," he managed, his voice raw. "Not this time."

"I do not care," she said, the breathy sweetness of her voice undermining his control. "Let us continue so we can bring this time to completion, then do it again," she added, taking him by surprise. "For I should indeed like to experience this ... this *joining* ... without the pain."

Duncan's passion surged anew, his shaft swelling and lengthening as he slowly eased himself back inside her. She tensed, her fingers clutching his shoulders, her soft moans urging him on.

But still, he held back, not yet ready to guide her into the age-old rhythm her untried hips instinctively sought to find.

"Relax," he coaxed, his hand sliding over her breast, gently kneading her fullness as he spoke. "Let your knees fall farther apart and give yourself up to what you're feeling. I'll try not to hurt you."

Linnet did as he said, opening her thighs wider to accommodate him, trying desperately to relax as he said she should, to will the tenseness from her limbs.

She *wanted* to, for the sensations spreading through

her were almost too exquisite to bear, but doing so wasn't easy.

It *did* hurt.

Much more than she'd expected.

Yet the searing discomfort was of scarce import compared to the way he made her feel and the exaltation flooding through her since she'd glimpsed the truth of his desire for her.

Indeed, 'twas writ all o'er his face and in the tender way he moved within her.

". . . good, lass," she heard him say, his voice somehow distant, blurred by the haze of passion swirling around her.

"Open yourself a wee bit more," he urged, using his hands to gently ease her thighs farther apart. "Dinna worry . . . I'll withdraw immediately if you but ask."

"That I shall not do," she said, smoothing her hands over the broadness of his shoulders, glorying in the feel of his hard muscles working beneath her fingers.

Faith, how could he think she'd want him to stop?

She couldn't bear it if he did.

Not now, just when she was reveling in his acceptance of her as a woman.

The blatant need raging in the depths of his eyes, the urgency in his touch, the huskiness of his deep voice, his concern for her comfort, all went straight to her heart, fair overwhelming her with a powerful surge of emotion, the likes of which she couldn't begin to comprehend.

'Twas a glorious feeling, and she wanted to savor each moment it lasted, relish each touch, memorize the wondrous feel of him inside her.

Give herself up to the heady sensations he awakened

in her, enjoy the feel of his magnificent body joined to hers.

Indulge herself in the sheer intimacy of his maleness moving ever deeper into that most secret part of her.

Aye, simply knowing he wanted her . . . *her*, Linnet, the plain one, made her spirits soar so high she feared she might never come down again.

"Am I hurting you?" his voice came again, this time so close to her ear his warm breath sent a delicious shiver down her neck.

"Aye, it hurts," she told him true, "but dinna cease, for the rest of it makes up for the pain."

He raised up at that, looking down at her with a triumphant smile spreading across his face.

The first smile she'd ever seen that fully reached his eyes.

Then the smile faded, replaced by an expression of intense concentration and something else . . . a heavy-lidded, smoldering look that turned her very knees to jelly.

Without taking his eyes off her, he slipped his hand between her thighs, touching her . . . *there* . . . where their bodies came together so intimately. She couldn't help but gasp, her eyes widening.

A faint ghost of the smile returned, flickering knowingly across his lips as he began to move his thumb in a slow circular motion that made her moan, so intense were the sensations.

"Shhh," he urged, and she suspected he knew full well what his intimate ministrations were doing to her. "Dinna fight it. Let me pleasure you, lass. *Feel* me touching you."

Breathing rapidly, incapable of speech, she turned her head from side to side, squeezing her eyes shut, and raised her hips, pushing herself against his hand, ever closer to his roving fingers.

An exquisite throbbing began deep inside her, the sensation centering in her very core, then spiraling outward, filling her with a warmth and heaviness almost too sweet to endure.

She opened her mouth to cry out, but he captured her lips with his, smothering any sound she might have made with a deep and sensuous kiss.

Desperately seeking, struggling to reach some elusive goal hovering just beyond her grasp, Linnet opened her mouth wide beneath his, welcoming the silken stroking of his tongue. She melted against him, wanting, *needing*, more . . . *burning* for all he could give her.

As if he knew what she sought and meant to aid her, Duncan slipped his other hand beneath her hips, drawing her higher, ever tighter against him.

Then he increased the caressing motion of his thumb.

Linnet screamed and dug her fingers deep into his shoulders.

Unable to do more than cling to him, she let him sweep her into an abyss of such intense sweetness she wondered if she'd die of it—so powerful were the sensations whirling through her.

All else faded away. The bed and its cool sheets of linen. The fine embroidered coverlets and many silken pillows. Even the darkened chamber with its faint scent of still-smoking tallow candles and damp smell of rain . . . its very stone walls seemed to fall away, ceasing to exist.

Naught remained save the tempest building inside her.

A storm a thousandfold more potent than the one still raging outside.

Then its fury broke, releasing a flood of pleasure such as she'd not dared to dream existed. As if from a distance, she thought she heard Duncan call her name, but wasn't sure, for the fierce sensations surging through her had stolen her ability to hear aught but the rushing of her own blood, the pounding of her heart.

She lost control, was powerless but to let this wondrous feeling carry her to a place she wished she could stay forevermore.

But gradually she became aware of the damp sheets beneath her . . . and the heavy weight of her husband sprawled atop her. His heart pounded, too. She could feel its thudding against her breast.

She felt his gaze upon her, too.

Opening her eyes, a task that seemed a tremendous exertion, she found him staring down at her, his face mere inches from hers.

Raising himself on his elbows, he said naught, only lifted a brow.

Linnet didn't need her gift to ken what he wanted to know. She'd grown up around too many brothers not to recognize the look a man wears when questing for praise.

She tried to speak, then to smile, but was too drained to offer him more than the weakest of smiles.

"Did I hurt you?" he asked when she remained

silent, his self-satisfied expression leaving no doubt he already knew he hadn't.

Or at least not so much to keep her from enjoying what they'd done.

"Aye,—you—did," she gasped, her breath coming too hard and fast to get more than a few words past her lips. "At first."

"And then?"

"I think you know."

"Tell me." He rolled onto his back and took her with him, settling her securely into the crook of his arm.

"'Twas . . . ah . . ." she stalled, snuggling closer against his side. "I'll tell you I've learned why my sisters would e'er blush and grow silent each time I asked them about . . . things."

"What *things*?" he persisted, an irresistible gleam in his eyes.

Trailing the tip of one finger down his chest, Linnet said, "I vow you know, milord. You only wish me to say it."

"Aye, I do." He captured her hand and brought it to his lips, kissing each fingertip in turn. "And will you?"

"Must I?"

"Nay, but hearing the words would please me." He turned her hand, placing a soft kiss in the middle of her palm.

"Very well." Her cheeks flamed to speak of such intimate matters, especially while she quivered at the touch of his tongue flicking lightly across her hand and the base of her wrist. "'Tis the sort of . . . *things* . . . I feel when you touch me thusly."

"How thusly?" he asked, almost too softly. "Do you mean so?"

"Sir!" Linnet jerked when he gently rolled the crest of one breast between his thumb and middle finger.

Heat shot straight to her core, bringing back the intensely exciting feelings that had only just subsided. Her nipple hardened beneath his fingers, and the same, languid waves of pleasure began stealing through her all over again, making her go limp in his arms.

"I see your meaning, lady. Your lusty response speaks louder than your words."

She glanced at him, embarrassed and aroused at the same time. "Lusty? Me?"

"Aye, you, and I canna recall when a lass has pleased me more." He gazed deep into her eyes, stoking her passion by continuing to toy with her breasts as he spoke.

His hands on her, working such delicious magic, whilst he held her captive with the heat of his eyes was almost more than she could bear. "Sir, I dinna think I can—ohhh . . ." her words trailed off as he replaced his fingers with his lips.

When finally he raised his head, a slow smile spread across his usually stern features, and Linnet's breath caught in her throat at the sight.

She'd always suspected his smiles would be deadly, but never, until this very moment, had she guessed how breathtakingly handsome he truly was.

Even his half brother Kenneth, whose looks were so noble and fine, paled by comparison. How blind she must've been that day in the yew grove to think him the comelier of the two.

". . . and do you still doubt I find you desirable?"
His words came to her as if through a passion-induced
haze, a *spell* he seemed to have cast over her.

He'd bewitched her, turned her from a simple and
virtuous maid into a brazen wanton. His touch filled her
with longings so strong, so undeniable, she was wont to
scream if he didn't soon resume his stimulating attentions.

To feel thusly was beyond intoxicating.

"Is aught amiss?" he asked, his voice half-teasing.
"Have I not yet proven my ardor to you?" As he spoke,
he began caressing the sensitive skin of her belly, moving his fingers in slow, sensuous circles. "Do you require
more proof?"

"Yes, please," she blurted, feeling much the harlot,
but not caring.

"Then so be it. Many are the ways I can show you.
But first we shall bathe."

Sliding from the bed, Duncan drew the coverlet
carefully over her, so she wouldn't catch a chill. But,
were he completely truthful, he also sought to shield her
sweet body from him, if only for a few brief moments.

Just long enough to regain hold of his emotions.

Blood of Christ! *Emotions.* Duncan recoiled inwardly. He hadn't thought he possessed any, believed
himself incapable of falling prey to such foolhardiness.

Yet his lady's passionate response to him, her sheer
innocence and desire to please, had awakened a part of
his soul he'd much prefer to keep dormant.

Although he felt her gaze on him as he busied himself lighting a few candles, he didn't turn around and

wouldn't until his barriers were safely erected again—or at least bolstered a bit.

Kneeling to stoke the dying fire, he fought to brace himself against the maelstrom she'd unleashed within his hitherto well-guarded inner self.

'Twas positively frightening, the ease with which she'd made him forget he didn't want to care, to *feel* again.

His lady wife with her angel's smile and unbridled, wild-blooded passion, had brushed aside his defenses as if they were no more substantial than cobwebs!

By Saint Peter's tomb, the mere act of looking into her eyes, seeing the trust and adoration there, was enough to bring any man to his knees. For a man like himself, long shunned and feared by the fairer sex, 'twas a potent brew she stirred.

Duncan bit back a bitter oath.

He didn't *want* to be adored.

Trusted, aye. Desired in a carnal way, of a certainty. But not adored.

Not in the way *she* understood such things. Soon she'd be all misty-eyed and talking of love if he did not tread carefully.

Lust was what he felt for her.

And all he meant to share with her.

Lust. Pure and simple.

Naught else.

So why did his infernal knees go weak when she turned those gold-flecked eyes on him? Why had it been so hard to pull himself from her arms just now?

Getting to his feet, he dusted the soot from his

knees, brushed a few clinging sprigs of meadowsweet from his calves.

Anything to prolong turning around.

By all that's holy, he'd only meant to fetch water and a cloth to cleanse the blood from her thighs, yet he'd found it nigh onto impossible to wrest himself from her side.

Worse, and by far the most dangerous aspect, was his inclination to climb back into bed with her now and simply hold her. Not take his ease again, but gently draw her into his arms and await the dawn with her curled against him.

Such desires could wreak more havoc than the strongest pull in a man's loins, cause more trouble than bedding a dozen willing wenches.

He wanted no part of such fool notions.

Duncan drew in a long breath. Linnet MacDonnell was more than he'd bargained for.

Much more.

She left him no choice but to banish the stars from her eyes, convince her she felt naught for him but lust. He knew he must lie and make her believe what had happened between them, what he hoped 'twould oft happen, was only of the flesh.

A need they shared and could reap much pleasure from, but one that had naught to do with love.

Pouring water into a small basin, Duncan only wished it wasn't so wretchedly difficult to convince himself. He set down the ewer. Scowling, he snatched up a few linen cloths, laid them over his arm, and steeled himself to face her.

Then he turned around.

His misgivings flew at him like a hoard of banshees the moment he saw her. She'd scooted up against the pillows, her naked skin gleaming, bathed by the soft glow of the rekindled fire.

Her hair spilled over her shoulders, even more tangled by their lovemaking, the peaks of her breasts poking through the silken strands.

Duncan's loins tightened in immediate response. It was all he could do not to cast aside the basin and towels, dash across the chamber like an untried and overeager squire, and fall upon her once more.

"By St. Columba's holy staff, woman, did I not cover you?" he said gruffly. "Do you want to catch the ague?"

"I dinna fall ill lightly," she said, that soft, dreamy look still on her face.

"Good. Then you willna take a chill when I wash you. And I would that we make haste about it, for 'tis weary I am and in need of sleep." The words came out more abruptly than he'd intended and her eyes widened in surprise.

"But . . . I thought . . . you said—"

"I ken what I said, but 'tis only a night's rest I desire now. I'm more tired than I realized." He deliberately avoided her eyes. The hurt he'd seen burgeoning there would've smote his heart if he'd had one. "There will be other nights for passion. A marriage of practicality need not be void of physical fulfillment. We can satisfy ourselves however oft if it pleases you. Lust—"

"Lust, sir, is the reason men seek out harlots," Linnet informed him, drawing the coverlet over her breasts. "It should not be a basis for a marriage."

"And it is not," Duncan countered, placing the basin on a small table next the bed. "Our union is based on my need for your sight as you well know." He paused to dip a cloth into the water, then carefully wrung it out. "But it is nowhere writ we cannot partake of physical love. I've shown you I desire you. I believe you enjoyed our coupling as well?"

She declined to answer him, and the injured look on her face dug into him like the tips of a thousand fire-heated daggers.

But as if ridden by the devil himself, he went on, "It will not be an unpleasant arrangement. 'Tis well suited we are for one another."

"And how so, sirrah? In the same manner as the bawd who barters her wares to any man in rut?" she asked in a cold, toneless voice.

Duncan swore beneath his breath. He'd extinguished the flame in her he'd so painstakingly kindled.

And he'd cast himself into a roiling sea of regret somewhere between heaven and hell.

In one short night, he'd coaxed her into her his arms, fair demanded a response from her, and when she gave it . . . what had he done?

Tossed her trust and adoration right back at her.

Even after she'd bestowed upon him the most precious gift a wife has to give, taken him closer to happiness than he'd e'er expected to go in this life.

Made him realize how easily he could fall in love with her.

And for that transgression alone, he had to temper the wild-hearted romantic dreams he knew swirled through her even now. Unlike his wife, he knew the danger of such folly. It was his task to spare them both later grief. Even if doing so was far from painless.

Saints, he'd become the heartless bastard the prattle-spreaders claimed him to be!

Striving to avoid the anguish he knew followed quick on the heels of love was one thing . . . hurting his new bride was another entirely.

He cursed himself for not having kept himself from her as he'd meant to do. But he hadn't expected her to tempt him so, couldn't have guessed she'd turn adoring gazes on him, thoroughly enchant him with her amber-colored eyes.

And he certainly hadn't thought himself capable of feeling so deeply.

Nor had he known this ridiculous farce he'd begun, this *pretending* to be unaffected by her, save for her bodily charms, would disturb him so.

Blood of Christ, but his conscience bothered him.

"Linnet, I—"

Lifting her hand, she made a quick, dismissive motion. "Please, sir, say no more. I believed you cared for me. Now I see exactly what it was you were after," she said, her voice cold and hard. "How silly of me to have thought otherwise."

"You do not understand. It isna—"

"You said you wished to bathe me for 'tis weary you are," she cut him off, snatching the damp cloth from his hand. "Dinna overexert yourself. I can wash myself and would rather. If you'll do me the kindness of turning around."

Duncan knew he should move away, but he couldn't take his eyes off her. She was so beautiful.

Holding the covers to her chin with one hand and clutching the washcloth with the other, she stared at him reproachfully. "I asked you to turn away."

Silently cursing himself, Duncan did as she bid and stood before the fire. Feeling more a bastard than his half brother, he stared in brooding silence at the flames.

Behind him, he heard the soft sounds of Linnet cleansing the traces of her virginity from her thighs. He remained standing where he was long after silence filled the chamber. Only when he was certain his lady slept, did he turn around. She lay with her back to him, the coverlet pulled high.

Duncan expelled a deep, ragged breath. On his life, he hadn't meant this night to end thusly.

But he had no one save himself to blame.

Stifling a curse, he lowered himself into a chair. The same one in which he'd spent most of his ill-fated wedding night.

12

Thunder rumbled in the distance, and the smell of rain seemed to seep through Eilean Creag's thick stone walls, permeating the great hall, making the cavernous vaulted chamber even more dank and cold than usual. 'Twas just before the hour of prime, and many of Duncan's men still slept soundly upon the rush-strewn floor.

Flickering light from the few wall torches lit at this early hour helped Duncan make his way through the darkened hall. Carefully, he picked his path around, or over, his slumbering men and headed straight for the high table where Sir Marmaduke sat staring into a pewter chalice.

Without uttering a word of greeting to the Sassunach knight, Duncan dragged back his chair and sat. Pointedly ignoring his friend, he tore off a chunk of bread, ate it, then washed it down with a hearty gulp of stale wine.

"And a good morrow to you, too," Sir Marmaduke

said, lifting his chalice in mock salute. "'Twas worse than I predicted, eh?"

Duncan took another sip of the flat wine, then wiped his mouth on a linen napkin. "Aye."

"Do you wish to speak of it?"

"Nay."

Marmaduke ran a finger slowly around the rim of his chalice. "Shall I speak with her? Mayhap I can vouchsafe you. She heeded my words the morn of your wedding."

Duncan slammed down his wine goblet. "I've already suffered enough of your interfering, you great lout," he said crossly. "'Tis the vilest of deeds I have done, and trying to make amends at present would bring naught but more ill feeling."

"Ill feeling I can see you stirring, for seldom has a man been less gifted with words than you. But vile deeds? Against your gentle lady wife?" Marmaduke shook his head. "Nay, I cannot believe it."

"And I am not asking you to believe me or nay, for I willna speak of it."

"Tsk, tsk," Marmaduke chided, "you've no reason to be wroth with me."

"Many are my reasons to be wroth with you, and 'tis grateful to the saints you should be that I dinna haul your English arse outside for an ordeal to the death," Duncan snarled. "Rain or nay, and *not* with blunted swords!"

Marmaduke's good eyebrow arched upward. "Pray share what transgression have I made to deserve your wrath?"

Struggling to control his temper, Duncan said, "I told you I shall not discuss it."

"You were not averse to discussing it yestereve," Marmaduke countered. "Not that I expect you will have taken a single word of my advice."

"Your advice was not needed, you blithering knave. The matter has naught to do with Cassandra and the painted boards bearing her infernal likeness," Duncan snapped, ripping off another hunk of bread. " 'Tis more grave than that."

"Then she wasn't unduly bothered . . . having seen the painting?"

"Of course, she was bothered!" Duncan replied heatedly, not caring if he disturbed those still sprawled upon the rushes. " 'Tis mightily aggrieved she was."

Marmaduke peered at him queerly with his good eye. "You spout nonsense. A moment hence you declared the panel-painting had naught to do with your foul mood, yet now you pronounce it upset the lady greatly." Leaning across the table, he rested his chin atop one hand. "Do you care to make your meaning more understandable?"

Duncan leaned forward, too. "By the Rood, you would extract a confession from a dead man! If you must know, everything you professed would happen, happened. As it usually does." Duncan paused to fix the Englishman with a withering glare. "My lady was sorely distraught, but I was able to console her."

Marmaduke sat back and folded his arms. "Indeed?"

"Aye."

"So you did follow my advice?"

"Nay, I did not," Duncan said impatiently. "I used my own methods."

"And they worked?" Marmaduke sounded doubtful.

"Too well."

"Too well?" Once more, Marmaduke quirked his one intact brow. "What do you mean *too well*?"

His brother-in-law was e'er mimicking his words, and at the moment his patience was less than thin.

"I *mean* I bedded her," Duncan snarled.

A lopsided grin lit Marmaduke's ravaged features. "And that has cast you into such a black mood?"

Standing, Duncan leaned across the table until he was mere inches from Marmaduke's face. "She was a maid, you conniving whoreson! A *virgin*."

Marmaduke's jaw dropped. "You mean you've only just claimed her?"

"Would she have been a maid had I already taken my ease with her, you empty-headed varlet?" Duncan brought his face so close to Marmaduke's their noses fair touched.

"But—"

"But *you* hoped locking me in her chamber whilst I was befuddled from hippocras, then parading a bloodied piece of linen before my men would convince me I *had* taken her!" Duncan seized Marmaduke by the neck of his tunic and hauled him from his chair. "And the ploy worked! I *did* believe I'd taken her. Still, I refrained from touching her again or so I thought since I obviously hadn't taken her at all. Until last night."

Letting go of Marmaduke, Duncan slammed his fist against the hard planks of the table. "Blood of Christ, Strongbow, your interfering has wrought more grief than I can undo!"

Straightening his tunic, Marmaduke regarded Duncan with consternation. "For the love of God, Duncan, 'tis pleased you should be to have a virtuous bride. I regret conspiring to push the two of you together prematurely, but my intentions were noble. Give me your sword, and I shall swear it upon the relic in its hilt."

Duncan sank back onto his chair. "I am sorry, my friend," he said. "And 'tis indeed grateful I am for my wife's virtue. Discovering it fair unmanned me." He paused and pulled one hand down over his face. "You dinna understand."

"Nay, I do not." Marmaduke refilled their chalices with wine as he spoke. That done, he narrowed his good eye, and asked, "Or did you take her so roughly you injured her?"

Heat stole up Duncan's neck at the Sassunach's words. He'd come closer to the truth than Duncan cared to admit.

Even to his most trusted friend.

Leaning back in his chair, Marmaduke crossed his arms. "Ah-ha. In your . . . eh . . . haste, you shocked and frightened her and now she wants naught more to do with your, eh, passion?"

Duncan pressed his lips together in a tight frown. If only his problems were so simple. 'Twould not be a hardship to spend his days and nights wooing his lady, teaching her the delights and rewards of love.

But, alas, such was not the issue.

His lady already possessed more passion than any female he'd ever known.

"Well?" Marmaduke pestered when Duncan remained silent.

"Well, *what*?" Duncan groused.

"Shall I give you lessons in properly courting a lady?"

Duncan emptied his goblet in one gulp. Just barely, he resisted the urge to fling the empty wine cup into the nearby hearth. "I am not a fumbling youth nor am I ill-bred. I ken how to woo a lady and . . ." He paused, leaning forward. "I dinna need instruction in how to awaken my wife's ardor. I'd wager my soul she's more passionate than any lass you've e'er had the pleasure to sample."

Falling back in his chair, Duncan crossed his arms. "Nay, that is not the problem."

"Let us see," Marmaduke said, holding up one hand and counting off fingers as he spoke. "The lady was pure, is possessed of heated blood, and is far comelier than she believes. On my honor, MacKenzie, I cannot see wherein lies the problem." Pausing, he began tapping his forefinger against his chin. "'Tis a riddle. Lest . . . lest you've fallen in love with her?"

"Love?" Duncan scoffed. "Such is only good for troubadours' tales on long and cold wintry nights. 'Tis *lust* I feel for Linnet, naught else."

"Think you?"

"Aye!" Duncan snapped, furious over the heat creeping into his cheeks at the Sassunach's insistent probing. "She fires my blood."

"And that is all?"

"Christ's bones! 'Tis enough! What man would not weaken at the sight of a fetching lass bare-bottomed and inviting upon his bed?"

The English knight took a slow sip of his wine, carefully studying Duncan across the pewter chalice as he drank.

Duncan squirmed under his friend's sharp perusal. Saints, the man could unnerve him!

Setting down his chalice as carefully as he'd partaken of his wine, Marmaduke asked, "And does she not stir your emotions as well?"

"By the Rood!" Duncan jumped to his feet. For a long moment he stared up at the vaulted ceiling. When he looked back at Marmaduke, the lout wore one of his knowing grins. "I dinna have emotions, so wipe that cunning smirk off your ugly face. 'Tis her *body* I desire. Such urges are natural and have naught to do with love."

Marmaduke's smile faded. "And did you tell her that?"

Duncan withheld the answer. Instead he drew a long, frustrated breath, then lowered himself into his chair. The accuracy of the Sassunach's words had hit him as if he'd been dealt a blow.

Aye, the truth stung.

"So that's the way of it."

Although it vexed him to admit it, Duncan locked his gaze with his friend's and nodded.

"Do you wish to talk about it?" Marmaduke asked, and Duncan heard the sincerity of his concern. "Mayhap, together, we can find a way to undo the damage you've wrought."

"You are a dreamer, English. Do you not realize what I'm saying?" Lowering his voice lest anyone else hear, Duncan said, "I robbed her of her maidenhead, initiated her in the pleasures of carnal desire, then, when she turned those damned eyes of hers on me—all soft and adoring—I panicked and told her I wanted naught but an occasional dip into the woman's flesh betwixt her thighs!"

"Pray tell me you did not use those words?"

"Not exactly, but I injured her feelings all the same." Duncan pressed his fingers against his temples. Just thinking of the callous way he'd treated her made his head ache. "She turned her back on me, Strongbow. I killed something inside her, do you understand?"

"Then you have no choice but to make amends . . . convince her you did not mean what you said. Show her you do care."

"But I do not," Duncan argued, feeling the weight of the cold, damp air pressing against his chest, curling around his neck as if to suffocate him, steal his very breath. "It *is* only taking my ease with her I care about. I canna tell her I love her when I do not. To do so would be a lie."

Marmaduke said nothing.

"I willna lie to her," Duncan insisted.

"Mayhap not," Marmaduke conceded, the look in his single eye, penetrating and wise. "But there are other things as ignoble."

"Such as?" Duncan asked, knowing he'd regret the answer.

"Lying to oneself."

With that, the English knight stood. He took a last draught of his wine, wiped his mouth, then strode from the hall without a backward glance.

Duncan stared after him, feeling soundly chastised. Faith, the all-knowing churl should've been a holy man, so good 'twas he at instilling guilt in the innocent.

But, Duncan admitted with a dark scowl, he wasn't an innocent.

He was a bastard.

Worse, he'd become a liar.

The most despicable liar in the Highlands.

Linnet woke to a dull ache between her thighs. Curling herself into a ball, she hugged her knees and shut her eyes, willing away the throbbing pain.

But the ache persisted, and sleep would not return.

Nor could she deny the weak bands of sunlight filtering through the shutter slats. 'Twas morn ... the morning after she'd lost her maidenhood, her heart, *and* all hopes of ever winning her husband's affection.

Refusing to give heed to the urge to pull the covers back over her head and ignore the day, she quickly scanned the room, making certain *he* was truly gone and not lurking in some dark corner, waiting for her to awaken so he could continue his lecture on the glories of bodily lust.

But the chamber was empty, she was indeed alone.

Linnet shuddered, feeling utterly used and betrayed.

Angry, too, because, despite everything, she couldn't deny the sharp stab of disappointment she'd felt upon discovering he'd already slipped from the room.

Stiffly, for it seemed every bone and muscle in her body ached, she climbed from bed and dressed as quickly as she could. With luck, she could pass unnoticed through the hall and spend the day in her herbarium.

Or perhaps she'd try to sneak past the sentries at the gate so she could walk in peace along the shore?

Naught would please her more than a pleasant stroll on the shingled banks of Loch Duich, where the towering castle walls would keep her well hidden from prying eyes and wagging tongues.

But all plans for a day spent in blessed solitude vanished the moment she pulled open the bedchamber door, stepped out, and collided with *him*.

"Saints, woman!" he exploded, trying to balance a large wooden tray of food. "Can you not watch where you're going?"

Linnet shrank back at his scowling countenance. "I vow, sir, I could not have known you'd be standing before the door."

Striding past her into the room, he set the heavy tray on a small table near the hearth. "I've brought victuals to break your fast. Oatcakes and a jug of fresh buttermilk." He folded his arms over his chest and frowned when she remained by the door. "Are you not hungry?"

"Aye," she admitted, uncomfortable under his gaze. "But I could have eaten in the hall. There was no need for you to fetch my breakfast."

He made a gruff noise, then pulled out a chair for her. "The fare in the hall wasna fit for the alms dish," he explained, obviously waiting for her to take her seat. "Besides, I . . . ah . . . thought you'd prefer to dine alone this morn."

Unsure of the motive for his gesture of courtesy, Linnet crossed the room. Mayhap he wanted to keep her from the hall? Hide her away as he did Robbie?

Was he afeared his men would be able to read her expression and see aught was not well between them?

More disturbing, could *he* see what troubled her?

Was it writ upon her face that her heart was breaking? That he'd taken her to the dizzying heights of all her hopes and dreams, only to let her crash to the ground, her most secret desires scattered around her like shards of broken pottery?

Avoiding his eyes, she sat and carefully poured herself a cup of buttermilk. "Thank you," she said quietly, keeping her head down, purposely avoiding his stern scrutiny. "'Twas thoughtful of you."

"Nay," he said, stepping forward and reaching toward her, then letting his hand drop, as if embarrassed he'd dare attempt to touch her. "'Tis as it should be and . . . and . . . not good enough. 'Tis more you deserve for what you gave me yestereve. I should have brought you a length of the finest cloth and a chest overflowing with jewels. I . . . 'tis . . . oh, by the saints, lady," he blurted, yet another frown creasing his brow. "Can you not see I am not adept at fancy words?"

"I've no need for fancy words." She glanced up at last, surprised by the deep flush coloring her husband's handsome face. "Noble gowns and glittering gemstones mean little to me."

He reached toward her again, this time smoothing the backs of his fingers down her hair. The light caress sent a sharp jolt through her and made her pulse quicken.

"Have you naught what requires your attention?" she asked coolly, hoping he'd leave her be whilst at the same time wishing he'd touch her again.

Faith and mercy, she wished he'd do more than simply run his hand o'er her tresses.

A strange look entered his deep blue eyes. "Aye, there is a matter of importance I must tend to," he said, taking the seat opposite her, his intense gaze holding her captive. " 'Tis why I am here."

"Oh?"

He nodded, the corners of his mouth curving upward in a seductive smile. "A matter of utmost importance."

"I do not understand," Linnet hedged, half-afraid to listen further. Tearing her gaze away, she turned her attention to the food before her.

Anything but lose herself in the depths of his bone-melting gaze, anything but abandon her heart to the whim of a devil's beguiling smile.

But already, that warm, soft feeling was spreading through her limbs, pooling in her belly, and making her all too aware of the strange power he held over her.

Worried he'd sense what she felt, and before she could regret the consequences, she blurted, "Be the 'matter of importance' that you wish to quench your bodily lust again? If so, I'll disrobe and spread my legs at once . . . I ken 'tis my duty."

Duncan shot to his feet so fast he knocked over the jug of buttermilk. For a brief moment, he stared aghast at the thick liquid spilling over the table edge onto the rushes, then, with one great swipe of his arm, he sent the earthen jug and all else upon the table to the floor.

Linnet jumped up, too. Extending her arms before her, she began backing away from him. But he caught up with her in two quick strides, seizing her by the shoulders and pulling her roughly against his chest.

"Must you e'er vex me?" he railed, fair lifting her off her feet. " 'Twas to apologize I came! To repay you—"

"For what? My *services*?" Linnet countered, her

voice a mere squeak, for he held her so tightly the neckline of her gown dug painfully into her throat. "The same as you'd pay for the favors of a stewhouse harlot?"

"Nay! 'Tis my *wife* you are. Dinna twist my words. I've told you I'm not good at pretty speeches." Letting go of her suddenly, he ran both hands through his hair, the gesture making him appear more desperate than angry. "You do not understand. I did not mean to hurt you. I—"

With trembling fingers, Linnet tugged her gown into place. "You're mistaken, sirrah. I do understand. 'Tis well I ken you did not mean to cause me undue pain."

"I—dinna—mean—*that*—kind—of—pain," he bit out, emphasizing each word. "And I think you know it. I meant it wasn't my intent to injure your *feelings*."

Linnet's heart turned over at his awkward attempt at apologizing, and at the sincerity in his eyes. Even so, she didn't dare make overmuch of aught he said or did.

He'd expressed his true opinion of her, of their marriage, the night before.

Squaring her shoulders, she fought to dispel the sweet sensations his nearness aroused in her. "I thought feelings held no interest for you?"

Taking her firmly by the shoulders, Duncan said, "I do care for you, Linnet."

"So you said." Waxing bolder than she would've thought she'd dare, she pressed on, "You care for me as a man cares for a finely honed sword or an obedient and worthy steed."

Duncan's face suffused a deep scarlet. "By the Rood, wench, can you not see I am trying to make amends? Have a care lest you taunt me too much. My patience has already been sorely tested this day."

A sharp rap upon the closed door spared her having to reply. Without further acknowledging her, Duncan strode across the room and yanked the door wide. Three young pages entered, each carrying leather pails of water.

A fourth, a wee lad no older than Robbie, carried a small wooden stool.

Two squires followed, one with a large wooden cooper's tub held before him, the other with a stack of folded linen toweling piled high in his arms.

"I ordered a bath brought up for you," Duncan said gruffly. Following the pages to the hearth, he dipped his hand in one of the buckets. "The water has been heated below, but 'tis not overly warm. I'll stoke the fire so you do not overchill yourself."

Linnet refrained from giving vent to a bitter laugh. The only thing in the room capable of chilling her was the cold expression on her lord husband's face.

Arms folded across his chest, his jaw rigidly set, he silently watched the young servitors line the tub with a huge length of linen, place the tiny stool inside, and drape it, too, with a linen cloth, before they began pouring rose-scented water into the bath.

When they were done, he dismissed them with a stern nod.

Heavens, but he appeared chiseled from granite! 'Twas no wonder the young pages scurried from the room, anxious to be gone, the older squires not far behind them.

They'd surely sensed the tense atmosphere hanging

in the air. 'Twas so thick Linnet could almost taste its bitterness on her lips. Sweet Mary have pity on her, even the brisk draught of damp morning air blowing in through the opened windows wasn't as frigid as the look her husband wore.

'Twas a foul expression she'd no doubt put there with her artless manner and loose tongue.

In all fairness, he *had* sought to appease her.

Regret at her harsh words ate at her from within as she watched him test the bathwater once more, his smile of only moments before gone, in its place a grim expression that revealed nothing.

"I told Fergus to have Cook add a few drops of rose oil. I trust that is to your liking?"

"Thank you, milord," Linnet said. "I favor roses."

A bit of the anger faded from Duncan's face, replaced by a look Linnet couldn't quite identify. "Have you forgotten I'd asked you to use my name?"

"Thank you, Duncan . . . sir," she said, sorely tempted to dive back into the bed and pull the bedcurtains to shield herself from the displeasure she could see thrumming through him.

"Duncan. Just Duncan," he said, his voice solemn. Coming to her side, he gently lifted a handful of her hair. "I am not an ogre, lady."

Letting the strands slip from his fingers, he cupped her chin. "I offended you last night, and I hereby ask you to accept my humblest apology."

Linnet gazed into his deep blue eyes, no longer dark and stormy, but now almost the same shade they'd been as he'd whispered tender endearments to her in the night.

The vivid memory of all he'd said, and done, in the

heat of his passion, sent a whirlwind of conflicting emotions swirling through her.

Could he truly be sorry he'd hurt her feelings?

Mayhap, but she still doubted he cared for her.

At least not in the way she wanted him to care.

She swallowed, for her throat had suddenly gone dry as cold ash. Let the angels have mercy on her, she wanted him to love her.

Truly love her.

With all his heart.

Not merely desire her as a convenient vessel for his masculine needs.

But was he capable of such emotions? And could he accept her feelings for him as well?

Or must she learn to be content with the bits and pieces of tenderness he'd surely grant her whilst in his arms?

Would such be enough?

Linnet smothered a sigh. It'd never be enough. She wanted more, so very much more.

"Well?" he prodded, yanking her from her dreams, back into the ice-cold present. When she didn't answer immediately, he quirked a brow at her. "Will you accept my apology? Will you have me as I am?"

She hesitated for a moment. "Aye," she consented.

Duncan smiled hopefully, then brought her hand to his lips for a kiss. "You will not regret this, I promise. Tonight, I shall love you until you are fair limp from passion and beg me to cease."

Still clutching her hand in his, he added, "If it takes till first light, I shall repay you for the injury I caused last night."

Linnet stiffened at his lightly spoken words. "'Tis not payment I wish. What I want canna be bought with coin nor replaced by physical, ah, . . . fulfillment."

A shadow passed over Duncan's face, and he seemed to withdraw from her even though he still held her hand. "Dinna wax sentimental on me, lady. I swear on all that's holy, I will cherish and honor you all our days as man and wife. Pray let that satisfy you. Romantic love, as I believe you covet, does not exist."

Letting go of her hand, he knelt to rebuild the fire. Over his shoulder, he continued, "You must accept me as I am. If you cannot, tell me true and I shall hie myself from this chamber and ne'er cross the threshold again."

His task done, he got to his feet. "It is not my wish to cause you pain. I ask you again, will my affection be enough for you?"

Resigning herself to the only option she had, Linnet nodded.

He rewarded her lie with one of his beatific smiles.

The rare kind she'd so seldom seen grace his lips.

It warmed her heart and sent a fluttery sensation straight to her belly despite the chill emptiness of what he was asking of her.

Looking pleased at her apparent acquiescence, he offered her his hand. "Then come, I will help you undress."

The moment she placed her hand in his, his smile turned wicked, stealing her breath. "Mayhap I shall help you bathe as well," he suggested, massaging her palm with his thumb.

And each round of his circling thumb stirred the cauldron of resistance bubbling deep inside her.

It would appear he believed he need only gift her with a smile and a spot of tenderness and she'd crumple to his feet, eager to do his bidding.

"Your bath awaits you, my lady," he said with a meaningful glance at the wooden tub. "Do we not want to discard your clothes before yon water grows cold?"

'Tis I who have grown cold, milord seduce-me-not. Linnet kept the sharp retort to herself. In truth, she wasn't sure she *could* resist him. Already his deft fingers had maneuvered her out of her gown! But when he sought to remove her only remaining garment, her thin chemise, the words of protest poised on her tongue could no longer be contained.

"Is this some new form of crude entertainment, sirrah? Stripping me naked and watching me bathe?" She curled her fingers around his wrists in a vain attempt to dislodge his hands from her undergown. "Did I not make clear last night that I prefer to be unobserved whilst making my ablutions?"

"God's wounds!" As quickly as the sharply spoken oath left her husband's lips, so did he break free of her grasp and have done with her chemise. Indeed, he divested her of its scant protection with such speed, she scarce noticed he'd drawn it over her head until she stood naked before him.

And as every time she'd done so before, it was a glorious feeling. Heady, potent, and much more powerful than the streak of rebellion that still glowed hot with fervor somewhere deep inside her.

Then he put his hands on her shoulders and began a slow and tender exploration of her body. Barely touching her, he smoothed his hands down her sides and up again, brought them around behind her and traced the length of her back, then cupped and felt along the curves of her lower buttocks. With the lightest of barely there strokes, he slipped his hands between her thighs and caressed her there as well.

The mastery of his touch made her womanhood throb with a pulsing need, and her heart forget every shred of resistance she'd meant to display.

Unable to resist, she gave herself up to the sensations he stirred in her. As if he sensed the exact moment of her capitulation, he pulled her close and, gladly, she slid her arms around him in return.

'Twas bliss beyond words simply being held in his embrace, close to his heart.

A heart she was determined to win.

Despite her pretense of accepting a life together on his loveless terms.

"Saints, but you tempt me," he murmured into her hair as he gathered her into his arms, lifting her off her feet. Gently, he lowered her into the silky warm waters of the bath. "Ne'er in my life have I desired a woman more."

Without taking his eyes off her, he lowered himself to his knees beside the tub. Tenderly holding her face between his hands, he leaned forward and softly brushed his lips back and forth over hers.

Lulled into contentment by the sheer magic of his kisses and the soothing warmth of her bath, Linnet felt herself melting, her limbs turning as liquid as the scented water. She sighed, and her breath mingled with his . . . a heady sensation that made her woman's flesh pulse with an intensely pleasurable feeling of warmth. Parting her lips, she begged him without words to deepen the kiss.

Duncan obliged, crushing her mouth beneath his, his lips and tongue taking heated possession of hers. When he let his hands glide down over her shoulders to caress her breasts, she could do naught but give in to the feverish desires building inside her.

A tiny voice deep inside scolded her for being a wanton fool. A brazen piece willing to barter her pride for a man's sensual touch, for the feel of his lips melding with hers, his hands moving so exquisitely over her breasts, and the earth-shattering release she'd found with him last night.

A shiver, unpleasant this time, rippled down her spine. In truth, she'd sunk lower than the cheapest whore.

Abandoned her morals for the thrill of a few moments in the arms of a man who'd boldly stated he'd never love her.

"Duncan, wait," she pleaded the moment he broke their kiss to feather lighter ones down the curve of her neck. "Please, I cannot do this after all."

"Shhh," he urged, "*of course* you can. Hush, dinna speak." He placed two fingers over her lips, silencing her. "Just *feel*. Let me pleasure you, show you how much I desire you, love you until you are weak from our joining and beg for mercy."

"But you do not—"

"I told you, we will not speak of love," he said, as if he'd read her thoughts. Pushing suddenly to his feet, he yanked his tunic over his head, tossed it aside, then bent to remove his shoes.

"Dinna do this," she begged again. She tried in vain to tear her gaze from his bared chest, even as the sight of its hard contours made her heart hammer wildly. "It is not right," she gasped, her voice a ragged whisper. "You do not love me."

"Hush, sweeting," Duncan protested, rolling his braies down his well-muscled legs as he spoke. He kicked them out of the way and stood facing her, hands braced on his hips, his arousal unmistakable. "I desire and ache with longing for you."

Linnet's heart turned over at his words, her pride screaming at her to look away or at least close her eyes, but she couldn't.

The hot throbbing deep inside her feminine core refused to be denied. That traitorous part of her begged, nay, *demanded*, she forsake all misgivings and surrender herself to the unbearably sweet pleasures she knew he could give her.

As if he sensed her yielding, a slow, seductive smile stole over his lips, and he reached for her hand. A strange sound, a raw and utterly primitive moan, escaped Linnet's throat when his strong, warm fingers closed over hers.

Not taking his eyes off hers, he brought her hand to rest against the flat plane of his abdomen. He held her hand there, her fingers splayed over his hot skin for an excruciatingly long moment.

Then he began edging her hand downward.

Her blood raced, every nerve ignited, on fire, as he skimmed her hand lightly back and forth over the thick mat of dark hair at his groin.

With a deep groan feral enough to have been made

by a wild beast and not a flesh-and-blood man, Duncan moved her hand to his maleness, closing her fingers tightly around the hot, pulsing shaft.

The feel of him, all searing heat and proud, rigid as steel yet satiny-smooth to the touch, sent a bolt of excitement shooting through her, stealing her breath and making her forget her cares.

Forget her objections to this . . . this loveless mating of their bodies.

Forget her pride.

She sighed, her fingers moving around the length of him. The man must be part-wizard, for surely it was not a small feat to whisk away her doubts and send her spiraling into a sea of such reckless longing she might soon perish from the sheer glory of it?

Indeed, her husband's caress, his kiss, touching him, even one glance from him was a more powerful mixture than the most potent mead.

More intoxicating than the sweetest of wines.

As if she had the same effect on him, his eyes darkened, fair smoldering with passion. Whispering soft words of encouragement, he carefully unclasped her fingers, then leaned down and placed her hands about his neck.

Linnet clung to him as he slipped his arms around her back and under her knees and lifted her from the tub. Water ran in rivulets down her limbs and the brisk sea wind coming through the opened windows brought gooseflesh to her skin, but she didn't care . . . she was oblivious to all but the wondrous feel of being held in her husband's powerful arms.

He'd carried her but a scant three paces across the

room when he stopped to claim her lips in a fiercely demanding kiss. Linnet melted against him, digging her hands into his hair, helpless to do aught but surrender to the wild fury of her own undeniable need.

Then, at the very moment she was certain something would shatter and spill deep inside her, a loud rap on the closed door broke through the haze of their ardor.

"Damnation!" Duncan cursed, sending a furious glance toward the door.

Still clinging to him, Linnet buried her face against his neck and bit her lower lip to hold back the deep sigh of pleasure she'd been about to give forth.

"Hush," Duncan whispered into her damp hair.

But the knocking came anew, persistent and unrelenting. "Lady? Be you in there?" a youth's voice called between the sharp raps.

"Damnation," Duncan repeated, easing Linnet to her feet.

Snatching a large drying cloth off a chair, he thrust it at her, and she gratefully wrapped it around her shivering body.

Heart in her throat, she watched Duncan stride angrily across the room and jerk open the door.

His nude body blocked her view of whatever hapless soul sought to find her, but she heard a sharp intake of breath, then a young male voice stammer, "A good . . . good morrow to you, sir."

"And a fine one it was till now," Duncan quipped, folding his arms. "What brings you to my lady's chamber at this early hour?"

"I dinna . . . I dinna ken you'd be here, sir." The lad shifted nervously from one foot to the other as he spoke, and Linnet caught a brief glimpse of him. Despite the high color staining his cheeks, she recognized him as her husband's youngest squire. "'Twas Fergus sent me. He bid me to fetch the Lady Linnet."

"Fergus?" Duncan shot a quizzical glance at Linnet. "And pray what does he want with her that could not wait till my lady wife finished her bath and made her own way belowstairs?"

The squire gulped noisily, then tried to explain. "He wishes to ask her blessing, milord."

"Her *blessing*?"

"Aye, sir," the young man confirmed. "I . . . I believe he means to marry the Lady Linnet's woman servant."

"*Marry her?*" Duncan asked, his tone incredulous. "Do you mean my wife's old nurse? The one called Elspeth?"

"Aye, she be the one, sir."

"Then tell Fergus my wife and I shall meet him and his intended in my former solar within the hour," Duncan ordered. "Now be gone from here and dinna disturb us again," he added, already closing the door.

Turning, he leaned against the heavy oak panels of the door. "Did you hear that?" he asked, shaking his head. "Fergus wanting to marry? The old goat! He never wanted aught to do with women, save his rare trips to the village to slake his . . . eh . . . needs."

Linnet hugged the linen drying cloth tighter about her body. "I've noticed they seem fond of one another. I canna say I'm surprised."

"But *marry* her? Next, he'll be claiming he's fallen in love."

"Mayhap he has," Linnet said. "Mayhap they both have."

"Bah!" Duncan gave a derisive snort. " 'Tis no such thing. And if they think so, they're both old fools."

Linnet shrugged. "Whatever you say, milord."

But, in truth, she couldn't disagree with him more.

13

Not quite an hour later, Duncan walked into his solar, or what *used* to be his solar, his lady wife following on his heels. A cheery fire burned in the hearth and it was more than obvious his dearest friend and brother-in-law, Sir Marmaduke, had laid claim to the chamber.

The romantically inclined English knight had cluttered the once-austere solar with all manner of useless trappings. Duncan pressed his lips together in a tight frown as he surveyed the many changes.

Indeed, were it not for the wicked-looking sword and other knightly attraments resting in a far corner next to the door to his former bedchamber, Duncan would've sworn he'd entered the quarters of a lady.

A fanciful one with naught but nonsense in her head.

Duncan spied the one-eyed lout leaning nonchalantly against the closed bedchamber door, his arms folded. Ever the gallant, Sir Marmaduke sprang to attention, coming forward to give Linnet a courtly bow. When he straightened and claimed Linnet's hand for a kiss, Duncan had had enough.

"Cease conducting yourself as if you're at court," he said irritably, whilst the Englishman fawned over his wife's hand. "'Tis instructing my squires in swordplay you should be at this young hour and not pandering about pretending you're the fabled Sir Lancelot."

Taking hold of Linnet's elbow, Duncan drew her closer to his side, away from the Sassunach. "Where is Fergus? I was told he wished to speak with my lady."

"Fergus and his intended should arrive any moment," Sir Marmaduke assured him, returning to his position in front of the closed bedchamber door. "You won't deny his request, will you?" he asked.

"Of course not," Duncan snapped. "Why should I? If he wants to tie hisself to a wife, 'tis his decision."

Beside him, Linnet stiffened. With a little jerk, she freed her elbow from his grasp and went to stand before the tall, narrow windows. Her back to the room, she clasped her hands loosely behind her and appeared to stare out at the waters of Loch Duich far below.

Marmaduke shot a quick glance her way, then turned his one-eyed gaze on Duncan. The look of reproach on the Sassunach's scarred face made Duncan feel as if he were once again a wee laddie and had just been dressed down by his father.

"I doubt Fergus sees it that way," Marmaduke said. "He's quite fond of Elspeth. I daresay he loves her." Pausing, he narrowed his good eye at Duncan. "As all men should love and cherish the woman they take to wife."

"And who made you an expert on marriage?" Duncan quipped sourly before remembering how deeply the Englishman had loved his late wife, Duncan's sister, Arabella.

How much he still mourned her death.

As so often of late, Duncan cringed at the harshness of his own words. By the Rood, what had come over him? Angry at himself, and embarrassed as well, he sought to change the subject. "Since when have you become Fergus's champion? 'Twas not long ago the two of you couldn't abide each other."

"Times change, people change, my friend. 'Tis a wise man who can admit he is wrong."

The neck opening of Duncan's tunic suddenly seemed inexplicably tight, and heat stole up his neck and into his cheeks. "If you're referring to—"

A knocking on the still-open door behind Duncan saved him from finishing. "'Tis good of you to meet with us," Fergus called from the door. "May we come in?" he asked, although he'd already stepped inside.

Duncan's jaw dropped. Never had Fergus asked his permission for aught. More oft than not, the bristly old seneschal spoke his mind and did as he pleased.

But something had changed him.

He even *looked* different.

So much so, Duncan highly suspected he'd taken a bath, a small miracle in itself. 'Twas glaringly apparent, too, that he'd tried, albeit without much success, to comb his shaggy mane of gray hair into a semblance of neatness.

He'd also donned his best plaid and polished the silver brooch holding it in place at his shoulder.

"What's this about you wanting to marry?" Duncan asked, his voice purposely gruff in an attempt to hide his astonishment at the old man's jaunty appearance. "Be that the truth?"

"Aye, 'tis God's truth, milord. I ken you willna deny me my happiness," he said, stepping farther into the solar, his intended close beside him, holding tightly to his gnarled hand. "With all due respect to you as laird, 'tis your lady wife's blessing I wish to have, as my Elspeth and I dinna want to do aught what doesna meet her approval."

Duncan crossed his arms and forced himself not to lose his temper.

Or let another rash statement pass his lips.

'Twould seem his entire world had been turned inside out since he'd fetched Linnet MacDonnell to be his bride: Sir Marmaduke had used trickery to oust him from his quarters, he couldn't open his mouth without putting his foot in it, he was master of his castle and rightful laird, yet everyone under his roof would lead him around by the nose.

And now his cranky old tale-spinner of a seneschal had spruced himself up like a lovesick squire and sought not his, but his wife's blessing to marry!

A wife who had yet to fulfill the one task he asked of her, to tell him the truth about Robbie.

A wife whose very nearness unsettled and excited him.

"Milord? Have we stirred your ire?" Fergus asked, causing Duncan to scowl even more.

Saints, the old buzzard had ne'er called him aught

but his given name. That, and a few choice titles Duncan didn't care to recall.

But never *milord*.

"Nay, you have not," Duncan replied with a vigorous shake of his head, trying in vain to rid himself of the persistent notion his entire household had gone raving mad while he wasn't looking. "'Tis merely surprised I am."

Turning to his wife, he said, "Lady, you've heard Fergus's plea. Will you grant them your blessing?"

Linnet took a hesitant step forward, her hands tightly clasped before her, her gaze intent on the older pair still hovering near the door. "Is this your wish, too, Elspeth?" she asked her former nurse. "Be you certain?"

Elspeth nodded, her gray curls bouncing. "Aye, child, it is, and 'tis more than sure I am. When Angus passed, I did not expect I'd meet a man I could care for again, but"—she paused to beam at Fergus—"I have, and it is my hope you'll be happy for me. For both of us."

'Twas all his lady wife needed to hear apparently, for she abandoned her cautious stance and fair charged across the room, throwing herself first into Elspeth's arms, then allowing Fergus, the bandy-legged old goat, to embrace her as well.

"Ahem," Duncan tried to catch their attention, to bring a spot of order, nay, dignity, to the moment, but the three ignored him.

Ooohing and aaahing, they continued to hug, kissing each other upon their cheeks as if he wasn't even present.

From his post by the bedchamber door, Sir Marmaduke shrugged. He wore an expression Duncan could only call a self-satisfied smirk and obviously found the situation highly amusing.

"Ahem!" Duncan tried again, louder this time.

All three stopped their silly prattle and turned toward Duncan. "Aye?" Fergus answered him, plucking his plaid into place, then drawing himself as tall as his somewhat-stooped frame would allow. "What's ailing you, boy? Have you lost proper use of yer tongue?" His bushy brows snapped together as if daring Duncan to shed ill favor on his newfound happiness.

"Naught ails me," Duncan countered crossly. "Naught at all."

Except wondering when every man, woman, and child under my roof had their brains pickled!

He turned to his wife. "You approve of this union?"

"Oh, aye," she said, smiling in a way she'd never smiled at him. "If Elspeth is so happy, how can I do aught but approve?" She grasped Elspeth's hands then, holding them between her own. "'Tis a fine pair they make. A bonnie pair."

"Then so be it," Duncan pronounced firmly.

He refused to be party to such gushing sentimentality.

'Twas a frivolous waste of time better left to women and his softhearted Sassunach brother-in-law.

Indeed, he'd let Marmaduke, with his unbridled love of French romances and constant gibberish about chivalry and courtly love, see to the reading of the banns and organizing a small wedding ceremony for the besotted old fools.

He, as laird, had more important matters to attend to.

Fixing the Sassunach with a pointed stare, he ordered, "You can help them make arrangements. I must hie myself below and dinna have the time. A patrol is due in this morn, and 'tis anxious I am to hear what tidings they bring."

Because it was no doubt expected of him, he strode over to the older couple and placed a hand on each of their shoulders. "'Tis pleased I am to see you both content. May God grant you many long and happy years together."

Stepping away from them, he heaved a deep sigh and made for the door. Without another word, and not looking back, he left them.

He truly did have much to tend to this morn. Reports of cattle snatching had been filtering in of late, as well as the scattered accounts of kinsmen being harassed. He couldn't spend the day dallying about planning a wedding when such trouble was underfoot, when his people needed him.

Besides, so much blissfulness as he'd just been forced to witness was hard for a man to bear.

Especially when his own heart ached for even a meager share of such happiness.

A fierce scowl settled over his face as he began the circular descent to the hall.

By the devil, the truth hurt.

Bad.

And knowing he was too much of a coward to do aught about it pained him even more.

*   *   *

An uncomfortable silence ensued after Elspeth and Fergus excused themselves a while later, leaving Linnet alone in the solar with Sir Marmaduke.

She could have left with them, and mayhap she should have, but something held her back. Her instincts told her the gallant Sassunach knight could answer many questions for her . . . if she could muster the courage to ask them.

And if he was willing to oblige her.

Moving to the small table near the window seat, she paused to admire the finely carved chessboard. Each piece was exquisitely rendered and well polished.

She picked up one piece, then turned to face the English knight. He still leaned against the closed bed-chamber door, the expression on his marred face unreadable but not unkind.

In truth, Linnet thought him a most kind man.

One she could trust, despite his English blood.

Clearing her throat, she said, "You have done much with this room, sir. And"—she fingered the chesspiece, peering at it as she spoke—"I dinna think I've e'er seen anything so fine as this. Is it from your home, from England?"

"Yes, milady, it hails from England."

The melancholy in his voice was not to be mistaken, so different was it from the jovial tone he often used when conversing with her husband. Linnet glanced sharply at him, the chesspiece forgotten.

His good eye seemed clouded with sadness, but he didn't flinch from her perusal. Instead, he pushed away from the door and came to stand before her, close, yet keeping a respectful distance.

Rather than look at her, he stared fixedly out the tall arched-topped windows. "My father carved the chess set. It is one of the few memories I have of him, as I have not seen him since I was but a young squire."

Emboldened by his apparent willingness to speak of his past, Linnet posed the question she'd oft wanted to ask but hadn't dared till now. "Sir Marmaduke, it is apparent my husband holds you in high esteem, you wear the MacKenzie colors, yet you are a Sassunach." Still fingering the chess piece, she plunged ahead, "Pray, how did you, an English knight, come to be here?"

He turned toward her then, but she could see he was looking back, into the past, and not at her. "'Twas my steadfast belief in being chivalrous to all members of the fairer sex, and not just those blessed with noble birth what brought me here, milady." With a sad smile, the best his disfigurement would allow, he went on, "Mayhap 'tis closer to the truth to say it was the unchivalrous behavior of my peers, and my refusal to condone it, what landed me in the MacKenzie household."

Linnet set down the chess piece, then settled herself on the window seat and drew one of the colorful silk cushions onto her lap. "I do not understand."

"Nay, and 'tis a blessing you have been sheltered from such things," he said, his voice turning cynical. "Mine is not a pretty story."

"I am still desirous to hear it," Linnet said, hugging the pillow to her middle. "If you dinna mind, of course."

"As you wish," Marmaduke agreed, clasping his

hands behind his back as he began to pace back and forth. "'Twas many years hence, the summer I earned my spurs. Truth tell, I was mightily proud and took my knightly vows most seriously. Much to the scorn of my fellow knights."

He paused to peer intensely at her. "Sadly, I was mistaken in expecting my peers to share my idealistic beliefs. And so, on my first foray into Scotland, I refused to participate in the ruination of village women. Worse, in the eyes of my peers, I took up my sword to defend the women against the atrocities my fellow knights would commit upon them. I—"

"You protected Scotswomen from your countrymen?" Linnet cut in.

"Yes. I sought to prevent innocent women from being violated. My punishment for such was swift and severe."

"Is that how your face came to be scarred?"

"Oh, nay," he said, shaking his head. "My face was defiled many years later. That is another story entirely. My punishment for attempting to aid the Scotswomen did leave me with scars, but they are upon my back. I was stripped and beaten by my own men, then left for dead. 'Twas Duncan's father who found me."

He paused then, absently rubbing the scar slanting across his face. "The good man, God rest his soul, carried me to this castle upon his own steed, where I was nursed to health by his lady, your husband's late mother."

A wistful smile played around the good half of his mouth. "It was my great fortune to have been welcomed into this household and I've worn the MacKenzie colors with pride ever since."

Inwardly, Linnet winced at the images evoked by his tale. And at her own initial fear of him. "I must apologize to you, sir, for I did you most unfairly when first we met," she said, heat springing to her cheeks. "'Twas greatly afeared of you I was."

Marmaduke smiled as best he could. "You've no need to apologize, lady. It is indeed a grim sight I present. You have shown me naught but kindness, and 'tis with great honor I serve you and your lord husband."

Still ashamed of her reaction upon first seeing him, Linnet changed the topic. "You have been friends with my husband since his father brought you here?"

"More than friends. 'Tis as brothers we are."

As brothers. The words stirred a memory, something she couldn't quite place.

As brothers . . .

Turning away from him, she glanced down at the wind-whipped waves crashing against the jagged rocks at the base of the tower.

As brothers . . .

Then it came to her.

Robbie had once called Sir Marmaduke "Uncle."

Looking back at the tall, once-handsome knight, Linnet asked, "Be that why Robbie refers to you as his uncle?"

"Nay, lady, that is not the reason," he said, then fell silent, a closed look settling over his features.

Embarrassed, afeared she'd gone too far with her probing, Linnet pushed to her feet and went to stand before the hearth. "Please excuse my curiosity," she said, staring into the flame. "I did not mean to pry."

When he remained silent for more than a few moments, Linnet stole a glance at him. He regarded her with a look of great intensity as if weighing whether or not he aught say more.

Finally, he shrugged and said, "You may as well know, as it is no secret. I am Robbie's uncle by marriage. My wife, Arabella, was Duncan's sister."

Linnet's mind whirled with snatches of conversation, bits of gossip she'd gleaned from servants. The pieces settled slowly, coming together one by one, their portent chilling her to the bone despite the warmth of the crackling fire so near where she stood.

Trembling, she cleared her throat and stated rather than asked, " 'Twas the lady Cassandra who killed your wife and Duncan's mother. She concocted a poison with herbs from the herbarium."

"It was never proven," Marmaduke said, joining her before the hearth. " 'Tis long past and should not be allowed to cloud your mind."

"It clouds more than my mind, it clouds my very life." She attempted a wan smile and failed. "Whatever marred my husband's first marriage casts a shadow o'er my own, dinna you see?" Swallowing her pride, she burst forth with her innermost fear. "I've wondered if he still mourns her, yet now, knowing this, surely he cannot? Not after what she'd done?"

Sir Marmaduke started to answer, then clamped his mouth shut. Spinning away from her, he strode to the windows. "Upon my word, lady, and pray forgive me if

I offend you, but you erred in even considering such a notion."

"I did? Then why does her likeness yet hang beyond yon door?" she asked, nodding toward the closed oaken door to Duncan's former bedchamber.

Sir Marmaduke ran a hand over his face as if he'd suddenly grown weary. "I cannot vouchsafe your husband's motives for keeping the panel-painting, but I can tell you mine and 'tis on any saint you care to name, I'd swear his reasons are similar."

Linnet waited, clenching her hands to lessen their shaking.

The Sassunach's broad shoulders sagged ever so slightly. "'Tis to remember," he said, bitterly. "To remember, lest I forget the misery she wrought unto myself and all who had the misfortune to know her."

Coming forward, he placed his hands lightly on her shoulders and turned his face first to one side, then the other. "Would you believe I was once considered handsome? That, at tourneys in France, and at court, fine ladies vied for my attention?"

"Sir Marmaduke, please," Linnet pleaded, the regret and sorrow in his tone squeezing her heart. "I beg you, forget I mentioned her. It was not my intent to distress you."

"And you have not, dear lady," he assured her, some of the bitterness gone from his voice. "With or without your being here, my face and my memories would be the same. Truth to tell, you have helped me as none before, for your healing skills have made a great improvement in my blighted appearance."

Lifting a hand to the puckered flesh where his left

eye should've been, he said, "'Twas her lover did this, 'twas Kenneth, your husband's bastard half brother."

Speaking slowly, as if the words had to be pried from wherever he kept them, he went on, "My wife had learned he and Cassandra were plotting to murder Duncan. They'd already done away with Duncan's mother, although we did not realize 'twas their doing at the time."

He made a low bitter sound. "Fool that I was, I confronted Kenneth. I challenged him to take his whore and be gone, warned him not to set foot on MacKenzie land again. But as so oft, my belief that there dwells a bit of good within all men was sorely misplaced."

Linnet tried to murmur soothing words, her own worries paling beside those the Englishman now confessed to her, but the words wouldn't come, refused to be pushed past the dryness in her throat.

"My interference cost me my wife and Duncan his sister," Marmaduke said, and Linnet was horrified to see a tear form at the corner of his good eye. "Whilst Kenneth led me to believe he'd follow my advice, he hastened back as swiftly as his mount could carry him, but not to fetch his harlot and leave Kintail for good. Nay, lady, they poisoned my Arabella instead."

Pausing, he swiped the back of his hand roughly over his eye, wiping away the tear before it could fall.

"Mayhap they feared she knew too much and would warn Duncan. I cannot say, and it scarce matters, for they killed her just the same. I am sure of it, even though their guilt can never be proven."

"Does my husband know this?" Linnet asked gently.

"Yes, he knows. He confronted her. She ran from him, fleeing to the battlements, Duncan chasing after her." He stopped to draw a deep, ragged breath. "She laughed as she ran, taunting him about Robbie, claiming the boy was Kenneth's child, not his. Then she tripped on the hem of her gown and plunged to her death before he could do aught to save her."

"Do you think he would have?" Linnet's voice was a bare whisper.

"Yes, had he been close enough. He likely would've questioned her, then banished her to a convent for the remainder of her days." He paused then, staring off into the distance before he continued, "May God forgive me, but had I been up there with her, I do not think I'd have made an effort to prevent her fall."

"And when did Kenneth do this?" Linnet gently touched a finger to his puckered scar.

"That same day. I caught him trying to steal Duncan's best horse. He'd learned of his ladylove's demise and meant to flee. We fought and, as you can see, he bested me." He stopped to take a deep breath, then tried to give her a smile, a rueful one. "He is an excellent swordsman, almost as masterful as Duncan."

"But Duncan has boasted of your skill with arms," Linnet protested. "He said he's seen you cut down five men at once."

"And so I have. In war," he told her, his voice burdened by a flat dullness that twisted Linnet's heart. "'Tis a fool I was that day for I broke the first rule a squire is taught when learning to wield a sword: I let my emotions get in the way. My rage made me clumsy."

"I am sorry." Linnet frowned. "'Tis a high price you paid for your loyalty to my husband."

"I did naught he would not have done for me. Duncan is my brother as surely as if his blood flowed through my veins. As for my face, and losing my eye . . ." Sir Marmaduke let his voice trail off, then sighed. "I'd gladly forfeit my remaining eye and all else I possess if by doing so my Arabella could return to me."

When Linnet said nothing, he peered at her with such intensity she feared he could see into the deepest reaches of her soul.

Shuddering under the weight of all he'd told her, she turned back to the fire, no longer able to meet the pain she saw on his face. Ne'er had she heard of a man sacrificing so much, nor of a husband whose love for his wife burned so strong.

"You loved her very much," she said at last, her gaze steady on the flames curling around the firelogs. "I canna imagine a love so enduring."

"Indeed? I have observed your gaze following Duncan, and I have seen how he watches you when he thinks no one is taking notice of him," he said, his voice seeming to come from a great distance.

Linnet strained to hear him over the unusually loud crackling of the fire. Shaking her head, she tried to rid her ears of the noise, but the popping and snapping of the fire only grew louder.

The wind, too, had become deafening, whistling past the windows with an unearthly howl, rattling the shutters in its wake.

As the din increased, the skin on the back of her

neck prickled and her hands grew damp. Still staring into the fire, she fought the uncomfortable sense of ill-ease creeping up on her and concentrated instead on making herself heard.

"You are mistaken," she said, her voice sounding strange, hollow, even to her own ears. "My lord husband has told me—"

"Lady?" The Sassunach rushed forward, catching her as she swayed and began to slump to the floor. "Sweet Mother of God, what is it?"

Linnet felt herself collapse into his arms. She could barely make sense of his words, so shrill was the buzzing in her ears. Her head fell back against his chest, and she tried to look up at him but saw only flames.

A dancing wall of fire surrounded her, its heat searing her, its roar drowning all other sound. Through the flames, and as if from many leagues away, she thought she heard someone calling her husband's name, but she was too weary, too deafened by the raging fire to tell for sure.

With great effort, she forced her eyes open, only to recoil in horror at the terrifying sight before her. Cringing, she cowered against the hard chest of whoe'er held her so securely. But she kept her eyes open, bound as if by a sorcerer's wand to stare at the figure standing in the flames.

'Twas a two-headed man.

A monster.

An abomination of nature.

Tall and powerful-looking, he stood with his legs apart, hands braced on his hips. His two heads were cowled, shielding his features from view, but she knew instinctively one of the heads smiled benevolently at her whilst the second wore an evil grimace.

A horrifying mask of fury aimed straight at her from the gates of hell.

And all the while, the other head smiled, benignly enjoying her terror.

Linnet screamed.

Wild shrieks ripped from her throat, torn from her very soul, straining her lungs and bursting forth until her cries grew louder than the roar of the flames.

Then all went still.

The flames vanished as if they'd never been there, mercifully taking the two-headed man with them, leaving her floating in a sea of darkness where all was quiet and still.

And black.

A blackness deeper and more impenetrable than the dark waters of a bottomless loch on a cold December night.

Through the darkness she heard the muffled sound of running feet and loud cries. A man's agitated shouts, peppered with curses and tersely barked orders. But despite her efforts, it was impossible to fully decipher the words or place the direction from which they came.

She heard mumblings, too. Softly uttered words, unintelligible murmurs.

Sounds of concern.

Then other arms took hold of her. Arms equally strong and powerful, perchance even more so. And her aching head was held against something hard and firm yet undeniably comforting.

Comforting and familiar.

Linnet tried to open her eyes to see who held her so tenderly, to discover where he was carrying her, for she could only tell they climbed round and round . . . in dizzying circles.

But her eyelids proved too heavy to lift and sleep pressed in on her with a relentless, overpowering seductiveness she couldn't resist.

Then she was floating again. No longer held and coddled, but on her own and resting upon a bed of such exquisite softness it could only be a cloud.

'Twas surely a dream.

But a nightmare, too, for the ghastly figure of the two-headed man appeared again, albeit only in the darkest recesses of her mind.

Hoping to will away the frightening image, she curled herself into a ball and kept her eyes tightly shut. Someone's gentle hands touched her, at times stroking her forehead, then pressing something cool against her cheek.

On occasion, whoever it was, would lift her head and carefully dribble fresh water onto her parched lips, or help her take small sips of cool water until sleep claimed her once more.

Then she'd drift deeper into the darkness, unaware of those around her.

Gone, the roaring flames. Vanquished, the fiendish two-headed man. Silenced, too, the shouts and curses.

Faded to nothingness, the hushed and guarded whisperings.

Naught remained but an all-encompassing quiet and the dark.

And the comforting feel of her hand, limp and cold, held tenderly between a pair of larger, warmer hands.

Strong hands, gentle and sure. Familiar, too, yet strange as well for their touch conveyed without question that, whoever it was, cared.

Cared deeply, for each time the fog thinned, the hands were always there. Oft simply holding hers, sometimes heartily massaging her fingers as if to chase away the cold.

Once, when the dark receded a bit, she stole a brief glance at the owner of the hands. 'Twas Duncan, her husband. But when she looked again, to make certain, the haze blurred his face, and she couldn't tell for sure.

With a sigh so weak she barely heard it herself, she gave herself up to the darkness. It was safe and pleasant to drift through a dreamworld where her husband watched o'er her.

A world where he held fast to her hands, caressing them.

As if they were cherished.

As if *she* were cherished.

Aye, for a while at least, she'd tarry in the netherworld between the place whence her visions came and the cold, unforgiving world in which she was naught more than a wife desired but not loved.

That decided, she let herself sink into the soft feather mattress of her bed—for she knew the bed was not truly a cloud—and savored her husband's gentle ministrations as he sat beside her, tending her as if he cared.

As if he loved her.

A tiny, contented sigh escaped her when he suddenly began massaging her fingers anew. She'd warn him of the two-headed man on the morrow when her head was no longer fuzzy.

After she'd had her fill of his surprisingly gentle touch.

Then would be time enough.

None could fault her for indulging herself in a few scant hours pretending her husband cared.

14

Linnet woke to a room cloaked in semi darkness. Weak sunlight filtered through the closed shutters, casting long blue-gray shadows across the floor and up the tapestried walls, letting her know it was late evening. Faith and mercy, but she'd slept many hours since her frightening vision in the solar.

An empty chair stood next to the bed, mute testament someone had indeed sat there, tenderly holding her hand, offering her comfort whilst she'd slept so fitfully, plagued by nightmares of a two-headed man surrounded by flames.

Could the compassionate soul who'd so lovingly looked after her truly have been her husband?

Dare she hope it?

Was Duncan MacKenzie, the formidable and mighty Black Stag of Kintail, capable of such great gentleness? Or was she deluding herself, adjusting her vague memories of the dark hours following the ghastly vision to better suit her secret desires?

Scooting up to a sitting position, she rubbed her throbbing temples and tried to think. Could Duncan harbor such concern for her or had she merely crafted a soothing lie to sweeten what transpired after she'd lost consciousness?

A sideways glance at the small table near her bed assured her the gentle hands, the loving ministrations she remembered, hadn't been imagined. Someone had cared for her, for atop the table stood an earthen water jug, a drinking cup, and a small metal basin, empty but for a few damp cloths.

She'd imagined naught, and it was indeed her husband who'd sat by her side, tending her so lovingly.

It had to have been him, for deep inside she knew his touch. A slow smile spread across her face at the revelation. She would ken his caress, the feel of his hands, amongst those of a thousand men. Mayhap more. He *did* care. Heat stole into her cheeks, joining her smile, as warmth spread through her, filling her with hope and banishing the lingering aftereffects of the disturbing visitation.

Slipping from the bed, she crossed the room and flung the shutters wide, eager to let in what meager light remained. But more than fading light and chill, briny air came in through the opened window. The sound of men's voices, low and troubled, entered as well, drifting down from the ramparts above.

Men's voices raised in anger, the words carried on the wind turning her blood to ice water.

". . . butchered every last one o' them, even the

bairns. The laird'll carve the bastard to pieces when he catches him . . ."

Linnet snatched her mantle from the back of a chair and tossed its warmth around her. With trembling fingers, she worked in vain to fasten the brooch at her shoulder, gave up, and hurried from the room. Clutching the cloak about her shoulders as best she could, she made her way to the great hall as fast as her legs would carry her.

Deep grumblings and furious shouts rose up to greet her as she descended the tower's circular stair. Pounding noises and loud thumps, too.

And the unmistakable hiss and clatter of steel.

The nearer she came to the hall, the more fierce the ruckus sounded. It was as if the entire assemblage were either slamming their fists upon the tables, stomping their feet, or unsheathing their swords.

Mayhap all three from the frightful din they made.

"*Cuidich' N' Righ! Save the king!*" The clan war cry erupted suddenly, bursting forth, resounding and ferocious, from the lungs of what sounded to be a legion of MacKenzie warriors.

Each one filled with rage.

Nay, rage was too paltry a word.

'Twas bloodlust she heard.

Bloodlust pure: cold, unforgiving, and bent on revenge.

"*Cuidich' N' Righ!*" 'Twas a chant now, the fervent cry deafening as it bounced off Eilean Creag's thick stone walls, echoing eerily in the stair tower as she rounded the last curve, finally reaching the great hall's arched entrance.

There, she stopped short, drawing back into the shadows to assess the sight before her.

In the center of the hall, her husband stood upon one of the trestle tables, his powerful legs arrogantly spread. With both hands, he held his sword high above his head as he led his kinsmen in shouts for justice.

Flickering light from scores of lit torches glinted off his black mail hauberk whilst little flames appeared to dance in the gleaming darkness of his wildly disordered hair.

Linnet's fingers tightened on the edges of her cloak as she stared at him. He looked savage, fierce, with great waves of anger emanating from every taut muscle of his warrior's body.

A bloodthirsty, brutal warrior demanding vengeance.

Repeatedly, he thrust his great sword upward, skill-fully whipping his men into a frenzy. As one, they re-peated the war cries he roared from his lofty perch.

Unable to move, frozen in place and transfixed by the spectacle before her, Linnet stared at him in awe. Every inch of him exuded sheer power. Light from the many raised torches reflected onto the steel mesh of his mail tunic, gilding his muscles and turning the close-fitting hauberk into a glittering shirt of flames.

Flames. Her breath left her in a rush and her heart slammed against her chest.

She'd near forgotten the two-headed man she'd seen standing in the flames! Terror seized her, chilling her to the very marrow of her bones. The message had to per-tain to whatever vile deed had unleashed such havoc upon the Clan MacKenzie.

She had to warn Duncan, tell him about the two-headed man.

Mayhap he could make sense of it.

Shaking anew, Linnet forced herself to leave the shelter of shadows in which she'd been hiding. On legs that felt too wobbly to carry her through the crowd of angry, jostling men packing the hall, she made her way forward.

With great effort, she pushed through the MacKenzie warriors to where Duncan loomed heads above them, now brandishing his sword menacingly in the air, jabbing ferociously at an unseen enemy. "Let none among us rest until the lives of those taken from us have been avenged," he swore, his outraged voice reaching even the farthest corners of the massive hall.

"Tomorrow, before first light," his booming voice rang out, "we shall descend upon the camp of the bastard Kenneth and have done with them afore they'll ken 'tis their time to take their places in hell!"

Resheathing his sword, he planted his hands on his hips and raked his men with a challenging stare. "No quarter! We'll slice every last one of the miscreants to ribbons. All save Kenneth. Sir Marmaduke alone shall have *that* honor."

He paused to draw a breath, his angry gaze sweeping the width of the hall before issuing further challenges. "*Cuidich' N' Righ!*" he shouted, his fist thrust high in the air. "Save the ki—"

The war chant froze on his lips when he spied his wife teetering through the crowd, her fiery tresses cascading unbound to her waist, her amber-colored eyes wide in a face gone deadly pale.

What the devil was she doing up and about? He'd ordered a watch placed on her door.

Hers and the lad's.

But instead of his orders being heeded, none had stopped her and she now struggled toward him through the tightly-packed hall. The sheer terror in her eyes made his gut clench.

Blood of Christ, he'd meant to spare her hearing details of the butchery wrought upon his people, meant to know her safely ensconced in her chamber, far from this gathering intended to stir the fires of revenge in his men.

Saints, but he'd not wanted her exposed to such madness.

The lad neither, his seed or nay.

Not that he'd admit any greater concern for the child than he felt for any of the other bairns under his protection.

Scowling, he dragged his arm over his damp forehead and watched her approach. As if they'd only just become aware of her presence, his men parted before her, clearing her way through their midst.

Unfortunately, Duncan's mood worsened with each faltering step she took forward. Holy St. Columba preserve him, but, as she neared, he imagined he saw her not as she appeared, healthy and whole of limb, but mangled and bloody.

Violated.

Her creamy skin streaked and crusted with blood, her lush curves horribly mutilated in the heinous ways his patrol reported Kenneth and his band had massacred his crofters' women.

And the poor crofters themselves.

Their innocent bairns, too.

Even the oxen and milk cows hadn't been spared. Naught had escaped their butchery.

Closing his eyes on the imagined horrors, Duncan threw back his head and let out a bellow of sheer rage. When he opened his eyes again, Linnet stood directly beneath him, her hands clutching the edge of the table for support.

"My lord, I must speak with you," she stammered, the words trembling as much as her body. " 'Tis a matter of grave importance."

Seeing her so close, so near he caught the sweetness of her scent rising up to him, pushed Duncan's control beyond its limits. The very thought aught could happen to her made his blood run cold. The possibility terrified him and undid the last vestige of his already waning discipline.

Jumping from the table, he landed mere inches from her and clamped his hands down hard on her shoulders. "Whate'er possessed you to hie yourself down here?" he shouted, his words echoing in the vastness of the vaulted hall. "Can you not see this is no place for a woman?"

Her trembling increased at his outburst, but she stood her ground. "Sir . . . *husband* . . . you did ask me to warn you if ever I foresaw danger."

"Lady, 'tis because of *danger* I ordered a guard on your door. I willna have you underfoot here, jostled about and hearing tales not fit for a lady's ears!" he fair boomed, his voice rising with each word.

"But—"

"No buts," he cut her off, half-mad from the silky feel of her hair beneath his fingers, for as he spoke he imagined her shining tresses brittle and matted with dried blood. "Naught you can warn me of matters now. 'Tis too late."

Linnet shook her head. "Nay, but it does. What I must tell you has naught to do with whatever wickedness has caused you to raise a hue and cry." She paused to wet her lips. "'Tis of a future evil I must warn you, a foretoken I beg you to hear."

Duncan swallowed his irritation. He didn't want to learn of more ill tidings. What he wanted was to know her safe in her chamber.

"Lady, I dinna ken what fouler deed can befall me than what already has. A full score of my kinsmen and their families have been killed, *butchered*," he told her, his voice ragged, drained. "Simple farmers who work the outlying reaches of MacKenzie land. 'Twas Kenneth's doing, and an even worse devastation than he'd wrought upon the Murchisons. In the wee hours, I'll ride out with a party of my best men. God willing, we'll find them before they can escape us."

His wife blanched upon hearing his words, but didn't lower her gaze. Instead, she slowly shook her head once more. "It was not Kenneth I saw," she insisted, digging her heels into the rushes when he tried to propel her from the hall. "'Twas a stranger, a two-headed man surrounded by flames."

Gasps issued from the men standing near enough to have heard her whispered words, and Duncan swept the lot of them with a furious glare, cowing them into silence.

'Twas nonsense his lady wife spoke, and he wouldn't have his men plagued by thoughts of two-headed monsters whilst Kenneth merrily hacked his way through those MacKenzie kin not dwelling within the safety of Eilean Creag's protective walls.

Gathering Linnet into his arms, he stalked toward the spiral stair at the back of the hall. His men fell back, making way for them, as he strode angrily through their midst. "'Tis no such thing as two-headed men. I'll hear naught of such drivel," he thundered, purposely raising his voice so his men would hear. To them, he called, "Sharpen your blades, then get what sleep you can. 'Twill be time to sally forth before you know it."

"I wouldn't discount the lady's words," Sir Marmaduke cautioned, stepping out of the throng and boldly blocking Duncan's way up the stairs. "It behooves you to listen to her warning."

Duncan's patience snapped. "Indeed?"

"Yes," the Sassunach replied, crossing his arms. "She wouldn't appear so troubled without just cause."

"And, pray, did you *hear* her warning? 'Twas of a two-headed man she spoke." Duncan heaved a deep sigh. "Mayhap such blighted creatures roam England, but I forswear I've ne'er seen one hereabouts. Furthermore, it behooves *you* to get yourself out of my way lest I be tempted to ask why my orders weren't followed. I told you to post a guard on my lady's door."

He paused to narrow his eyes menacingly at his friend. "Is it possible you also neglected to send a guard to the lad's chamber as well?"

"Think you I'd shirk my duties?" Sir Marmaduke asked, a look of mock astonishment on his scarred face. "Nay, my liege, never would I ignore your wishes, 'tis only a bit late I am in implementing them . . . with just reason, of course."

"And what might that be?"

Rather than answer him, Sir Marmaduke nodded to someone in the crowd behind Duncan. Before he could turn around to see who it was, Thomas, the tongueless lad, pushed his way forward, Robbie perched high atop his broad shoulders, a child-sized wooden sword clutched tightly in the boy's hand. Mauger, Robbie's ancient hound, followed close on Thomas's heels.

Duncan's heart turned over in his chest. If e'er he'd doubted he possessed one, he knew it now. As with Linnet, for one sickening moment, he imagined the wee lad limp and lifeless, bloodied and bruised.

For a moment, Duncan lost his footing on the loose rushes, slick as they were with ale spilled from his men's tankards. He stumbled and would've dropped Linnet had she not clung to his neck. Truth to tell, he was nigh onto losing the last victuals he'd eaten, so wrenching was the thought of Robbie meeting the same fate as he knew had befallen his crofters' innocent bairns.

"What's the meaning of this?" he demanded of Sir Marmaduke, venting his rage on him rather than face the demons riding his back.

Keeping his gaze averted from young Thomas and Robbie, he thundered on, "Why isn't he in his chamber with a guard watching over him?"

"I dinna need a guard," Robbie piped up, brandishing his little toy sword. "Uncle Marm'duke said I must protect the ladies."

"And so you shall, little mite," Sir Marmaduke addressed the child, his good eye twinkling with mirth.

Duncan winced inwardly at the look of adoration Robbie bestowed on his uncle. How long had it been since the lad had looked at him thusly?

Saints help him, he couldn't remember, and admitting such was akin to having a white-hot blade thrust deep into his belly.

His lady wife twisted in his arms, turning toward Thomas and Robbie. "I vow 'tis no man I'd trust more to defend me," she said warmly, her voice, for the moment at least, no longer shaky and frightened.

Stealing a glance at her, Duncan saw her lips were gently curved as she gazed lovingly at the lad. Faith, she had the face of an angel when she smiled like that. 'Twas a look she'd gifted him with, too.

Once or twice. Mayhap more often.

And each time he'd managed to banish it with the bitter utterance of his harsh and foolhardy words.

"I asked you a question, Strongbow," he said tightly, tamping down the shame he felt at his own actions and aiming a heated glance at his Sassunach brother-in-law. "I would that you answer it."

For the space of a heartbeat, Duncan thought the Englishman would try to outstare him, but he finally complied. "Be our intent not obvious? We were making haste to bring Robbie and your lady's maid to your wife's chamber."

He paused, arching his one intact brow. "It was surely an oversight on your part to order two guards posted at separate doors when in truth it is wiser to have the Lady Linnet, her woman, and Robbie, safely ensconced in one chamber, with one guard?"

Heat crept up Duncan's neck at the wisdom of his

friend's words and at his own neglect in seeing it himself. He'd meant to spend what few hours remained till he'd must rouse his men, sleeping peacefully in his lady's arms.

Right or wrong, naught else had concerned him.

The saints knew he'd need his rest, and all his wits, afore it was time to lead his men in pursuit of Kenneth. But the good Lord knew no peace would be his with Elspeth and Robbie sharing the chamber.

"I—" Duncan snapped his mouth shut, swallowing the sharp protest he'd been about to voice when he caught sight of Fergus and his lady hovering on the edge of the circle of men gathered round them.

Although she tried to hide it, he could tell the old woman was frightened. 'Twas writ all o'er her face and in the way her gaze kept darting to the wicked-looking mace Fergus held in his gnarled hands.

"Aye, 'tis right you are," Duncan conceded, watching Elspeth as he spoke. Sure enough, the taut lines around her mouth relaxed upon hearing his words.

Turning first to Sir Marmaduke, then young Thomas and Fergus, he continued, "Marmaduke, you help me escort the women up the stairs. Thomas, you'll follow with the lad, then stand guard at the door. And you, Fergus, see the men stop quaffing ale. Send a few extra up on the wall walk and to the gatehouses and make certain the rest bed down to sleep. 'Twill be a short night."

His commands issued, he nodded briskly at his seneschal, then began the circular climb up the stone steps, Linnet cradled securely in his arms. The others followed close behind, the burning torch Sir Marmaduke held aloft casting eerie shadows on the wall as they went.

"I must speak with you," Linnet whispered close to his ear, her warm breath sweet against his skin, and stirring more than his hair. "You misunderstand the portent of my vision. It was not a true two-headed man I glimpsed, but a veiled warning. My gift always works thusly, and I can do naught but guess the meaning of such messages."

Curling her fingers around his neck, she tried to draw him closer. "I canna speak louder lest the others hear, and I do not wish to frighten Robbie, but you must heed the warning. Please, I beg you."

Without slowing his pace up the cold and damp-smelling stair passage, Duncan shifted her in his arms, pulling her tighter against his chest. He held her so close his heady male scent filled each breath she took, and the hard, unyielding links of his mail shirt pressed into her skin despite the thickness of her woolen mantle.

As if he hadn't heard her plea, or chose to ignore it, he remained silent until they came to the door of their bedchamber. Halting before it, her husband ordered Sir Marmaduke to open the door, then, without releasing her, he stood back to allow the others to file inside.

Rather than follow them into the darkened chamber, he remained looming near the arched opening, saying nary a word as the Sassunach busied himself rekindling the fire and Elspeth bustled about like a mother hen, lighting tallow candles with shaking hands whilst murmuring reassurances to Robbie. The boy sat by the hearth, his arms wrapped tightly around the neck of his dog.

The strapping youth, Thomas, hovered just inside the door, his long arms hanging loose at his sides while he repeatedly nudged the floor rushes with the toe of his well-worn boot.

Stepping away from the opened door and into the deep shadows of a wall embrasure, Duncan finally set Linnet on her feet. He took a firm hold on her elbows and looked deep into her eyes. "So, my sweeting, what is this dire warning I must heed? What meaning do you see behind this two-headed man of flame?"

"He was not of flame," she said, uncomfortable even recollecting the frightening image. "The flames surrounded him. 'Twas as if he stood in the very mouth of hell itself."

Duncan folded his arms across his broad chest. "And what do you make of that? Do you foresee a fire? Shall I have wet hides and buckets of water made ready?"

Linnet glanced downward at her tightly clasped hands. How could she tell him she didn't know the vision's meaning? Had he not listened when she'd told him she could but guess?

"Well?" he asked, leaning back against the stone wall.

"I know not, my husband," she said after a moment's hesitation, the words barely audible even to her own ears.

He gave her a penetrating look, the kind that made his deep blue eyes appear black, as dark as the hair sweeping back from his proud forehead. "Then, pray what do you *think* the vision meant?"

Linnet wet her lips. It was hard to concentrate, even

difficult to breathe, when he stood so near and peered at her with such an intense look upon his handsome face.

"I think—I think," she began, fair stumbling over her own tongue, "it was a warning."

"So you've told me," he said, capturing her face between his warm hands. " 'Tis what you fear may happen I would know."

"I—I fear the flames meant the two-headed man is of the devil. A man filled with evil," she told him, giving voice to her fears. "And I believe the two heads speak of one who would betray you. A friend you dare not trust."

"A friend?" Her husband looked doubtful, almost amused. He didn't believe her.

She could tell.

"You doubt me," she said the words as a statement, not a question.

Duncan dropped his hands from her face, catching her own in his larger ones, lacing his fingers with hers. "I vow I wish to believe you, lady, but a *friend*?"

She nodded. "So the message feels to me. I cannot say who would do you false, but of the two heads, one smiled whilst the other was vile. Evil." She squeezed his hands, trying to make him understand. "Please, 'tis important. I know it. Someone you trust speaks with two tongues. You must beware."

To her great relief, a look of dawning comprehension stole across his face. "And so I shall. 'Tis no doubt Kenneth you saw. He is a master of deceit who would seek to charm you whilst hiding a well-honed blade behind his back," Duncan reasoned.

"He fooled my father thusly, ever playing on our

sire's largesse," he went on. "When we were young, he had me deceived too. For a time."

Linnet shook her head, she *had* to convince him. "Nay, it was not Kenneth I saw. 'Tis certain I am, and whoe'er he was, he bodes ill and . . ." Her words trailed off when he slipped a hand beneath her hair and began caressing the back of her neck.

"Linnet," he said, his voice cajoling. "It can be no other. Kenneth is a haveless nithing who would defile any and all things what, in his twisted mind, keep him from attaining what he wants."

"Nay, ple—"

Duncan silenced her by placing two fingers against her lips. "I'm thinking the warning came because of this most recent terror he's wrought unto my people. Never has he dared go so far and he willna get away with it. 'Tis nary a soul amongst my men who'll rest until he's breathed his last."

"You mean to kill him?"

"There can be no other way. I cannot turn my back on such carnage as he's allowed himself this time," her husband vowed, his voice cold. "His vicious acts cannot be undone, but we shall claim retribution, and it will be swift and without mercy."

Botheration welled inside Linnet's chest. He still didn't believe her. The saints knew her husband must exercise vengeance on his onerous half brother, but *she* knew the two-headed man in her vision hadn't been Kenneth.

Nay, the wretched creature foretold a danger yet to come.

A danger her lord husband refused to see.

Tears of frustration pricked the backs of her eyes, but she blinked them away. From somewhere close behind her, footsteps approached, then a man cleared his throat as he neared the alcove where she and Duncan stood in the shadows.

"Your lady's maidservant and the boy are settled, the fire stoked," the Sassunach told her husband. "By your leave, I shall see who Fergus has sent to the battlements."

"Aye, go. I'll join you shortly," Duncan said, stepping forward but keeping her in the shelter of the deep wall embrasure with a firm hand to her elbow.

From outside the alcove, Sir Marmaduke peered at her as if he meant to say something, but he must've decided otherwise, for he gave Duncan a brisk nod, then left them alone.

The moment he disappeared up the turret stairs, Duncan turned back to face her. He, too, peered at her strangely, but unlike the look Sir Marmaduke had given her, *this* look sent heat coursing through her and made her feel as if she'd soon melt into a puddle at her husband's feet.

Without a word, he drew her tight against him. Her hands splayed against the solid wall of his chest, the hard coils of his black mail shirt pressing into her palms. Crooking his fingers under her chin, he lifted her head, forcing her to look at him. The unbridled desire in his eyes ignited an equal fire deep in her own core.

Still silent, the passion in his eyes all the words he needed, he brought his mouth dangerously close to hers. "I'd meant to spend these hours in your arms, loving you," he said, his each word sending a whisper of warm breath over her lips, "but I canna pleasure you as I am wont to do when all and sundry occupy our bedchamber."

Linnet raised her hand, placing it gently upon his jaw. He drew in a sharp breath at her touch, as if she'd scorched him. Then he slowly turned his head and pressed a gentle kiss into her hand. She sighed, her knees almost going out on her when he began flicking the tip of his tongue back and forth across the tender skin of her palm.

"Aye, lass," he vowed, his voice ragged, "I burn with need for you, but a kiss must suffice for I dare not tarry in joining Marmaduke on the battlements."

"Will you be long?" Linnet almost did not recognize her own voice, so breathless were her words. "Shall I await you here?"

He seemed to consider, but then shook his head. "Nay, I will not return this way. 'Tis best I bed down in the hall with my men."

"Must you? Can you not sleep in our chamber? The others will surely be deep in slumber by the time you return, they will not disturb us," she coaxed, emboldened by the insatiable hunger he stirred within her.

Of a sudden, she was athirst for more than just his kisses, blissfully forgetful of the dangers lurking so near. And willing herself blind to the pained look she'd seen pass quickly o'er his face when she'd mentioned Elspeth and Robbie. "Please," she tried again, melting against him, her skin tingling in anticipation of his touch. "Please reconsider."

"You tempt me beyond all bounds," he breathed, lowering his lips to hers. He slanted his mouth over hers in a fierce kiss, claiming her lips, her passion, her very soul, in a way she could no longer deny.

She opened her mouth beneath his, inviting the sensual sweep of his tongue against hers. Desire flared inside her, a raging, all-encompassing fire.

An unquenchable need.

An unbearably sweet ache.

"Saints, but I burn for you," he breathed, moving his lips over her face, neck, and shoulders. With the tip of his tongue, he licked at the sensitive skin beneath her ear, then gently nipped his way up and down the curve of her neck.

The place between Linnet's thighs began to throb with a heavy, pulsing warmth she could scarce endure, so intensely pleasurable was the sensation.

"Did I not know better, I'd swear you've cast an enchantment over me," Duncan vowed, threading his fingers through the unbound mass of her hair. He lifted great handfuls to his face and breathed deep as if he meant to savor the essence of her tresses. *Of her*. Letting go of her hair, he smoothed his hands over her shoulders, easing down her still-unfastened cloak until it pooled at her waist.

Chill air washed over the heated skin he'd bared, passing without resistance through the thin barrier of her linen kirtle to caress her as enticingly as if unseen hands would ply her nakedness, tease and taunt her with a deliciously cool and smooth length of finest silk.

"Touch me," she whispered, and he obliged, closing his hands over her breasts. He kneaded them, gently at first, then in a more bold manner, toying and plucking at her nipples through the linen of her gown until they hardened beneath his fingers and her entire body quivered with sheer pleasure.

Lowering his hands to her hips, he pulled her close against him. Before Linnet could release a single sigh of contentment, he hoisted up her skirts and slipped one hand between her thighs.

"'Tis soft as an angel's sigh, you are, lass," he breathed into her hair, while his fingers caressed the moist heat of her most private place.

With a sharp intake of breath, he stilled the gentle probing of his fingers and simply cupped her, pressing his hand firmly against her woman's flesh. Then he began moving his palm over her in a slow, circular motion. A floodtide of exquisite tingles washed over Linnet's mound, whilst a spiral of pulsing excitement whirled inside her, threatening to spin out of control and shatter any moment.

As if a score of the devil's own mischief-makers spurred him on, Duncan used his fingers again, simply stroking her at first, then idly toying with her damp nether curls as if he had all night to pleasure her.

But he didn't, so when she gave a sweet sigh and arched herself against his hand, Duncan moved a single finger, his middle one, over the tight little bud of her sex—and rubbed.

Her eyes widened and her musky, woman's scent rose up to swirl around them. "This is passion," he told her, his voice husky with his own raging ardor, his senses set afire by the intoxicating scent of her desire.

With his free hand, he took one of hers and pressed it hard against his rigid shaft. "When this madness with

Kenneth has found an end, I shall keep you abed for seven days and seven nights.

"I shall love you until you beg me to cease." He watched her carefully as he spoke, waiting for the instant her eyes would grow heavy-lidded with desire. When the moment came, he increased the pressure of his touch, moving his finger in an ever-faster circle over her need until she sagged against him, trembling, her breath leaving her in one long, shaky gasp.

"Merciful saints," she whispered, clinging to him.

"Nay, my lady, I vow such pleasures are more of a devilish nature," he said, withdrawing his hand and letting her gown drop back into place. "Keep yourself safe while I am gone. There is much more of passion I would teach you, but I cannot if you are not here to learn. Do not even think to attempt anything foolhardy in my absence, or I shall be greatly aggrieved upon my return."

He leaned forward to kiss her, and in that moment, a commotion could be heard on the ramparts above. He drew back from her, his handsome face gone pale.

Unable to bear the way he stared at her, Linnet took hold of his arms and clung to him, refusing to let him brush her aside. His expression frightened her, for he stared at her as if he'd never seen her before. 'Twas as if he'd just discovered he'd been dallying with the bride of Lucifer and not his own lady wife who deeply cared for him.

"Please . . . please do not look at me that way," she implored him, wishing she had the courage to voice her true feelings, beseech him to cease punishing her for another woman's sins.

If Cassandra was the reason for his stony-faced expression.

She wanted to supplicate him, nay, urge him, to fight his inner demons as bravely as he would face his physical foes, beg him to seek not only the quenching of their bodily needs, but those deeper still as well.

The most important needs, the needs of their hearts.

But she remained silent, the closed look on his face turning any words of protest she might dare utter to dust afore she could even form them coherently in her mind, much less give voice to them.

Shifting uncomfortably under his fierce perusal, she drew her mantle up over her exposed shoulders.

"I must leave you now." He reached out to adjust the woolen cloak for her. "Go to your chamber and heed my words. We've tarried here overlong. I've much on my mind and shouldn't have given in to my baser desires."

His words doused whatever longing still lingered within her as surely as if he'd tossed her into the icy waters of Loch Duich.

Baser desires?

Linnet bristled. "Am I naught but a vessel to you, my husband? Do you see in me only a means to take your manly ease when the lust to do so overcomes you? Am I but a burden to be borne, a wife to feed and clothe, but not care about the rest of the time?"

By the Rood! Duncan's eyebrows rose in astonishment at her accusation. Did she not ken the sounds of his men manning the walls had smote him with sheer dread o'er the possibility of harm being done her? Did she not realize he'd pulled away from her because he was appalled at *himself*?

Shocked to the core he could think of lust whilst a score of his people lay slain and maimed, awaiting his vengeance?

Had she so quickly forgotten the tenderness he'd bestowed upon her whilst she'd recovered from the disturbing vision she'd had in his former solar?

"Think you truly I care naught for you?" he asked, unable to keep the accusing tone from his voice. "That I almost lay with you here, upon the stone floor, without even the comfort of strewn rushes, because I need a '*vessel*' to slake my manly needs with?"

To his dismay, she nodded.

"Christ's bones!" he roared, too angry to care if all under his roof heard him. "I vow you have held your hands o'er your ears each time I've told you I am not good with words. I am a man of deeds, not pretty speeches. 'Tis up on the wall walk with Marmaduke I should be, not standing here feeling sick at the thought of harm coming to you."

He paused to catch his breath. "For one blessed with a gift such as yours, 'tis beyond belief how dense you can be. Do you not ken I kissed and touched you to banish the horrors of this day from my mind? So I could take sweet memories of you with me when I ride out of here?" He caught her chin, gently forcing her to look at him. "And do you know why?"

The stubborn vixen shook her head again.

He opened his mouth to tell her 'twas because he cared, but the words lodged firmly in his throat. She might construe caring with *loving*.

And he did not love her.

He loved no one.

An uncomfortable silence settled over them, and to escape it, Duncan withdrew a two-edged dagger from a leather sheath attached to his belt. "Thomas will be standing guard outside your door," he said, handing her the knife. "Give this to him and tell him not to give entry to any save myself, Marmaduke, or Fergus."

She stiffened visibly, but took the blade. "You think we are in danger of being attacked?"

"Nay. None but a fool would attempt a siege against these walls. Kenneth is many things, but not a fool."

"Then why such precautions?"

"Because," he said, trailing his knuckles down her cheek, "naught but a fool would not ascertain his loved ones' safety when peril, real or imagined, is near. And I am even less a fool than my bastard half brother."

Turning away from her, lest he be tempted to reveal further sentiments best kept to himself, he made to march up the turret stairs to join Marmaduke, but his lady wife rushed after him.

"Wait, please," she called, sounding flustered.

"Aye?" He stopped on the third step, but didn't turn around.

"Does Robbie count as one o' your 'loved ones'?" she asked, taking him completely by surprise.

Once more, the gruesome image of the wee lad, pale and lifeless as he knew his poor crofters' bairns to be, flashed before his mind's eye. The very thought turned his blood cold, made his innards quake and his hands tremble.

Sweet Jesus, he'd *said* his loved ones. Wasn't it enough to have spoken the words? Was she so blind, so deaf, she couldn't hear the truth when he'd fair bellowed it at her?

He would not voice the sentiment again.

Not when he himself wasn't prepared to accept the words his lips had spewed forth almost of their own accord and afore he'd even realized he'd spoken them.

He heard her come up behind him, felt her place a hand on the back of his arm. "Is he?" she breathed, her voice eager, expectant. "Are you telling me you do care about the boy?"

"Is he my son?" Duncan asked, the turmoil inside him finding release in the coldly spat words.

"Would it matter?"

Kenneth's face, so like his own but marred by a gloating sneer, chased the sickening image of Robbie, his small body bloodied and twisted, from Duncan's mind.

"Aye, it matters," he said, hating the way his stomach turned inside out at the lie. And hating himself more because he was too cowardly to admit, even to his own self, he did indeed care about the lad.

"Is he mine?" he demanded once more.

"I canna say," Linnet said in a small voice, disappointment weighing heavily on each word.

Duncan stood, ramrod straight, holding his shoulders and neck so rigidly he might as well been carved of stone. He would not turn around, would not let her see the pain he knew had to be mirrored in his eyes.

After what seemed an eternity, she took her hand off his arm and walked away. He waited until he heard her repeat his instructions to young Thomas outside her

door, then trudged the rest of the way up the stone steps
to the battlements.

Bile rose in his throat.

Had he truly claimed he was not a fool?

15

An unceasing and exceedingly annoying thumping noise disturbed Duncan's much-needed sleep. Determined to ignore the infernal sound, he flung out his arm, intending to draw Linnet to his side, but his outstretched hand encountered only matted straw, not his sweet wife's slumbering form.

"What the—" he began, only to leap to his feet, wide-awake, when he realized where he was and why.

As quickly, the source of the loud thumping became apparent when two of his men lumbered into view from the base of the turret stairs. They carried a limp MacKenzie in their arms.

A bloodied MacKenzie with an arrow shaft protruding from his neck!

"Saints, Maria, and Joseph!" Duncan yelled, girding on his sword belt. "Fergus! Rouse the men! We're under attack!"

"*Cuidich' N' Righ!* Save the king!" Fergus shouted in answer, scrambling to his feet as swiftly as his age-bent legs would allow. At once, he began scurrying about the hall, delivering a sound kick in the ribs to any kinsman not yet awake.

"Get yer arses off the floor!" he scolded, waving his mace in a wild circle above his grizzled gray head. "Cease lolling about like witless varlets wi' their feet caught in a sea o' muck!"

"Man the walls!" Duncan thundered, running toward the two kinsmen bearing the injured man. Halting before them, he cleared the nearest trestle table with a broad sweep of his arm.

Duncan leaned over Iain, the wounded clansman, the moment the others lowered him onto the table. He'd meant to offer him a bit of comfort, but the intended words stuck in his throat when he got a closer look at Iain's blood-drained face and the unnatural stillness of his broad chest.

Although he knew what he'd see, Duncan carefully lifted Iain's eyelids. Sightless eyes gazed up at him, their vacant stare piercing him with dread, filling him with rage, and making him aware as naught else could, of the danger lurking outside Eilean Creag's thick walls.

A danger he would not allow entry.

An enemy who'd soon suffer Duncan's vengeance, taste his fury, and rue the day he'd dared thought to lay siege to the MacKenzie stronghold.

"God's blood!" Duncan hissed, thinking not only of Iain's spent life, but also of the young wife and four small bairns left without husband and father.

His mouth set in a grim line, Duncan eased down

Iain's eyelids, then covered his waxen face with a linen napkin. Closing his own eyes, he shook his head to rid himself of the white-hot fury threatening to consume him.

After a moment, he opened his eyes and scanned the hall for his first squire. The youth stood about twenty paces away, tucking all manner of weapons into his belt and boots. "Lachlan," Duncan called, "hie yourself over here."

He came at once, leaping over a table and knocking down a bench before skidding to a halt on the slick rushes. "Aye, sir?" he panted, nigh breathless.

Duncan rested a hand on the lad's shoulder. "Becalm yourself, boy. You willna be able to aim your crossbow if your chest is heaving with each breath you take."

A dark stain colored the squire's cheeks, but he nodded in acquiescence. "What would you bid of me, my lord?"

"Have Cook boil lard and see the kitchen boys gather whatever nastiness they can find," he ordered, his voice steady despite the heated anger coursing through him. "Tell the pages to fill buckets from the cesspits, then make haste getting it all to the battlements." Duncan paused, tightening his hold on the lad's shoulder. "But not afore you've taken a few deep breaths."

Lachlan bobbed his head in answer. His cheeks still flamed, though Duncan suspected his high color came more from nerves at seeing his first true fighting than over embarrassment at having been told to compose himself.

Bracing his hands against his hips, Duncan watched the squire hurry toward the screened passage and the kitchen beyond. On sudden impulse, Duncan halted him with a sharp cry before he disappeared through the darkened archway.

The lad spun around so quickly he almost collided with two burly warriors hastening past him. "Aye, sir?" he called, his arms flailing wildly as he sought to regain his footing.

"Dinna fret, laddie," Duncan's deep voice boomed across the hall. "Whoe're would attempt to breach these walls will taste the bite of our steel . . . or gag to death on the muck we're going to dump on them!"

Hearty cheers went up at Duncan's words. Lachlan's face turned a deeper red, but he made Duncan a low bow before turning and dashing off about his task, a most obvious new bounce to his steps.

Satisfied, Duncan waited until Lachlan disappeared into the shadowy kitchen passage, only then allowing his own face to settle back into a tight grimace.

Once more, he leapt onto a table, this time loudly banging two tankards against each other to get his men's attention. "Cease bellowing, lads, and take your positions!" he roared, tossing aside the tankards when the cheering stopped and all eyes turned his way. "We'll soon have hot oil and refuse enough to drown the bastards in! Now, be off, and may God be with us!"

No sooner had the words left his mouth, than the sounds of angry shouts and the furious clash of steel against steel reached them from above.

'Twas a clamor so earsplitting, if he didn't know better, he would've sworn men were coming to blows in the far end of the hall. Duncan cast a quick glance at each of the hall's dark corners before jumping down from the table.

Impossible though it would have been for an enemy to gain entry to the sanctity of his hall, a great surge of relief washed over him at seeing none but his own men hurrying about, arming themselves or hastening to their posts.

Nay, the loud ruckus echoing through Eilean Creag's cavernous hall, bouncing off the cold stone of its massive walls, came from above, not within.

Men were fighting on the ramparts.

On the ramparts!

With the realization, an unholy chill seized Duncan, curdling his blood and sending icy fingers around his neck. Fingers of dread, cold and unerring, hailing from the blackest pits of hell.

And if he didn't soon free himself of their stranglehold, they'd cut off his air, squeeze the very life out of him.

Saints sustain him, if the attackers had gained the walls, they had scaling ladders and might, even now, be laying one against Linnet's window. Might be attempting to reach her chamber and lay waste to all that was dear to him.

With sickening clarity, the images that had plagued him since first learning of Kenneth's attack on the crofters came back to revisit him.

Only, this time, a thousandfold more frightening.

"Alec! Malcolm!" he thundered, stopping two of his most stalwart men before they could charge up the turret stairs. "Go at once to my lady's chamber. Make certain her windows are shuttered and barred. Kill any who would dare attempt entry. And tell young Thomas to keep his post at the door and to guard it with his life."

Both men nodded, then bounded toward the circular stairway leading to the tower chamber Duncan shared with his wife. Duncan's fists clenched as he watched them take the stairs two at a time.

Hellfire and damnation, but he wanted to race past them; 'twas *his* task to see to his lady's safety.

And the child's, the thought coming as one with his concern for Linnet.

Seeing naught but their beloved faces before him, Duncan barreled his way through the hall. He made straight for the tower stairs, roughly shoving aside any who had the misfortune to happen across his path.

But the weight of duty halted him on the fifth step.

God's blood, what had come over him? He was laird and as such, was honor-bound to see to the safety of his clan.

His entire clan.

Every man, woman, and child, under his roof.

Yet here he was hightailing himself to his lady wife's side, forgetting his responsibilities, and turning a blind eye to his duties as clan chief.

Duncan heaved a great, calming breath and dragged his hands through his sweat-dampened hair. Never would he have thought mere lust, simple physical need and mayhap a spot of affection, would drive him to act so rashly.

Truth tell, and 'twas well he knew, only in commanding his men, in fighting at their sides, could he ensure the safety of all within his walls.

Including Linnet and Robbie.

Knowing what he must do, he cast one more glance up the darkened stairwell. He could still hear Alec and Malcolm's hurrying footfalls. Both would defend his lady and the child with their last breath if need be.

As he, too, would do . . . from the battlements.

Next his men.

His resolve clear, he turned to face the hall. With his hands planted firmly on his hips, he surveyed the chaos unfolding around him.

Praise the saints, it was an orderly chaos.

Fergus still dashed about brandishing his mace and ranting at Duncan's men, barking orders, and doing his best to spur them into action.

Not that any amongst them could be called a laggard.

Nay, far from it.

To a man, they'd roused and armed themselves. With pride, Duncan noted even his youngest squires had heeded what they'd been taught and disposed of their scabbards. Their naked swords gleamed at their sides, unsheathed and battle-ready, thrust through naught but a simple ring attached to their belts.

Not a one would be hindered by an unwieldy scabbard dangling empty at his side.

And none would fall without a fight.

His men were feared as bold and courageous warriors. They ranked as some of the fiercest e'er known to walk the Highlands.

Whoever was foolhardy enough to attack Eilean Creag would pay dearly for their daring.

With pride, Duncan watched his best archers race to man the walls. Others equally skilled, hurried toward umanned wall embrasures whilst those already in place raised their bows, aiming them with deadly intent through arrow loops cut deeply into the thick stone walls.

Duncan curled his fingers around the leather-wrapped hilt of his sword. A trusty weapon, light and perfectly balanced, it's double-edged blade was sharp enough to slice off a man's arm without even taking a notch in its steel if wielded properly.

And Duncan wielded it well.

Better than most.

His hand tightened around the leather grip. 'Twas soft and smooth, growing warm beneath his touch, welcoming him almost as seductively as a woman would her lover's caress.

Duncan's lips curved upward in a bitter travesty of a smile. His intent wasn't that of a lover's. His purpose was earnest.

Deadly earnest and meant to be dealt swiftly and without mercy.

With the strength of mind he'd mastered through years of battle, Duncan pushed all thought from his mind. All thought but protecting his own and driving the enemy from his castle walls. Quickly, he descended the few steps he'd climbed, then crossed the hall with great strides, eager to join his men on the battlements.

But before he could mount the turret stairs, Sir Marmaduke came barreling down them. Breathing hard, his scarred face glistening with beads of sweat, the Sassunach came to an abrupt halt beneath the arched entrance to the hall.

Duncan didn't wait for his friend to catch his breath.

"Who?" was all he asked, though deep inside, he already knew. It could be no other. Still, he repeated the single word. "Who?"

"'Tis Kenneth, the bloody whoreson," Marmaduke panted, dragging the back of his arm across his damp brow. "With the devil's own stealth, they've left their galley anchored out of firing range and used one-man coracles to sneak ashore. It would seem they're trying to undermine the walls."

"And our defenses?"

"We're prepared," Sir Marmaduke reported, breathing hard. "We've been letting loose a steady barrage of arrows upon them, but they're using their boats like shields, holding the upturned coracles over the sappers whilst they pick at our walls."

"And fired arrows?" Duncan asked, stepping aside as two laundresses hurried past, clutching baskets of linen, obviously come to tend poor Iain's body.

"It wouldn't be worth the effort to set the arrows aflame. They've covered the coracles with wet hides. I *did* set fire to a few of the vessels before they could toss hides over them," Marmaduke boasted, his lips twitching in an attempt at a wicked grin. "But I didn't do it with flaming arrows."

Duncan quirked a brow at the Englishman, a sudden suspicion stealing into his mind. "Pray then, what did you use?"

Marmaduke clamped a large hand on Duncan's shoulder. "Something much better, my friend," he said, his voice smooth, fair oozing contentment. "Something we should have consigned to the fires of hell long ago."

"You didn't," Duncan said, his suspicion confirmed

by the look of satisfaction on Marmaduke's ravaged face.

"Indeed I did," Marmaduke acknowledged, a twinkle in his good eye. "Now lets hurry her nithling lover and his pack of misbegotten buffoons on their bloody way to join her. As I recall, she could get quite cross when left waiting overlong."

"Aye," Duncan agreed, a smile spreading across his own face. "'Tis a journey long overdue."

Marmaduke gave a hearty laugh and thwacked Duncan on the back, then both men began the circular climb to the turret wall walk. "Have they gained the gatehouses?" Duncan wanted to know, as they ascended the curving stone steps.

"Nay. Our guards are keeping a hail of arrows and stones raining upon them; they won't venture near either gatehouse or the causeway."

"How many scaling ladders have you seen?"

"Only a few, and they aren't setting them up where they'd do the most good," Marmaduke puzzled. "So far there have been no tries to reach the lady Linnet's window, and Kenneth must know its her chamber."

"Yet they attempt to sap our walls?" Duncan frowned. Something wasn't right. "Kenneth knows this castle cannot be assailed. It's built on solid rock. 'Tis a fool's errand he's on." He stopped in his tracks, turning around to face his brother-in-law. "Or else he means to distract us. But why?"

The Sassunach rubbed his chin. "Hmmmmm . . ."

"Hmmmmm is not an answer."

Marmaduke began tapping his cheek with his forefinger. Finally, he said, "Iain was struck down."

The man was going daft on him. Heat shot into Duncan's cheeks and his pulse leapt with aggravation. "I know that," he snapped. "His body's not yet gone cold, rest his soul. Now, think and dinna tell me what I already ken."

"Iain was one of our best archers."

Now he *was* angry. "So?"

Marmaduke drew a deep breath before speaking. "I would swear upon my beloved Arabella's bones they *chose* to slay Iain. Kenneth had laid his hand above his eyes and appeared to study the men lining the wall walk, then said something to the crossbowman standing beside him. The man took aim, and Iain went down."

Duncan thought a moment. It made no sense. "Mayhap Kenneth had a quarrel with Iain? I know of naught ever falling betwixt them, but I canna conceive any other reason Iain would've been sought out to die."

"Red James was attacked as well."

"Red James?" Duncan fixed Marmaduke with a penetrating stare. "Do not tell me he, too, is dead."

"Nay, he lives. The man is stronger than ten oxen." Marmaduke cast a quick glance up the stairwell before continuing. "One of the miscreants climbed a scaling ladder and slashed open his right arm. The bastard nigh cut him to the bone."

Anger welled in Duncan's chest. Red James was one of his best warriors. "By the Rood," he swore. "Will he lose use of the arm?"

"That hardy knave?" Marmaduke arched his good brow. "It would take more than a mere cut, deep though it be, to slow Red. He hardly blinked! He cast aside his crossbow, drew his sword, and skewered the mangy whoreson. Ran him clear through, then sent his foul carcass and the ladder flying."

Of a sudden, the noise increased. The sound of running feet and the furious clatter of steel against steel warned them the fighting had taken on a new fervor. Men's shouts rose above the din.

Shouts and sharp screams.

Screams of pain.

The kind a man only emits when a blade bites deep.

Deep, sure, and deadly.

"Come, English," Duncan said, yanking his sword from its ring. "We've tarried too long."

With speed born of anger, Duncan charged up the stairs, the Sassunach close on his heels. From behind, Duncan heard the hiss and zing of cold steel as Marmaduke, too, freed his great broadsword.

At the top of the stairs, Marmaduke's hand closed over Duncan's elbow, preventing him from bursting onto the battlements. "Hugh's been hit, too," he said, raising his voice above the clamor.

Duncan swore. "Saints preserve us. Is he down?"

"Nay, only wounded. The arrow passed cleanly through his shoulder."

"Damnation," Duncan swore again. "We have no finer archer than Hugh."

Marmaduke nodded. "True, and 'tis his *right* shoulder—like Red James."

The nagging suspicion that had been dancing so elusively on the edge of Duncan's mind flared and took form. "Iain, Red James, then Hugh," he said, his fury curling into a tight, black knot deep in his gut. "The whoresons are picking off our best warriors apurpose!"

"So it would seem."

"Then let us return the favor."

"With the greatest pleasure, my friend," Marmaduke said raising his sword.

"*Cuidich' N' Righ!*" Duncan shouted, brandishing his own blade. Then he stepped onto the battlements and into complete chaos.

In her tower chamber, Linnet paced like a caged animal. "You canna mean to keep me locked in here," she railed at the two brawny warriors who blocked the room's only exit. They stood unsmiling before the locked door, their muscular arms crossed forbiddingly over their massive chests. "There will be injuries, mayhap deaths. My husband would want me in the hall to tend his men."

" 'Twas the laird himself who declared you shall not leave this chamber, my lady," the taller one, Malcolm told her, his voice so calm and courteous Linnet wished to hurl something at him.

"Please, lady, you must becalm yourself," Alec, the other one tried to coax, a pleading note underlying his deep voice. "We canna go against the Black Stag's orders. 'Tis for your own good."

Linnet bristled. Angrily, she cast a glance at Elspeth, who sat by the fire, holding the sleeping Robbie against her ample girth. The boy's old mongrel, Mauger, slept, too, curled on the floor at Elspeth's feet.

'Twas apparent from the way Elspeth pointedly avoided her gaze that her old nurse sided with the two giants sent to keep her from her duties.

" 'Tis well and good to keep my lady and Robbie

safe behind barred and guarded doors, but I am lady of this castle. 'Tis my place to tend the injured." She paused, then aimed her next words at Elspeth. "Your betrothed is likely in the middle of the fray as well. Would you not that I be there to tend him should be struck down?"

"I am but a servant," Elspeth said, the humble words foreign to her usual self-assured demeanor. "It would not be seemly for me to dispute the laird's wishes."

Fair desperate and spurred to action by a series of hollow-sounding thuds as arrows thwacked against the closed window shutters, Linnet dashed across the room and snatched up her herb satchel.

Near tears, she waved it under the odious guards' noses. "In this bag is everything needed should harm befall my lord or a single one of his men." Pausing, she blinked back the stinging moisture burning her eyes. "And you would keep me from aiding them."

The men grew still, nodding in silent admission they'd heard her, but not budging from where they stood.

"Do you not care if one of my husband's men dies for lack of proper care?" she pressed, clutching the satchel close to her chest.

The look they exchanged told her more than spoken words.

"Who?" she demanded, dropping her bag of herbs and rushing up to them. With trembling hands, she clutched at the tunic of the one called Malcolm. "Who is—" she broke off, panic seizing her. "Not my husband?"

Malcolm swallowed and slid a sideways glance at Alec.

"You will tell me," she cried, pulling on Malcolm's shirt. "I demand it."

"Naught has happened to Sir Duncan, lady," Alec spoke up. "'Twas Iain. He took an arrow in his neck. Naught would've saved him."

"There will be others, and they deserve my care," Linnet said, letting go of the warrior. She stepped back and straightened her shoulders, her determination growing upon hearing this dire news. "Mayhap even my husband."

"You've no need to fret over the laird," the more talkative one, Alec, tried to reassure her. "A more able warrior never lived. I've seen him cleave a man in two with one stroke of his broadsword."

"And if he cannot wield it? If he takes an arrow?"

"He'd fight on. Your husband is a masterful opponent, my lady," Malcolm said, breaking his silence. "He fears naught and would challenge the devil himself to defend his own."

"I can fight, too," Robbie piped up, suddenly awake. He sprang from Elspeth's arms, his little wooden sword held high. "I will fight Uncle Kenneth to the death."

"And surely you will," Elspeth granted, pushing herself out of her chair and gathering Robbie up in her sturdy arms, toy sword and all. "'Tis a fine and noble warrior you'll no doubt be. *Someday*," she crooned, settling herself back in the chair, the lad held firmly upon her aproned lap. "But first you've a mite bit of growing to do."

"Well, I *am* grown," Linnet boldly proclaimed. "And I can fight well. My brothers taught me."

At Elspeth's shocked gasp, Linnet defiantly lifted

her skirts and displayed the finely honed dirk tucked into her boot. "'Tis sharpened, and I ken well how to use it." She paused to glare at Alec and Malcolm as she let the hem of her gown fall back into place. "Dinna make me show you."

"My lady, you go too far," Elspeth warned. "Have you forgotten the tales of Sir Duncan's valor? He does not need your help to fight off his enemies. As for the wounded, *if* there be any, Fergus will have thought to see such needs are taken care of."

Linnet shot her lady a furious look and resumed her pacing. But after three rounds of the chamber, she halted in the middle of the room. "Do none of you hear the shouts and screams out there?" she cried, wringing her hands. "Are you all deaf?" Her frantic gaze raked first Elspeth, then her husband's two men. "I can't bear it, do you hear me? How can you expect me to stand here and do naught?"

The old hound, Mauger, stirred at her outburst. As if unsure of the welcome he'd receive, he crept forward, his head low, his straggly tail held between his legs. Whining softly, he nudged her, pressing close against her legs.

"Mauger," Linnet breathed, the one word almost too thick to get past her painfully constricted throat. The dog gazed up at her, his brown eyes filled with concern and adoration. Not taking his gaze off her, he gave another pitiful whine, then bathed her hands with kisses.

His display of devotion snapped the tenuous threads holding Linnet together. With a little cry, she dropped to her knees and wrapped her arms around the ancient mongrel, burying her cheek against his shoulder. "Oh,

Mauger, why will they not listen?" she murmured against the soothing warmth of his rough coat. "'Tis important . . . so important . . ."

Holding tight to Mauger as if only he understood, she kept her eyes squeezed shut, refusing to let her tears fall. Even when Elspeth laid a gentle hand upon the back of her head, she kept her cheek pressed firmly against the dog's shoulder, clinging to him and drinking in the solace he so lovingly offered.

If only something would drown out the horrid sounds reaching them from the battlements.

Then something did.

Something infinitely more terrifying for its portent.

'Twas Sir Marmaduke's voice, loud and gruff, ordering young Thomas to unlock the door.

Linnet scrambled to her feet at once. She remained where she stood, frozen to the spot, whilst Alec slid back the heavy bolts barring the door from inside, for it had been secured against intruders both within and without.

An unnatural silence fell heavily over the chamber as the door creaked open to reveal the tall Sassunach. His formidable presence filled the archway, but it was the grim expression on his scarred face that struck terror into Linnet's heart.

That, and the pity in his one good eye.

"Nay!" she cried, her world crashing around her feet. "My lord? Is he . . ." She let her voice trail off, unable to put her fear into words.

Sir Marmaduke shook his head, then drew an arm over his begrimed forehead. "I am sorry, my lady, but I must escort you to your husband. He lives, but I fear he will not much longer if he does not have his wounds tended." He paused. "The fool refuses to leave the battlements."

No! He must not die! Linnet didn't know if she screamed the words or if they sounded only in her head. She couldn't tell, for the floor had tilted crazily beneath her feet, and the room seemed to be spinning around her.

Ever faster, a dizzying whirl of colors and blurred faces, all crowding around her, staring at her.

He must not die!

The English knight's strong arm went around her, supporting her, and someone . . . Elspeth? . . . pushed her herb satchel into her arms, then draped her mother's *arisaid* around her shoulders.

And somewhere behind her, a young boy cried.

"God go with you," one of the guardsmen said, but she didn't ken which one.

Then Marmaduke was guiding her from the room, urging her toward the stairs to the battlements. "The wounds are not so grave, my lady, do not fear," he sought to console her. " 'Tis only he will not stop fighting and his movements are causing him to lose too much blood. You must convince him to leave the battlements. He will listen to you."

He must not die!

Linnet's knees gave out halfway up the stairs. Before she could crumple to the stone steps, Sir Marmaduke caught her, easily lifting her into his arms.

"He will live," he assured her, "and I will not let any harm come to you. Do not be afraid."

Holding tight to her herb bag, Linnet pressed her lips together and said nothing.

"All will be well," he promised as they rounded yet another curve in the stairs.

He must not die!

"We are almost there." Marmaduke halted before the door to the wall walk. "Lady, have you listened to me? Have you heard a word I've said?" he asked as he eased open the door with his foot.

"Aye, I hear," Linnet whispered, her voice ragged.

But she didn't mean his well-meant words of comfort.

Nay, Holy St. Margaret have mercy on her, she only heard the words in her head.

Over and over again.

He must not die!

She simply wouldn't allow it.

16

"**I** dinna believe my own eyes!" Duncan raged, glaring at his addlepated Sassunach brother-in-law. "Has your brain turned to mush, English?"

Bold as day, Sir Marmaduke stood before him, Linnet fair crushed against his mailed chest. With his brawny arms and broad shoulders, he all but swallowed her, one arm wrapped tightly about her waist, the other holding a shield over her head and upper body.

Only a fleeting glimpse of her lustrous red-gold hair and the bulge of her herb bag peeking from beneath the shield revealed just who the English knight cushioned so protectively with his great, lumbering form.

Duncan swiped at the blood dripping into his eyes and let loose a string of vicious oaths. He didn't give a pig's arse *how* carefully the witless dolt sought to shield her from the arrows whizzing all about them, his lady wife did not belong on the battlements.

He'd given strictest orders she was to be kept under guard.

In her chamber.

Safe.

Away from danger.

Not here on the wall walk exposed to a hail of fire arrows and broadsword-wielding assassins bent on slashing anything that moved.

Still cursing, Duncan cast aside his crossbow and, heedless of the blood on his hands, yanked Linnet from Sir Marmaduke's grasp and thrust her to her knees before the crenellated wall. Gritting his teeth against the searing pain the effort cost him, he shoved her down, lower and lower, until she was completely sheltered by one of the stone merlons.

Staunchly ignoring his agony, he straightened and snatched the shield away from Marmaduke. "Cover yourself and dinna move," he barked, shoving it at Linnet. "Do as I say," he snapped when she started to protest.

"But, my lord—*Duncan*—plea—"

"Silence!" he cut her off, whirling to face Marmaduke. "Have you lost your wits, you fool? What were you thinking bringing her up here? If aught—" he broke off suddenly and clutched his side. A fresh stream of hot blood spilled onto his hands.

He'd been clipped by a crossbow bolt.

This time it was Sir Marmaduke who swore. His arm shot around Duncan, supporting him. "'Tis not I who would be a fool this night. If you will not heed my advice and abjure yourself below, then pray listen to your lady."

"Aye, Duncan," his wife pleaded, her head popping up above Marmaduke's shield. "Merciful saints, you've an arrow in your arm and I do not want to know how many other wounds. 'Twill serve no pur—"

"Get down, I said!" An arrow whistled through a gap between the merlons, barely missing Linnet's head. A sickening thwack and a pain-filled grunt bore testament to the arrow's having found another mark.

Glancing quickly to his right, Duncan saw one of his younger squires go down, the arrow shaft protruding from his back. Rage as red as the blood trickling into his eyes surged through him at the sight.

Beside him, Sir Marmaduke muttered a quick prayer.

The squire was but a lad.

A boy who, mere days before, had proudly showed Duncan the first signs of facial hair sprouting on his youthful chin.

And now he was dead.

Duncan threw back his head and roared out his anger.

Turning back to his wife, he found her creeping on hands and knees towards the boy. "Crucifix, woman, stay where I put you! I will not see you killed."

"Yet you would have me a widow before morn," she argued, still moving toward the fallen squire. "If you dinna care to have your own wounds tended, I shall lend my talents to others." She glanced defiantly at him over her shoulder. "And you willna stop me."

"You cannot help the lad. He is dead."

Linnet froze and stared at the inert youth. Her face paled as if she only just noticed the queer bend of his limbs, only now realized the arrow had surely pierced a lung, mayhap even the lad's heart.

She opened her mouth, perhaps to scream, but no sound came forth. Her stomach fair turning inside out, she could do naught but stare at the slain squire.

Heaven help her, 'twas the one who'd reminded her of Jamie, her favorite brother.

As Jamie'd looked in his youth.

'Twas fond she'd been of the young squire, a cheery lad who'd oft gifted her with a broad smile, then blushed furiously when she'd smiled back.

"Nay!" Denial burst from her throat. Blind and deaf to the pandemonium going on all about her, Linnet hurriedly scrambled the last few paces to where the boy lay so still.

"He is not gone," she insisted, rolling him onto his side. "He is not."

But the loll of his head and his blank stare told another tale.

Horror washed over her, colder and more biting than the chill sea wind tearing at her hair and whipping the loose folds of her *arisaid*.

Her gaze flew from the dead squire to her husband. He'd retrieved his crossbow and now leaned heavily against one of the square-toothed stone merlons, struggling to discharge a quarrel through the open space between.

His concentration was apparent in the tight set of his jaw, his waning strength in the way his powerful frame trembled as he cocked the bow with his foot, took aim, then loosed the deadly weapon.

From below, a sharp yelp of pain proved he'd hit his

target. Duncan sagged against the merlon and let the cumbersome crossbow slip from his bloodied grasp. "God willing," he breathed, his normally booming voice, ragged and weary, "God willing, that was the brigand who took young Ewan's life."

Linnet swallowed hard, her heart aching at the anguish she saw in his eyes. Pain she knew came from seeing his young squire meet such an untimely death and not from the grievous wounds he bore.

Tears of anger and fear jabbed into the backs of her eyes but she refused to let them fall. She could weep later, now she must get her husband to safety, see to his wounds. Pushing to her feet, she ran forward and clutched his uninjured right arm.

"Have done with this show of MacKenzie valor and come inside, my lord," she begged, pulling on him in vain. Though gravely injured, he stood as immovable as the stone of his castle. "I beseech you."

His face set in tight, grim lines, he shook her off as if she were naught but a pesky fly. Ignoring her pleas, he stooped to retrieve his discarded crossbow, his chest heaving with agony as he slowly straightened. Clenching his teeth, he made to reload it, but Sir Marmaduke wrested it away from him.

With a mastery that made the breath catch in her throat, Linnet watched the Sassunach right the unwieldy weapon, fix his bolt, draw, take aim, and release the lethal quarrel before she could let out her pent-up breath.

Then he propped the crossbow against the crenellated wall, boldly placing himself between the weapon and Duncan. "You will not live to use that crossbow or any other bloody weapon again lest you remove yourself from here at once.

"Duncan, please," Linnet pleaded anew. "'Tis covered with blood you are. Ne'er have I seen a—"

A fierce scowl darkening his blood-smeared face, Duncan suddenly lunged forward, grabbing Linnet by the elbow and yanking her out of the way as two kitchen boys hurried past carrying a large vessel of hot, bubbling grease. "Careless whelps," he called after them, "watch what you're about!"

He held her tight, his grip no less powerful for his injuries, and kept her out of harm's way as two of his men took the vat of boiling oil from the kitchen lads and hurled its contents over the wall.

Screams pierced the night as the scalding brew rained onto the heads of those unfortunates who happened to be in its sizzling downward path. Duncan gave the men who'd tossed the hot oil over the wall a grim nod, then loosened his hold on Linnet.

"See her back whence you fetched her," he said tersely to Marmaduke, fair pushing her into the Sassunach's arms. "And do not even think to disobey me," he added, then limped toward a small cluster of men clashing swords with two of Kenneth's miscreants who'd gained the wall walk. He drew his own blade as he went.

"Lady, come," Sir Marmaduke said, wrapping his arm about her shoulders. "Allow me to return you safely belowstairs. I should have known it would do no good to bring you here."

Linnet held back. At the far end of the battlements, Duncan wrangled with a man lashing furiously around himself with an ugly-looking battle-ax. And Duncan's movements were slow, hampered by his injuries.

Yet he fought on.

Despite the hail of fire arrows arching overhead, trailing acrid smoke behind them before clattering on the stone floor of the wall walk in a shower of sparks and ashes. Pages dashed madly about, their sole task stamping out the flames with their feet.

But the mighty Black Stag of Kintail fought on—just as his guardsmen had told her he would.

"Lady, come," Sir Marmaduke urged again, trying to drag her away. "'Tis not safe for you here."

"Nay. I will not go," Linnet argued, stiffening in the Sassunach's iron hold on her, straining against him.

Her heart pounded hard within her breast as she watched her husband fend off his assailant's vicious attack. 'Twere he hearty and whole, uninjured, he would have skewered his enemy and sent his corpse sailing over the wall afore the man had even lifted his ax.

But he wasn't whole and hearty.

And he was getting weaker by the moment, she could tell. If naught happened, he'd soon be felled.

He must not die.

She'd sworn he wouldn't, vowed it to herself, and if the saints so deemed it, she'd perish keeping her vow.

God willing, neither of them would die.

A fire arrow whistled past, coming to a sputtering halt near the edge of her cloak, and Sir Marmaduke loosened his hold on her to stomp on its smoking shaft. Linnet seized the moment to tear away from him and dash to the wall.

Before any of the men could stop her, she snatched

up Duncan's forgotten crossbow and heaved the cumbersome weapon into place, aiming it downward through the open space of a crenel.

"Kenneth MacKenzie," she called to the men below, "I challenge you to show yourself!"

"Lady, cease or you will be killed." Sir Marmaduke slid his arms around her from behind and began pulling her away from the wall.

Linnet dropped the crossbow and grabbed hold of a merlon, clinging to it while arrows whistled through the crenels and over their heads, sailing into the castle wall behind them with loud thwacks.

"Leave her be," a deep voice rose up from the rocky shoreline beneath the battlements. And with the words, all fighting stopped.

A lone fire arrow clattered to the stone floor near Linnet, then an eerie hush fell over the men assembled on the ground below as well as those manning the turret walls. For a long moment, the only sound was the gusty sea wind blowing over the ramparts and the rhythmic whoosh of waves smacking into the jagged rocks lining the base of the tower.

"Let the lady come forth and speak her piece," the voice called again.

"Do not heed him, 'tis madness," Marmaduke whispered above her ear. "He would think naught of seeing you killed."

"God's teeth!" her husband bellowed, his bloodied fingers curling around her arm in a viselike grip. "Go inside at once!" he commanded, yanking her arm with such force, she tumbled away from the merlon and out the Sassunach's firm hold.

"Leave me be," she shrieked, unconsciously mimicking Kenneth's words. The blood on Duncan's hands made them slippery, and she took advantage, squirming nimbly from his grasp. "I ken what I am about," she breathed, pouncing on the crossbow where it rested against the crenellated wall.

"Seize her!" her husband shouted at the men closest to her.

"Stay back!" Linnet warned as they closed in on her. Then, feigning acquiescence, she bent down, making as if to adjust the folds of her cloak. She whipped out her dirk instead. Raising it calmly to her throat, she said, "Dinna think I will not use it. I would speak with my husband's half brother, and none shall hinder my doing so."

Muttered curses and grumbles answered her, but the men, Duncan and Marmaduke included, remained where they stood.

Keeping her gaze steady on the circle of fiercely scowling MacKenzie warriors, she placed the dirk on top of the nearest merlon. Then she swept them with a dark look of her own. "Those of you who've seen me teaching Robbie to throw a blade know how fast I am with this dagger. Do not force me to show you again."

When they said naught, she nodded and lifted the crossbow. "I have come," she called to the tall man standing below, his broad shoulders and arrogantly cocked head raging high above his men, who still hunkered beneath the shelter of their upturned boats.

She peered down at him, wishing fervently she could set him aflame with the heat of her stare.

Even at this distance, he looked so much like her

husband, 'twas only the strength of her will that kept her from glancing over her shoulder to make certain Duncan stood yet behind her and hadn't somehow found his way belowstairs and outside.

But she knew beyond a doubt her husband hadn't left the wall walk. She could feel his fury burning holes into her back.

As she could feel the bemused smile his loathsome half brother bestowed upon her. Linnet shuddered, steeling herself against his unsettling resemblance to Duncan. Briefly, the greenish black glow she'd seen around him that long-ago day in the yew grove, flared, reminding her of the kind of man he truly was.

She shuddered again and willed her hands steady on the bow.

"I am come, Kenneth MacKenzie," she repeated, "to bid you and your men begone from this place." She paused to cock the crossbow with her foot. "If you willna, I shall fire a bolt from this bow into your bonnie knee, and your men can carry you away."

Kenneth inclined his head and deepened his smile. A gust of briny air carried his men's snickers up to Linnet and those standing upon the battlements.

"Tell your men to cease their laughing—or have you brought different brigands with you than those present when we first met?" she challenged.

Kenneth raised a hand and his men fell silent. "'Tis not you they find amusing, fair lady," he called up to her, his rich, deep voice so like Duncan's her blood nigh curdled. "They—*we*—find it humorous that my brother would hide behind your skirts."

Behind her, Duncan fairly roared his outrage. Linnet

heard his struggles and knew his men were holding him fast. The Sassunach admonished him in a low voice, "Be still, you fool. 'Tis to rile you he speaks thusly. He would that you storm forward so one of his assailant's can take you down before you could draw your bow."

"My husband is not here," Linnet returned, her voice firm and steady though her heart beat wildly at the lie. She heard Duncan swear, then the black oath was cut off sharply as if someone had clapped a silencing hand over his mouth.

"He is gravely wounded, and his men have taken him below," she barged on, afraid she'd expose herself as a liar if she didn't speak the untruth swiftly.

"What a shame," Kenneth crooned, the timbre of his voice smooth as thick cream. Once more, he inclined his head.

"Kenneth MacKenzie," she rushed on, "you claim to be a chivalrous man. Will you prove your words by granting that, as lady of this castle and with my lord husband fallen, 'tis my duty to oversee these walls?"

His displeasure floated upward like a dark cloud, coming at her in great, undulating waves. He stared up at her, hands braced on his hips, then finally made her a low bow. "I concede, lady. Under one condition."

"I will not bargain with you," Linnet countered, fixing and drawing an arrow as she spoke. "Go forth from here and dinna return."

Without taking his gaze off her, Kenneth placed his right foot upon a nearby boulder. "And if I do not, you think to shatter my knee?"

"So I have said."

"Your courage impresses me, milady, but I do not

believe a mere lass, *any* lass, can wield a crossbow." He patted his knee and smiled again. "Most assuredly not with the accuracy you profess to master."

Linnet said naught and took aim.

"Throwing a dagger is a gypsy's trick," he taunted. "As a healer and seeress, 'tis not surprising you are possessed of such talent. Handling a man's weapon . . ." his voice trailed off and he chuckled. "Nay, I dinna believe it."

Linnet kept her silence, her fingers inching toward the lever under the bow's crosspiece.

"Send down my son, and I will leave you in peace." All mirth now gone from his voice. "My claim to this castle can wait for another day."

Angry rumblings issued from the men crowded around Linnet, jeers from those below.

"You have claim to neither," Linnet shouted, her fingers finding the lever. "Not the boy nor these walls. I bid you once more to be gone."

"I think not," came Kenneth's reply.

"Then I shall send you," Linnet said under her breath and released the quarrel.

A sharp cry of pain rent the night. As her husband's men cheered, Linnet propped the bow against the wall, satisfied even though the bolt had missed its mark.

Instead of striking Kenneth's knee, the quarrel had lodged deeply into the bastard's thigh.

"I vow, woman, if you e'er dare disobey me again, I shall hie you over my knees and whip your bare arse afore all my men who care to look!" Duncan snarled at his lady wife as she, irritatingly unperturbed, continued to torture him with her poking and prodding at his wounds.

Ignoring him, she went about her task. Even his men seemed to have forgotten to whom they owed their loyalty, turning deaf ears to his objections and ruthlessly holding him prisoner upon one of his own trestle tables.

"By the Rood, have a care!" he railed when Linnet jabbed her infernal blade deep into his injured thigh. "Saints, would you finish what Kenneth and his band of outlaws started?"

"Your lady seeks to *help* you, my friend," Sir Marmaduke chastised. The English lout leaned against a nearby table, his arms smugly crossed.

Duncan shot him a glower, but he merely lifted a pewter tankard in mocking salute, then calmly took a deep draught of ale.

"Had you heeded our plea to get yourself off the battlements, you would've had fewer wounds needing attention."

"Think you?" Duncan's ire swelled. His ugly knave of a brother-in-law bore nary a scratch.

"I have no cause to think it," the Sassunach drawled. "I know 'tis so."

"Is there aught you dinna kno—" Duncan snapped, his words ending in a sudden intake of breath as Linnet dug deeper into his torn flesh.

Sir Marmaduke shrugged and took another sip of ale.

"Hush now," Elspeth soothed, using a cool, damp piece of linen to dab at a gash on Duncan's temple.

"If you'd drink the wine we've been trying to pour down yer uncooperative throat," Fergus scolded from the far end of the table, "'tis far less pain you'd be in about now, laddie."

"I am not in pain," Duncan barked, shooting an angry glare down the length of the trestle table.

"Be that so?" the old seneschal quipped, meeting Duncan's stare undaunted.

Then he tightened his hold on Duncan's ankles. "'Twere that the truth, why do you need six o' your most braw kinsmen to hold you down?"

Duncan opened his mouth to reply in kind but snapped it shut, wincing as the tip of Linnet's probing dirk unexpectedly scraped along his thighbone.

"Saints alive!" he bellowed, bucking wildly against six pairs of restraining hands. "Lachlan," he called out, "fetch me that jug of wine!"

The squire hurried to his side, a large earthen ewer in his hands. "Give the wine to Elspeth," his wife told Lachlan, not looking up from her task. "Then lift his head so she can help him drink."

Lachlan glanced at him then, a worried frown creasing his brow.

"Do as she says," Duncan hissed through gritted teeth.

At once, the squire relinquished the jug.

A moment later, the blissfully soul-and-pain-easing wine flowed down his throat. After he'd guzzled the entire contents of the jug, Elspeth gently lowered his aching head back to the table.

"I would have more," Duncan said, then expelled a great sigh.

But not before he'd glared at Fergus, daring the old goat to utter another of his barbed comments.

He was laird, after all, and he'd have all the wine he wanted.

Anything to dull the pain.

Putting on a show of bravura be damned, Fergus and his offensive banter or nay.

Some hours, 'twould seem, and the blessed Apostles only knew how many jugs of wine later, Duncan came awake. Through a shadowy haze of pain, he peered up at his lady wife.

She leaned over him, staring down at him, and he did not care for the troubled expression clouding her amber-colored eyes. Nor did he like the taut lines of tension and fatigue etched onto her sweet face.

But mostly, he didn't care for the way she looked at him.

It bode ill.

For him.

"Are you not yet through sticking your damnable blade in my flesh, woman? How much longer do you think to keep me here, naked and trussed up in linen bandages like a rotting corpse?" he asked crankily, secretly shocked by the rasping, broken sound of his voice.

Rather than answer him, Linnet slid a worried look at his English brother-in-law. The great all-knowing lackwit stood beside her, also gawking down at him.

"Well?" Duncan snapped. "Dinna try my patience, for I've not much left."

"Your lady and Elspeth have worked well, my friend," Sir Marmaduke answered for her. "They've cleaned and bandaged most of your wounds. God be praised, they were able to remove all the little bits of mail, cloth, and leather embedded in your flesh. That should spare you any festering."

Duncan focused on one word of the Sassunach's pretty speech. "What do you mean *most* o' my wounds?"

"We couldn't pull the arrow from your arm," his wife said, her soft and gentle tone in sharp contrast to the disquiet in her eyes. "To do so would cause more harm than is already done."

With effort, Duncan lifted his head and peered at his left arm. True enough, the arrow shaft still raged out of his arm and the skin around its entry point was puffy, the swollen flesh an angry shade of red.

"You'll have to push it through," he said, his gut clenching at the thought.

Linnet nodded solemnly. "'Twill hurt."

Duncan let his head fall back onto the hard surface of the trestle table. "Think you I am daft?" he wheezed, weak from the effort of holding up his head. "I know it will hurt. Just have done with it."

"Aye, we must," she agreed, "the skin around the shaft doesn't look good. The wound may not heal as cleanly as we'd like."

Duncan drew in a breath through clenched teeth. The mere act of talking about what must be done made the hot, throbbing ache in his arm increase tenfold. "Have-done-with-it," he said.

Linnet took her lower lip between her teeth and nodded grimly. Once more, her gaze slid to the Sassunach. He inclined his head in answer and ordered the men still gathered around the trestle table to tighten their hold on their laird.

Then Linnet took one of Duncan's hands, lacing her

fingers through his. When Sir Marmaduke closed his large hand around Duncan's upper arm and grasped the arrow shaft with the fingers of his other, Duncan shut his eyes.

"I am sorry, my friend," he heard the Sassunach say . . . then Duncan's very innards caught fire, and all went black.

"Praise God, he's passed out," Linnet said on a rush of breath as she clung to her husband's suddenly limp hand. She turned her face away from the bloody arrow Sir Marmaduke had just pushed through Duncan's arm, her breath coming in quick, little gasps as she fought the nausea churning inside her.

At the head of the table, Elspeth clucked like a mother hen and pressed yet another cool cloth to Duncan's forehead. Glancing up at Linnet, she said, "We will have to cleanse the torn flesh and apply one of your warmed yarrow poultices, then bandage his arm."

She paused a moment to turn over the damp linen she held against Duncan's head. "Fare you well enough to help, lass, or should I tend him myself?"

Linnet squared her shoulders and willed her lower lip not to tremble. She'd kept herself from crying all through the long night whilst caring for her husband and his injured men.

She'd cleaned wounds, stitched and poulticed jagged, torn flesh, spoon-fed soothing broth and her pain-killing tinctures to countless wearied MacKenzies, all whilst not once giving in to her own desire simply to curl up next to her husband's broken body and offer him the comfort of her arms.

Once or twice she'd slipped up to her chamber to

look in on Robbie. Blessedly, the lad slept soundly behind the drawn curtains of the massive bed she shared with Duncan. And, to her, relief, though she knew 'twas a might foolish, the mute giant, Thomas, still stood watch at the door.

Aye, somehow she'd kept on. She'd even managed to bestow wan smiles on the uninjured warriors as they'd sat about quaffing ale and recounting with glee how Kenneth and his brigands had made a hasty retreat, disappearing into the heavy fog in their little boats just moments after the quarrel from her crossbow had slammed into their bastard leader's thigh.

She'd shared their glee, too. 'Twas with great satisfaction, she'd watched Kenneth limp toward a boat one of his men held ready for him. But she couldn't laugh and share in their boasts whilst so much remained to be done—while so many men lay about the great hall, writhing in agony or moaning until their voices became so hoarse they could do naught but lie still, their pain-glazed eyes staring up at all who passed.

And through everything, she hadn't shed a tear.

Nor would she now.

Not so long as her husband needed her.

But the saints knew she wanted to.

'Twas unthinkable what would have happened had Duncan's wounds been more serious. *Had he been taken from her*. Gooseflesh broke out on her arms and a hefty shudder skittered down her back at the thought.

She couldn't lose him . . . not now.

Not after she'd come to care so very much for him.

Rough edges and all.

Not after she'd fallen so very deeply in love with him.

So much so she'd rather die, too, than live without him at her side.

"Lady?"

Linnet started, Elspeth's voice bringing her back to herself. "Aye?" she asked, blinking at the old woman.

"'Tis a-dreaming you were," Elspeth said, "I've done washed your husband's arm and his squire's fetched the last of your poultices—can you apply it and wrap the wound or shall I? Mayhap 'tis best you go abovestairs and sleep."

"Nay." Linnet shook her head. "I'll see to him myself." Reluctantly letting go of Duncan's hand, she took the warmed linen packet Lachlan offered her. As gently as she could, she eased it around Duncan's upper left arm, then secured it in place with a band of clean linen.

"Thank you, Lachlan," she said, carefully lowering Duncan's newly-bandaged arm to the table. "We'll redress all his wounds afore he awakens."

The squire inclined his head. "Is there aught else I can do, milady?"

"Aye, there is." Linnet briefly touched her fingers to his arm. It trembled, and she noted he still bore an unhealthy pallor. "You can rest yourself."

Turning, she stooped and withdrew a small flagon from her opened herbal satchel. "I'm going to give my husband some wine laced with valerian. It will help him sleep through the morn, mayhap longer. You can lift his head so I can get the brew past his lips."

She paused and touched the back of her hand lightly

to the lad's cold cheek. "Then I'd like you to take a wee draught of it as well."

Color shot into Lachlan's cheeks, and he bobbed his head again. "I thank you, lady."

Together, Linnet, the squire, and Sir Marmaduke managed to get a goodly portion of the valerian concoction down Duncan's throat. And, luckily, he didn't stir but continued to slumber deeply.

Sir Marmaduke glanced at her, his good eye filled with concern. "Lady, you have done all you could this night and more. You command my deepest respect and admiration." He laid a gentle hand on her shoulder. "Dawn is nigh upon us, and as you have sent Lachlan to rest, I vouchsafe 'tis wise we both follow him and see to our own."

Linnet's gaze flew back to her husband, his body still half-naked save for linen wrappings. He rested well, she knew, for the rise and fall of his broad chest was steady, and he even issued forth an occasional light snore.

But she didn't want to leave him.

The Sassunach lightly squeezed her shoulder. "'Tis best we leave him where he is. We would do him no favor by waking him through our efforts to transport him elsewhere."

"But—"

"Do not worry, lady, he will be fine," he assured her, using the side of his callused thumb to brush away a tear that had slipped from the corner of her eye. "He is too stubborn to be aught else."

A painful constriction in Linnet's throat prevented

her from replying, but she gave him a shaky smile in gratitude.

"Fergus and his lady will soon return with the woolens you asked them to fetch. They will make Duncan and the other wounded men comfortable. There is naught else you can do. Not this night. Duncan would want you to rest."

He stepped back then and offered her his arm. "Come, I will escort you to your chamber."

After a last troubled glance at her sleeping husband, Linnet took the Sassunach's arm and let him lead her away. When they reached her room, Thomas quickly opened the door for her, but before she could enter, Sir Marmaduke stayed her with a hand to her elbow.

"Would you that I sit by the fire while you sleep?" Flickering light from a nearby wall torch clearly showed the concern on his ravaged face.

"'Tis kind of you, but I will be fine," Linnet declined, at last accepting how tired she was. She wanted naught but to slip into bed, cradle Robbie in her arms, and sink into the mind-numbing bliss of sleep.

"You are certain?"

"Aye."

"As you wish, lady." Sir Marmaduke nodded respectfully and left her alone.

She watched him go, bid young Thomas a good night, then let herself into her room, bolting the door behind her.

Nigh asleep on her feet, she arched her lower back and stretched her aching arms above her head.

Then she crossed the room and pulled back the bed-curtains.

Robbie was gone.

A smiling man lounged upon the bed in his stead.

Before she could scream, a steely arm slid around her waist from behind, and a foul-smelling hand clamped tightly against her mouth, thoroughly stifling any sound she might have made.

"Fair lady," Kenneth drawled from the bed. "I thought you would never come."

"It would not be wise to bite Gilbert's hand," Kenneth warned, falsely guessing Linnet's intent. "His manners are crude, and he would not handle you as gently as I'd prefer should you sink your teeth into him."

Linnet shuddered, fair gagging, her skin nigh onto crawling off her bones in sheer revulsion. The hand clamped so suffocatingly tight across her mouth reeked far too much like rotting fish for her to dare attempt such a deed.

The stench was bad enough. She wouldn't torture herself further by *tasting* the lout's stinking flesh!

She *did* narrow her eyes to glare at the smug bastard still reposed atop her bed, though. He'd crossed his feet at the ankles, folded his arms behind his head, and it was obvious someone had tended and dressed his injured thigh.

"It will do you naught good to shoot daggers at me

with your eyes, lovely though they may be," he said, his voice low and silky, rife with amusement.

His dark blue eyes, so like Duncan's, gleamed whilst he slid his gaze lecherously over her breasts, then to her feet and back again. "On my honor, lady, I vow you are possessed of many, ah, *lovely* attributes. I shall enjoy savoring them all."

Wresting herself free of Gilbert's meaty hand, Linnet fumed, "You will burn in hell afore you lay a hand on me! And dinna speak of honor, for you do not know what it is. 'Tis what you've done with Robbie I wou—" the fishy hand clapped over her mouth again, cutting off her protestations.

"The lad is unharmed. Think you I bear ill will toward my own son?" Kenneth affected a look of mock astonishment as she struggled wildly against the bear of man who held her captive.

"You will soon be reunited with the child, my sweeting," he crooned, Duncan's pet name for her a travesty on the bastard's lips. "If you would becalm yourself, we can be gone from here. Indeed, your resistance surprises me. I thought you desired my attentions?"

His lips curving into an arrogant smirk, Kenneth brought one hand from behind his head. A lock of glossy black hair dangled from his fingers. "Why else would you have let this token of my admiration fall upon the woodland path? Lest you hoped I would happen upon it and be honor-bound to return it to you?"

Outrage made Linnet's heart race and her cheeks flame. Even the tops of her ears burned with seething anger.

She shook, too.

Badly.

Only her fury and concern for Robbie kept her standing upright.

And angry she was.

Mightily so.

Enough to disregard her repugnance and bite deeply into Gilbert's grime-covered hand.

"Oooooow!" he howled, letting go of her to bring his foul-smelling appendage to his own mouth.

Whipping up her gown, Linnet grabbed for her dagger but steely fingers curled around her arm, staying her hand. Despite his wounded leg, Kenneth had sprung from the bed with a speed and agility she'd hitherto seen only in her husband and the Sassunach.

Breathing hard, her heart pounding, she had no course but to watch helplessly as her malefactor plucked the dirk from her boot.

"My most humble thanks, lady. I was about to insist you surrender your weapon." Still smirking, he tucked her blade beneath his belt, then drew her flush against the broad expanse of his chest. "Now cease squirming," he instructed, covering her mouth with his own hand, "and dinna scream or I shall silence you with my lips and hold you still by mounting you."

Linnet promptly swallowed the cry she'd been about to let loose.

She froze, too, standing perfectly still, as if carved from stone, in the miscreant bastard's unyielding arms.

"That is better. Much better." He smoothed a hand down her back as he spoke. "Do not make a sound as we leave here," he advised her, hooking the fingers of his other hand under her chin and forcing her face to within inches of his own. His hot breath grazed her skin and turned her stomach.

"Should you choose not to heed my warning, I shall cast you to the ground where we stand and have you just to spite my brother." His mouth came so close to hers she feared he'd plunder her lips any moment. "Have I made myself understood?"

Linnet nodded, fighting off the waves of revulsion washing over her at his nearness, at the feel of his vile hands touching her body. She could not be sick . . . she had to keep her strength and wits about her until she was rejoined with Robbie and could plot their escape.

"Good," Kenneth replied to her nod. Then he loosened his hold on her and stepped back. Folding his well-muscled arms across his chest, he arched one brow and ran his gaze over her breasts again. "Dinna think I would not do as I've said. 'Twould be an act I'd relish under any circumstances, and partaking of your sweetness afore my brother's affronted eyes would only heighten the pleasure."

Still eyeing her breasts, he motioned toward the tapestried wall next to the hearth. "Free the passage, Gilbert. If we do not exit this chamber now, I will need to explore the lady's treasures here, and I wouldna deprive myself of the sheer bliss of anticipation."

To Linnet's amazement, the brigand named Gilbert strode to the wall, pushed aside the hanging tapestry, and exposed a half-opened door in the stone wall.

At her sharp intake of breath, Kenneth chuckled. "So you dinna know of the secret passage?" he breathed just above her ear, nudging the door with his foot until it swung fully open to expose a dank-smelling set of stone stairs spiraling downward into blackness.

He leaned closer still, pressing heavily against her as he forced her into the darkness and they began a slow, circular descent. "You mustn't feel alone for not being aware of the passage. I am not supposed to know of it either," he boasted, his voice full of barely suppressed mirth. "But, alas, my brother was e'er the fool . . . the dullard never guessed I'd oft seen him slipping in and out of it in our youth."

Her eyes not yet accustomed to the dark, Linnet slipped on one of the slick, moss-covered steps. "Ho, lady," Kenneth chided, his arm snaking about her waist, his iron grip preventing her from tumbling down the stairs.

"Slow and cautious if you will, fair one. The bolt you fired into my leg has left me a wee bit unsteady on my feet. I may not be able to catch you should you slip again."

Lifting his hand, he let his fingers glide through the loose strands of her hair. Linnet shuddered and tried to pull away, but he only tightened his hold on her. Even without seeing his face, she could sense his gloating.

As if her ill ease pleased him.

"Aye, so is better, lass. Nice and *slow*," he breathed and Linnet knew he did not mean her hesitant steps on the curving stone stairs. "I would not wish to see you battered and bruised. Such an unfortunate state would spoil my pleasure later on."

The tone of his softly whispered words, smooth and cajoling, made Linnet cringe. He'd spoken as if they sat across from each other in a finely appointed solar sharing a trencher of victuals and a jug of good wine.

Like lovers.

Bile rose in her throat at the very thought.

He chuckled again, undoubtedly aware of her discomfiture, relishing it. His low laughter echoed grotesquely off the cold, dank walls of the dampish passage. "Nay, I dinna care to see you marred," he said again. "I mean to enjoy your favors."

Of a sudden, he took a handful of her hair, twisting the strands cruelly, pulling until she gasped from the pain. "Afterward . . ." He let his voice trail off and released her hair.

Linnet said naught even though his unspoken threat struck terror through her. She bit down hard on her lower lip to keep from flinging angry words at him.

And to keep from crying.

Tears and bursts of temper would scarce help her now.

She needed to *think*, not provoke him. Her mind raced, frantically seeking a means to get herself and Robbie away from him and back to safety.

At her silence he plunged on, taunting her with apparent glee. "Is it not amusing I am snatching you from beneath my brother's self-righteous nose . . . and by way of a passage he thought none but his arrogant self knew existed?"

Duncan. Her heart screamed out his name as they descended ever deeper into the cold, dark bowels of Eilean Creag. They passed several low-ceilinged passages leading off from the curving stairwell, and Kenneth must've sensed her desire to flee, for he paused briefly beside the entrance to one of them.

"This tunnel leads to your husband's solar and beyond, ending in the chapel," he told her, nodding toward the impenetrable blackness looming beyond the passage's arched entrance. " 'Tis nary a stone of this castle I dinna ken, no matter how well my brother thought to keep its secrets to himself," he jeered. "A man can move unseen throughout the entire holding, and disappear afore one is missed. Long afore one is missed," he added in a sinister tone surely meant to unsettle her.

But Linnet kept her tongue, glancing about her as they passed several other tunnels on their winding way downward. Each one smelled ranker than the last. 'Twas a cold, damp smell. An unpleasant one reeking with the stench of rotting sea kelp and dead fish, all blended with the sharp tang of brine and the musty odor of stale air.

Gooseflesh rose on Linnet's arms. Had Duncan used these secret passages to appear so unexpectedly in her chamber at times? Aye, she supposed he had, making use of them to gain entry when she would ne'er have unbolted the door to him.

Searing, stabbing heat, like the pricks of a hundred tiny needles jabbed painfully into the backs of her eyes, and she blinked rapidly, chasing away the tears she wasn't wont to shed. Instead she dwelt on her memories of Duncan coming upon her, seemingly out of nowhere.

How often had he surprised her awake with tender kisses and gentle hands?

More often than she could count.

A fierce surge of longing and regret rose within her,

nigh robbing her of her breath in its intensity. How could she not have known he'd meant to court her, woo her?

Saints forgive her, she hadn't. Not truly, not till now, this very moment.

In the darkness of the stairwell, his face flashed before her: his deep blue eyes stormy with passion, then with the skin around them crinkled in merriment, and yet again, this time his proud brow furrowed in frustration as he sought to put his feelings into words and couldn't.

Without warning, a strong gust of cold, briny air swept up the stairwell from below, its bone-deep chill sending shivers down her spine.

A chill slid over her heart, too. And it grew colder with each downward step. Its icy fingers seized her in a grip tighter, more inescapable, than Kenneth's firm hold on her arm.

Holy Mother of God, would she ever see her husband again?

E'er be able to tell him she didn't care that he fair stumbled over his tongue whenever he attempted to speak his heart? Would she ever have the chance to assure him it mattered naught?

That she finally realized he cared?

Would she ever have the chance to reveal she found his bumbling way with words endearing? Sweeter even than the bonniest prose an accomplished bard could sing?

A hot lump rose in her throat, and she pressed her lips firmly together, willing the constriction to dissolve. When it did, she took a deep breath and squared her shoulders.

She had to be strong. If not for herself, for Robbie.

She had no other choice.

The cold wind increased then, accompanied by a hollow wail and the sound of waves washing over rocks, then receding. Kenneth hurried their steps, practically dragging her around the last few curves of the stairs until they emerged into a good-sized cave.

Deep shadows and flickering light from a small brazier cast eerie, shifting images on the glistening walls and domed ceiling. The sea wind was stronger here, whistling unhindered through a tall crevicelike opening on the far side of the cavern, the chill gusts whipping her cloak against her legs and tangling her unbound hair.

Sea spray dampened her skin and burned her eyes, whilst dampness from the wet, sandy floor seeped through the leather soles of her boots until her toes felt like clumps of ice.

Rubbing her hands together to keep warm, she glanced around. Two men guarded the narrow entrance, each one holding a sputtering, smoke-spewing torch. Gilbert, the smelly giant who'd seized her when she'd stepped into her chamber, remained hulking on the bottom step of the stairwell.

His towering bulk blocked all hope of snatching Robbie and disappearing into one of the secret passages, ruined any chance of escape.

Even worse, Robbie was nowhere to be seen.

Straining her eyes for a glimpse of him, Linnet tried to peer past the two men lurking near the cave's entrance. She hoped to see the child somewhere on the rock-strewn shore beyond, but she saw naught except whitish curtains of fog drifting across the jagged boulders and the choppy, pewter-colored surface of the loch.

Ill ease curled through her, settling in the pit of her stomach like a coiled, venomous snake. "What have you done with Robbie?" she demanded, finally finding her voice.

"I woulda thought your special talent would've taken you straight to his side," Kenneth quipped, his tone full of mockery. "Or is your sight as false as my brother's supposed valor?" he added, releasing her to limp hurriedly toward the two men guarding the entrance.

Linnet ignored the insult to her husband for Kenneth's taunting words about Robbie, and his sharply barked orders for his men to ready boats for a swift departure, sent alarm coursing through her.

She must find the lad.

Frantic, she scanned the cavern, peering deeply into its shadows, desperately searching for some sign of her stepson, half-afraid of what she'd find.

Her sight was no help. She'd attempted to look inside herself, but had glimpsed naught but darkness and cold.

Then her gaze fell upon a dark, rounded lump in the farthest corner of the cave, and her worst fears were confirmed.

Almost hidden behind a cluster of black, glistening rocks jutting out from the cavern's sloping wall, the wee lad huddled, knees drawn to his chest, his wooden sword clenched tightly in his hands.

Linnet ran to him, dropping to her knees on the wet sand. "Robbie, lad, praise God you are not hurt," she cried, hugging him to her breast. "They will take us from here, laddie," she whispered, holding him close, "but dinna you worry. I will find a way for us to escape, and your da will surely come looking for us. "

Robbie twisted in her arms, turning away from her. "I won't go," he sniffed.

"But you must, we both must—we don't have a choice," Linnet said, taking his chin between her thumb and forefinger, forcing him to face her.

She drew a sharp breath at her first good look at him. Pale and drawn, his cheeks streaked with tears, his eyes filled with pain, the lad appeared to have aged years. His lower lip trembled, and the hands clutching his toy sword shook.

His usual hardy spirit was gone without a trace.

Thoroughly vanquished, the bold bravery he was always wont to display.

A fresh burst of tears spilled down his cheeks, and he tore away from her grasp, lowering his head to stare at the cave's sandy floor.

"Robbie, lad, you mustn't be afraid," Linnet crooned, smoothing a hand over the warm silkiness of his bowed head. "I will not let aught happen to you."

He looked up then and a spark of his old self flared in his dark blue eyes. "'Tisna for mesself I cry, lady," he said, his voice breaking as if a world of sadness bore down on his small shoulders. "'Tis Mauger"—he sobbed then—"the bad men killed him."

"Oh, Robbie." Only then did she notice the old dog, barely discernible in the deep shadows behind Robbie. Silent and unmoving, naught more than a tangled heap of fur and bones, his dome-shaped head matted with blood, his ever-trusting eyes, closed. "Oh, laddie, nay.

'Tis so sorry I am," she breathed, now spilling tears of her own.

"Uncle Kenneth kicked him."

"Aye, and he deserved to be kicked," Kenneth said, closing his fingers tightly around Linnet's arm and yanking her to her feet. "The mangy beast meant to bite me."

"I hate you, you're bad!" Robbie sprang to his feet and began thwacking at Kenneth's legs with his wooden sword.

Kenneth laughed. He grabbed the neck of Robbie's tunic and hoisted the boy high above the ground so his spindly legs dangled loosely in midair. Robbie's toy sword slipped from his hands as he thrashed about trying to strike his uncle with his balled fists.

"Take him—I grow weary of the pesky brat." Kenneth fair tossed the child into Gilbert's arms. "'Tis time we are on our way."

The foul-reeking giant slung Robbie over one shoulder, crossed the cavern with a few long strides, then disappeared through the narrow opening.

Kenneth gave Linnet's arm a sharp tug. "Your boat awaits you, milady."

"You will not live to savor this foul deed. My husband will come for us."

"Think you?" Kenneth shot her a wolfish grin, then shoved her through the mouth of the cave. "Did you not say the man is gravely wounded?" he asked with a wicked smile, stepping through the opening.

"That will not stop him," Linnet swore, as Kenneth pulled her across the rocky shore toward one of the tiny coracles.

"We shall see, lady, we shall see."

Then he shoved her into the small boat, climbed in after her, and began rowing them away from shore. Nearby, Gilbert practically flung the still-struggling Robbie into another of the round, little boats, whilst Kenneth's remaining men followed suit close behind them.

Thick curtains of fog pressed in all around them, swallowing Robbie's high-pitched squeals of protest and eventually closing in around the solid bulk of Eilean Creag's thick gray walls.

Soon the forbidding MacKenzie stronghold vanished from view, slipping behind the enveloping swirls of mist, disappearing as thoroughly as if it'd never been there.

And all Linnet heard was Kenneth's heavy breathing as he rowed them farther and farther away, the rhythmic slapping of the oars hitting the water, and the overly loud beating of her anxious heart.

"Can you hear me, laddie?"

Duncan opened his eyes a crack and glowered at his old goat of a seneschal. "Of course, I can hear you," he groused, "the way you've been blaring in my ear, a deaf man would hear you, and I am not deaf."

That said, he promptly shut his eyes again.

There wasn't a single part of his body that didn't ache, and his head throbbed as if he'd downed Eilean Creag's entire store of spirits.

Nay, he did not want to be disturbed.

Not by Fergus, not by anyone . . . not even his sweet lady wife.

The way he felt, he wouldn't even stir for the

blessed St. Columba should the highly revered holy brother care to pay him a visit.

"Be you still awake, laddie?" Fergus shouted into his ear, bellowing as if he sought to rouse the dead.

Duncan's hands curled into fists, and his eyes shot wide open. "If I was not, I am now, you dolt! Can you not let a man rest?"

"Someone's come to see you," Fergus, still leaned low over the trestle table, bellowed into Duncan's ear.

"If it is not God the Father Himself, send him on his way," Duncan ground out, each word, each movement of his lips, sheer agony.

He tried to close his eyes again, but Fergus, the persistent wretch, started rattling Duncan's uninjured arm. "You canna keep sleeping. 'Tis nigh unto vespers, you've slept the day through and your visitor brings us grim tidings."

With a great effort, Duncan pushed himself up on his elbows and tried to focus his hurting eyes . . . they burned as if someone had poured sand into them. "What tidings? Has my bastard half brother marched into the hall and laid claim to the high table?"

"It is grave news, sir." This from Fergus's lady, and Duncan did not care for her tone.

Following her voice, he squinted up at her. The expression on her face was worse than her tone. Her nose glowed bright red, and her eyelids were puffy. The woman had been crying.

Sobbing, from the look of her.

As he peered at her, she gasped, clapped her hands over her mouth, and wheeled away from him, her rounded shoulders heaving.

Duncan forgot his wounds and sat straight up. "What madness has befallen us whilst I've slumbered?" he wheezed, fire shards of pain shooting through him.

To a man, the kinsmen gathered around the trestle table avoided his gaze, each one suddenly shuffling about as if their feet were afire or plucking at their clothes as if they'd been beset by a horde of man-eating fleas.

Even Fergus. The grizzled old seneschal stood half-turned away from Duncan, scratching furiously at his elbow.

"What goes on here?" Duncan boomed, now fully awake and furious himself.

" 'Tis your lady, Laird MacKenzie," a great hulk of stranger said from the foot of the table. "Your brother has her."

"You lie!" Duncan made to leap off the table but white-hot pain knifed through him. Black rage nigh blinding him and sheer terror squeezing the very air from his lungs, he doubled over in agony, tightly clutching his middle.

Fergus, his gnarled hands firm and strong, eased Duncan gently backwards until he was once more in a prone position on the table. "Becalm yourself, laddie, we dinna ken aught for certain. Not yet. Marmaduke's gone abovestairs. We'll soon hear if any harm has come to your lady or the wee lad."

Inclining his head toward the stranger, the seneschal continued, "He be Murdo, of the MacLeod clan. Says he was on his way here with a message from his laird. The MacLeod would bid us to send men. They need help rebuilding their hall after a fire and—" Fergus paused to rest an arm about his weeping lady's shoulders, "—on the way here, he came across some of Kenneth's men. They boasted the whoreson had your lady and Robbie and meant to ransom them," he finished in a rush.

For a long moment Duncan said naught. He couldn't, for terror constricted his lungs, and each one of Fergus's words had been like a nail hammered into his heart.

Lifting his head as best he could, he narrowed his eyes at the stranger. Something about the man struck him in a bad way, and it wasn't just the grim tidings he brought. "I ken John MacLeod well. His men, too, but I dinna recall ever meeting you."

Murdo nodded, then withdrew a gleaming golden brooch from a leather pouch suspended from his belt. With grimy fingers, he held out the finely wrought piece of jewelry for Duncan's inspection. A large red gemstone in its middle winked and sparkled in the reflection of a nearby rushlight.

'Twas a choice gem and a brooch of rare beauty.

Duncan knew it well . . . he'd seen it oft as the MacLeod laird wasn't wont to go about without the brooch fastened to his cloak.

'Twas a charmed piece, John had sworn.

One he always wore.

Murdo must have seen the recognition in Duncan's eyes, for he dropped the brooch back into his pouch and gave Duncan a broad smile.

Duncan didn't return the smile. "I canna believe John would part with that brooch."

The stranger's smile dimmed, but only for a moment. "Oh, aye," Murdo disagreed, bobbing his shaggy, unkempt head. "He knew you wouldn't know me and sent along the brooch to vouchsafe for my identity."

"I see." Duncan didn't believe a word of the man's story. He slanted a glance at Fergus, but the bristly old fool was still scratching his elbow.

Looking back at the stranger, Duncan hissed out a sharp breath before he opened his mouth to speak. Saints alive, just turning his neck sent sizzling bolts of pain shooting down his spine. Wincing, he forced his lips to move. "What of a fire? How many men does John need?"

"So many as you can spare. All but the bare stone walls are ash and soot. Oh, aye, 'twas a fierce fire," Murdo said, rocking back on his heels. "You'll be wanting to send a party after your lady first, though. My lord willna begrudge you looking after your own afore you send help."

Apprehension, cold and disturbing, slithered over Duncan's skin as the man spoke, but his thinking was too fogged from pain to place what bothered him.

"And you will tell us where to look?" Alexander, one of Duncan's kinsmen, spoke up. Duncan glanced sharply at him. His brows were furrowed, and he stood rubbing his chin, peering suspiciously at the tall man called Murdo.

"Aye, I can. Way I done heard, Laird MacKenzie's brother means to head by galley to one o' the northern isles." Murdo's barrel-like chest swelled with importance. "Whilst I'm here, I can ride north with you. I have some kin on the coast and can help secure a boat."

Despite his aching bones and suffering, Duncan pushed himself up on his elbows. "I think not," he wheezed. "My men will ride out *if* my lady and the child have been taken, but you will not go with them. You and John's brooch shall remain here. In my safekeeping, if you will."

Murdo's face suffused a deep red. "You canna keep me prisoner here."

Duncan only lifted a brow.

"'Tis a breach o' hospitality!" Murdo sputtered. "My lord is a trusted ally of—"

"If John is your lord, he will understa—" Duncan cut into the man's speech, then snapped his own mouth shut at the sound of pounding footsteps. He turned toward the noise just in time to see Sir Marmaduke burst into the hall from the tower stairs.

The Sassunach plowed his way through the men standing about, not stopping until he reached Duncan's side. "Mother of God preserve us, 'tis true," he panted. "The lady Linnet and Robbie are gone."

A loud roar sounded in Duncan's ears, increasing in volume until he could scarce hear aught else. "Nay! It canna be." His words were barely audible, drowned out by the noise he now recognized as the rush of his own hot blood coursing through him.

The sound of his world crashing down around him.

"It canna be," he repeated. "Thomas wouldn't have left his post."

"He didn't. The door was bolted from within, we had to break it down," Marmaduke said, dashing Duncan's last hope. "They were taken by stealth." His gaze flickered briefly over Murdo. "I do not know how the deed was done, but they are gone."

Duncan pushed himself to a sitting position, easing

his legs off the table and clutching its edge for support. He didn't know what whirled faster, the sickening dread spinning through him, or the hall itself. Both spun madly, out of control. And through it all, he kept hearing the Sassunach's terrible words.

They are gone, they are gone. . . .

And Duncan knew how they'd been taken.

Aye, he knew.

Damnation but he'd been a fool. He should have known. Kenneth was clever. He would've known he could ne'er have taken Eilean Creag, was well aware its walls couldn't be breached.

His attack had been a ruse.

A clever stratagem so his men could clear the rocks blocking the entrance to the sea cave. Somehow the bastard had discovered the secret Duncan thought only he knew. And once they'd gained access to the hidden passage, they'd stolen his lady and Robbie.

Darkness closed in on him in dizzying waves, washing over him, pulling at him from the outside, whilst his insides twisted in unspeakable agony.

As if from a great distance, he heard a woman's high-pitched wail, then Fergus grousing at him to lie back down. Other voices, shouts and murmurs, merged with theirs until his aching head was filled with naught but confusion.

Someone . . . Marmaduke? . . . pushed him down, pinning him onto the trestle table with hands as unyielding as steel. He struggled to break free, but couldn't. He was too weak. The pain, his anguish, his *rage*, was nigh onto unbearable.

It lamed him, was too formidable an opponent to fight.

And naught hurt as fiercely as the gaping, bleeding wound Kenneth's evildoing had left in his chest.

For along with his lady and the lad, they'd stolen that which he hadn't truly believed he possessed till now.

His heart.

They'd ripped it, bleeding and raw, from his breast, leaving him bereft . . . empty.

Clarity dawned even as blackness claimed him, the weight of its truth almost crushing him, pressing the life from him, robbing him of his very breath.

They'd taken his lady and his son, for suddenly it mattered naught whether the lad was truly his or nay.

All that mattered was their safe return.

He had to get them back.

Both of them.

He'd never be whole again until he did.

18

Your brother has her.

Laird MacKenzie's brother . . .

The stranger's words drifted in and out of the darkness swirling around Duncan, cleverly weaving themselves into the confounding whirl of raised voices so he couldn't decipher aught what made sense.

Gritting his teeth, he pressed the flats of his hands against the cold wooden planks of the trestle table and strained to concentrate.

Strained, too, against the iron-hard grip holding him down.

But his efforts were of no avail.

The din only increased, becoming a cacophony of discord irritating enough to drive the wits from a saint, blurring the elusive words dancing in and out of the shadows on the very edges of his consciousness.

And whoever held him to the table possessed the

strength of ten men and dinna appear willing to loosen their grip.

Duncan drew in a breath through clenched teeth and willed his agitation aside. He'd deal with the lout and his steely fingers soon enough.

After he'd made sense of the garbled jumble of words careening in and out of his aching head.

Keeping his eyes tightly shut, he fought to ignore the shouts of his men, the chaotic sounds of a hall filled with confusion, and focus on Murdo's words.

He had to. They were important.

Vital.

He pressed his hands harder against the table, so hard his forearms shook with the effort. But, devil be damned, the words and their meaning kept eluding him.

His eyes still shut, he tried to swallow but couldn't. His lips were dry, split and parched, and his tongue felt thick, swollen. More annoying still, the inside of his mouth tasted foul, as bitter as soured wine.

Duncan's lips compressed into a tight grimace.

He *was* sour.

And he intended to stay that way until he could figure out what vexed him so, unravel the clue lurking in the outer fringes of his mind, tantalizingly close one moment, distant as the moon the next.

Your brother . . .

Murdo's words penetrated the blackness again, repeating themselves like a monk's morning chant, growing ever louder until the other voices and sounds receded into nothingness.

The two words pelted him like icy, needle-sharp rain, taunting him, pushing him to the brink of madness.

Then another voice chimed in, soft and gentle, sweet, but insistent in its urgency. His lady wife's voice. Clear and bright as a ray of sun on a fine spring morn. Strong enough to dispel the other voices, powerful enough to chase away the fog clouding his befuddled senses.

'Tis of a future evil I must warn you . . .

It was not Kenneth . . .

Someone speaks with two tongues . . .

As quickly as they'd come, Linnet's prophetic words faded, but he'd heard enough.

Suddenly he knew.

And with the knowledge came sanity.

Sanity and determination.

His eyes shot open. His grimace deepened. As he'd suspected, the hands holding him down were English hands. Those of his all-knowing one-eyed brother-in-law.

He fixed the lout with a fierce stare, one that would send most men scurrying for their mothers, but Sir Marmaduke merely stared back, his one good eye as unblinking as Duncan's two.

"Release me at once." Duncan pushed the words through his teeth, refusing to acknowledge the agony it cost him to move his lips. "I am well."

The Sassunach quirked his brow and said naught.

"I am," Duncan insisted, temper giving him the strength to break free of Marmaduke's grasp and sit straight up.

Nausea rose high in his throat at the sudden movement. By sheer force of will, Duncan quelched the hot waves of dizziness threatening to pull him back into a sea of grayness and pain.

"Can you not see I am fit?" he snapped, flexing his fingers, defiantly wiggling his bare toes.

"I see an unfit man borne on the wings of anger," the Englishman said, folding his arms. "Naught else."

Duncan scowled darkly and eased his legs off the table. Doing his best not to wince, he stood, then leaned against the table's edge.

Every muscle, every *bone*, in his body hurt. His head would surely burst asunder any moment, and his hall seemed wont to spin and dip around him.

But for naught in the world would he admit it.

Blinking to clear his vision, he searched the throng, looking for Murdo. To his relief, he didn't need to search long. The accursed mucker still stood near the foot of the trestle table.

And he had the effrontery to bestow another of his yellow-toothed smiles on Duncan. "Be you hurting, Laird MacKenzie?" he wanted to know.

"Nay, but you will be," Duncan fair growled. "Soon."

Murdo's nostrils flared. "Yer makin' a grave error. The MacLeo—"

"Is not your laird," Duncan finished for him. "'Tis Kenneth's man you are."

The stranger's coarse features hardened, and his hand stole beneath the gathered folds of his grungy tunic. His blade flashed and gleamed for but an instant before Malcolm wrested it from him, then pressed the wicked-looking blade against the man's throat.

Marmaduke positioned himself at Malcolm's side,

his own sword drawn and at the ready, the look on his scarred face, feral.

"If you harm me, Kenneth will slit yer lady wife's throat . . . after he's had his way with her," Murdo swore. "You'll never see—"

Duncan slammed his fist on the trestle table. "'Tis you who'll ne'er see aught again lest you answer my questions, and dinna ask what'll happen if I don't care for your answers."

"I'll tell you naught," Murdo sneered.

"Think you?" Duncan's lips curled in a sneer of his own.

He pushed away from the table and made straight for Murdo. One grueling step at a time. Only the heat of his fury enabled him to cross the short distance without his knees buckling, without giving voice to his pain.

Leaning so close to the officious cur's face, the man's hot, foul-reeking breath meshed with Duncan's own, Duncan snarled, "There wasn't a fire at John MacLeod's keep, was there?"

Murdo clamped his mouth shut and stared fixedly at a point somewhere beyond Duncan's shoulder.

"The fire was a ploy, a ruse to make me send my men on a fool's errand," Duncan breathed, his tone icy, his deep voice calm, without a trace of the raw anger coursing through him. Nor of the bone-jarring pain each movement, each word cost him. "Do not lie if you value your life."

Murdo remained silent.

"Very well," Duncan said, his voice low, his every nerve taut. "I grow impatient with you. Admit you lie."

Murdo spat on the floor.

Duncan's anger surged anew. "You are a brave man," he said simply, then nodded once to Malcolm, who still held the loathsome churl's own dagger to his throat.

The tall kinsman obliged, pricking Murdo's throat with the sharp tip of the dagger. A dollop of bright red blood appeared, another followed, turning into a slow, steady trickle.

Duncan nodded again and Malcolm pressed the blade deeper.

Murdo's eyes bugged and he wet his lips.

"Where did Kenneth take my wife and the boy?" Duncan asked coldly.

Murdo fidgeted, but when Duncan's gaze slid back toward Malcolm the miscreant lost his nerve. "I dinna mean you no harm," he said in a rush. "'Tis following orders, I was, dinna you see?"

"I see more than you ken. Where is my wife?"

"To . . . to the south," Murdo stammered, trying to lean away from the knife. "To the south."

Duncan feigned a look of mock surprise. "Did you not say 'by galley to the northern isles'?"

Beads of sweat dotted Murdo's forehead. "'Twas as you say, a ruse. I was to escort you north, some of your men were to go to MacLeod's, and whilst your men were scattered elsewhere, Kenneth meant to ride south without you on his trail."

"And my lady? The boy? They are to be ransomed?"

Murdo gulped, his face paling.

"Speak or die."

"I dinna ken," the man blurted, "on my life, I dinna ken what he means to do with them."

"Your life is forfeit, but it is not here you will lose it," Duncan said, his voice flat, toneless. "Take the pouch," he bade the Sassunach, jerking his thumb toward the leather purse hanging from Murdo's belt.

Marmaduke handed him the pouch and he peered inside it. John MacLeod's brooch winked up at him, its red gemstone catching the light from a nearby wall torch.

"This brooch was stolen," he said, closing the pouch and tossing it to Alec. "You shall return it. Alec and Malcolm will escort you. What John MacLeod does with you is none of my affair. If he does not kill you, be warned lest you e'er set foot on MacKenzie land again, for I will not hesitate to have done with you myself."

To Alec and Malcolm, he said, "Be off with him, he's sullied the air in my hall long enough."

Duncan stood ramrod straight until they disappeared from view, then he sagged against the nearest table and closed his eyes. His left arm throbbed and burned and he didn't need to glance at it to know the wound had started bleeding again.

But the fire in his arm was naught next to the smoldering flame burning inside him.

Rage over the taking of his loved ones and fear for their safety fired his blood, filling him with a fury so intense the pain of his wounds seemed paltry by comparison.

"I vow that whoreson was your lady's two-headed man," Sir Marmaduke said, resheathing his sword. "The one in the flames."

Duncan cracked his eyes open and slid a sideways glance at the Sassunach. "Aye, and for once I didn't need *you* to figure it out for me."

One corner of Marmaduke's mouth lifted into a twisted smile. "And so I observed, my friend. Mayhap there is hope for you yet."

Duncan's brows snapped together. "I am not a dull-wit. 'Twas his use of the word 'brother.' No friend or ally would dare grant Kenneth such status to my face."

Marmaduke glanced at Duncan's left arm. "Your arm bleeds."

"'Your arm bleeds,'" Duncan echoed grouchily. "Think you I am not aware of that? 'Tis a wonder my whole body is not bleeding considering all the holes in it."

"Aye, laddie, and Elspeth will want to re-dress your wounds, especially your arm. It doesna look good," Fergus agreed, stepping up to them. He tilted his head to the side and peered sharply at Duncan's injured arm. "I'm a-thinking we should cauteri—"

"And 'a-thinking' about it is all you're going to do," Duncan groused, pushing away from the table's edge and fixing Fergus with his most intimidating glare.

Undaunted, Fergus affected a look he'd used with much success in Duncan's childhood.

It didn't impress Duncan the man.

"You canna walk about with that arm spewing blood all o'er you," his seneschal pressed.

"I can and I shall." Duncan stood firm. "Now cease blathering on over a few wee drops of blood, you grizzled-headed old graybeard. If you desire to be useful, see our swiftest horses saddled and made ready to ride."

Fergus's bushy brows shot upward. "Mounting a horse will be the death o' you, boy, and your men need to rest their bones," he protested. "We'll send out a party of our most braw men on the morro—"

"On the morrow is too late. We ride now, through the night," Duncan vowed, refusing the notion he might not have the strength to carry out his plan.

Searching the throng for his first squire, Duncan signaled the lad to come closer when he spied him. "Lachlan, fetch my clothes and weapons," he ordered, his voice surprisingly strong.

"And dinna drag your feet," he added, glancing irritably at the irksome yards of linen wrapped around nigh every inch of his aching body. "I tire of being swaddled like a newborn babe or a corpse awaiting burial."

Rather than dashing off to do Duncan's bidding, Lachlan remained rooted to the floor, worriedly seeking out Marmaduke with his eyes. Scowling, Duncan planted his balled fists on his bandaged-wrapped hips. "*I* am laird, not Sir Marmaduke," he said, the harshness of his tone smothering the gasp of pain he'd almost let loose. "Do as I say, or would you have me ride out garbed in naught but rags?"

Two spots of color appeared on Lachlan's pale cheeks, but he inclined his head and took off at a run.

Duncan watched him go, then blew out a shaky breath, releasing some of the tension coiled within him. Turning back to Fergus, he said, "Send a party of men to my bedchamber. Behind the largest tapestry, they'll find the door to a hidden passage. It leads to the base of the tower. Be sure they seal it at both ends. *Permanently* seal it."

Beside him, Marmaduke drew a quick breath. Duncan couldn't resist flashing the all-knowing lout a triumphant smile. "Aye, my good friend, it would appear there were a few things you didn't know."

To the rest of his men, he said, "Lads, I know you are weary, some of you wounded. I will not ask those too fatigued to join me. Nor can I vouchsafe you will return whole if you ride with me. Kenneth is a daring and able warrior. His men are no less adept as we've seen. Any of you who choose to stay behind, I bid you seek your pallets now so you are well rested and can best protect these walls in our absence."

He paused, waiting.

No one moved.

Then, from the back of the hall, someone called, "*Cuidich' N' Righ!* Save the king!"

Others joined in, and soon the MacKenzie war cry filled the air until the walls fair shook. Duncan clasped his hands behind his back and nodded in approval.

The saints knew he couldn't do much more. Not with his throat painfully tight and the backs of his eyes afire, so moved was he by his men's stout showing of support.

When the ruckus died down, a firm hand grasped his elbow. "Let me lead the patrol," Sir Marmaduke offered, leaning close to Duncan's ear. "No one will look askance if you stay behind. 'Twould be madness for you to sally forth. Fergus is right, you are in no condi—"

"*My* lady and *my* son have been taken," Duncan said, his voice as cold and unyielding as steel. "I mean to fetch them."

Sharp intakes of breath issued from those gathered near, then low mumbles spread throughout the entire hall, followed almost immediately by stunned silence.

To a man, his kinsmen stared gog-eyed at him, their fool mouths hanging open as if they sought to catch flies.

And Duncan knew exactly why they gawked.

What he didn't know was why the words had slipped so easily from his tongue. He hadn't meant to say them, still doubted Robbie had sprung from his loins.

But of a sudden, now that the wee lad was gone, his true parentage mattered naught.

Only his safe return.

Then the silence was broken . . . someone sniffled.

A loud and sloppy wet sound, made louder by the awkward silence hanging over the hall.

The noise came again and to Duncan's amazement, he saw it was old Fergus. The bandy-legged seneschal rubbed his nose with the back of his sleeve and turned quickly away.

But not before Duncan caught sight of the telltale moisture glistening in the old man's eyes.

Heat crept up his neck and he swept the lot of them with a furious glare. "Cease gaping like witless varlets and make ready to ride," he chided them. "And dinna think to start telling tales about me going soft. Naught has changed."

To his great annoyance, his men didn't look like they believed him.

Her legs stretched before her on the chill, damp ground, Linnet leaned against the trunk of a tree and rested her weary bones. Ever since Kenneth had unbound her, she'd been forced to wait upon her captors, coerced by threats upon Robbie to heed their constant demands and tend those wounded in the siege.

Seeing no choice . . . for the moment . . . but to ac-
quiesce, she'd bowed to their will, catering to their every
whim until her back ached so fiercely she'd begun to
walk like a crone, one hand pressed to her hip, her shoulders hunched in pain.

'Twas sometime in the mist-hung gray hours before
dawn on the second day since they'd been taken and for
the first time, she'd been allowed to sit with Robbie.
Sleeping peacefully, praise the saints, the boy curled
next to her, covered with a threadbare blanket one of
Kenneth's men had deigned to toss over him.

Most of the brigands slept. To Linnet's dismay, Kenneth was amongst the few who did not. He lounged near
the low-burning fire, nursing a cup of wine and conversing in low tones with one of his men, a shifty-eyed
weasel of a lout who suddenly held his cup aloft and motioned for her to refill it.

Rather than scramble to her feet as the miscreant
surely expected, Linnet sent him an icy glare.

Truth to tell, she was too fatigued to stand.

" 'Twould seem the lady's grown tired of serving her
lessers," the weasel taunted.

Kenneth made a coarse huffing noise. "Mayhap her
attitude will change once we've all had a turn at showing her how pleasurable servicing the lowborn can be.
Once we've covered a bit more ground, we shall enlighten her."

"Och!" The other man slapped his thigh. "Wait'll
she's seen the size o' yer—"

"Enough," Kenneth admonished. "I wouldna want
her to suffer from yearning. There will be time a-plenty
for her to explore my maleness, and yours, later."

He glanced at her then and the raw lust in his gaze nigh curdled Linnet's flesh. "She may find herself so taken with our charms, she'll prefer us to my loathsome brother."

His gaze still on her, and in a most disconcerting way, Kenneth pushed to his feet. Linnet willed her fear not to show as he came toward her. Beneath the folds of her cloak, her cold fingers found and closed around a small, leather-covered flagon.

A flagon she'd almost forgotten she had with her, secured as it was in a small linen pouch beneath the many layers of her clothes.

A flagon filled with pure essence of valerian.

Filled, too, with her only hope of escape.

Kenneth loomed over her then, saying not a word, but prodding her hip with his foot. When the foot caught and lifted the hem of her cloak, exposing her ankles and calves to the brisk night air, and any leering eyes that might be gawking at her, Linnet forgot all pretense of appearing calm and frowned up at him.

"Leave me be, you swine," she hissed, her hand curling tighter around the flagon. "Dare touch me, and I shall unman you at the first opportunity."

Snickers and ribald comments issued from those men still awake. Kenneth's face suffused a dark red. "You need the sharpness stolen from your tongue. I vow my brother did not break you well enough!" he fumed, barely restrained anger heavy in his every word.

He leaned close. "'Tis an oversight I shall enjoy rectifying. And in *his* bed . . . once I've ousted him from what would have been mine had his whorish mother not stolen our father's affection."

Linnet pressed her lips together and glowered at him.

Her silence seemed to fuel his anger, for he grabbed her arm and yanked her roughly to her feet. His fingers digging deep into her flesh, he jerked his head toward the unwashed cur who'd waved his cup at her.

"Replenish our wine." The words were curt, his gaze, thunderous.

Linnet returned his glare. "I canna fetch aught lest you release my arm."

He did, but not before narrowing his eyes at her. "Watch your manners, *lady*. I've had done with less bothersome bawds than you."

Linnet made a deliberate show of dusting off her sleeve. Then, her chin high, she made for the messy heap of supplies just beyond the circle of mostly sleeping men. 'Twas where her captors kept their store of near-rancid wine, and not far from where their horses were tethered.

Horses too noble-looking to be aught but stolen. Not that she cared . . . she meant to steal one, too.

As soon as she tainted the wine with valerian and Kenneth imbibed enough of the sleep-inducing brew to fall into a deep slumber.

"Make haste," he called to her. "Our thirst is great."

Linnet smiled.

A hearty craving for the soon-to-be potent brew would suit her well.

Her back to the men, she plucked an earthen jug from the untidy pile. The moment her fingers touched the vessel, cold waves of ill ease crept up her spine, but she forced herself to remain calm as she withdrew the flagon from its hiding place beneath her cloak.

Then, after a quick but wary glance over her shoulder, she removed its stopper and tipped the entire contents into the sour-smelling wine.

Kenneth extended his cup at her approach. "You make a comely serving maid. 'Tis good, for soon you shall be offering up more than mere wine," he drawled, his gaze sliding down the length of her. "*Much more.*"

Linnet said naught and filled his cup to the brim.

Again and again until his eyelids drooped and his words slurred.

Then she returned to her resting place by the tree and waited.

Waited and watched.

For what seemed hours, she kept her vigil, her assessing gaze touching lightly on each slumbering man. Especially the one who, in sleep, looked so much like her husband, her heart twisted painfully within her chest.

Then . . . *finally* . . . a hush settled over the campsite. The fire burned low, the brigands' restless tossing and turning ceased, and only a few hardy souls amongst them still snored.

All slept.

'Twas time.

Half-afraid to breathe, lest she make a noise, Linnet gently nudged Robbie's shoulder. His eyes fluttered open, the wariness in them giving sad testament to how heavily the ordeal of the past two days weighed on him.

He opened his mouth to speak, but Linnet quickly pressed two fingers over his lips. "Hush," she whispered close to his ear, " 'tis time for us to be gone from here.

Can you be very quiet? Not make a sound no matter what happens?"

Robbie regarded her with rounded eyes and nodded.

Linnet returned the nod and ran the backs of her fingers down the boy's cheek in what she hoped to be a reassuring gesture. Then she pushed slowly to her feet, gathered Robbie into her arms, and stole into the trees.

She paused beneath the spreading branches of a large yew until her eyes adjusted to the damp, earthy-smelling darkness of the wood, then strode toward the horses as fast as she dared. They stood quietly, only one bothering to glance her way and whicker softly in greeting.

At the noise, Robbie squirmed in her arms. "Are we going to steal a horse?" he piped, obviously forgetting his promise to keep quiet.

Linnet clamped her hand over Robbie's mouth and froze, fear of discovery sending her heart straight to her throat.

A great bear of a man slept nearby, his head resting on a saddle, his slack mouth emitting a sputtering chorus of snores.

Praise be the saints he slept on.

Unfortunately, his resting place was but a few steps away from her chosen mount, a fleet-footed courser she'd had her eye on.

Linnet eyed the proud-looking horse again, weighing her chances, but when the man groaned and rolled onto his side, she abandoned any and all designs she'd had on the courser and lifted Robbie onto the bare back of the nearest beast, a gentle-eyed palfrey.

The only horse among the lot who appeared to be long of tooth and swaybacked.

It scarce mattered. With a last glance at the sleeping giant and a silent warning to Robbie to keep still, she used the moss-covered trunk of a fallen tree as a mounting block and scrambled up behind him. Sliding an arm about his waist, she drew him against her. To her immense relief, he appeared calm.

Would that *she* were calm.

Ne'er had she ridden without a saddle.

Truth to tell, she doubted she could, ancient-looking nag or nay.

At least the beast wore bridle gear. Saving her relief over that particular blessing for another time, she took the reins in her free hand and urged the horse forward.

God willing, the palfrey possessed a stout enough heart to carry them a goodly distance before Kenneth regained his senses and discovered them gone.

19

𝒟uncan reined in his mount as soon as he spied Sir Marmaduke galloping his horse down the slope of a nearby hill, thundering back from his scouting foray with a speed greater than if all the hounds of hell were upon his heels.

Such haste bode ill, and Duncan wasn't wont to ride ahead and hear dire tidings a moment sooner than necessary.

Then the Sassunach was upon him, jerking his steed to an abrupt halt before Duncan's. "They are not among them," he reported, dragging his arm across his damp brow.

The words hit Duncan with the ferocity of a well-executed blow to the gut. He stared hard at Sir Marmaduke, searching for a sign, any evidence his friend was mistaken.

Sadly, he found no such indication.

Sir Marmaduke sat straight in his saddle, the expression on his scarred face, stony . . . *grim*. Further, his mount's heaving sides and sweat-lathered coat bespoke the truth of his words, gave proof of the urgency with which he'd hastened back with his grave news.

Duncan's heart—the selfsame one he nigh wished he'd ne'er rediscovered for the suffering it now brought him—lurched cruelly within his chest.

"You are certain?"

The Sassunach nodded, and Duncan knew what it was like to die.

Anger, rage, and stark terror—a darker fear than he'd ever known—consumed him. Dread welled up inside him until he almost gagged, and a red haze of fury clouded his vision, near blinding him.

When the haze cleared, he felt naught. Not the agony of his still-fresh and aching wounds, nor the jagged shards of fierce pain lancing through his very soul.

"How far?" he asked, his tone flat . . . cold.

"A short ride. The whoresons yet sleep, with but a few seasoned men, I can dispatch them with ease."

" '*I*'?" Duncan pushed up in his stirrups and leaned towards his friend. "Think you I would allow other men to avenge the taking of my wife, my child? Whilst I stand peaceably aside? God's blood, 'tis dead they may be, now, as we speak!"

Clamping his mouth shut, Marmaduke wheeled his horse to face the line of grim-faced MacKenzie warriors. " 'Tis by the good Lord's grace, your laird has ridden thus far without sliding from his saddle." He shot a reproachful look at Duncan. "His wounds bleed anew, and his anger, justified though it may be, dulls his senses. Should he continue, should he fight, we may lose him."

Duncan eyed his men and waited.

Not a one spoke.

"I was asked to ride ahead and locate Kenneth's camp," Marmaduke went on undaunted, his tone compelling. "I have done so. The lady Linnet and Robbie are not there."

He raised a hand for silence when angry words rose from the gathered men. "That does not mean aught has befallen them. I propose some of you accompany me to exact our revenge. The remainder, including Duncan, shall stay behind and search for them."

Again, thick silence met his words.

"Fergus," he called, "'tis a wise man you are. What say you?"

Once more, Duncan waited. Only this time he held his breath. Fergus was e'er fond of gainsaying him. But the old goat sat firm, his bony shoulders thrust back, the glint in his hawklike eyes, fierce.

"Well?" Sir Marmaduke prodded.

Fergus edged his mount a few steps forward, then spat on the ground. "I say you have a bonnie way with words, and yer a good man, but Scotsman ye ain't."

To a man, the clansmen roared their approval, and Duncan let out his pent-up breath.

"So be it," the Sassunach conceded. Duncan thought he heard him mutter something about a "band of stubborn fools" before he grudgingly bid all follow, spurred his horse, then tore off in the direction whence he'd come.

They'd covered but a few leagues before Sir Marmaduke signaled a halt. "They are there." He indicated a thick wood in the distance. "Their camp is—"

Duncan dug his knees into his horse's sides, not waiting to hear more. He gave his mount its head, allowing the swift courser to charge unrestrained toward the enemy camp.

His men chased after him in fast pursuit while he pressed onward, not even slowing as his horse plunged into the trees. Branches slapped into him, one almost unseating him, but he rode on, spurring his mount until the great beast burst into a clearing.

Kenneth sprawled near the smoldering fire. Roaring his fury, Duncan kicked his horse in the sides, driving the courser straight at the bastard. He reined in at the last possible moment, and so sharply, the animal reared, its powerful front legs cleaving the air.

Now fully awake, Kenneth scrambled wildly to the side, barely avoiding the horse's hooves as they slammed into the earth where he'd lain a mere heartbeat before.

Heedless of the screaming agony of his reopened wounds, Duncan flung himself from his saddle. "Here's a foretaste of hell, you bastard," he swore, kicking hot ash into Kenneth's face.

The bastard yelped and scooted backward. "You've blinded me, you son of whore!" he bellowed, grinding his fists into his eyes.

"Nay, he has not, but I shall," Sir Marmaduke corrected, swinging down from his own steed and drawing his sword. "'Twill be a fitting revenge. For myself and for my lady wife, whose blood stains your foul hands."

"Awaken, you fools! Seize them!" Kenneth called

frantically to his men. Still scooting backward, he clawed at his eyes. "Kill them! My whoreson brother before his bawd's very eyes!"

Several of the men stirred and groped for their weapons, but the thundering sound of approaching horses stilled them. "*Cuidich' N' Righ!*" Duncan's men cried as their horses crashed through the underbrush. "Save the king!" they repeated, their swords drawn and ready.

"Cowards!" Kenneth cursed his men, squinting furiously at them, fumbling wildly for the dagger tucked beneath his belt. "Can you not see the bastards mean to kill me?"

Duncan slammed down his foot on Kenneth's left arm. "'Tis you who are the bastard, and 'tis blinded you are to be, not killed. Your fate is Sir Marmaduke's call, not mine. I will not soil my hands by taking the life of my own father's seed, much as you deserve to die."

"E'er the noble," Kenneth sneered, his voice dripping contempt. "Yet you'd have my eyes put out whilst you pin me down?"

Duncan ground his foot into the bastard's arm. "Tell me what you've done with my wife and child, and you'll be allowed to stand and fight like a man."

"I've done naught with them," Kenneth rasped. "Take the prickly wench and the snot-nosed brat. 'Tis more trouble they make than they're worth."

Duncan dug his heel into Kenneth's arm until the bone cracked with a sickening snapping noise. "Where are they?"

"You've broke my arm!" Kenneth howled, writhing on the ground.

"Cease shrieking like a fishwife and answer me," Duncan roared. "Where—are—they?"

"Have you grown as blind as the one-eyed worm you call friend? The sharp-tongued ogress and the whelp yet sleep by yon tree," he sputtered, nodding toward a tall birch at the edge of the clearing.

A tattered and soiled blanket lay on the ground at the base of the tree . . . nothing else.

Kenneth's jaw dropped and his eyes widened. "What witchery is this? They were there," he stammered. "I vow they we—"

Duncan's anger surged. "Do not insult me with the worthlessness of your word. If my lady or the child bear one mark, I shall forget my honor and slice you to ribbons."

Barely keeping his temper in check, Duncan withdrew his foot and stepped back. Glancing at Sir Marmaduke, he said, "Give him a sword and do with him what you will. But make haste. I would that we scour every hillock and vale for my wife and son."

One of Duncan's men stepped forward with a spare blade, but Kenneth sprang to his feet, shoved the man aside, and lunged at Duncan just as he turned away. "'Tis you who'll die this day," he cried, raising his dirk.

His face contorted in rage, he made to plunge the dagger into Duncan, but the blade slipped from his hand, tumbling to the ground as Kenneth doubled over, a bloodied sword protruding from his gut.

His eyes bulged, already glazing, as he gaped, disbelieving, at Duncan. "I'll wait for you in hell," he wheezed, then fell silent.

Behind him, Sir Marmaduke withdrew his blade, allowing Kenneth's body to topple to the ground. "I would've much preferred taking his sight," he said simply, wiping the blood from his sword with the edge of his tunic.

To Duncan's great surprise, he felt a flicker of remorse, a twinge of sadness, if only for the youthful companion his half brother had once been. But the feeling was gone as soon as it had come, replaced by the more urgent need to find Linnet and Robbie.

An uncomfortable silence descended upon the clearing, and Duncan's hand went instinctively to the hilt of his sword. He scanned the faces of Kenneth's men. Some appeared stunned, others showed no emotion at all. None seemed bent on avenging their leader's death.

"Where is my lady?" he asked, his tone icy.

"'Tis the God's truth Kenneth told you," a giant of a man spoke up, hitching his ill-fitting braies into place as he stepped from the trees. "Stole a horse, yer lady wife did," he added. "They must have escaped in the night."

Relief washed over Duncan, swelling his throat and making his heart slam roughly against his ribs. "The men you lost whilst attacking my castle shall serve to avenge the lives of my crofters. Should any of you care to seek revenge for Kenneth's death, step forth now," he challenged Kenneth's men as soon as he could speak. "Otherwise, cast down your weapons and be gone. You may go in peace. But be warned, if e'er you set foot on MacKenzie land again, you will not live to regret your mistake."

One by one, Kenneth's men nodded humbly, relinquished their arms, and departed. When the last one was gone, Duncan turned to Fergus. "See he is properly laid to rest," he ordered, glancing briefly at Kenneth's still form.

To the rest of his men, he added, "We shall search without cease until we find my lady and child. Pray God they are unharmed."

She'd taken the wrong direction.

For hours, it seemed, they'd ridden in circles, covering a great distance but going nowhere. Linnet's frustration reached unbearable proportions as her surprisingly able mount carried them past the same landmarks . . . over and over again.

Let the plague take her if her ineptness caused them to fall back into Kenneth's hands!

Then, just when the shards of her dwindling hope began to give way to desperation, riders crested a far-off ridge. They rode slowly, obviously searching, scanning the landscape.

Linnet's breath caught in her throat, and sheer joy filled her to bursting. 'Twas Duncan. Even at such a distance, she could tell. He'd come for them at last. And with him, what appeared to be his entire household.

Nay, *their* household, for ne'er had she felt more a MacKenzie than at this moment as her husband shielded his eyes and pointed in their direction before tearing down the hill toward them.

"Robbie, we're saved! 'Tis your father," she cried, kicking the palfrey into a swift canter. "Hold on, laddie, we'll soon be home."

Impatient to reach Duncan, Linnet repeatedly dug her heels into the horse's sides. When a rock-strewn burn suddenly loomed up out of nowhere, 'twas too late to swerve, too late to do aught before the palfrey sailed across the stream, flinging them both from its back.

"Nay!" The denial ripped from Duncan's throat as he witnessed Linnet and Robbie hurtle through the air, then plummet to the ground . . . his lady onto a grassy embankment, his son headfirst onto the ground near a large boulder.

Dizzy with horror, sick with dread, he spurred his horse toward where they lay, still and unmoving, near the innocent-looking burn that might have brought about what Kenneth had failed to do: rob him of his loved ones . . . his life.

His men rode heavy behind him, but his was the first horse to plunge into the burn. Duncan swung down from his saddle midstream. "Linnet! Robbie!" He crashed through the rushing waters, his chest so tight with anguish he could scarce breathe.

When he reached them, he took one quick look at Robbie then tore his gaze away, unable to bear the sight of the lad, his body limp and twisted, his head resting at an odd angle against a large rock. Terror and remorse clawed at his insides, killing him as surely as Kenneth's dagger would have done had the blade sank into his heart.

Bending over Linnet, he grabbed fistfuls of her cloak and buried his face in the silken warmth of her hair. "God in heaven don't let them be dead," he pleaded, his voice thick with pain. "Dinna take them from me now."

"Duncan?"

His wife's voice, faint but oh-so-precious, reached

through his grief, a shining beacon spilling light onto the darkness threatening to consume him.

If she'd survived the fall, mayhap Robbie had, too.

Unable to stand it otherwise, and his throat too constricted for him to speak, Duncan scooped them both into his arms, holding them as tightly as he dared, *willing* them whole.

He had no idea how long he held them thusly, but of a sudden the pounding of horses' hooves, the sound of splashing water, and a chaos of men's raised voices was all around them.

"Have a care, laddie, or would you squeeze them to death?" Fergus scolded, reining in beside them.

The old man's voice held a peculiar note, causing Duncan to glance up at him. "Close yer mouth, boy," Fergus snapped, wiping a tear from his leathery cheek. "Or have you ne'er seen a man show his feelings? 'Tis something I'd hoped you'd learned by now."

Learned by now?

Saints a-mercy, could the old fool not see the tears swimming in Duncan's own eyes?

Did he not ken Duncan held his dear ones so fiercely because he feared what he might see when he released them?

Dreaded he might discover Robbie's chest no longer rose and fell with the sweet breath o' life?

"'Tis hurting me, you are," Linnet breathed, her words so soft he scarce heard her. "Let me see Robbie," she urged, her voice stronger.

Duncan released her at once, then watched, his fear a cold weight on his shoulders, as she slowly pushed to a sitting position and eased Robbie onto her lap. Gently, she smoothed her fingers over an ugly bluish lump on the boy's forehead.

Then a tiny smile curved her lips.

Before Duncan could digest what the fleeting smile meant, she clutched his arm. "We must be gone from here, Kenneth could be upon us any moment."

"Kenneth is dead," Duncan said, his half brother's fate far from his mind as he continued to stare at the knot on Robbie's head. The lad's eyes were closed, his face, pale and waxen. And, saints preserve him, his wee chest still.

Too still.

'Twas just as he'd feared.

With great effort, Duncan tore his gaze from the boy, his heart unwilling to accept what his eyes would have him believe. "Is he . . . will he live?" he forced himself to ask. "Can you . . . can you see if my son will live?"

His wife returned his penetrating stare, a question of her own in her eyes. "Did you say your *son*?"

"Aye, my son," Duncan said, his voice loud and bold, as if he'd dare any and all gathered round them to deny it. "He is my son no matter from whose loins he is sprung."

No sooner were the words spoken than Linnet's eyes filled with tears. She gave him a wobbly smile and simply stared at him, her lower lip trembling, whilst his men pressed closer, the lot of them making all kinds of womanish noises.

Sniffles and snorts.

· Babble.

Duncan glared at them, then wished he hadn't.

There wasn't a dry eye amongst them.

He looked back at his wife. "I asked you a question. I would that you answer it."

"And I shall. With the greatest pleasure. Robbie will live. I have seen and am certain." She paused, beaming at him. "Your *son* will live."

A great resounding cheer rose from his men, and it was a good thing, for Duncan himself was speechless. The heart he'd been cursing but hours before swelled to a most painful degree, and the tears he'd been trying not to shed flowed freely down his cheeks.

His *son*, she'd said.

His son!

A fool wouldna missed the import of those two words, the way she'd said them.

And he wasn't a fool.

"So, my lady," he struggled to push the words past the hot lump in his throat, "just how long have you known that?"

"From the beginning," she said. "From the very beginning."

epilogue

Eilean Creag Castle, The Great Hall
A Fortnight Later . . .

"Does she not make a bonnie bride?" Linnet peered down the length of the high table at Elspeth. "I dinna think I've e'er seen her so happy."

Duncan took a swallow of the hippocras made especially for Fergus and Elspeth's wedding feast before he answered. "Aye, she does, but her old goat of a new husband looks a wee bit too comfortable in my chair."

"'Tis only for this night. You ken neither of them would ever—" Linnet began, then snapped her mouth shut and smiled when she saw the teasing glint in Duncan's deep blue eyes.

But then his expression changed, turning solemn, as his gaze slid past her to settle on Robbie. The boy sat at the opposite end of the table, and appeared to enjoy being held on his lady wife's eldest brother's lap.

Ranald MacDonnell was whispering something in the lad's ear and whatever it was must've been highly amusing, for Robbie giggled so hard his shoulders shook with laughter.

Across from them, Linnet's favorite brother, Jamie, and Duncan's first squire, Lachlan, both seemed spellbound by whate'er tall tale Sir Marmaduke was weaving for them.

Duncan purposely caught the Sassunach's attention and lifted his chalice in a silent toast.

In honor of the sanctity of the day, he'd generously desist from telling the two young men to believe only half of the Englishman's silver-tongued tales of romance, chivalry, and honor.

"You've grown quiet, my lord," his wife's soft voice called him from his musings. "Are you truly not displeased with me for keeping silent about Robbie for so long?"

Duncan glanced back at his son. The lad was now showing Ranald his wooden sword. A surge of fierce pride flooded Duncan as he watched him. "And why," he said, his gaze still on his son, "did you not tell me sooner?"

"But I have told you, because it should not have mattered. I wanted you to love him for himself."

"And I do. I have always done so," Duncan said, and knew it to be the truth. "I was simply too stubborn to admit it."

Linnet laid a hand on his arm. "And you give me your word naught else is amiss?"

He turned to look at her then and, as so oft of late, his heart swelled at the mere sight of her.

And his heart wasn't all what swelled.

"'Tis more than my word I am wont to give you,

lady," he said, adjusting his tunic to hide the telltale bulge in his braies. That accomplished, he trailed his fingers up the length of her thigh. "Naught ails me what will not be seen to in our chamber this eve."

She blushed, her sweet face turning pinker than Elspeth's. "But your wounds, I dinna th—"

"My wounds are healed," Duncan insisted, offering Mauger a choice tidbit of roasted meat as he spoke. "Think you I am less hardy than Mauger?" He smoothed his hand over the old dog's head, careful to avoid the newly healed scar above the mongrel's right eye.

" I will not tell you what I saw him doing this morn," he added with a bold wink.

The pink tinge on his lady wife's cheeks deepened to crimson. " 'Twas good of you to let my brothers stay to see Elspeth wed," she said, artfully changing the subject.

"I told you long ago, I am not an ogre. It was good of them to inform us of your sire's passing, and a noble gesture to offer help with the rebuilding of the burned crofters' cottages. Ranald will make a fine laird. He tells me he's made peace with John MacLeod, too." He leaned toward her and gently brushed her lips with a kiss. "Aye, your brothers are welcome here, and, come spring, I shall take you to visit your sister Caterine."

"I never thought I'd see any of them again."

"And I ne'er thought I'd see Fergus wed," he said, grazing his fingers over her hair.

"They do look happy," Linnet said, a strange thickness in her voice. "I believe they are truly in love."

Duncan sat back and crossed his arms. "I daresay they are."

"And you, milord?" The words were hesitant, barely audible.

"I what?" He glanced sharply at her.

"I was wondering if . . . ah . . . if you love me?"

"If I love you?"

"Aye." She nodded. "I should like to know."

"Well, then, I shall tell you. Aye, I love you. I believe I have since the moment we clasped hands through the marriage stone."

Linnet's brows lifted. "Ah . . . so you do believe in the legend's magic?"

"I believe in *your* magic," Duncan said, and smiled. "You restored everything I'd thought lost to me. My heart, my life, my very soul."

An infinitely pleased look settled over his wife's sweet face. "You did not make it easy for me to do so," she said.

"Nay?" Duncan gave her a look of feigned surprise. "I would think just the opposite to be true."

Leaning forward, he took her face in his hands and kissed the tip of her nose. "By the staff of St. Columba, lass, and I shall admit this only once, you enchanted me so thoroughly, I didn't stand a chance."

In Scotland's Misty Hills, Love Blossoms